Also available by Nancy Revell

The Shipyard Girls
Shipyard Girls at War

Secrets of the Shipyard Girls

Nancy Revell

arrow books

1 3 5 7 9 10 8 6 4 2

Arrow Books
20 Vauxhall Bridge Road
London SW1V 2SA

Arrow Books is part of the Penguin Random House group of companies
whose addresses can be found at global.penguinrandomhouse.com.

Penguin
Random House
UK

First published in Great Britain by Arrow Books in 2017

www.penguin.co.uk

A CIP catalogue record for this book is available from the British Library

ISBN 9781784754662

Typeset in 10.75/13.5 pt Palatino by Jouve (UK), Milton Keynes
Printed and bound in Great Britain by Clays Ltd, St Ives Plc

To my mum, Audrey Walton (née Revell),
who has always encouraged me to follow
my dreams. With all my love.

Why YOU love Nancy Revell

Acknowledgements

Since starting the Shipyard Girls series I have been bowled over by the amount of support I have had from so many people and organisations. Special thanks must go to John Wilson, owner of Fulwell Post Office, Sunderland, and his lovely staff for their continuing support and promotion of the Shipyard Girls series; Rachel Emmett, of the Salvation Army, for helping me with my research into Ivy House – the country's first unmarried mothers' maternity hospital; Meg Hartford, for unearthing specific historical facts and information on my behalf; Jackie Caffrey, creator of the Facebook group Nostalgic Memories of Sunderland in Writing; the ever-supportive Beverley Ann Hopper, of The Book Lovers; the National Maritime Museum; the Sunderland Antiquarian Society, especially Linda King, Norm Kirtlan, and Philip Curtis; and journalist Katy Wheeler at the *Sunderland Echo*.

I would also like to thank Pauline Martin, of South Tyneside Libraries and Dr Trish Winter, of the 'Putting Southwick on the Map' research project, for allowing me to indulge my passion of spreading the word about the forgotten women who worked in the Sunderland shipyards in World War Two.

I must also say a really big thank you to my editor Viola Hayden and assistant editor Cassandra Di Bello for their invaluable editorial advice and guidance, and to the rest of the talented team at Arrow.

As always, I am indebted to the fabulous Diana Beaumont, who really is the best literary agent anyone could wish for.

And, of course, to my mum and dad, Audrey and Syd Walton, and my husband, Paul, who keep me fuelled with so much love, care, support and encouragement.

Thank you.

*We make a living by what we get, but we
make a life by what we give.*

Winston Churchill

Prologue

Monday 4 August 1941

Jack Crawford desperately tried to stay afloat.

But as yet another angry wave of freezing cold sea-water washed over him, his flailing body was forced back down into the darkened, soundless underworld of the North Atlantic.

Jack fought back and seconds later he managed to battle his way to the surface, but the numbness presently creeping up his limbs told him his time was running out. As he gasped for breath, he inhaled salt water and started spluttering. Choking. With his last ounce of energy he strained his head up to the skies, frantically trying to take in the fresh, pure night air. But his thick tweed trousers felt like lead weights dragging him back down, and, despite having freed himself of his jacket shortly after being thrown – or rather blasted – into the ocean, even his cotton shirt now felt like it was tailored with metal.

It might have been Hitler's Luftwaffe that had caused Jack to be floundering around in a debris-strewn expanse of sea, with planks of wood from the ship's deck bobbing next to him, and a smattering of lifeless bodies lolling aimlessly face down on the surface of the water. It might have been their bombs that had successfully sunk the steamship which had been taking him back home to the woman he

1

loved, but, as Jack felt Nature close in – claiming him – drawing his body down into the quietness of its watery womb, his eyes closed.

Jack had lived and worked within a stone's throw of the sea his entire life and he loved it with a passion – yet, after a lifetime of adoration, it had turned on him, and like a spurned lover baying for blood, it was trying its utmost to kill him.

And it was succeeding – slowly but surely.

As Jack opened his eyes to take one last look at life, he saw a bright, round, yellow light. It was the middle of the night – he was in the middle of nowhere – and, until this moment, the only illumination had come from the starry sky and the waning moon above.

Jack felt Nature close in – claiming him – drawing his body down into the quietness of its watery womb, his eyes closed.

Jack knew he was dying.

He felt his body closing down, but as it did so his whole being was flooded with the most comforting warmth, and all around him he could smell a sweetness; like jasmine on a sultry summer's eve. As his grip on life loosened, the door of his mind's eye opened and he was gifted with a wonderful vision – a beautiful, newly born baby girl. Her eyes were still cloyed with sleep, but as Jack stared in awe at this ethereal apparition, the baby's eyes opened and looked back into his own with unguarded love.

A ripple of surprise – then recognition – hit Jack, and he smiled, for the wide, grey-blue eyes gazing back at him were a replica of his own.

And it was then he knew.

He knew who the child was.

And at that moment Jack's world went black. And quiet. And he knew Nature had won.

Death had come for him.

Chapter One

The Ford Estate, Sunderland

Three weeks later
Wednesday 27 August 1941

'*Happy Birthday to you . . . Happy Birthday to you . . .*'

Dorothy bent over the crib in the middle of Gloria's neat front room and sang softly to the baby girl who was snuggled up on her side, her little thumb just touching her tiny bud-shaped mouth. Hope was sound asleep, her breathing only broken by the occasional snuffle.

Gloria was putting a tray laden with two cups of tea and a plate of shortbread fingers down on the oblong wooden coffee table. As she sat down on the sofa she pushed her thick, slightly curly, brown hair back behind her ears, and pulled her favourite cardigan around herself. She'd given up trying to convince herself it had shrunk; the fact of the matter was it wasn't only her waist that had expanded with this pregnancy, but just about every other part of her body.

'Honestly, Dorothy, she's only two weeks old. It can hardly be classed as a birthday!' Gloria said, looking at the sugar-speckled shortbread before guiltily taking a piece and dunking it in her tea.

Dorothy straightened up and put her hands on the belted waist of her denim overalls that had been pulled in tight to accentuate her tiny waist and womanly hips. She frowned at Gloria. Her friend. Her workmate. The mother of her goddaughter. She would never have guessed a year ago, when they'd all started working at Thompson's shipyard as trainee welders, that it would be Gloria with whom she would form the closest bond.

'I swear, Glor, if I said something was black you'd argue it was white.' She left the side of the crib and went to her holdall and pulled out a small present, which had been neatly wrapped in pink tissue paper and adorned with a white bow on the front. She had purchased the little present from Risdon's, which had the reputation for being the best baby shop in town.

Dorothy handed the gift to Gloria.

'You open it on Hope's behalf,' she demanded.

Gloria pursed her lips, a little embarrassed, as she took the present. 'You should be saving your money,' she reprimanded her friend. This was so like Dorothy, as frivolous with her money as she was about life. But, she also had a heart of gold. And, more than anything, she was one of the most loyal people Gloria had ever met. Take away all the bluster and showiness and you were actually left with a surprisingly solid and steadfast young woman, someone who would stand by your side, whatever the circumstances.

'I told you . . . ' Dorothy sighed dramatically, untying her headscarf and allowing her raven-coloured hair to tumble untamed around her face and over her shoulders ' . . . when Hope was born, I was going to be the best godmother *ever*. That means spoiling her rotten – even if she's not awake to appreciate it.' As she spoke, she looked over at Hope to make sure she had not woken up.

'Anyway . . . ' she continued, 'I didn't haul myself all the way over here – from the other side of the town – *after an entire day spent welding the hull of a great big bloody ship together* – to be told how to spend my hard-earned money!' Dorothy pulled a comical 'so there' pout, sat down, picked up her cup, and took a big slurp of tea.

Gloria watched Dorothy nestle up in what had been *Vinnie's* chair, and smiled to herself. The tatty brown armchair had always been her husband's – or rather, her soon-to-be ex-husband's. They must have had the wretched thing for almost twenty years: it was probably as old – and definitely as worn out – as their marriage. And during all that time, no one but His Majesty King Vinnie had been able to park their bum in it. Gloria could honestly not remember a single occasion when anyone else had used it. And now, even after she'd finally found the strength to chuck Vinnie out of the marital home at the end of last year – Gloria could still not bring herself to sit in it. It was almost as if by doing so she would feel him near – and that was the last thing on earth she wanted.

Gloria's mind spun back four months, to when Vinnie had called round at the house after work and lost it with her; he'd smashed her so hard in the face it was a fluke her nose had not been broken. She had not seen hide nor hair of him since then and she had the sneaking suspicion that someone had put the frighteners on him. She'd heard through the grapevine that not long after he'd tried to rearrange her face, he had been given a right battering himself. He'd claimed he'd been mugged, but Gloria knew no one with half a brain would bother trying to rob Vinnie – especially after he'd been to the pub. Even if he'd had any money on him in the first place, it would be safely tucked away in the landlord's coffers by the time it was last orders.

Seeing Dorothy sitting there now, drinking her tea, all cosied up and still in her dirty overalls, Gloria was glad she had kept the chair. She would love to see the look on Vinnie's face if he were to see her workmate – and a woman, at that – now commandeering *his* throne. *His* chair that no one had ever been allowed to use – not even their two grown-up boys. Seeing others sitting on it without a care in the world, especially someone like Dorothy, who, she knew, Vinnie would hate with a passion, gave her a sliver of revenge.

Gloria held her daughter's birthday present for a moment before carefully tearing the tissue paper to reveal the cutest, smallest brown teddy bear she had ever seen.

'Ah, Dorothy, it's lovely. Thank you. She's going to love it. Why don't you give it to her yourself when she wakes up,' Gloria said, helping herself to another finger of shortbread and taking a big bite.

Dorothy looked at her friend and laughed, 'Eee, I see your sugar craving's not left you then?'

Gloria popped the rest of the biscuit into her mouth and brushed the crumbs off her skirt. 'I know. I've already used up all my sweet rations. Anyway, I vaguely recall you telling me when I was in labour that you were going to buy me "the biggest cake ever" once I'd given birth!'

Dorothy let out a theatrical sigh at the mention of Hope's birth, when Gloria had gone into labour in the shipyard in the middle of an air raid. It had been one of the most terrifying but also most wonderful days in their lives. They'd all run around like headless chickens, with the air raid sirens screaming out their warning for everyone to take cover, and bombs dropping just half a mile away in Fulwell. They hadn't even had time to get to the yard's shelter as baby Hope had been determined to make her entrance into the world in the middle of all the pandemonium.

'God, I think I'll remember every second of that day for as long as I live!' Dorothy said, helping herself to a biscuit and casting another look over at Hope.

'Same here,' Gloria agreed, her mind immediately tripping back to Hope's traumatic birth; it still made her feel incredibly emotional thinking of how Dorothy and all the other women welders had risked life and limb to get her to the relative safety of the painters' shed that had ended up becoming a makeshift delivery suite.

'Anyway, come on, tell me the latest gossip from the yard,' Gloria demanded, pushing away the tears which had started to prick the backs of her eyes. She was annoyed at herself for being so overly sensitive but it was hard when she remembered Dorothy's face after she had delivered her goddaughter, and the look of both relief and elation on the rest of the women's faces.

'How's our "little bird" getting along?' Gloria asked. 'She still happy working in the drawing office?'

Hannah had been taken on as a trainee draughtsman just a few weeks before Hope was born. It had been her saving grace as she really was like a little bird, petite and fragile, and in no way cut out to do any kind of physical work, never mind something as gruelling and back-breaking as welding. They'd all been amazed she'd stuck it out for as long as she had, as she'd struggled from the moment she had first switched on her welding machine, but, much to their amazement, she had continued to slog it out for nearly a year.

Thankfully, Rosie had spotted some drawings that Hannah had done of one of the ships that was waiting to be launched in the dry dock and had taken it across to Basil, the head draughtsman. He had jumped at the chance of taking Hannah on, as not only were her sketches, in his words, 'technically brilliant', but, like just about everywhere nowadays, his department was desperately short of workers.

Dorothy's eyes lit up. 'Oh yes, *more than happy*.

Apparently Rosie says she's taken to it like a "duck to water". She's even got some colour in her cheeks, quite something for Hannah. I've never known anyone with such translucent skin . . . But, anyway, I digress –' Dorothy sucked in air for added effect '– our little bird has not only got a few roses in her cheeks – but, more importantly, she's got quite a sparkle in those big brown eyes of hers.'

Gloria almost choked on her tea. 'No . . . Hannah? . . . Really? I can't believe she'd have her head turned by anyone.'

'Well,' Dorothy said, grabbing a biscuit from the plate, 'it would appear so, or at least Ange and I think so.'

Gloria chortled, 'Oh, honestly, you two are terrible. Not everyone's man-mad you know? I'm surprised either of you ever get any work done the way you're constantly on the lookout for new talent. Hannah's not like you two. The poor girl's probably got a "sparkle in her eye", as you put it, because she's simply cock-a-hoop she's not having to weld any more.'

Dorothy sat back in her chair. 'Well, there's something up. Every time I see this Olly he's practically glued to Hannah. He's obviously got the glad eye for her.'

'Mm.' Gloria took a sip of tea and got up to check on baby Hope. 'Well, if that *is* the case, and you and Ange *are* right, then you'd better make sure she's all right. She's far too young for any kind of shenanigans . . . And I don't want you and Angie encouraging her. The next thing we know, she'll have had her heart broken, or worse still, have gotten herself in the family way.'

Dorothy spluttered with outraged laughter. 'God, you're a right one to talk! . . . Anyway, Glor, "that girl" is the same age as Ange and me. Hannah's not far off nineteen. She's a young woman not a child!'

'That may well be,' Gloria pursued her point, 'but

she's *different* to you two. She's had a different upbringing. And she's so naïve. And on top of all of that, she hasn't got anyone around her – apart from her aunty Rina, who, by the sounds of it, is a lovely woman, but she's getting on a bit and she's not very – how can I put it – worldly-wise?'

All the women knew Hannah had had a sheltered upbringing in her native Prague; that her middle-class Jewish upbringing in Czechoslovakia couldn't have been more different to being raised in an industrial, working-class town like Sunderland. The only reason she was over here, instead of sat at a desk studying Latin, or learning to play the piano, was that Hitler had decided Hannah's homeland was to be a part of his Third Reich.

'Hannah's got us,' Dorothy reassured her friend. 'Anyway, don't worry, I'll keep an eye on her – *and* this lovelorn work colleague of hers.' Dorothy stood up and noisily put down her teacup, causing Hope to stir. Dorothy smiled; she had succeeded in waking the baby.

'Hurrah! She's woken up . . . wants to see her fairy god-mother,' Dorothy said as she strode over and picked Hope up out of the cot, cradling her in her arms and cooing.

Gloria shook her head at Dorothy as she pushed herself out of the sofa. Last week when Dorothy had popped in to see Hope, she'd used similar tactics to wake the baby.

'Well now, seeing as we're *all* up and awake I'll make you some sarnies,' Gloria said. 'You must be starving. I know I'd be after a day's work at the yard. Bring Hope into the kitchen and you can keep telling me all the news.'

Gloria plodded into her little kitchen, which, as always, was spic and span. Since she had got shot of Vinnie, she had enjoyed keeping her newly built council house pristine and well ordered. There wasn't room in her life for any more chaos.

'So, Glor, have you made up your mind when you're

going to get this little one christened?' Dorothy asked, following behind her with Hope cradled in her arms.

Gloria sighed. Dorothy had asked her the same question last time she came round. She wasn't quite sure whether it was because Dorothy genuinely thought her daughter should be baptised, or because it would be a good excuse for a bit of a social – and one where she would be the centre of attention.

'Not yet,' Gloria said, slapping two slices of white bread down on the wooden chopping board. 'So, how's everyone else doing?'

'Well . . . ' Dorothy paused, looking down at Hope and pulling a funny face. The baby's little clenched hands reached up and tried to grab at some imaginary object in front of her godmother's face. ' . . . Polly's just got a letter from lover boy, so she's all happy.'

'Oh, that's good,' Gloria said, genuinely pleased. Polly's fiancé, Tommy Watts, who she'd met and fallen in love with when he was working as a dock diver at the yard, was now removing limpet mines from the bottom of Allied ships. Being on the list of reserved occupations, Tommy could have stayed at home, but he'd been determined 'to do his bit'. Gloria couldn't work out if he was a brave man, or a mad one. Probably both. But regardless, Polly adored the lad, and every time she got a letter from him she'd read it out to them all.

'He still based in Gibraltar?' Gloria asked.

Dorothy nodded. 'Polly says she can't see him being moved anywhere else. They can't risk losing the Rock. If they do they'll lose control of all shipping in and out of the Mediterranean and the Atlantic. Then we really will be done for.'

Any talk of the Atlantic or the war being waged on the sea made Gloria anxious. Thoughts of her own two boys, who were also in the Royal Navy, pushed themselves to the fore, as well as her increasingly desperate worries about Jack. It had now been three weeks since his ship had gone down and still there'd been no word as to whether or not he had been one of the lucky few to survive.

Gloria forced her mind back to Thompson's and their squad of women welders. 'And Rosie?' Gloria asked. 'How's she doing?'

'Mm,' Dorothy mused, 'she seems all right . . . although you know Rosie, it's always hard to tell. She's such a closed book.'

Gloria opened up a can of spam. 'Mm, she's a deep one is Rosie.'

'I know,' Dorothy said as Hope managed to grab a strand of her shoulder-length thick black hair and yank it with surprising force. 'I thought she might have opened up a bit more after that trouble with her uncle . . . ' Dorothy gently tugged her hair free from Hope's determined grasp. 'Especially after she told us about her *other work*.' Dorothy spoke the words quietly as if they were in danger of being overheard.

Gloria sliced the spam up and layered in on to the thickly buttered slices of bread. Neither woman had to say anything. Nor wanted to. After that awful night last year when Rosie had nearly been killed by her uncle in the shipyard, they'd learnt about Rosie's 'other job' – her night-time work at a place called Lily's bordello in a posh area of the town just next to the Ashbrooke cricket club. Rosie had worked there for years, although after the night she'd almost died she'd stopped working as one of the girls and, by the sounds of it, was now practically running the place.

'She's not mentioned anything more about that copper she seemed to be getting friendly with? What's his name . . .

11

DS Miller? God . . . memory like a sieve . . . Can't remember his first name . . . '

Gloria knew that Rosie had felt more than friendship towards the detective; knew that they had been meeting at a little café called Vera's just up from the south dock.

'Peter,' Dorothy said, 'DS Peter Miller . . . No, not a peek. I know for a fact she's not seeing him every week like she used to. Shame. I thought he was quite scrummy – in an older man type of way.'

'Maybe it's just as well,' Gloria said. 'I mean, it's not as if she could ever have a proper relationship with the bloke. If he ever found out about . . . you know . . . Lily's place and what goes on there, it wouldn't just be Rosie who would be up to her neck in it – but everyone working there. No,' Gloria surmised, 'Rosie's a wise woman. She would know there would be too much at stake – "scrummy" or not,' she said, cutting up Dorothy's sandwich and putting it on a plate.

'That may well be,' Dorothy added. 'But what if she's fallen madly in love with Mr Scrummy Detective?'

Gloria chuckled. 'God, Dorothy, you go to see too many of those daft romantic films. I know Rosie, she's got her head far too securely screwed on. Anyway, come on, let's do a swap,' she said, hauling Hope out of Dorothy's arms. They went back into the lounge and between mouthfuls of sandwich Dorothy continued to tell Gloria all the latest.

'Oh, how could I forget. You'd never believe Martha. She's getting really chatty lately!' Dorothy exclaimed. Gloria's eyebrows rose in surprise.

'Well,' Dorothy said, ' "really chatty" might be a bit of an exaggeration, but she's definitely talking a lot more than normal. I reckon it's because Hannah's not really about all that much. I know she's missing her like mad – you know how close they were – but I think, in a way, she's come out of her shell more since Hannah's defected to "the other side".'

Gloria chuckled. There was definitely a division in the shipyard. A real 'them and us': Those who worked outside in all weathers, building the actual ships – and those who worked in the comfort and warmth of the offices.

'Either that,' Dorothy added, 'or seeing little Hope being born has shocked her into speech!'

Gloria laughed. Hope's birth really had been blood, sweat and tears.

'Sounds like she's opening up more. That's good,' Gloria said, and she meant it. She had a soft spot for Martha, who really was the epitome of a 'gentle giant', with more muscle on her huge frame than most men, yet possessing the quietest and mildest of natures.

As Hope started to wriggle in her mother's arms, Gloria chuckled, 'I bet you she's still not uttering a word to any of the blokes, though?'

Dorothy laughed. 'No, not that any of them mind. I think they all find her a bit scary, although they'd never for one minute admit that.'

'And . . . ' Gloria said tentatively, 'dare I ask if Helen's been causing any more trouble?'

Dorothy's face dropped. They were all well aware that the yard's acting manager Helen Crawford hated them. Her animosity was mainly due to the fact that she had not got what she'd so desperately wanted – Tommy Watts, and that he'd not only fallen for Polly, *but had proposed to her*. Since then Helen's need for revenge had applied to them all, and she'd tried every trick in the book to break up their squad – and what's more, had nearly succeeded. Over the course of the past six months she had repeatedly used her position at Thompson's to push Martha across to the riveters, and make Hannah's life unbearable by making her do some of the hardest welding jobs. When Helen had found out Gloria was pregnant, and that legally she could get rid of her at the drop of a hat, she had almost succeeded in her aim of systematically ripping apart their gang of all-women welders. It would have left Rosie with just Polly and Dorothy, giving Helen the green light to place the women in different squads at opposite ends of the yard.

It had only been thanks to Rosie that they were all still together now. She had brought in the Union, who had stipulated that contractually Martha's employment was as a welder – and not a riveter; she'd then orchestrated a job swap with Gloria and Angie, a crane operator.

But, even though Helen had failed in breaking them up, that was not to say she had given up.

'For once that horrible vindictive cow is not on our backs,' Dorothy said, adding, 'but that's only because she's not been at work these past couple of weeks. I'm guessing because of Jack . . . ' Dorothy let her voice tail off.

Helen was Jack's daughter, something everyone found quite hard to believe. The apple had truly fallen a long way away from the tree. Helen's spoilt, self-obsessed nature could not have been more different from that of her father, and it was generally agreed by those who knew the family that Helen was the replica of her mother, Miriam. Still, it was her father Helen adored and she had pulled every string possible to get herself a job at Thompson's as she had been determined to follow in his footsteps. Miriam, of course, was horrified that her beautiful daughter should go to work in the shipyards, but Helen had, as usual, got her own way and wangled herself a job in the administration offices, where, much to everyone's surprise, she had made her mark. So, when Jack had gone off to America to educate the Yanks about the new Liberty ships which the yard's owner Cyril Thompson had designed, Helen had been promoted to acting yard manager – and, in doing so, had become a deeply embedded thorn in the women's sides.

'Helen's never off work,' Gloria worried. 'I wonder if that means they've heard something about Jack. No one's said anything at work, have they?'

Dorothy shook her head. 'Sorry, Glor.'

Gloria looked down at Hope and felt her heart start to beat faster. Since she had been told that Jack's ship – the SS *Tunisia* – had been sunk somewhere off the coast of Ireland, she had been filled with a sense of terrible foreboding. Baby Hope had brought light and joy into her life, but that could not obliterate the worry and the dread she felt whenever she thought about Jack – a worry and dread that plagued her just about every minute of every day.

When she had started work at the yard, she had done so to escape her unhappy and abusive marriage; all she had wanted was a respite from Vinnie. An escape. She had never expected to fall in love with Jack – for the second time in her life.

Twenty years previously he had broken her heart when he'd dumped her and married Miriam. They had barely seen each other during that time. She had married Vinnie and had two boys. Jack and Miriam had had a daughter, Helen. But then Gloria had started work at Thompson's. She had known he was yard manager there, but not that she would see so much of him. But she had, and it had been as if there was a magnet pulling them together. Their love had been reignited – a love that they realised had never really died, and they had become lovers. Jack had told her that his marriage to Miriam had never been a happy one and had been dead for many years. He'd been desperate for them both to come clean about their love for each other, especially as he now knew about Vinnie's violence and how it had been, and still was, both brutal and frequent. But Gloria had told Jack to wait until after he had returned from America. Their new lives together would start after he came back.

But ever since hearing that his ship had been hit, Gloria had felt in a cruel limbo, her mind swinging between hope that Jack was alive – then back to mentally preparing herself for news of his death. It was driving her insane, and it was for this very reason that she was going back to work tomorrow. She couldn't stand to be alone with her own thoughts a moment longer. She needed the distraction. And on top of everything else, she needed the money – not just to get by on, but also because she was determined to get a divorce. And in order to do that, she had to seek legal advice – and that kind of professional help didn't come cheap.

Her decision to return to work had been made that much easier when Polly told her that her sister-in-law, Bel, would be more than happy to look after baby Hope while Gloria was at work. When the war had really got going last summer, Polly's mother, Agnes Elliot, had been determined to 'do her bit' for the war effort, and, after the government had stuck up posters emblazoned with the plea: 'If you can't go to the factory, help the neighbour who can', she had transformed her home into a makeshift crèche, now known affectionately by those around the doors as 'Aggie's nursery'.

Gloria knew Hope could not have been in better hands.

'I hate to even utter that man's name . . . ' Dorothy said with a look on her face as if she had eaten something rather unpleasant, 'but have you heard anything from Vinnie?'

Gloria shook her head.

'Well, fingers crossed it stays that way,' Dorothy said sternly.

Half an hour later, after relaying more snippets of gossip doing the rounds in the yard, Dorothy said her farewells in a whirlwind of hugs and kisses, which Gloria allowed her to bestow on Hope, but which she herself rejected.

'Dinnit be so soft and get yourself home,' she berated her.

'Home?' Dorothy gasped in mock outrage. 'It's far too early to be going home, Glor! Ange and I are off up the town. Apparently there's a load of RAF blokes out on the tiles – living it up before their next mission.'

Gloria tutted her disapproval but couldn't quite suppress a smile as she watched her workmate make her way down the path and out the front gate – her leather hobnailed boots sounding out her departure, her long shiny black hair falling down the back of her dirty overalls.

A few minutes later Gloria was settling herself down on the sofa so she could give Hope her evening bottle of milk when the doorbell rang. Thinking it was Dorothy and that she must have forgotten something, Gloria got up out of the comfort of the cushioned settee, and, with Hope cradled in her arms, went to open her front door.

As soon as she did so, though, she immediately regretted it and tried to slam the door shut again – but it was too late. Vinnie had already jammed his steel toe capped boot in the doorway.

Gloria cursed herself. *Why hadn't she put her safety latch on?*

It had never occurred to her that it could be Vinnie. Whenever he turned up, he either bashed on the door or pummelled it with his fists. She had never known him to use the bell.

'Dinnit worry, Glor,' Vinnie said, keeping his foot in the door, 'I'm not ganna kick off.'

Gloria's hand instinctively went to shield Hope's head – and her vision – from the sight of the man she both hated and feared, and who was now standing on her doorstep.

'What you doing here?' Gloria demanded, half turning away, protecting herself and her babe-in-arms from the man she had been married to for twenty long years – from the man who thought this bundle of innocence she now held in her arms was his.

'What the hell do you think I'm here for? I want to see my bairn?' he shouted, his face starting to contort with anger.

Gloria swung her face round to look straight at Vinnie. Her mouth was set hard and her eyes daggered into him.

'Ooh, if looks could kill . . . ' Vinnie's face turned mocking.

'I wish,' spat Gloria. 'You're not wanted here, Vinnie. Not ever.' Her words were said with complete conviction.

For a second she had a flash of memory; of the pain she had felt as his bare knuckles had smashed on to the bridge of her nose. She could still recall the taste of metal as blood gushed from her nose and down her throat. Gloria had not heard a whisper from Vinnie since then, and she was sure that wasn't because he'd all of a sudden developed a conscience, but because someone had warned him off. Someone, she was sure, had given him a dose of his own medicine, although she still had no idea who.

As if reading her thoughts, Vinnie stepped forward.

'Dinnit worry, Glor, I'm not ganna hurt you. You can tell yer mate that.' He looked at his wife, trying to read her but not succeeding. He still wasn't entirely sure whether or not it was Gloria who had got the balaclava-clad man to give him a good hiding, and looking at her blank face now, he was still none the wiser.

'I just want to see my little girl.' He leered into the doorway, trying to see the baby encased in his wife's arms.

'I heard from the auld gossipmongers you've called her *Hope*. What kind o' a name's that?' he sneered.

'I'm telling you this just the once, Vinnie.' Gloria added volume to her voice. 'I don't want you anywhere near me or *my* baby. So, get yer foot out of my door before I start screaming blue murder.'

'All right ... ' Vinnie slid his booted foot back. Gloria immediately clashed the door shut in his face and with shaking hands rammed across the bolts she had installed herself, before swinging the safety chain on to the latch.

Vinnie stood speechless. His face was just inches away from the wooden front door. He felt himself flush with anger and humiliation. It took a second or so for him to find his tongue. 'I'll be back, Glor! Yer can't stop me seeing my own daughter!'

Gloria remained standing quietly in the hallway, barely allowing herself to breathe until she heard Vinnie stomp back down the short garden path. She only turned to go back into the lounge when she heard him pull the little wooden gate shut with such force it nearly took the hinges off.

His retreat felt like a victory for Gloria – even if, like her gate, it was a fragile one, and had left her more than a little shaken.

Chapter Two

Tatham Street, Hendon, Sunderland

'Oh my,' Bel's soft voice sang out when she opened the door the following day to see Gloria standing on the pavement, one hand holding on to her pram, the other cradling Hope. It had just gone a quarter to seven but already the cobbled street outside the door of the Elliots' home in the heart of the town's east end was teeming with a mass of flat caps, all moving in the direction of the numerous shipyards lining the River Wear.

Reaching out to gently take the sleeping baby out of Gloria's arms and into her own, Bel gazed down at the little face, barely visible through the layers of blankets Gloria had wrapped her in for her early morning journey to what was to be Hope's second home.

'How she's changed in just two weeks,' Bel said quietly, trying not to wake her new charge. But it was no good, baby Hope had sensed the crossover and knew she was no longer in her mother's arms. Her eyes opened and Bel gasped in delight at the slightly startled baby, 'What a beautiful girl you are!'

Bel's face became sombre as she looked up at Gloria and quietly asked, 'Any news about Jack?' She knew only too well the true awfulness of waiting to hear about a loved one.

Gloria shook her head, and Bel automatically reached out with her free hand and squeezed Gloria's arm gently.

'Anyway,' Bel said, forcing her voice to become more cheerful, 'come in. Everyone's up.'

Turning with the baby to walk down the long, tiled hallway and into the warmth of the kitchen, she announced to the whole house, 'Look everyone! It's baby Hope!'

As Gloria followed Bel down the hallway, she was touched by her words, but she couldn't stop herself feeling a little emotional watching another woman take command of her baby – even if it was Bel. There was a part of her that wanted to snatch Hope back, but she knew she was being stupid.

As Gloria walked into the hub of the warm kitchen she was greeted by a room full of upturned faces: Her workmate, Polly Elliot, who was just pulling on her overcoat and taking a last sup of tea, her older brother Joe, who was hobbling through from the scullery with the aid of his walking stick, their mother, Agnes, who was pulling a pan of porridge off the stove to serve up to Bel's three-year-old daughter, Lucille – and Arthur Watts, Tommy's grandad, who was pushing himself out of the armchair positioned next to the range.

Gloria smiled over to the old man and thought how well he looked despite his seventy-odd years. His recent move from the Diver's House down by the south docks, where he had lived most of his life with Tommy, to the Elliots' home here in the east end had done him well.

'Me see baby?' Lucille asked, her little face straining up towards Hope. Her question was more a demand, and Joe went to pick his little niece up by the waist and held her aloft so she could have a bird's eye view of the newcomer.

'*My* baby!' she announced on seeing Hope. Everyone chuckled. Lucille was going through a stage of declaring anything new or of interest to be hers, and hers alone.

'What's all the commotion about?' Everyone turned to see Pearl, standing in the doorway, her faded pink cotton dressing gown wrapped around her scrawny body. Gloria had met Pearl, Bel's mother, just the once at the next-door neighbour's birthday party a few months back and she had sussed her out pretty quickly, although her reputation had preceded her as Polly had bent all the women's ears back at work with her regular laments about how outrageously out of order Pearl could be – and had been most of her life.

'Ma, go and have your fag,' Bel said, spotting the unlit cigarette between her mother's fingers. 'I know you're gasping for one, and it's not as if you're a real baby person, is it?' Bel snipped at her mother.

Gloria looked at Polly and they both raised their eyebrows in unison.

Pearl peered across at the gurgling baby in her daughter's arms and sniffed, 'Aye, yer right there . . . I mightn't be a "real baby person" as you put it,' she paused, 'but *you* are, Isabelle.' Pearl's eyes shifted mischievously up to her daughter's pretty face and across to Joe who was standing with his back to the wall, allowing the women to 'ooh and ah' over the new baby.

'So,' Pearl added, 'don't *you* be getting any ideas, *will ya?*'

With a half laugh, half cough, Pearl bustled to the back door and out into the yard to smoke her cigarette.

Gloria looked at Bel, who was looking at Joe. Their look of exasperation at Pearl's inappropriate comments was plain for all to see. Gloria knew, of course, that Bel and her brother-in-law, Joe, were now an item. They had admitted they had fallen in love to Agnes on the day when Gloria had given birth to baby Hope.

Poor Agnes. She was surprised the woman was still of

one mind; in the space of just a few months her only daughter had started work in the shipyards – the target of just about every bomb dropped on the town so far – then her son, Teddy, had been killed out in North Africa – and her other son, Joe, seriously injured.

Bel, who had been married to Teddy, had plummeted into a terrible depression, but had thankfully come out of it. She had helped to nurse Joe during his convalescence at home and their friendship had developed into love. Luckily, from what Gloria had gathered from Polly, Agnes had given her blessing to their union, but, still, she was sure Agnes's head must be a minefield of mixed emotions.

'She's a bonny bairn.' Arthur's deep voice caused them all to look up. The old man, like his grandson Tommy, had a low, calm voice. Gloria smiled, and watched as Bel held Hope out to Arthur who put his hands up as if he was surrendering.

'Nah, Bel, I'll only drop the wee thing,' he said, leaning forward to take a peek. As he looked at the baby girl happily cuddled up in Bel's arms, his pale blue eyes widened. Hope was the spit of her father. It was uncanny.

'Eee, well, we best be getting off then, Pol,' Gloria said, trying to be strong and not give vent to the well of tears she felt were building up inside her at the thought of being without her beloved baby all day long.

Polly looked at Gloria and understood her workmate's need to make her parting as quick and as painless as possible.

Agnes seemed to have cottoned on quickly too. 'Yes, get yourselves off to that yard.' She ushered them out of the kitchen. 'I don't want you both to be late otherwise the stingy buggers'll dock yer wages.' She smiled as she pushed Polly's sandwiches into her hand as they made their way down the hallway and out the front door.

Gloria stepped out on to the busy street, now full of the sound of men's voices and the smell of burning tobacco that followed the blanket of cloth-capped heads moving towards the Borough Road.

As she did Agnes quickly grabbed Gloria's arm. 'And don't you be worrying about Hope,' she said, her latent Irish accent coming to the fore. 'She'll be just fine here. No need to fret . . . And if anything *were* to happen to the bab, I'll make sure you'll get word straight away,' she told her, adding with a cheeky smile on her face, 'I'll send Pearl – with the promise of a pint. Guaranteed she'll be there faster than the speed of light!'

Chapter Three

The North Atlantic Ocean

Monday 4 August 1941

'Look! Out there!' The skipper's panicked but excited voice sounded out into the blustery night as he spun the trawler's steering wheel quickly to the left and powered the vessel forward.

Their boat was the first to make it to the wrecked SS *Tunisia* after responding to a Mayday call which had come across the airways: A British steamship had just been bombed out of the water by a German FW200 aircraft. The cargo vessel had been transporting manganese ore, desperately needed for iron and steel production, but 350 miles off the west coast of Ireland it had been spotted by the Luftwaffe. Within minutes the immense weight of its cargo had made the ship sink like a lead balloon into the depths of the Atlantic.

The ship had been made up almost entirely of Merchant Navy sailors – although there had been a few passengers who, like its cargo, were being transported back to British shores.

'Quick! Get the light on him!' the skipper shouted to the young lad whose hands were clamped on either side of a large, round light from which a strong beam was laying a yellow path across the turbulent waters.

Behind him a burly-looking older man stood stock-still,

staring intently as the moving path of light caught a snatch of life being dragged under the waters.

'I'm going in!' the broad-shouldered, bearded fisherman yelled, as he swiped off his cap, tore off his waxed cotton gaberdine, and pulled his thick polo neck jumper over his head, before freeing himself of his rubber boots. Before anyone had time to object he had tossed his long thick woollen socks aside and had climbed barefoot, wearing just his vest and trousers, on to the side of the boat.

'Jim!' the skipper shouted out, but it was too late. His mate had dived, torpedo-like into the moving grey sea and disappeared.

The old skipper and the young lad stood transfixed, holding their breath and staring intently into the choppy waters. It seemed like an age, but must have only been a few long-drawn-out seconds before Jim reappeared, gasping for air. He swam towards the end of the beam of light and upended himself back beneath the water. The light caught his white, bony feet as they disappeared where his head had been just moments before.

'Holy Mary, Mother of God,' the skipper said aloud. 'Jim, yer a bloody eejit yer are!' He mumbled as he gripped the boat's large wooden steering wheel, keeping the trawler on track and chugging slowly to where he had seen his lifelong friend disappear. The silence felt deafening as the old man and the young boy stared, their eyes glued to the spot where the brave fisherman had dived beneath the surface.

There was a joint intake of breath as their mate reappeared; one of his arms was wrapped around a man's chest, while his other arm floundered behind him as he fought the water, swimming on his back, towing the man's lifeless body in his wake. Waves kept submerging them both, but the fisherman and his human cargo kept bobbing back up to the surface.

This was one battle Mother Nature was not going to win.

'Bejesus!' the skipper shouted out jubilantly. 'Let's get the great big lummox back on board,' he shouted to the young lad, as he powered off and swiftly wrapped a length of rope around the steering wheel to keep the rudder steady.

By now Jim had grabbed a piece of timber bobbing about on the water's surface and was using it like a float, his feet kicking out furiously to keep himself and the lifeless man buoyant. As the boat neared its human catch, the young lad dangled the top part of his skinny body down the side of the hull, desperately trying to grab the shirt that the lifeless man was still wearing.

'Got him!' the youngster shouted out, as he took a firm hold of the shirt before reaching out and grasping Jack's thick leather belt. Summoning all his wiry strength, the boy hoisted Jack up, over and into the boat, landing him on deck like a monster-sized catch. But unlike the fish the men were used to hauling on board, all thrashing around and gulping for air, there wasn't a flicker of movement from the man.

The skipper dropped the ladder across the side of the boat and threw a thickset arm down to grab his mate's out-stretched hand. Clutching the skipper's hand, Jim managed to pull himself out of the water, clamber up the ladder and over the vessel's railings, before collapsing on to the deck next to Jack. Water trickled from his grey-speckled black beard as he heaved to fill his lungs, his chest rising and falling as he sucked in the night's air.

Now the skipper dropped to his knees and started pushing with all his might down on Jack's chest.

'Come on, man!' he shouted. Taking Jack's lolling head in

27

his hands, the skipper cleared his airway before blowing into Jack's mouth and giving him the kiss of life. But there was no sign of life.

'Come on, yer bastard! We've not done this fer bugger all!' The man's voice was frantic as he took another gasp of air and blew once more into his lifeless catch.

The young lad was standing nearby, hands on his knees, retching with adrenaline. Jim was laid out on his back, too exhausted to even sit up. The strength was draining from the skipper's arms, and in a fit of desperation he turned his head upwards and muttered a quiet prayer to the starless skies above. The old man hoped someone up there was listening.

Suddenly Jack's body convulsed, and as it did so, a huge spray of salty seawater erupted from his mouth.

'Thanks be to God in the Highest Heaven!' the skipper voiced his relief, before rolling the sodden weight of Jack's semi-conscious body on to its side, allowing more of the sea's deathly liquid to spew back out and on to the deck.

He looked across to his mate, who was still breathing heavily and still flat on his back. 'You okay there, Jim?'

Jim looked at his old friend and smiled.

'Aye, I am, Shamus,' he coughed, spat out seawater, then forced himself to sit up. 'But I think we're getting too old for this game.' Jim let out a loud bark of laughter as the young lad hurried round, stepping over crab pots and a heap of nets to help his dripping-wet workmate to his feet.

'Best get some blankets wrapped around the both of them – and quick, laddie,' Shamus commanded the young boy as he himself lurched unsteadily back into the confines of the small cabin, climbed behind the wheel and began steering the boat back to dry land. 'The sea mightn't have got 'em, but the cold might yet,' he muttered to himself.

*

A quarter of an hour after the three fishermen had hauled Jack's lifeless body out of the sea, the small trawler was joined on the water by a converted freighter bearing the red and white insignia of the Red Cross.

It was a great relief to the crew to hand over the unknown man to the Order of St John volunteers.

'We think hypothermia's set in . . . he's barely conscious,' Shamus told one of the medics tending Jack, who was now shaking violently from the freezing temperatures he'd been exposed to.

As Jack's stretcher was winched from the trawler and swung on board the rescue ship, the medic shook the hands of the skipper, the fisherman, and the young lad in turn. 'If he lives, it'll be down to you three,' he said solemnly.

'Aye, well, she took an old friend early this year,' Jim said, nodding over the side to the lapping ocean, now surprisingly calm. 'She wasn't gonna have anyone else – not on my watch anyway,' he said with a clear determination in his voice.

'We'll be having a dram or two when we get back to shore,' Shamus added, ruffling the messy mop of dirty amber-coloured hair on the young boy standing next to him. 'Won't we, lad?'

The pale, freckle-faced youngster smiled and nodded enthusiastically.

'Let's just hope this one gets to enjoy the burn of a good whisky again,' the skipper nodded up to Jack as the stretcher he was strapped into disappeared from sight.

As the two fishermen and the boy watched the Red Cross ship power away from them they knew they would probably never find out what happened to the unknown man they had saved from certain death. They could only hope and pray that he survived – for his own sake, and for the family they presumed he had waiting for him at home.

*

As Jack's eyes flickered open momentarily he saw a brass lantern dangling above him and felt the gentle sway beneath him and he knew instinctively he was in the bowels of a ship at sea.

The glow of the light bobbing above him seemed so bright. Too bright. He closed his eyes.

He was almost sure he was still alive. He had a sense that he had somehow escaped death – that he had beaten the odds and survived. He had a vague recollection of drowning, of being dragged down into a watery grave. But then he had felt the pull of something, or someone, above him and seconds later he was breathing in air – not water.

What had happened after that was sketchy. He remembered darkness and then seeing an old man's face next to his. The man had had a distinctive Irish accent and he had shouted some kind of profanity at him. Then he remembered his body starting to shake – and shake. His whole body had felt like it was bouncing off the stretcher he'd been put on. The shaking had spread to his jaws and he had heard his teeth repeatedly clashing together.

There had been patches of black. Jack realised he had been swinging in and out of consciousness and that he had no idea how long he had been in the belly of this ship.

For a moment a part of his muddled mind wondered if he was, in fact, dead, that this was some kind of strange afterlife and he was being transported to 'the other side' – whatever or wherever that was; that was until he heard voices around him, voices that were very clearly human.

'How many were on board?' a voice to his right asked. Jack hadn't realised he was not alone; he tried to turn his head to see the person who was speaking, but his head wouldn't move. Jack felt like he was sinking slowly down into a dark pit and that there was nothing he could do to stop it.

'I think I heard there were forty-three,' another, deeper voice on his left replied with what sounded like a guttural north-west accent.

'And how many survivors?' the first voice asked.

'Apart from this one – if he makes it,' the lilting voice answered, 'just four.'

The people on either side were now moving about around him, and Jack could feel the odd bump as the ship rode waves.

There was silence and Jack again tried to open his eyes a fraction. It was all he had the energy for. Even his eyelids felt heavy. He caught sight of two men, now with their backs to him, bent over another stretcher with a lifeless-looking body laid on it. It seemed so quiet now, and so dark – or was that his eyes closing?

He was now back in the darkness and he could feel his mind and his body welcoming the deep sleep that he sensed was just about to take him. It was a heavenly feeling and he couldn't wait to embrace it. But just before he did – before the darkness came and he fell willingly into its embrace – he saw the cherub again.

The baby.

The child he somehow knew was his.

And then the darkness came and took him away.

Chapter Four

J.L. Thompson & Sons Shipyard, North Sands, Sunderland

Thursday 28 August 1941

'Welcome back!' Rosie said, handing Gloria her very own welding helmet that had her name painted on it in big white lettering. All the women welders now had their own personalised headgear. The idea had been Martha's, although it had been Dorothy, of course, who had jumped at the suggestion as soon as it had been made, and had wondered out loud why on earth *she* hadn't thought of it, before promptly galloping off to find a spare pot of white paint and a brush so she could do the honours. Having their names emblazoned on their helmets had made them all feel like they had finally made their mark in the shipyard. It was proof that they were here to stay.

Just a year previously the yards were more or less a totally male-dominated environment. But now, despite shipwrights being exempt from conscription, the number of shipyard workers had become depleted, and despite objections from some of the town's bigwigs, there'd been no choice other than to bring the women on board.

'Look,' Martha declared to Gloria, causing her to turn around and face the rest of the women welders. 'We've got our names on our masks!' As she spoke Martha threw her thick muscular arm around in a semicircle as if she was introducing a new stage act.

Gloria stared at Martha. This was the first time she had really heard her normally less than verbose workmate speak a full sentence, never mind sound so animated. Dorothy had been right. Something really had propelled her into the world of words.

'Eee, it feels good to be back,' she said, looking round at Martha and then at Dorothy, Angie, and Polly, all proudly clutching their personalised metal helmets like gladiators holding their shields. A big smile spread across her face. 'Feels like I've been away ages, not just a couple of weeks.'

Dorothy was just about to say something when her voice was lost in the sound of the bellowing klaxon. It was seven thirty on the dot. Time to start building ships.

'Saved by the horn,' Gloria ribbed Dorothy, who responded by scrunching her face up into a scowl.

'I'll make up for it at lunchtime,' she promised, before they all put on their newly decorated helmets, pushed them down and got to work.

As the deafening sounds of the shipyard started up, there seemed to be a particular buzz in the air. It had been noticeable for some time now. It might well have been down to the fact that they had just finished building the SS *Empire Liberty*, the first British emergency war-built ship.

There was a great communal sense of pride. J.L. Thompson & Sons shipyard was leading the rest of the world.

As well as the sense of achievement and status their own yard had, everyone knew all of the town's shipyards were crucial to the war effort. Naval fleets and merchant vessels were falling victim to enemy attacks with worrying frequency and, as a result, Sunderland, which was known as 'The Biggest Shipbuilding Town in the World', was playing an essential role in producing new ships and repairing those damaged in battle.

Rosie watched the women and thought they all looked like they had been doing this job all of their lives. It was hard to believe that they had only joined the shipyard a year ago. She had done a good job. She was pleased with herself.

Rosie had worked hard to build a strong squad of women welders. And it hadn't been easy. Not only had she had to train them all up from scratch, but she'd also had Helen to contend with.

As Rosie watched the women climbing up on to the staithes to weld together the hull of the yard's new commission from the Ministry of War Transport, the cargo vessel SS *Empire Brutus*, she silently congratulated herself. Now that Gloria had returned to work she had her entire team back. She had only lost the one – Hannah – but that had ended up being a blessing in disguise as she was now putting her education and natural skill for technical drawing to good use in helping design the ships that they all hoped were going to win them this war.

When lunchtime arrived, the women welders switched off their machines, put down their rods and helmets and marched across the yard to the canteen, all the while bombarding Gloria with questions about baby Hope. Each of them also made a point of telling Gloria quietly that they were keeping their fingers firmly crossed for Jack's safe return.

Rosie had been waylaid chatting to Jimmy the head riveter about what needed to be done in the afternoon, and was jogging to catch up with the women when she spotted two of the yard managers looking uncannily solemn heading for the admin office. Catching sight of Rosie, who was wearing a particularly vibrant red headscarf that was successfully keeping all but a few strands of her naturally blonde hair away from her face, the men both stopped in their tracks.

'You got a minute, Rosie?' Harold, the older of the two, asked, waving his hand to beckon her over. Rosie slowed down and veered away from the women and towards her two superiors.

'Yes, of course,' she said, walking briskly over to them. As Harold opened the main entrance door and allowed Rosie to step into the warmth first, Rosie took one look at his face, and asked, 'It's about Jack, isn't it?'

Her question was answered with a silent nod.

As they made their way up the stairs to the first floor, Rosie felt a rush of apprehension. She knew Gloria was worried sick about Jack, but she too cared deeply for her boss. He had fought her corner when she had started working at the yard just days after her sixteenth birthday, helping her become the only woman at that time to be employed to do what was considered a 'man's job'.

As they approached Jack's office, Rosie wondered why she had been summoned. Harold and Donald knew Rosie thought the world of Jack, and had been waiting on tenterhooks for news of his welfare, but she was not management.

On entering the office Rosie came face to face with someone she wasn't best pleased to see. The woman's dark blue jacket and skirt had the right balance between fashionable and professional, and her figure was slim and still gave off a slight youthfulness despite her age. It was just her hands, as she stretched one of them out regally towards Rosie, which gave away her forty-four years. No amount of good living and expensive hand creams, Rosie thought, as she took hold of the woman's hand, could hold back the show of time.

'Ah, Rosie, good to see you.' The woman's words were perfectly enunciated, without the hint of an accent.

'Mrs Crawford,' Rosie said, clearly and politely, 'how are you doing?' She tried to sound as sincere as possible, although she felt no kind of warmth or genuine care for this woman she had known and met only very occasionally during her eight years working at the yard.

Miriam Crawford was Jack's wife, mother to Helen – but, most importantly, she was the wealthy daughter of one of the north-east's top industrialists who had close connections with all the Sunderland yards.

She was also one of the most stuck-up women Rosie had ever come across.

'I'm very well, thank you, Miss Thornton.' Miriam's voice sounded as cold as her hand had felt, and her words were clipped as if she resented wasting words on someone as lowly as a welder.

'And Jack? Has there been any word . . . ' Rosie hesitated, not sure how to ask whether Jack was alive or dead. ' . . . Has there been any news of his well-being?'

Rosie knew she was probably speaking out of turn by enquiring about Jack, but he was – had been – her boss, after all, and more than anything, she was desperate to find out what had happened to him, for Gloria's sake. The poor woman needed to be put out of her misery. Rosie had only seen Gloria the once since Hope had been born, due to her work at Lily's demanding every spare minute she had outside of her employment at the yard, but it was quite clear that Gloria was worried sick about Jack. Rosie's heart had gone out to her friend, and it had put into perspective her own private misery over the ending of her relationship with Peter.

'*Mr Crawford's* well-being . . .' Miriam put the stress on 'Mr Crawford', subtly reprimanding Rosie for being over-familiar, ' . . . is why I'm here today.'

Rosie was much taller than her boss's wife, but Miriam still managed to give the impression of looking down her nose at her, and not just at Rosie, but just about anyone else she deigned to converse with.

Rosie looked at Harold and Donald, and saw that they too clearly felt uncomfortable in Miriam's company. Standing solemnly to attention either side of the large metal desk behind which Miriam stood, they gave the impression of being Miriam's minions, rather than men who were in charge of a business that produced more ships than anywhere else in the country. But their serious, straight faces did not hide their concern for Jack, which was not surprising as they had, after all, known him all of their working lives. In fact, just about everyone who knew Jack, and had worked with him over the years, liked him and respected him.

'As you know, I try to leave the shipbuilding business to the men,' Miriam said, 'but as Mr Crawford's wife, I felt it only right that I come here personally to impart the news.'

She took out a cream lace handkerchief and dabbed her nose.

Rosie knew Miriam thought the shipyards – and any kind of industry, for that matter – were solely the domain of the menfolk. So much so that she had actually voiced her opposition to women working in the town's shipyards, agreeing with the argument that they should 'protect' the so-called shipbuilding traditions, and that the men's jobs should be kept open for them when they returned from war. The only reason, she guessed, why she'd allowed her daughter Helen to work for Thompson's was because she had an office job.

'Well,' Miriam began as if she was about to give a sermon, 'I have come here today to tell you the news that I am sure you will all be pleased to hear – Jack is alive.'

Rosie felt a surge of pure joy. Jack was alive!

'Oh, that's wonderful news.' Rosie couldn't help the words spilling out of her mouth.

'Yes,' Miriam said, her voice still in lecture mode, 'it is "wonderful news", but he has had a rather difficult time of it all, and the doctors aren't sure when Mr Crawford will be well enough to come back to work.'

Rosie's heart sank. Had Jack suffered some terrible injury? Lost limbs, like so many others who had been caught in the war's crossfire? Rosie had to bite her tongue to stop a demand to know more.

Luckily, Harold plucked up the courage to ask, 'Is he going to be all right?'

Miriam dabbed her nose once again. Rosie couldn't help but think that Miriam was enjoying this moment of being in control. Of standing behind what had been Jack's desk and acting like she owned the place.

'Mr Crawford was very fortunate in that he was one of the few to survive the direct hit the SS *Tunisia* suffered on the fourth of this month.'

Miriam took a breath; a pause for dramatic effect.

'He was rescued, but had been in the water for some time and, not unusually, he suffered hypothermia.'

Miriam looked at both managers – and then at Rosie. 'Which is caused by being exposed to freezing cold temperatures for a prolonged period of time.'

Rosie wanted to shake the woman. Any idiot knew that if you were dumped in the middle of the ocean there was a good chance that, if you didn't drown, you'd freeze to death.

Just spit it out, woman! she wanted to scream. *Is Jack all right?*

Perhaps sensing the atmosphere in the room was getting a little tense, Miriam continued at a brisker pace.

'And, although he is still alive and still managing to breathe on his own, it would appear that due to either his near drowning, or the hypothermia – or, indeed, both – his body has shut down. Mr Crawford is in a coma.'

Rosie was stunned. Her head spun as she tried to get an understanding of whether what she was hearing was good news – or not.

'The doctors,' Miriam said, her voice starting to shake a little, 'will not say whether or not he will wake up. And if he does,' another dab at her nose, ' . . . what state he will be in.'

Her voice started to warble slightly.

'That's where my daughter is now. With her father. By his bedside, praying he wakes up.'

Rosie couldn't help but feel Miriam's ladylike sobs were crocodile tears, and she chastised herself for being so hard. Jack was the poor woman's husband, after all. She wasn't totally heartless, was she?

Miriam sat down, and both managers looked over to Rosie, giving her a hard stare and then shifting their look to Miriam.

So that was why they had invited her up to the meeting. Now she understood. They had wanted – needed – another woman there, having anticipated Miriam's outpouring of emotion. Obeying the wordless command of her superiors Rosie walked around the table to where Jack's wife was now seated and in tears.

'Mir— I mean Mrs Crawford, I'm sure he'll come through it.' Rosie tried her best to sound sincere, but just as she reached her side, Miriam waved her away with the hand in which she still had her scrunched-up lace hankie.

'Just spread the word, Miss Thornton,' she said, adding, with barbed bitchiness, 'I'm sure you and your *girls* will do a good job of making sure everyone in the yard knows.'

Rosie glowered down at this woman who had barely looked at her in all the time she had stood just yards away. All her comments had been addressed to the two men.

Miriam looked up with sorrowful, puppy dog eyes at Harold and Donald. She had made sure she hadn't cried so much that her mascara ran. Harold shuffled awkwardly forward and tapped his hand on her back by way of comfort.

Rosie knew she had been dismissed, and took the staged breakdown as her cue to slide quietly out the door and back down the stairs of the office to the ground floor then into the yard.

She stood for a moment and breathed in the sea air which was particularly pungent today. There was something about being indoors, and especially in the confines of an office, that made Rosie feel as if she was being deprived of air. Now she was outside, she filled her lungs, and listened to the overwhelming sounds of the shipyard – of man, metal and machinery. She had been in the meeting longer than anticipated – hadn't even been aware of the klaxon going off. Rosie looked across to the dry basin and spotted her women welders hard at work, all of them encased in an umbrella of sparkling, red hot molten metal.

Rosie spotted Gloria straight away. Now that the women had their names emblazoned on their helmets there was no need to guess who was who. She took a deep breath and walked purposefully over to the dock.

She had to tell Gloria the news about Jack at once.

It was only fair.

Chapter Five

' "A coma"? What does that mean? I mean . . . I *know* what a coma is, but . . . ' Gloria's head felt like it was spinning. Her brain was muddled. She didn't seem to be able to think straight.

She felt Rosie take her hand and give it a gentle squeeze. The pair of them were seated in the canteen. It was quiet, save for the noise of the dinner ladies clearing up from the lunchtime rush. Pots and pans were being banged about and leftover food scraped off plates and slopped into large metal waste bins.

'Does that mean he's going to live?' Gloria implored.

'I don't know,' Rosie said. She felt so helpless. She didn't know whether to be positive, and in doing so perhaps give Gloria false hope, or be more honest, and admit that in all truthfulness the little bit of information Miriam had imparted had not sounded good.

'Did Miriam say anything else? Anything about what the doctors said? People come out of comas, don't they?' Gloria asked desperately. Gloria rarely uttered Miriam's name, she hated the woman so much, but at this moment in time she didn't give a damn. Every drop of her mind was focused on Jack, and every ounce of emotion taken up with her feelings for the man she had fallen in love with as a young girl, and who she had fallen in love with all over again this past year.

For want of words Rosie squeezed Gloria's hand again. She then poured her a cup of tea from the pot she had bought when they came in, adding a good heap of sugar. She wished she had a hip flask of brandy or whisky like the ones some of the men kept in their overall pockets.

'From the little I know I think it's just a case of wait and see,' Rosie said, pushing Gloria's cup towards her. Gloria took a sip, but didn't put the cup down, instead keeping it suspended just inches away from her mouth. Her eyes looked lost and forlorn, but, unlike Miriam's, her eyes were dry. There were no tears.

Although Rosie had never seen Jack and Gloria together as a couple as their love affair had been clandestine (no one, not even any of the women welders, had known they were seeing each other – let alone had become lovers – until after Jack had left for America), but all the same, Rosie could tell they'd make a good couple; she'd seen them chatting in the yard on a number of occasions and it was obvious how at ease and happy they were in each other's company.

But Jack and Miriam as husband and wife? They were an odd mix. Like chalk and cheese, but not in a good way. Not in an 'opposites attract' way. Jack was a nice bloke, whereas Miriam was not a nice woman. And their daughter Helen was most definitely not a nice girl. Rosie leant back in her metal chair and the two women sat in silence and tried their best to digest the news they had been given this last hour.

'At least he's alive,' Rosie ventured.

'Yes, of course,' Gloria muttered, still staring ahead, her cup in hand. 'There is that . . . God, this is the last thing I expected. I should really be thanking my lucky stars that he's not dead – but being in a coma doesn't really feel like he's actually alive. Does it?'

Rosie nodded her agreement. 'I know.'

'Either of you two need a top-up there?' a harsh, but friendly, heavily accented voice shouted over. It was

Muriel, one of the older women, who worked in the canteen.

'We're fine, thanks,' Rosie shouted back over. She looked at Gloria, who had put her teacup down but had not drunk more than a sip.

'You heard anything from Vinnie lately?' Rosie asked. It was an often repeated enquiry. That man was trouble. And his temper was dangerous. She had seen for herself the marks left by his fists on her workmate's face, and the bruises round her neck where he had tried to squeeze the living daylights out of her. It made her blood well and truly boil. After the last episode, when Gloria had come into work with a black eye and a mouth so bruised and puffed up she could hardly talk, Rosie had been livid and determined to put a stop to him – although she'd had to admit she was at a loss to know exactly what to do.

Gloria herself had got a legal letter drafted at the end of last year threatening him with the law if he was violent towards her again, and that had worked for a while, but it had proved to be just a temporary solution to the problem.

Rosie had gone as far as discussing the problem with Peter who, she could tell, had been equally horrified that a man could be so violent to a woman, let alone his own wife. A week or so later they had heard through one of the caulkers, whose girlfriend worked with Vinnie at the ropery, that he had apparently been mugged and given a good going over. It had seemed too much of a coincidence that he'd been given a bashing so soon after he had done the same to Gloria. Rosie had tentatively broached the subject with Peter, but he had remained straight-faced, and she hadn't known how to interpret the words he used on hearing the news. 'Divine intervention,' he had said. A perfectly innocent comment – or one infused with irony? She still wasn't sure.

'Funny you should ask about Vinnie,' Gloria said, distractedly, 'but he turned up last night. Shortly after Dorothy left . . . she came round to give Hope a two-week-old birthday present . . . ' Gloria's mind was wandering.

'What did he want?' Rosie pursued. She was worried. It had been months since he had seen Gloria. Why turn up now?

'Oh, he said he wanted to see the baby,' Gloria mumbled, looking out the canteen window at a pair of young lads – one heating rivets with a big pair of tongs and then throwing them to his mate. It was like some strange game of catch, only played with a red hot metal bolt.

'And did he – *see the baby*?' Rosie asked, taking hold of Gloria's hand and trying to draw her attention back to the here and now. She looked miles away. Totally lost in thought.

Gloria turned her focus back to Rosie.

'God, no! Over my dead body.' As she uttered the words they looked at each other, imagining the scene: Vinnie stepping over Gloria's lifeless body to get to the child he believed was his. Neither Gloria nor Rosie was in any doubt that if Vinnie was riled up enough – and inebriated enough – he would be capable of losing it so badly that he might indeed take a life. And there would be no question as to whose life that would be.

'The problem is,' Gloria continued, 'I know this is just the start and there'll be more visits. As long as he thinks the baby is his, he's going to be determined to be a part of her life. Even if it's just to cause me grief.'

Gloria sighed heavily.

'I was all set to come clean about who Hope's real father was when she was born. That day here in the yard, when I held her in my arms and we were all bawling our eyes out –' both women automatically smiled as they remembered the scene '– I vowed to myself,' Gloria continued, her voice becoming thick with emotion, 'that as soon as Jack was back – *if* he came back alive – I would tell him Hope was his. And that I would be open and honest about everything . . . Which, of course,' Gloria added ominously, 'meant telling Vinnie that the child was *not* his. That I had been with another man.'

'Not that that should have mattered,' Rosie jumped in. 'I mean, he had been seeing – *and sleeping with* – that Sarah for a whole *two years* behind your back. And then you finally chuck him out and say "no" to any more beatings – and in a blink of an eye – or rather the time it took him to walk from the Ford estate to Grindon – he's shacked up with his bit on the side.'

Rosie felt herself getting annoyed at the injustice of it all. She knew no one would condemn Vinnie for moving in with his mistress, but God only knew what kind of vicious gossip Gloria would be subjected to if people found out she had borne a child by a man who was not her husband.

'I know it's wrong,' Gloria added, 'but it's just the way it is – one rule for them and another for us. The thing is, I was more than willing to take the flak for it, to be looked at like I was some harlot –' she looked at Rosie and wished she could have taken the words back.

'Sorry, I didn't mean . . . ' Gloria apologised.

Rosie immediately dismissed her comments with a wave of her hand, saying, 'But now you really are stuck between a rock and a hard place. It wouldn't be fair to declare that Hope is Jack's – not with him being in a coma – and you cannot really tell Vinnie that the baby's not his, because . . . God knows what would happen. It doesn't bear thinking about. If you tell him, you *have* to have Jack by your side . . . I think at the moment,' she continued, 'you've only got one option – and that's to keep mum.'

Gloria looked back at her boss, her friend and her confidante, and smiled dejectedly.

As they left the canteen and trudged back to the dry dock in silence, Rosie's mind was swinging between thoughts of Jack lying in a coma, and Vinnie's dark and threatening re-emergence. If only Jack and Vinnie could swap places. As it was, she would not like to be in Gloria's shoes. Not for one moment.

When they'd climbed down into the dry dock where the women were working this afternoon on a frigate that had been caught in a mine blast and had suffered serious, but not irreparable, damage to its underside, Rosie walked over to Angie and tapped her on the shoulder. Her weld had died on her and when she lifted her mask her face was full of angry frustration.

'You're holding your rod too far away from the plate. That's why your arc keeps going out.' As she spoke, Rosie bobbed down so she didn't have to shout over the commotion of the yard. 'And if you loop the lead around your arm it'll take some of the weight off,' she advised. Angie was still learning the ropes when it came to welding, but she was a quick learner and only ever needed telling something the once.

Angie nodded her understanding but didn't bother to speak; she had learnt fairly soon after starting work at Thompson's that talk was pretty pointless as the noise of the yard was simply too much to contend with.

Sensing they had company, the women broke off from their welding and looked up to see that Rosie and Gloria had returned. Dorothy immediately pushed her helmet up and opened her mouth to speak, but before she had time to say anything, Rosie beat her to it.

'The Admiral. After work!' she shouted out, knowing

that if the women couldn't hear her they had probably lip-read her words, something they were getting quite adept at doing.

Dorothy closed her mouth and looked over at Gloria with concern. The women pushed their helmets back down and worked steadily through until the end of the shift. They all guessed that there must be some news about Jack, and judging by both their workmates' faces, it was not good.

Chapter Six

Borough Road, Sunderland

Later on that evening, Rosie hurried out of her basement flat as quickly as she could in her new red leather peep-toe shoes. The weather was just on the turn. There was a nip in the air and the approach of autumn was making itself felt, even though it was still a good few weeks away. Most nights Rosie was happy to walk the mile from her flat to Ashbrooke, but tonight she was running late after going to the Admiral, and had decided to catch the bus.

As Rosie hurried along the main road, she thought about her women welders and how supportive they had been of Gloria – all telling her not to worry and that Jack would surely come out of his coma. The expressions on their faces, though, belied what she knew they had really been thinking: the prognosis for Jack did not look good.

The seriousness of the situation had been further forced home when Hannah had asked what 'coma' meant, and Polly had explained, 'It's when the body closes down and goes into a really deep sleep.'

'Ah *bezvědomí*,' Hannah had murmured the word in her home tongue, adding, 'So, he might not wake?'

The women had all looked into their drinks, apart from Dorothy, whose deep concern for Gloria was etched on her young, pretty face, as she had exclaimed, 'Oh, but he *will*. He's *got* to. I just know he will.'

As Rosie continued to hurry along the road, she swung

her head back hoping to see a bus or a tram. This evening, like most these days, she had a lot to do at Lily's. She had started to do the bookkeeping and it was not easy, but it was necessary if she was to get to grips with how a business was run – even if that business wasn't a legitimate one. And as Lily was now so busy schlepping up and down the country to London and back, more and more of the managerial side of the bordello was being left for Rosie to sort out, which meant she had to put in all the hours she could outside of her work at the yard. She didn't mind, though. She was already seeing the financial benefits. The long hours were more than worth it; she had achieved what she had worked so hard to do, and the reason she had started working at Lily's all those years ago: she had ensured that her little sister would never see the inside of a workhouse – or some godforsaken children's home.

As Rosie checked again behind her for a bus, her mind, as it was wont to do when she thought about Charlotte or the past, threw up an image of her uncle Raymond. Her body gave an involuntary shiver that had nothing to do with the cold. Rosie had accepted that she would never be able to erase her uncle from her consciousness, nor the night when she was just fifteen years old, just days after she and Charlotte had been orphaned when their mum and dad had been killed in a hit-and-run accident. The night her uncle had violated her. When she had been forced to allow him to defile her body in order for her younger sister, who was then just eight years old, to keep her innocence.

Rosie knew she would never be able to get rid of the scars he had left her with – both the ones on her face and those you couldn't see – but at least she was alive and he was dead.

Finally he had got his comeuppance after nearly killing

her just nine months previously by forcing her head over a live weld. If her women welders hadn't come to her rescue, and her uncle hadn't stumbled and fallen into the river, Rosie would not be here now.

Rosie was well aware of the irony that it was due, in part, to her uncle that she was now in such a favourable financial situation, and that she was no longer working as an employee at the bordello but now part-owned it. Rosie knew her life had been cursed by her uncle but at least something positive had come out of his death, as she had been able to reclaim all the money she had been forced to hand over to him during the months he had been black-mailing her.

As Rosie strode up the slight incline to the bus stop she pulled her belt tight around her waist and tucked the large collar of her trench coat across her neck to keep out the early evening chill. She was glad she was wearing her new cream slacks that her old schoolfriend Kate, who had recently become the bordello's unofficial seamstress, had made for her. They were so comfortable and practical, and because they were now in vogue, she could get away with wearing them.

Lily had told her that she did not agree with women wearing trousers, but she'd added that as Rosie had man-aged to look ladylike in hers, and not like one of those 'butch women', she would let it pass. Rosie had laughed out loud at the outrageousness of Lily's comments, remind-ing her that they were now joint owners and if she wanted to wear a coal sack to work she would. Rosie chuckled to herself as she recalled how Lily had actually blanched at the thought.

As she hurried towards the bus stop, the number seven drove straight past her. 'Damn!' she cursed out loud.

As she did so, she saw the dark outline of a figure that

had been walking along the unlit street just ahead of her, suddenly turn around. Rosie stopped dead in her tracks when she saw who it was.

'Peter!' she said, her shock and surprise audible.

'Rosie!' DS Miller also sounded taken aback.

There was a moment's awkward silence.

'How are you keeping?' the detective asked. His voice sounded unsure and faltering. It had been over a month since Rosie told him she no longer wanted to see him, and not a day had gone by when he had not spent a good part of it thinking about her. His work with the Dock Police and for the town's civil defence might be time-consuming, but it was quite boring – which meant he'd had too much time to stew over why their courtship had ended so abruptly. The hours he had spent mulling it over, however, had not resulted in any kind of answer.

'Yes, I'm well, thank you, Peter.' Rosie could feel her face flush red. Her heart had suddenly started to beat like a drum and was causing her to sound a little breathless.

'And, yourself?' Rosie asked, self-consciously pulling her coat tightly around her. Peter had never seen her in anything but her work overalls, and she suddenly worried that he would notice she was dressed up and wonder where she was going. She should have known better, though. Peter was a detective, after all. She followed his gaze as he looked down at her red shoes.

'Yes, yes, all good,' DS Miller said, a little distractedly. The way Rosie was done up had caught him off guard. *Where was she going?*

'I see you're off up the town,' he went on, dragging his gaze away from her footwear and finding himself looking into her made-up face. Her hair also looked different. Rosie was now sporting a short, thick bob. And she was wearing perfume, too.

'Yes, yes, I am,' Rosie mumbled. She had never been a great liar and her mind had frozen. She couldn't think quickly enough to make something up, so she offered no explanation.

A wave of jealousy hit DS Miller as the possibility struck him that she was going on a date – with another man. *If she wasn't, why not tell him where she was going?*

'Rosie,' he started, 'I've wanted to see you since that day . . . '

Rosie looked down the road, hoping another bus would come along and save her.

'I really wanted to chat to you. Talk about why you said what you said.'

Another pause.

'I still can't understand why?' DS Miller was trying hard to keep any sign of desperation out of his voice. This wasn't going the way he had wanted. 'I honestly thought there was something between the two of us.' He could sense he was losing her, knew she just wanted to get on her way.

'I'm sorry, Peter,' Rosie began. 'I just . . . can't.' She was at a loss for words.

'Please, Rosie . . . ' DS Miller couldn't stop himself, ' . . . meet me at Vera's on Wednesday? Let's talk about this properly. Over a cup of tea . . . I think we owe it to each other.'

At the mention of Vera's, he saw a flicker of emotion cross Rosie's face. He could see her shoulders drop a little, and her face soften. He was surprised at how well the make-up hid the tiny scars scattered across her face. She had told him on the day he had first met her – when he had gone to inform her about her uncle's untimely demise – that the burns were the result of 'a weld gone wrong'.

Every minute of their first meeting was still fresh in his

memory; how she had touched her face self-consciously as she explained to him that she was a welder at Thompson's and that she'd had 'a bit of an accident'. Was it then that he had fallen for her? She was like no other woman he had ever met.

DS Miller took a deep breath.

'Please?' he implored, gently taking hold of Rosie's hand. To his joy, Rosie did not pull away. Instead he felt her fingers touching the rough skin on his hands. It took all of his willpower to stop himself pulling her towards him and kissing her. But, of course, he could not – not after what had happened last time. It would be the worst thing he could do. He had scared her off then. He couldn't make the same mistake again.

Just then he saw Rosie divert her attention from him. She was looking behind him. He swung his head around to see a bus chugging its way up the gently sloping road, its beam dimmed and headlights covered by what looked like huge plastic eyelids, as required by the government's blackout regulations.

DS Miller kept a hold of Rosie's hand, but she gently tugged it away, her fingers trailing across his open palm as she broke free from his grasp. Her face looked a picture of indecision, before she threw her arm out to hail the bus. DS Miller could hear the brakes being applied and watched as Rosie turned in anticipation of leaving him.

The bus came to a halt and Rosie climbed on board, but just as the driver put the engine into first gear and started to pull away, she turned to DS Miller. 'All right, Vera's. The usual time,' she agreed.

And with that the bus gathered momentum – and Rosie was once again taken from him.

Standing there in the darkness, his woollen coat flapping open in rhythm with the cold breeze coming in from the North Sea, he realised that, not for the first time, he was at a loss as to what to make of their encounter.

Of course, he was elated that Rosie had agreed to meet up with him. It would give him the chance to really talk to her, work out why exactly she did not want to continue their courtship, especially when he felt she *really* did want to see him – that she did have feelings for him.

He had to admit that he was totally baffled by this woman he had fallen for. Since the beginning of the year they had spent just about every Wednesday teatime cosied up in Vera's café, chatting, laughing, philosophising. They had got on like a house on fire, and it was clear that this was more than friendship. Friends didn't look at each other the way he looked at Rosie and the way, much as she tried to disguise it, she looked at him.

He had an overwhelming urge to run after the bus and follow Rosie into town to see where she was going, and if she was seeing another man, but he forced himself not to.

'Argh!' Detective Sergeant Miller sounded out his frustrations into the night air.

When Rosie walked through the front door of Lily's she was hit by a warm gust of smoky, perfumed air and the tinkling of a piano being played in the reception room. It was the complete antithesis of the sounds, smells and sights of the yard.

As always, whenever Rosie stepped over the threshold of the bordello, it was like being transported from a world of black and white and into one painted in Technicolor. And this evening Rosie sensed an added hum of excitement in the air.

'Oh, *ma chérie*!' Lily cried out as she came out of the back parlour and spotted Rosie. She almost broke into a trot, but was prevented by the confines of her tightly fitted fishtail skirt

'You wouldn't guess what?' she asked, looking over the half-moon spectacles that were perched delicately on the bridge of her small but perfectly shaped nose.

Rosie looked at her friend, who was now also her business partner, and smiled. Lily's dyed-auburn hair was, as usual, carefully crafted into an elaborate bun, but in the flurry of the evening's events, various strands had broken free.

'I have no idea, Lily,' Rosie said, 'but I am sure you're going to tell me. Let's go into the office. You can tell me your news there.'

The reason Rosie wanted to seek sanctuary in the front room, which had been converted into a very resplendent office, was that it was usually quiet there and she had a half-full decanter of Rémy Martin. And after bumping into Peter, she needed a drink.

Lily agreed to a tipple, but looked a little surprised to see Rosie pouring herself a drink so early – on top of which she was using the expensive brandy from the thick crystal cut-glass decanter that was usually kept for the sole consumption of the clients who came in to settle their bills.

'Come on then. What's happened?' Rosie asked, glad of the distraction from her own panicked thoughts about agreeing to meet up with Peter at the café.

'Well, *ma chère*.' Lily took a quick sip of her drink, before she continued. 'Old Mrs Pemberton, you know – our neighbour on the right, has passed away.'

Rosie spluttered on her brandy. 'God, Lily! You could at least pretend to be a little sad.'

'Oh, I know, that came out all wrong, sorry, anyone would think I was a heartless old cow.' Lily's cockney accent came to the fore as it always did when she was excited, angry, or a little inebriated.

'No, I am really, truly sorry. Poor woman,' Lily rested her hand on her ample bosom, which had been squeezed into a stylish, but rather risqué, black corseted top, 'but she *was* nearly ninety,' she added. 'And at least now – what do people like to believe? – she'll be together again with her dear husband Ernest.'

Rosie pursed her lips, feigning disapproval.

Just then the sound of the front door shutting could be heard and the distinctive sound of a walking stick hitting the polished parquet flooring of the hallway. Lily jumped up from the chaise longue she had been perched on.

'Perfect timing! It's George!' And she tottered to the half-open doorway of the drawing room.

'George, come in.' She waved her hand. Rosie thought she caught her giving George a rather cheeky, secret wink. One day Rosie would get to the bottom of what was really going on between the two of them. Were they really just friends, like they purported to be? Or was there more to the relationship than they were willing to disclose?

As George entered the room, dressed in a dapper deep blue three-piece suit and swinging his walking stick energetically, he made a beeline for Rosie and performed his usual ritual of taking her hand and planting a kiss on it. George was nothing if not a true gentleman.

'I was just telling Rosie here about poor Mrs Pemberton from next door,' Lily said, sitting back down on the small sofa and patting the place next to her, signalling George to join her.

'Oh, yes, Mrs Pemberton,' George said by way of encouragement but wanting Lily to carry on talking.

'But now you're here,' Lily said, 'you can tell Rosie

yourself about your plan.' She was clearly determined that George be a part of the conversation.

'*Our* plan,' George corrected, getting out a large cotton hankie, on which his initials were embroidered, and wiping perspiration from his forehead and the side of his face where a deep white scar was the permanent reminder of his time spent fighting in the First World War.

'Well, Rosie, I think what Lily wants to tell you is that she and I are going to buy next door!' George declared grandly, before continuing, 'As you know, I'm not exactly short of a few bob and I've a load of money just sitting doing nothing in the bank so I thought it was about time I spent it.'

'Why that's great news, George.' Rosie paused and looked at Lily with a curious smile on her face. 'So, does this mean you two will be "cohabiting" – is that the correct turn of phrase?'

Lily almost choked on her brandy. '*Mon Dieu!* Rosie, I think you must have love and romance on your mind at the moment!' She took another sip of brandy as if to steady her nerves at such an outlandish suggestion. 'I wonder what could make you think that I would do something as scandalous as "living in sin".' As Lily spoke, a wide, mischievous grin spread across her face.

Sometimes Rosie really struggled to know how to take Lily. She did think it interesting, though, that she had not reacted in shock, or even rebuffed the idea that she and George might live together as a couple.

'*Non, non, ma petite,*' Lily said, 'George and I are simply going to be joint owners. Partners in property, should I say.' She took a deliberate swig of her brandy and continued. 'We're not sure what we're going to do with the house just yet, but we think it's a good investment for the future. Some may think us mad with all the bombs being dropped around our ears, but we reckon we're going to be safe here in Ashbrooke. Hitler's more interested in obliterating the shipyards. Not much over this way Jerry wants shot of.'

'I suppose you could rent the house out,' Rosie volunteered. 'Or were you thinking we'd branch out. Extend the bordello?'

George nodded in agreement. 'We're definitely thinking along those lines. See,' he turned to Lily, who was now sitting by his side, 'natural business head on this one. She's going to go far.'

'I know, George,' Lily said in her most uppity of voices. 'And don't forget I was the one to bring her on board. I was the one who actually spotted Rosie's business acumen all those years ago when she first came here. But, of course, as always, no one listened to me.'

Rosie smiled, but her mind had started to wander back to her meeting with Peter. She did not want to tell Lily. She would only start to worry that their romance might be reignited, condemning them all to a good few years in some grotty prison cell.

'Well, some of us better get on and do some work.' Rosie opened up one of the drawers and pulled out her heavy accounts ledger, dropping it on to the leather-embossed desktop with a thud.

'All right, my dear, we'll leave you to your numbers, but before I go, there is just one more piece of exciting news I have to communicate to you.'

Rosie raised her eyebrows. 'More?' she asked.

'Yes, I've got to head back down to La Lumière Bleue.'

La Lumière Bleue was Lily's second business, which she had started up earlier in the year in London's red light district. It was also the reason why Rosie's responsibilities had increased so much of late, for Lily was creating what she called a '*magnifique*' Marie-Antoinette-themed

bordello in the heart of Soho. For its name she had un-
ashamedly copied the so-called 'blue-light' brothels that
had started up in Paris and were catering for a higher class
of clientele.

'I've a lovely, quite exquisite young woman who has
recently come under my employ in London. She's quite
divine; petite, so colourful, so full of life. And what is more
exciting is that she has asked to come and work here!'

Rosie looked puzzled.

'Well, that's a turn-up for the books. It's usually the
other way round – the girls wanting to go to London. I
mean the money's better and, let's face it – it's easier to
keep yourself to yourself there. What's made her want to
come up north? And to Sunderland, of all places?'

'Exactly the same questions I put to her,' Lily said, getting up to refill George's glass as well as her own. 'She
says she has relatives up here who she's been meaning to
come and see for some time – to "reacquaint" herself with
them. That's the way she speaks – ever so la-di-da . . . My
guess, though, is that she's probably running away from
something – or someone. But, who am I to meddle in the
business of others?'

Rosie let rip a laugh of pure scepticism, while George
forced himself to suppress a chuckle.

'Let me just interpret,' Rosie said with more than a little
mischief in her voice. 'This "exquisite" young woman is
going to be a great – and more than likely bankable – asset,
and you don't really give two hoots why she is heading up
north – only that she *is* – and that it's going to benefit you –
and the business – massively?'

'How did you get to be cynical, Rosie?' Lily shuffled up
next to George, who went to put his arm around her but
stopped himself.

'Spending too much time here!' Rosie joked back, but

she hadn't missed George's near show of affection for Lily, and for a short moment she stared at the pair of them with a question on her face.

They both looked away.

'Well,' Rosie said, filling the embarrassed silence. 'I look forward to meeting this "exquisite, colourful little bird" . . . but,' she said, putting on a matronly voice and shooing them away with both her hands, 'in the meantime, go and see our guests and let me get on with some work.'

Chapter Seven

Hendon Beach, Sunderland

April 1913

The tide had turned and seemed to be coming in quickly. The sea was lively and the waves seemed more frothy than normal. Pearl stood at the bottom of a sloping hill that was more mud and rock than grass, and which led up from the shingly sand of Hendon beach.

She wasn't alone as she bent down and picked up small round black nuggets of coal; on either side of her there were others, mainly women using their long skirts and aprons as makeshift bags in which they would carry their loot back home.

Pearl's heart leapt as she spotted a particularly large chunk of jet black stone. Her dirty hand quickly reached out to grab it, but she was too late – a large, callused hand belonging to one of the local fishwives got there first.

'You'll have to be quicker than that, bonny lass,' she cackled.

Pearl was caught between outraged anger and the need to cry with despair and tiredness. She looked at the older woman whose rotund body was protected from the bitter autumn cold by layers of skirts, petticoats and shawls.

'Yer dinnit need any coal with all that fat on yer,' Pearl spat out, wanting to hurt the woman for stealing what should have been hers.

The old woman simply laughed at the young girl's cheek, and shouted back as she hauled her black treasure in her large wicker basket up the hill.

'Come down to the docks and I'll put some meat on those skinny bones of yours. I'll boil yer up some nice tasty fish heads!' she shouted over her shoulder. The seagulls above her squawked as if in anticipation of such a feast.

The thought of any kind of food, even if it was a couple of smelly fish heads, had Pearl's mouth watering. She was starving. If she could just get enough coal, then the sooner she could get back home and get something in her belly the better. If she was lucky, her ma might have got some cut-offs of meat from the butcher's to make into a hot stew.

As soon as the thought flitted through her mind, though, it was dismissed.

'Chance'd be a fine thing,' Pearl muttered to herself.

The small rocks of washed-up fuel that had dropped from the local colliers heading out to sea would, at most, warm her, but any food which came her way would more than likely be a bit of bread and lard. At best she could fry the bread up once the fire was going.

Pearl's stomach started to growl.

Half an hour later, her small sack was almost full, which was just as well, as the light had nearly gone, and the tide had almost reached the pebbles at the bottom of the hill. Her bare feet were sore and had gone way beyond cold.

Pearl walked up the steep slope along with the last couple of remaining coal pickers – an old man, and a young woman who was clearly in the family way. Pearl looked at the girl's swollen belly and her worn-out face; she recognised her from around the doors, and knew her to be just seventeen, although she looked years older.

Pearl knew she still only looked her fourteen years of age, but at this moment in time, with her numb feet, her hands cut to shreds, and her aching back, having been bent scouring the beach like a man-sized crab for the last few hours, she felt the same age as the old fishwife she'd set her lip up to.

As she half carried, half dragged her bag of washed-up coal back along the cobbled pavements to the slums near the south dock, to the tenement where she lived with her ma and da and six other siblings, she fought back the terrible feeling of dread that had been growing inside her for the past few weeks and instead she concentrated on simply getting home, getting warm, and finding something to eat.

Then she would be able to work out what to do.

'Is that you, Pearl?' Her ma's voice was louder than need be and there was the hint of a slur. Pearl's mum, Edna, was drunk which, Pearl knew, with a sinking heart, ruled out any chance of a hot stew, even if it had been a watery stew, made with just fat and offal.

'Aye, it's me, Ma,' Pearl shouted down the hallway.

'About bloody time,' her ma yelled back. 'Ger in here with that coal 'n get the fire gannin . . . and put the bar down while yer at it. Everyone's in for the night now.'

Pearl wearily put her bag down and turned back to the thick wooden front door. With her scrawny arms she reached down and picked up a large plank of wood which she then put across the door. She had never really understood why they had to do this every night as it wasn't as if they had anything to steal, but all the same, the family upstairs and her own ma and da seemed to view it as a must.

'Well, come on. Dinnit take all day!' her mother shouted through from the back kitchen. When Pearl entered the dark, candlelit parlour, she saw her three youngest siblings cuddled up on the threadbare sofa. They were play fighting and scratching their heads at the same time. Pearl knew what that meant, and made a mental note not to go near them.

Her ma had her baby sister in her arms, and judging by her partly exposed breast she had just fed the baby, which was probably why she wasn't screaming her head off like she did most of the time. She could hear her father and her older brothers out the backyard. God knew what they had been up to, not that she particularly wanted to know. If they had just come in over the back wall, they'd probably been out on the rob, which might also explain why her ma wanted the door secured so quickly. Either way, it didn't make any difference to Pearl. If there was any loot to be had, or enjoyed, she was never privy to it.

As she knelt down to stack up the little bundle of kindling she had gathered earlier on in the day, a blast of cold air rushed through the room as her father and two siblings came in from the cold, rubbing their hands and laughing loudly at some shared joke. Her brothers Johnnie and James were a few years older than Pearl, and had inherited their father's strong physique and dark looks, just like Pearl had her mother's bony frame and fair hair.

'Ah, yer a good lass, Pearl, getting us our warmth fer the night. Stick the kettle on while yer there. Me and the boys are in need of a nice hot brew.'

It would never occur to her father that his sons do anything in the house, even something as simple as making a pot of tea. It seemed to be an unwritten law of the land that a man did not lift a finger in his own home. The man was the king of the castle. The lord of the manor. And it was up to the women of the house to serve him.

As Pearl prepared the fire, the room became alive with the animated talk of men discussing the ins and outs of the FA Cup final, which had seemed to whip the whole of

Sunderland up into a frenzy. The excitement and anticipation had been followed by a thick, depressive air of gloom after the town's revered football team was beaten by a team called Aston Villa at some place called 'Crystal Palace'. Football held no interest for Pearl, but the venue of the game had conjured up wonderful images of a sparkling, magical wonderland.

As the men's talk got louder and louder, so did the shrieks and cries of Pearl's three younger siblings now fighting more than playing on the sofa. Pearl got to work getting the fire going. Tonight she was tired, and just wanted to put something in her belly and then crawl off to bed. She could tell her da and brothers had been to the Welcome Tavern just across the road from where they lived on Barrack Street. It meant they must have had some success in whatever wrongdoing they had been up to.

As Pearl reached for the matches across the old Victorian range, she accidentally knocked over her mother's cup, which had been left on the floor. Quick as a flash her mother turned on her.

'Watch it, yer clumsy clot!' she said, grabbing the mug and sucking the last few drops out of the bottom. By the smell Pearl could tell it was gin. Her ma had probably got it from the bloke down the street who brewed it in his backyard.

As Pearl worked the blower with the last bit of strength left in her arms, and the flames slowly started to lick up and create a yellowy-orange glow, the banter between her mother and father started up; as it always did. It would begin in a jokey fashion and could be quite amusing sometimes – but then it invariably turned nasty.

Pearl was determined to have her bread and lard and get to bed before the atmosphere soured.

As she stood up from the fire, which had now caught and was starting to throw out heat, she felt a twinge in her stomach. She knew it wasn't the deep gnawing pain of hunger that could be remedied with a piece of stale bread or a gulp of milk – no, this pain was something else entirely, which she knew could not be so easily cured – if at all. She had tried these past few weeks to find a solution to her problem, to put an end to what was happening to her body, but she had so far not succeeded. She had sneaked into the public baths up the road and sat for ages in the hottest water she could endure until she had been shouted at to 'Gerr out!', but nothing had happened. She had pinched some of her mother's gin and drunk as much of it as she could, but all that had done was to make her sick. There was another option, but that needed money, and she didn't have any. And besides, going to those places down the back lanes of the east end scared her. She had heard horror stories of young girls bleeding to death or dying in pain slowly with the fever.

Pearl pushed through her da and her brothers who had formed a human barrier across the front of the stove so as to warm their backs on the now roaring fire, and headed to the cupboard in the corner of the room. She had to tiptoe to open the doors and look in. Her heart sank when she saw there was nothing in there. As she looked down, she saw a slice of bread had fallen by the side of the little wooden table and on to the dirt floor. Quickly she picked it up and slid it into her pocket and hurried off to her bed in the front room.

She was so tired and she was so cold, she didn't even attempt to take her clothes off and put on one of her mother's old raggedy dresses she used as a nightie. Instead she pulled back the blankets on top of the dirty lumpy mattress to check for cockroaches. They were one of the few things that really frightened her – which was stupid, as she should have been used to them by now. After all, they had been her bedfellows for as long as she could remember, but still, she had never got used to them. They never once failed to make her jump like a right old scaredy cat. She took great pleasure in killing them, but they were resilient buggers and sometimes took a good hammering before they stopped wriggling about. But it was the rats which really terrified her. It wasn't very often they got into the front room, but there had been one or two occasions when they had, and she had screamed the house down.

Feeling assured that there were neither cockroaches nor rats to disturb her tonight, Pearl sat in her bed and ate her slice of bread. She knew that, at the moment, her mother and father had no idea about her condition. She put her hand on her stomach and thought about the woman on the beach picking coal and how huge her tummy was. It panicked Pearl to think that she too would be that size in a few months. She didn't know how far gone she was, only that she hadn't had the curse for a couple of months. Why it was called 'the curse' she would never know. She would give anything to be cursed to kingdom come; every time she went to the lavvy she begged for a visit from what some called their 'lady friend'. God, what she would give for her to come knocking now.

As Pearl felt her eyes droop with the heaviness of sleep a part of her wished she simply wouldn't wake up. At least that would be an answer to her problem.

Chapter Eight

Vera's Café, High Street East, Sunderland

Wednesday 3 September 1941

It had been exactly six days since Rosie had bumped into Peter on her way to work, and during that time every spare moment she had – when she was not either working or doing the books at the bordello – she was thinking about her meeting with Peter.

As Rosie made her way up to Vera's café halfway along High Street East, just up from the south dock, the threatening dark clouds started to drip and the air was filled with a thin sheen of spittle, hinting at heavier rain to come. Rosie barely noticed the greying skies, nor the fact that her bare face was now wet; her mind was totally focused on what she was about to do, what she had planned to say – and how she would say it. A surge of nerves and excitement suddenly rushed through her at the thought of seeing Peter, but she stopped them dead in their tracks and immediately reined them back in. She could not allow as much as a hairline fracture let her true feelings break through.

Six weeks ago she had told Peter that she did not want to carry on their courtship – albeit their very chaste courtship, but still a courtship all the same. She realised she had tried to ignore what was happening, to pretend that she and the detective could simply be friends who met up every week for tea and a chat. Even when Peter had started to hold her hand and walk her home, Rosie had kept on lying to herself. But when he had tried to kiss her, she could no longer continue to live in her world of denial and she'd had to tell him straight that there was no future for them together, and that they could not continue to see each other.

She would never forget the look of complete and utter shock – and worse, the look of heartbreak – on Peter's face that day. She had fobbed him off with a muttered excuse, but she had not really offered up any kind of explanation. Instead, she had turned her back on him and disappeared into her flat.

She hadn't seen hide nor hair of him until the other day. But this was a relatively small town; she should have realised it was likely they would meet again. She should have been more prepared.

Well, Rosie said to herself as she walked towards the café, *at least I am now.*

Rosie knew that they had crossed a line and, even if they wanted to, they could not step back over it. By his actions Peter had left no room for doubt as to what his intentions were: he wanted Rosie as more than just a friend. Much more. And what was even more frustrating was that she too also wanted more. She could no longer ignore the incredible pull of attraction she felt – something she had never felt for any man before in her life.

That she had to have those feelings at this stage of her life – and for someone who worked for the local constabulary – was just so bloody typical. She'd always known it would be tricky to embark on a relationship with someone who was not, in some way, a part of the life she lived at the bordello – but it might have been viable. Stepping out with a copper, though, and one she knew was fervent about law and order, was, without a doubt, one hundred per cent impossible.

Why hadn't she nipped it in the bud at the start? She had been foolish in the extreme. If Peter had found out about the bordello, her whole stack of cards would have come tumbling down, destroying everyone else's lives around her – as well as her own. She had been playing with fire and, in many ways, was lucky she had not got burnt. She was ashamed of herself not just for having put her own livelihood at risk, as well as that of Lily and all the girls, but most of all for jeopardising her sister's future. Her life.

One night, just before she had called it a day with Peter, she had overheard Lily talking to George, expressing concerns about her continuing dalliance with the detective.

'George,' she'd said, 'if Rosie's copper finds out about her work here, it'll be me and her who'll be looking at a fine so big it'll wipe us out financially, and we'll be on the streets for sure – as will Rosie's little sister. And that's the "best case" scenario . . . If the law throws the book at us, there's a good chance we could even end up in the slammer!'

Rosie cringed as she recalled George's reply: 'Rosie would never risk everything – especially Charlotte's future – *for a man*. That much I know.'

But she nearly had – hadn't she?

Well, here she was now, paying the price for her sheer stupidity.

As Rosie reached the glass-panelled front door of the café, she threw a quick glance through the large floor to ceiling windows that were starting to run with rivulets of rain, but they were masked by steam from the heat inside, making it impossible for her to tell whether Peter was already in there. Placing her hand on the wet brass handle and clicking the latch, she felt a wave of nervousness. She had gone over what she was going to say dozens of times throughout the day.

She knew what she *had* to say – she just had to be convincing in the *way* that she said it. She had to get Peter out of her life for good. For all their sakes. After their meeting today she had to know that if they spotted each other again he would either pretend not to have seen her, or would simply walk the other way.

As soon as she entered the hubbub of the café, Rosie saw Vera's apple-shaped face look up from what appeared to be a brand new copper urn. The old woman's eyes lit up, and her mouth looked about to break into a smile, but it was quickly pulled back lest she tarnish her reputation for being a cantankerous old mare.

It had been two months since Vera had seen Rosie and her detective together; she had thought they were a couple, or at least two people on the verge of being a couple, but then one day Rosie simply hadn't turned up, and the look on the copper's face had spoken a thousand words.

Now, here they were – back in the café.

Vera nodded over to Rosie in acknowledgement of her arrival. She flicked up the tap on her new water dispenser and filled one of her brown ceramic teapots, secretly pleased that the day DS Miller had sat forlornly on his own had not been the end of their affair.

Rosie smiled at Vera and then looked over to the corner table.

When Rosie saw Peter, she took a sharp intake of breath. Why was her instant reaction to hurry over to him, touch his slightly weather-beaten face, and put her mouth to his?

Rosie ripped the thought from her head and dropped her metal guard down firmly in place. She had done it often enough in the past when she needed to do something she didn't want to. It was second nature to her.

'Hello, Peter.' Rosie tried to keep her voice pleasant but without a trace of intimacy in it.

Peter stood up at her arrival. He had already taken his trilby off, otherwise he would have removed it on seeing her. After Rosie pulled out her chair and sat down, he followed suit. As if timed to perfection, Vera arrived at their table and unceremoniously plonked the tin tray down between the two of them and proceeded to offload cups and saucers and a pot of brewed tea. She had also cut them two slices of the Victoria sponge that she had just made that morning and put them on separate plates. She placed a fork next to each.

'Thank you, Vera,' Peter said with a genuine smile.

Rosie looked at the old woman and added her thanks, then Vera grunted her response and shuffled off with her tin tray dangling by her side.

'I hope you didn't mind me ordering the cake,' Peter said. 'I thought it looked too good to pass up on.'

Rosie smiled, although eating was the last thing she felt like doing. She took hold of the pot and with a steady hand poured out their tea.

'Peter,' she said, 'I don't want you to get the wrong impression about why I am here.'

'I know . . . ' Peter butted in, picking up the little white jug and pouring a splash of milk into each of their cups. He couldn't help but look at Rosie now, in her dirty work overalls, her hair bundled up in a bright red headscarf. She didn't have a scrap of make-up on – unlike the other night – and he could clearly see the dozens of scars on her face.

'And I do appreciate you taking the time to talk to me . . . ' he stopped, again at a loss for words, 'well . . . about what happened that day.'

Rosie looked at Peter and was hit by the image of when he had pulled her close and tried to kiss her. She had relived that moment many times in her imagination and each time it had not ended with her rebuttal of his advance. Quite the reverse.

'I guess I just don't understand why ...' another pause – 'well, why an earth we are not sitting here as a courting couple? I honestly thought that we both felt the same ...'

Rosie looked at his handsome face and knew she had to let him have his say.

'I wondered if perhaps it was my age? I know there's a bit of an age gap ...' He caught Rosie shaking her head from side to side. Encouraged, he carried on with his entreaty.

'I want you to know that I don't consider myself too old for a family.' As he spoke, the image of Rosie holding Gloria's baby on the day of the air raid rushed to the forefront of his mind.

'I want you to know,' DS Miller continued, driven on by her silence, 'that I was – that I *am* serious about us – that I would never have tried to – ' he dropped his voice so the old couple behind them could not hear, ' – kiss you, had I not been entirely serious. I want you to know that I have not so much as touched another woman since my wife died six years ago. Haven't wanted to. Have never met anyone I wanted to even go for a cup of tea with. Until you.'

Rosie felt her heart break. Wished she had stopped him talking so the words would not be indelibly imprinted on her consciousness. What she would give to be with this man. His words were true and full of love. A love she so wanted. But a love she could never allow herself to have.

She forced air into her lungs. She knew it was time for her speech. For her lies.

'I'm so sorry, Peter,' she began, pushing down her

feelings and replacing them with the most sincere but une-motional face she could muster. 'That is such a lovely thing to hear. And I know you mean what you said. That you are an honest and good man. And I have so much respect for you and how you conduct your life . . . '

There was a pause. Neither of them had so much as sipped their tea, never mind had a bite of Vera's fresh Victoria sponge.

'Why,' Peter broke in, 'do I sense that there is one almighty "but" about to come . . . '

Rosie forced a smile.

'*But*,' she said, 'I'm afraid I really do not feel the same way for you as you do for me.' She hoped she sounded convincing.

'I'll be honest, Peter,' she added, quickly. She needed him to believe her. 'To start with I did feel an awful lot for you. I myself also thought that I would like to be with you, but – I'm sorry, but it is a "but".' Rosie could feel herself getting muddled. Her words weren't coming out the way they should. She took another deep breath.

'What I'm trying to say in the nicest possible way, Peter, is that I made a mistake, or rather I changed my mind, which sounds awfully fickle, and I don't mean to be – I'm not a fickle person. It's just that I thought I had feelings for you – but I'm afraid I don't.'

There. She had said it. Please God let her have been convincing.

Rosie looked at Peter. He seemed at a loss for words.

'Oh,' he said, 'well, I guess I have to thank you for *your* honesty. Brutal though it may be.' He gave a sad laugh. 'There's not anyone else on the scene, is there?' he asked. He had to know. 'It was just the other night when I bumped into you and you looked so dressed-up . . . so gorgeous . . .

74

I couldn't help but wonder . . . ' He didn't need to say any more, Rosie was already shaking her head.

'No, no, of course not. I would have said if there was.' Peter looked at Rosie as she spoke and thought they were the first words she had said in all the time they had been sitting there that sounded true.

Why did he not feel she was being genuine?

'So, it really is because your feelings have changed? I just thought—' he stopped himself from saying any more.

'I'm sorry, Peter. I really am,' Rosie said, trying her hardest to sound credible. She cursed herself for being such a bad liar.

Peter looked at Rosie. What more could he say? She had told him straight. She did not want him. It was as simple as that. He couldn't exactly argue that she was wrong, and that her feelings were wrong – and that she did, in fact, feel something for him. How could he tell her that? It was absurd. 'I guess . . . ' he started again, ' . . . that it wouldn't be appropriate for us to simply stay friends?' He hated himself for saying it. He felt as if he was begging, but he couldn't stop himself. If that was the only way he was going to be able to keep seeing the woman he had fallen in love with, he would take it.

Rosie shook her head. 'I don't think that would be a good idea, for either of us, do you?'

Of course, Peter knew it would not be possible. That it would end in disaster and yet more disappointment. Logically he knew you couldn't be friends with someone if you knew that other person was in love with you.

And he was in love. There was no other way round it.

'Of course not. You're right. It wouldn't be at all practicable,' he forced himself to agree.

Rosie looked at Peter and knew she could not stay

another moment or her resolve would leave her. She would break down and tell him her true feelings – and then she really would be in a state. 'I'm afraid I have to go now,' she said, standing up.

Peter, forever the gentleman, immediately got up.

'Well,' he said, wanting so much to grab her hand, pull her to him, and kiss her with the passion that was always simmering on the surface whenever they were near each other. Instead, he said simply, 'Well, then, I guess this is goodbye.'

'Yes, Peter.' Rosie swallowed hard. She looked one last time into his blue eyes and he looked back into hers, as if still searching for an answer, or at least for a different answer to the one she had given him.

She tore her eyes away from his and turned her back and walked away.

Peter watched her weave round the rest of the small tables, now all full with other couples, workers, or young families. Why was it he seemed to be forever looking at her back, as she walked away from him?

He watched as Rosie turned her head and mouthed 'goodbye' to Vera, who nodded in return.

His sight was still glued to Rosie as she left the café, leaving a blast of cold in her wake. He followed the blurry outline of her body through the steamed-up windows as it disappeared up the road through the rain and the thick fog that was starting to roll in.

What he could not see, though, as Rosie carried on walking up the road, was that within seconds of leaving the café her face had crumpled, and the rain starting to wet her cheeks was soon mixed with salty tears as the dam she had erected for this evening's performance collapsed and her true sorrow and heartache broke through and flooded every part of her being.

*

Peter felt no compulsion to leave the café. It was as if his whole being had sunk into a deep depression. He looked down at the two untouched pieces of cake.

'Excuse me,' he said, and gently tapped the old gentleman who had his back to him and was sitting at the next table with his wife. He was sure they had been earwigging in on his conversation with Rosie. The man turned round with a face full of irritation.

'Would you and your wife like these two pieces of Victoria sponge? My eyes were clearly bigger than my belly. They haven't been touched.'

The old man's face softened. Unused to such generosity he kept repeating his thanks as he turned to take the plates of proffered Victoria sponge. As the elderly couple ate they started to chatter for the first time since their arrival.

At least, Peter thought, he had brought a little pleasure to someone this evening. He just hoped he could lift his own spirits enough to get himself out of this chair and off to work. Still, he had a good hour to spare before he started his night shift with the Dock Police.

As he sat there stirring his tea but not drinking it, he mulled things over in his head. Why couldn't he just accept what Rosie had told him? Something just didn't make sense. He'd questioned enough people in his long career to know when someone was not telling the truth, and although he would never have had Rosie down as a liar, he felt that she was not being honest.

Just leave it, Peter, he reprimanded himself. *Just walk away. It's over. Accept it. Rosie couldn't have made it any clearer. She does not want you!*

Peter looked up from his tea and stared out the window. An image of Rosie from the other night sprang into his mind. The way she was dressed. She looked incredible. But it seemed so unlike Rosie to have make-up on – and those red shoes? Still, what did he know? They'd only known each other a few months. Had never gone out on a proper date as such – always just meeting up after work for a cup of tea and a bite to eat.

Besides, what was so unusual about her getting done up and going out on an evening? She was young and full of life. She worked hard. Why shouldn't she dress up for a night on the tiles? *But then, why had she been so cagey about telling him where she was going?*

'You all right there, hinny?'

Peter snapped out of his reverie. Vera was looming over him. Her wrinkled face had momentarily lost its hardness. Was that pity he saw in her pale blue eyes?

'Yes, thank you, Vera. I'm fine. Well, I better be getting myself off. Been hogging the table too long. Sorry about the cake,' he added, knowing Vera didn't miss a trick and would have seen him handing the two plates over to the old couple on the next table. 'It looked delicious, but I don't think either of us were that hungry after all.'

Vera leant closer as she moved the barely touched cups of cold tea and the brown ceramic pot on to her battered tray, and whispered conspiratorially, 'Aye, why, least it's given the two old miseries something to talk about.'

Her words gifted Peter a genuine smile, which he tried to maintain as he got up and said his goodbyes, making sure, as always, that he left a generous tip.

When he stepped out on to the pavement and into the dark, rainy night, a young Merchant Navy sailor and his girl hurried past him, their arms wrapped around each other, laughing as they tried to dodge the puddles and keep dry. They seemed locked into each other's worlds, as if no one else existed.

When he and Rosie had started seeing each other, they

too had talked like they were in their own private bubble. Only the words they spoke to each other mattered during the hour or two they were together. He had daydreamed about her during his waking hours, and as he fell asleep at night he had imagined her body next to his. He had such hopes that the two of them could share a future together.

But, then, he had tried to kiss her – to do what felt so natural and so right for them both – and in that second, his hopes and dreams had shattered. Afterwards he'd convinced himself that if he could just see her again – talk to her – she would admit she had been hasty – scared perhaps of commitment.

From the moment she'd stepped into the café, though, he could tell that she was not going to welcome him back with open arms. She had not minced her words. Why was it then that he still did not seem to be able to accept what she was telling him?

Why didn't he feel her words rang true?

Chapter Nine

'Listen,' Joe told Bel in a hushed tone.

Bel was bent down gently stoking the open fire in the middle of the black lead range that took centre stage in the Elliots' kitchen-cum-living room. She immediately straightened up and looked at her brother-in-law – the man she had fallen in love with even though she had tried her hardest not to. He had just got in from his Home Guard duties and was still wearing his khaki green uniform; his face looked deadpan and earnest.

'I can't hear anything. What is it?' Bel whispered, now curious. They were standing within inches of each other in what was normally the hub of the three-storey Victorian terrace they had both lived in most of their lives. 'It's the sound of silence,' Joe whispered back as his mouth widened into a broad smile.

'A real rarity these days,' he added, still speaking softly.

'Never a truer word.' Bel laughed gently. 'Even Lucille went to bed without much of a fuss tonight. I can't believe everyone's out this evening. There must be something on we don't know about . . . ' As she spoke, Joe took hold of Bel's hand and gently pulled her into his arms. The heat from the range had caused Bel's normally pale face to flush a little. Joe wrapped his arms around Bel and looked down into her pretty, heart-shaped face. He still couldn't quite believe this woman was his. The woman he had adored his entire life, the woman he had loved from the moment his sister Polly had brought her back to their home after finding her crying and shut out of her own home when they were all just children.

Bel allowed herself to enjoy the feel of Joe's lips as he gently kissed her neck.

'Someone might come in,' she worried, but she didn't struggle free from his embrace. Since she and Joe had admitted their feelings for each other, she felt as if she now lived for the moments when they were together – and alone. She loved the feeling of being in his arms, and his tender kisses. The guilt she had felt whenever he held her or caressed her had slowly diminished these past few weeks – but not vanished. There were still moments – both when she was alone and when she was with Joe – that she thought of Teddy and felt an overwhelming sense of betrayal. But, she told herself, these feelings were to be expected. Teddy had been her first love; the man she had married and with whom she'd had a child. It was normal for her to feel this way. But Teddy was dead, killed in the so-called 'Desert War' out in North Africa, and for a long time she too had felt like dying. Gradually, though, she had clawed her way out of what had seemed to be a bottomless well of grief – and had done so with the help of Joe.

And as she had emerged from the darkness and into the light, without intending to, or wanting to, she had found herself falling in love.

'I think there's something special in the air tonight.' Joe looked at Bel, who returned the look with a questioning furrow in her brow. 'Well,' he explained, his large hands, roughened by years spent riveting in the yards in all weathers, starting to lightly trace Bel's neck, 'I really don't think there has been a time since I got back from Africa that the house has been so quiet and empty. Even Arthur must be out on the razz tonight.' Bel giggled at the thought of Arthur whooping it up.

'He's with Polly,' Bel said, 'he went to meet her off the ferry after work and they've gone to Albert's to get some vegetables from his allotment.' She paused.

'Well, we're not totally alone,' she said, looking down at the floor at Tramp, the stray Agnes had adopted, and her one remaining puppy.

Tramp and the runt of the litter that no one had wanted were lying curled up together as near to the grate as they could possibly get without singeing their fur. When Bel looked back up she put her hand to Joe's face; it had now lost its desert tan and had aged much faster than it should have in the two years he had been away fighting in foreign lands. Her slender fingers slowly traced the side of his face, from the top of his forehead, down the side of his prominent cheekbones and ending on his lips.

Joe's eyes closed, and as he always did whenever Bel touched him, he entered a world of sensuality he never wanted to come out of. He stooped to reach her lips and when he found them, they stood there kissing, their bodies pressing closer together, betraying their yearning for each other. Only the soft snuffling of the dogs and the odd spit from the fire infiltrated the quietness.

'God, Bel,' Joe mumbled through the kisses. 'I so want you.'

Bel felt herself blush at Joe's words. The past month they had kissed each other more times than she could count, but that was all. Their bodies had told them how much they wanted more, but their minds were firm. Or at least Bel's was. She could allow herself to love Joe and to enjoy his kisses, his embraces and caresses, but there was no way she could give herself to him. It had always been her belief, and always would be, that love-making could only ever happen within the legitimacy of a marriage. Her upbringing had made her resolute. She had seen enough of her mother's shameless behaviour with other men to vow from an early age that she would never follow in her footsteps.

Bel knew she didn't have to explain herself to Joe, because he knew already. He too had seen Pearl's drunken and promiscuous behaviour as they had grown up on this very street and he understood exactly why Bel was the person she was. She had been brought up – no, she had been *dragged* up – by a woman who had no right to be a mother, and because of this Bel had ensured that she grew up to be the antithesis of Pearl in all ways.

When their lips finally parted, Joe cupped Bel's face in his hand. Their passion for each other had left them both breathless, but reluctant to part.

'I think you know how I feel, Joe, but I just can't. I know neither of us are exactly young and innocent – I've got a daughter, after all – but it's just that . . . well, it just wouldn't be right . . . I'm sorry, Joe.' Bel started to say more, but Joe put a finger to her lips.

'Never be sorry. I'm glad you are the way you are. And I love you the more for it,' he told her. Bel's startling blue eyes were glistening with love and also with tears. Whenever she was with Joe like this, her emotions seemed to overwhelm her. She had never felt so happy, so alive, yet also so tearful as when she was in Joe's arms.

'Bel,' Joe said, his voice becoming serious. 'I've something to ask you. Something I have wanted to ask since the moment you accepted my love. Something I know I should wait longer to ask you, but I'm afraid I just can't.'

Bel looked up at Joe and then watched, slightly puzzled, as he took a faltering step backwards. Joe's injured leg had healed, but at the expense of its ability to bend, which meant Joe required a cane to walk. As he hobbled a little to the side, he stretched out his arm to grab his walking stick that was propped up against the wall, before placing it firmly in front of him. As he did so Tramp and the pup started to stir, disturbed from their slumber by the sudden movement; one of Tramp's mismatched coloured eyes opened lazily to see what was going on and the dog watched curiously as Joe put both hands on the top of the cane's wooden handle, and slowly lowered himself on to one knee.

Bel stared down at him. At first she thought he was playing the fool, like he often did, using his stick as though he was Charlie Chaplin, or hamming it up to make her laugh. But, on seeing the very solemn look on his face, she realised Joe was not about to act out some comic scene.

'Joe?' she asked. She saw pain shoot across his face as he manoeuvred his bad leg into place so he was properly down on bended knee. Bel reached forward to help him back up. 'What are you doing, Joe?' she said. 'You're going to hurt yourself.'

Joe took hold of Bel's hand, which felt warm and soft in his own.

'Bel Elliot,' he said. His voice was steady but gentle. 'Would you make me the happiest man alive by becoming my wife?'

Bel froze. She looked down at Joe. For a moment her mind couldn't comprehend what he was asking her, and then the full force of his monumental question hit her like a ton of bricks.

And then panic set in. Everything was happening too quickly: Teddy's death. Her grief. Her love for Joe – a love that had blindsided her, but had also made her come alive again. Her fervent rallying against the way she felt. The shame. But in her battle to stop the onward march of her feelings for Joe she had been defeated and beaten down by the joy their love had brought – a joy that cascaded into

84

her own life and into that of Lucille, too. She felt tears spring to her eyes unchecked. She felt so confused. Of course, she wanted to be with this man now kneeling before her. Not only did she love Joe, but she had known him all of her life.

In a split second a hundred thoughts bombarded her. Images of her beloved Teddy, also down on one knee, saying words practically identical to the ones Joe had just uttered – only that had been years ago when she was just seventeen. And just like that, all her feelings of guilt flooded back to the surface.

'Bel,' Joe said, seeing the mass of confused thoughts racing across her face. 'I know this may seem too soon. And I know you must be thinking about our Teddy. But I don't see any reason to wait. We love each other. We've known each other our entire lives. It's not as if we need to get to know each other. There is no doubt in either of our minds ... I know that ... I can read you just as you can read me.'

As Joe kissed Bel's hand, she looked at him and knew every word he spoke was true. She had tried to run away from his love but it was a race she was always going to lose. In her heart she knew that she and Joe would be together for the rest of their lives. Over the past few weeks since they had admitted their love for each other, it had been uncanny how quickly they had become almost insep-arable. And it wasn't just the pull of attraction they both clearly felt, it was so much deeper. It was as if they both knew they belonged together.

Yes, in reality they had only been together a few weeks. Yes. If these were ordinary times, this might well seem more than a little hasty – far too short a courtship for him to be asking for a woman's hand in marriage. But these were not 'ordinary' times. Far from it. No one knew if they would be there from one day to the next, with the amount of bombs being hurled down at them from the skies above.

'It's really simple,' Joe kept on. 'I love you – and you love me . . . Ma said something when we told her that we loved each other that day in the air raid shelter . . . '

Bel looked at Joe. That day would be etched in her mind for ever.

'I remember it word for word,' she interrupted. 'She told us "If there is a love there between you and Joe, you can't fight it. Our lives are too short and too unpredictable."' Tears were now rolling down Bel's face and Joe squeezed her hand in an attempt to comfort her. He too would never forget his mother's words. His ma may not have served on the front line, but she had been changed by the war, had lost the man she loved in the First War and a son in the second. She was as hardened and as battle-weary as any soldier.

Joe looked up at Bel.

Tramp and the pup were now fully awake. Seeing Joe with one knee on the floor, they had scurried over to him.

'Will you, Bel? Will you take me as your husband?'

As Bel opened her mouth to give Joe his answer the kitchen door was flung open.

'Oh, my goodness!' It was Polly. She had stopped dead in her tracks in the doorway. Behind her was Arthur.

Bel and Joe turned to see two shocked faces gawping over at them.

Joe tried to get up, but struggled a little. Bel moved towards him and gently helped him back onto his feet. The shock of being interrupted had stopped her tears, but they had left their mark on her face.

'Well then?' Polly asked. Her voice was full of excitement and anticipation. *She had certainly not expected to find this on her return home.*

Bel and Joe looked at Polly blankly.

'Don't look at me as if you have no idea what I'm talking about,' Polly said, her eyes glued to her brother and sister-in-law.

'Is it a "yes" or a "no", Bel?'

Bel felt herself gulp for air. Joe was looking intently at her.

'*Yes*, it's a yes, Joe . . . Yes, *I'd love to be your wife.*' A big smile spread across Bel's face and another batch of tears started to tumble down her rosy cheeks. Joe grabbed hold of the woman he couldn't quite believe had agreed to marry him and kissed her on the lips.

'I love you, Bel Elliot. You won't regret this. I promise you,' he said, giving her another kiss.

'I just hope *you* don't regret it!' Bel said, half laughing through a blur of tears.

Polly strode over to the newly engaged couple and gave Bel an almighty hug. She was still in her dirty overalls, and her thick-soled work boots that made her even taller than she already was were now causing her to tower over Bel. Polly put her hands on Bel's shoulders and beamed at her.

Her smile was genuine, although a rush of sadness had accompanied her happiness for her brother and Bel. A sadness that Teddy had been deprived – not only of his life, but of love as well.

'Congratulations, Bel!' Polly said, forcing back thoughts of one brother and turning towards her other. 'And you too, Joe. Although heaven knows what Bel sees in you! She needs her head testing, if you ask me,' she teased.

'Aye, congratulations, the both of you.' Arthur stepped forward. 'You make a lovely couple,' he said, grabbing hold of Joe's hand and shaking it energetically before taking Bel's small, slender hand into his own gnarled bear's paw and giving it a kiss. The words he spoke were, as always, sincere. Arthur never said anything he didn't mean or feel.

'What's all the fuss about?' Everyone turned round. It was Agnes, back from her evening cup of tea and gossip with Beryl, their next-door neighbour. The faces that greeted her were full of emotion.

'Our Joe has just proposed to Bel.' Polly couldn't get the words out fast enough.

They all looked at Agnes, waiting her response. Needing her approval.

For a second her face went blank while she digested the words she had just heard, then her mouth creased upwards into a wide smile.

'Well, thank goodness for that,' she said in a mock-matronly manner. 'I was just starting to worry you two might be thinking of – what's that expression . . . "living in sin"?'

She went over to give Bel a big hug and a kiss, before turning to Joe and demanding, 'Well, what're you waiting for? Get the brandy out. This calls for a celebratory drink . . . Polly, get yourself cleaned up, you look like an overgrown chimney sweep. And Arthur, put those vegetables by the sink and get the wireless tuned into something cheerful. No news tonight, thank you very much!'

Agnes turned on her heel and walked back out of the kitchen.

'And where're you going, Ma?' Joe asked as he opened the cupboard door in the scullery to locate the brandy.

'I'm going to get Beryl and the girls. Can't have a knees-up without them. I'll be back in a jiffy.'

Agnes hurried down the hallway and went to open the front door but as she did so, Pearl was reaching to open it from the other side. The two women almost came head to head.

'Whoa!' Pearl said. 'What's the rush? Did I miss the air raid siren go off or what?'

'Ah, Pearl.' Agnes couldn't stop the disappointment showing in her face, but quickly covered it up. She knew this was probably the last person either Bel or Joe wanted to share this special moment with. Pearl was guaranteed to throw a big bucket of cold water over their excitement. Still, she couldn't exactly stop her from coming in. Pearl had made it quite clear that this was now her home, and one she was happily ensconced in for the foreseeable future. Besides, Bel was her daughter. Much as that pained Bel.

'I thought you were working at the Tatham this evening?' Agnes asked, unconsciously blocking her way into the house.

'Aye, I was,' Pearl said. Agnes could smell whisky and cigarette smoke on her breath. 'But it was dead as a doornail tonight. Bill told me to get myself home. No point in just standing around like a lemon deeing nowt.'

Agnes thought it more than likely that Bill, the landlord of the Tatham Arms, didn't want Pearl helping herself to free drinks all night, like she normally did, which he turned a blind eye to as Pearl was a good barmaid. She was quick on her feet, and could add up the cost of a round of drinks quicker than anyone he had ever known, and when she did make mistakes, they were intentional – but the till always tallied up at the end of the night, and that was all Bill was concerned about.

'Well,' Agnes forced out the words. 'You're just in time for a little impromptu party.'

Pearl's face lit up. Agnes knew her excitement would be down to the lure of free booze.

'Well, I'm taking it that you're off to get Beryl and her

girls, so I'm guessing it'll be all right for me to nip out the back and get Ronald round.' It wasn't a question.

Ronald was Pearl's new 'friend'; his house backed on to the Elliots' and Pearl was forever toing and froing across the back lane to see Ronald, or more often than not to smoke his cigarettes and drink his whisky. Ronald didn't seem to mind, nor was he under any illusion as to why Pearl was a frequent visitor.

As Agnes stepped outside and Pearl hurried in to the warmth, she turned round. 'So, what's the occasion?' she asked.

Agnes looked at her daughter-in-law's mother in her short skirt, low-cut blouse, and pair of Mary Jane shoes – all of which looked slightly ridiculous on someone of her age. There had been a time when Pearl would have looked good, more than good – attractive, even – wearing such an outfit, but not now. The years had taken their toll on Pearl, although she seemed oblivious to the ravages of time.

'I'll let Bel tell you,' Agnes said as she leant across the small stone wall and knocked loudly on her neighbour's front door.

As she did so she heard Pearl let loose a phlegmy cough before bellowing down the hallway, 'Isabelle!'

'So, then, *Isabelle* . . . ' Pearl said as soon as she stepped into the kitchen. Her eyes swept the room to clock Arthur sitting at the kitchen table, and Joe hobbling out of the scullery, one hand on his walking stick, the other clutching a bottle of brandy. Bel followed with a tray of sparkling clean glasses, and Polly was giving Tramp and the pup a bowl of water and some scraps of leftover food.

' . . . What's the big occasion?' Pearl asked, as she started scrabbling around in her bag for her packet of cigarettes. She couldn't wait to get out the back and have a smoke and then get Ronald round. He was bound to have a bottle of whisky she could persuade him to bring along.

'Ma, I thought you were working tonight?' Bel said.

Pearl noticed that her daughter's face had, as usual, dropped on seeing her.

'God, for the second time tonight, *Bill let me go early*, there was no one about, dead as a doornail . . . so, come on, why the party?'

'Well, it's not exactly a party, Ma,' Bel hesitated. 'Just a little drink to celebrate.'

'Party? Celebrate? Same thing. So then, what's going on?' Bel had freed a cigarette from its packet and was standing, fag dangling unlit between her fingers, her other hand clutching her lighter.

Joe came over to Bel and put his arm around her.

'Pearl, I'm pleased to tell you that your daughter has accepted my hand in marriage.' He sounded very formal, and looked serious, as if daring Pearl to spoil the occasion.

'Eee, well I never!' Pearl looked genuinely surprised, then her eyes narrowed and she looked from Bel to Joe and back.

'Ah, I get it,' she said as if she had just solved a complex puzzle. 'Has this one forced your hand, Joe? Is this going to be what they call a "shotgun wedding"?'

Joe grabbed Bel's hand and squeezed it tight.

'No, Pearl,' he said, before Bel had a chance to bark a retort. 'No one's forced anyone's hand here. It's much simpler than that. Your daughter and I love each other and want to be with each other for the rest of our lives. And that is the reason – the *only* reason – why I have asked her to marry me this evening.'

'Ah, love, is it? So no bun in the oven? No younger brother or sister for little Lucille?'

'God, Ma, not that it's any of your business, but there is

no "bun in the oven", other than the ones Agnes makes and you happily stuff down your gob.' Bel couldn't hold her tongue any longer. She just hated the fact that her mother always managed to take what was good and honest and turn it into something demeaning and dirty. Bel took a deep breath. Since her mother had decided not to return to Portsmouth to be with some bloke she'd been shacked up with, Bel had been trying to simply accept her for who she was, to finally get it through her thick skull that Pearl would never be the Ma she wanted, and to try – hard though that might be – to stop herself getting so wound up by her.

'Now go and have your fag. It might shut you up for five minutes,' Bel said, looking down at her mother's claw-like hand. 'And, no,' she added, knowing exactly what Pearl had in mind, 'you can't invite Ronald round.'

As Pearl left the kitchen and walked out the back door, she let out a loud laugh. As always, she had to get the last word in.

'Ah, you're a good girl, Isabelle, take after your old ma here,' she cackled at the irony. 'Waiting until there's a ring on your finger. Clever girl.'

Anger flared up inside Bel, but she beat it down. Her mother's words had stung – not least because they were hardly the words of congratulation a parent would normally bestow on a child, but also because, as was often the case with Pearl, they had an element of truth to them, in that, unlike her dear old ma, she would never give her body to a man if they weren't married.

Ten minutes later Pearl was back with Ronald in tow. Bel knew she couldn't push the poor bloke back out the door and the men seemed more than happy to have him as part of the evening's soirée as he'd come armed with a bottle of single malt.

Beryl also arrived clutching a bottle of port, which was drunk in favour of Agnes's cheap brandy. And Beryl's two girls, Audrey and Iris, were allowed a glass of port and lemonade, which had the effect of making them very giggly, especially around Joe.

It didn't take Lucille long to wake up and realise that there was a party going on. When she came tottering into the kitchen – all bleary-eyed, clutching her raggedy pet rabbit – Pearl was the first to spot her.

'Ah, you feeling all left out?' she said, bending down to pick her granddaughter up. 'Your nana knows that feeling only too well. Come on, let's get you some lemonade.'

Pearl's voice always softened when she talked to her granddaughter. Pearl had really taken to the little girl. The love she felt for Lucille had crept up on her unwittingly and had been a surprise to everyone – no one more than Pearl herself.

Lucille was happily surveying the party with her little legs wrapped round her grandmother's thin waist, but on spotting Joe she shouted out, 'Doey!' and flung her arms out towards him.

Pearl sighed. 'Go on, then. Go to the golden boy,' she said, handing Lucille to Joe as he hobbled over to them.

'Doey! Party! Party!' Lucille exclaimed, now wide awake.

When Bel saw her little girl in her fiancé's arms she smiled. Her mind tripped back momentarily to when Joe had first arrived back and she had hated the fact that Lucille had adored him so much. Bel sighed to herself. So much had happened in such a short space of time.

'Well,' she said, getting up from the table where the women were chatting away animatedly about just about everything and anything to do with weddings, ' . . . look who's joined the party.'

Joe laughed. 'Shall we tell her? Do you think she'll understand?'

Lucille turned her head to her mum, sensing something was afoot. Bel looked at her daughter and pushed a blonde curl away from her eyes.

'Mummy and Doey ... ' Bel said, 'are going to be husband –' she pointed to Joe '– and wife.' Bel pointed a finger at the middle of her own chest.

'So, that means,' Joe added, 'that we three,' his hand circling between them all, 'are going to be a family.' Lucille giggled, enjoying the attention, even if she wasn't quite sure what it was all about. But as Joe put her down so she could play with the dogs, she suddenly declared, 'Daddy!' and started excitedly chasing Tramp and the pup around the room.

As the music and chatter became louder and more raucous, Joe whispered in his fiancée's ear, 'So, how soon can I make you my wife?' He looked at Bel and added, with a cheeky grin, 'I'm not keen to have one of those long-drawn-out engagements.' Bel looked at Joe. For a brief moment she thought of her engagement to Teddy and how they had both been just seventeen when he had proposed to her and Agnes had persuaded them to wait until they were eighteen.

'Let's do short and sweet,' she said, as Joe grabbed her head gently between both his hands and gave her a kiss.

In the corner of her eye, Bel saw Agnes slip out of the kitchen, then heard her hurry upstairs to her bedroom. A few minutes later she returned with a very small blue velvet box. As she sat herself down next to Bel and Joe, it was clear to all that the matriarch of the house wanted to say something.

Agnes's eyes twinkled with more than a little emotion as she took hold of her son's hand and pressed the small box into it. 'This is my gift,' she said softly. 'Or rather, it is a gift from both me and your father,' she looked at Bel, 'to the both of you.'

The room was now so quiet you could hear a pin drop. Agnes very rarely mentioned her husband, Harry, to anyone. Despite all the years that had passed since his death in the First World War, it was as if it was still too painful for Agnes to talk about him.

Sensing the seriousness of the occasion, Lucille stopped racing around and settled herself on the thick clippy mat, with Tramp by her side and the pup squashed in her arms.

Even Pearl and Ronald came in from the yard and were quietly watching the moment.

Joe looked at his mother before opening the box. There inside was the most gorgeous, gleaming blue sapphire ring. It was framed by four tiny diamonds and set on a rose gold band.

'Ma, that's lovely,' he said and looked at Bel, whose sparkling eyes perfectly matched the glinting stone.

'Are you sure, Agnes?' Bel asked a little breathlessly.

She knew this was more than just a very beautiful, and very expensive, ring. It was Agnes's way of saying that their marriage had her blessing. And Bel knew it must be difficult for Agnes. She had never wanted anyone after Harry had died and Bel had often worried that she might well judge Bel for falling in love so quickly after Teddy's death – and with her other son, at that. But if she had had any reservations she had never shown them.

'I wouldn't have offered you it, if I wasn't sure, Bel,' Agnes said, smiling, 'you've always been like a daughter to me.' The words were out before she had time to pull them back in and she glanced a little guiltily over at Pearl.

'Besides,' Agnes added quickly to fill the awkward gap, 'my old fingers are now twice the size they were when I was married, so it's not as if I can ever wear it again, is it? It needs a new home, and I think it suits you down to the ground.'

'Oh Agnes,' Bel choked back the tears.

'Go on then, Joe,' Polly chipped in, 'put it on her finger.'

They all watched entranced as Joe slipped the ring on to Bel's finger. It fitted perfectly.

Bel held her hand out in front of her so everyone could see.

'Agnes, I can't thank you enough, I really can't.'

'Me too,' Joe added, giving Agnes a kiss on the cheek before she had time to bat him away.

'I think this requires another toast,' Arthur chipped in, as Ronald happily unscrewed the top of the whisky bottle and splashed a generous amount of golden amber into everyone's tumblers.

'Happiness!' Polly declared

'And Health!' Beryl added.

'And don't forget Wealth,' Pearl chipped in, gawping at the ring and wondering how on earth Agnes had managed not to sell it, or at least pawn the thing.

By the end of the evening Ronald's bottle of whisky was empty, a good part of it having been consumed by Pearl, who had spent a substantial part of the evening out the backyard with Ronald as Agnes was still holding firm to her somewhat unusual rule of no smoking in the house. She had been going to relent, especially as Pearl was now a permanent lodger, but had been firmly stopped in her tracks by Bel, who didn't so much hate smoking per se – she just hated her mother's smoking. As the evening had worn on Pearl had seemed determined to smoke every cigarette poor Ronald possessed and had even made him go home to fetch more from his home across the back alley.

When everyone had drunk and talked their way into the early hours, they all finally turned in for the night. Bel kissed her fiancé goodnight outside her bedroom, before he dragged himself away and into his own room next door with the words: 'I love you. And always will, Bel.'

Bel kissed him again in reply and closed her door.

As she changed into her nightdress and climbed into bed she looked across at Lucille, sleeping soundly next to her in her open cot. Her head was spinning as she lay down. She would never have thought in a million years that she would be getting married again – least of all to her husband's brother.

Upstairs on the first floor, Agnes had gone to bed holding her faded sepia photograph of her husband Harry, remembering when he had proposed to her as they had lain on the beach one sunny day looking up into a cloudless sky. Sometimes it just seemed like yesterday – other times it seemed a lifetime ago.

Arthur had lain in his bed and chatted to his Flo, who had been gone for more than two decades but who he still kept alive in his head and in his heart, and who he firmly believed was still very much with him.

And just before sleep took her, Polly had re-enacted every second of the evening when Tommy had proposed to her after he had told her he had joined up and she had vowed to wait for him. She couldn't wait to write and tell him the news.

Even Pearl, lying in her bed in the small bedroom overlooking the backyard, was thinking about someone she had loved so very much, and who was no longer with her. It was not some old lover, though, but someone no one else knew anything about, and about whom she could never talk, even if she wanted to.

Chapter Ten

The Slums, Sunderland

June 1913

'You? Working in some posh hotel? And in London? God knows how you wangled that one!' Pearl's mother sneered at her.

'Enid wrote.' Pearl stuck her chin up as she looked her ma defiantly in the eye. 'Said she'd got me a job, like she promised she would. At the same hotel. Said it's only till the end of the summer – but yer never know, might be longer.'

Pearl, of course, was lying her socks off. Had rehearsed her story dozens of time in her head. Everyone knew her old schoolfriend Enid Wallis was a cockney and that her ma and da had just upped sticks and taken her and her brothers back down to the Big Smoke. It was a convincing lie. Had to be. If her ma and da knew the truth, Pearl would be beaten to within an inch of her life by them both, and then chucked out on to the street for good measure.

She had tried to think of a solution to her problem for just about every waking minute of the past six weeks and had finally found the answer. Or rather, she had been given the answer as it had come to her totally by chance – had literally been handed to her by a stranger in the street.

'Well then,' Pearl's ma said with a vindictive smile on her face, 'if yer gonna be some skivvy in some hoity-toity hotel, ya better get yerself something decent to wear otherwise they'll take one look at ya and give yer the elbow before ya even start.'

Pearl looked down at her grubby, torn dress and made a resolution to somehow find something halfway decent to wear before she left the next day.

'Aye, why, good luck to ya, Pearl,' her da said. 'And good on ya. Better than sitting all day on yer lazy backside drinking yerself into a stupor like someone not a million miles away here.' He threw a derisory look over to his wife.

Pearl caught the return look in her ma's eyes and knew it would just be a matter of minutes before her mam and dad worked themselves up a treat and began screaming at each other like banshees. She forced a compliant smile at her da and made quick her escape.

Besides, she had things to do before she left the next day. Her ma was right. She needed to get herself a dress that didn't make her look like she had just stepped out of the workhouse – and she knew just where to get one.

A few hours later Pearl had acquired herself a nice-enough pinafore dress she'd pinched from a washing line in one of the backyards in Hendon. As well as this she had managed to put aside enough money for her train fare from the odd jobs she did for some of the Jewish families living on Villette Road. It was at times like this she was glad there was such a thing as God and religion, and for something called 'the Sabbath', which in Pearl's basic understanding meant that if you were a Jew, you couldn't do any kind of work from a Friday to a Saturday night. Even something as simple as lighting a fire or washing up was prohibited. That, in turn, had meant girls like Pearl, if they acted proper and watched their ps and qs, would be employed to do what the Jews weren't allow to do.

After counting her money out and folding her new dress loosely and putting it at the bottom of her bed, Pearl finally put her head down, although she wasn't at all tired. She couldn't decide whether her nerves were jangling from fear of what the next few months would bring, or excitement at leaving the town she had never set foot outside of her whole life.

After barely sleeping a wink, when the early morning light started to peep through the thin, threadbare curtains of the room she slept in with her siblings, Pearl got up and got ready. She waited until everyone else was up before saying her farewells. Her three young siblings ran up to her to give her a cuddle and Pearl hugged them back, keeping her head as far away from them as possible.

Her brothers joked that if the streets were really paved with gold, they would come and join her.

And her ma and da had actually stood at the door and waved her off.

Pearl had felt a little sad, wishing that they could have been like this more often, but then she imagined the scenario if they had known about her condition and she didn't feel quite so sentimental.

It only took her about twenty minutes to walk the mile from her home in Barrack Street, up High Street East and on to High Street West, before taking a sharp left into Station Street. And then she was there. At the entrance of the town's main railway station. At the start of her journey that she knew was going to change her life.

After paying over the majority of her 'Sabbath' money to an elderly gentleman at the main counter, she was given her ticket. She made her way down the two flights of stairs to platform number one. It was early so the place wasn't heaving, although more people started to arrive as the hands on the massive round clock hanging from the station's ceiling moved towards eight o'clock.

Half an hour later she was standing on the platform along with a swarm of other travellers. In one hand she was holding on tightly to the tatty carpet bag her mam had given her and which was now stuffed with her meagre belongings – in her other she clutched her one-way ticket to London.

Twenty minutes later she'd boarded the long, black Pullman steam train and found herself a seat near the window in one of the third-class compartments. The remaining bench seats were soon taken by three sole travellers – two elderly men and a young woman. The men curtained themselves off behind large newspapers, and the woman kept her gaze firmly fixed on events on the other side of the window.

As was the English way, they all avoided eye contact and no one spoke, which suited Pearl just fine.

As the train slowly pulled away from the steam-filled platform, only then did Pearl start to relax. She had made her escape. She knew she couldn't have waited a day longer. Her belly had grown quickly over the past few weeks, as had her breasts. It wouldn't be long now before she could no longer hide her condition.

Pearl stayed wide awake for every minute of the eight-hour journey, fascinated by the changing landscapes, but also wary that someone might want to nab her bag – not that there was much in there to steal.

When the train finally arrived in London, squealing to a dramatic halt and emitting a huge plume of steam, Pearl stepped out on to the platform at King's Cross station and was immediately hit by the buzz of life, a mixture of smells – some pleasant, some not – and a cacophony of noises – from shouts and laughter to high-pitched whistles and the slamming of carriage doors.

As Pearl looked around her she felt that she had stepped into another country – never mind another city. Even the people pushing past her to get on the train she had just got off seemed different. Some of the women she spotted were wearing the most amazing skirts made from enough material to clothe a family of ten. Even the voices crisscrossing around her were peculiar.

As Pearl joined the choppy sea of bodies, she held her bag to her chest and edged forwards, at last reaching the end of the platform and handing her now crumpled ticket over to a man, whose uniform had the brightest gold buttons Pearl had ever seen.

After passing through the rotating barrier, Pearl found herself chucked out into another swirl of men, women and children – some running, some idling, some simply standing. She looked around for a few minutes before finding the 'Way Out' sign.

The crowds started to thin out and for the first time Pearl was able to take in the immense building that was King's Cross railway station. She looked up at the huge ceiling which to her mind resembled the inside of an upside-down ship with its arching metal ribs. She could even see pigeons nestling in the framework, cooing and looking down at the tableau below.

As she neared the huge pillared exit, Pearl heard a load of women's voices shouting in unison. Wondering what all the kerfuffle was about, she swung round to see a group of a dozen or so women, all well dressed, and all waving large placards in the air.

Pearl squinted and read: 'Votes for Women'. Another read 'Ballots not Bullets'.

Pearl had heard about these women – these 'suffragettes' – but had not given them much thought. Her da said they were 'a bunch o' mad cows causing trouble'. Now seeing them for real, Pearl thought they didn't look at all mad. In fact, they seemed quite normal – and not short of a few bob either, judging by what they were wearing.

Pearl stood, rooted to the spot, captivated as the women passed her by. Once they had gone, she merged again with the moving crowd of fellow travellers.

She had never felt so small, so insignificant, or so anonymous.

Chapter Eleven

Thursday 4 September 1941

'Never?!' Dorothy's voice sounded out across the early morning quietness of the shipyard. A few of the plater's helpers who stood smoking and chatting around their five-gallon barrel fire instinctively looked across at the sound of Dorothy's loud exclamation before going back to their own conversations.

Oblivious to the attention she was drawing to herself, Dorothy looked around at the women welders who were standing around their own burning steel drum, and inhaled theatrically.

'Oh ... My ... Goodness!' She enunciated the words with increasing volume. Her face was animated with pure drama.

'Did you hear that, Ange? *Joe's gone and proposed to Bel!*' Dorothy's voice was somewhere between a shrill and a screech. The low-flying seagulls on the lookout for early morning titbits squawked as if in response to the melodrama unfolding below.

Angie had just turned up at the women welders' work area that consisted of a large wooden bench and a scattering of metal rods and welding equipment. She dumped her gas mask and holdall down by the side of their workbench.

Dorothy took another good suck of air. 'This is sooo exciting! We want to hear every teeny-weeny detail.'

Her head swung around to her best friend. 'Don't we, Ange?'

Polly wanted to laugh at Dorothy's pantomime performance at this time in the morning, but the banging in her head made her wince. She was suffering the worst hangover ever, and Dorothy's less than dulcet tones had her mentally reaching for the volume control. Last night had been great, but she was paying for it now, as she guessed everyone else in the Elliot household would be too. All apart from Pearl, who had the tolerance of a man mountain when it came to alcohol.

'Ooo, Dor, keep it down a notch, will you. My head's throbbing me. And I feel as rough as a badger's backside,' Polly pleaded, putting her hands to her temples as if that would somehow ease the loud internal knocking in her head. She wished she had held off telling them about Bel and Joe's engagement until it was lunchtime, when she would hopefully be starting to feel a bit better. But she had been so buoyed up that it had just come tumbling out as soon as she had seen her workmates.

Rosie chuckled. 'That'll teach you to drink on a work night. What was it? Brandy?'

Polly groaned. 'Port – but Bel and I did have a tiny sniff of whisky towards the end.'

'Argh,' Gloria sounded her disgust. 'I'm glad I'm not in your shoes.'

'Hannah'll want to know.' Martha's comment was a veiled request.

'Go on then,' Rosie said, 'nip over there quickly and tell her to get herself over to the canteen this lunchtime. A bit of good news for a change.'

The words were barely out of Rosie's mouth before Martha was loping across the yard, stepping over large coils of steel chains and dodging the incoming tide of workers heading off to their own work areas around the huge expanse of the yard.

'And tell her to bring her new *friend* if she likes,' Dorothy shouted after her.

Angie laughed. 'Dinnit wind her up, Dor. Yer know she can't stand young Olly. Bet ya she tells Hannah it's girls only.'

'I don't know why you two call him "young Olly",' Gloria butted in as she picked up her welding mask and gave the filter a clean with a piece of rag. 'He's older than you two. He must be in his early twenties. At least.'

'So, Polly,' Rosie spoke across the women and the growing level of noise and chatter as it neared the half past seven start time, 'I'm guessing Bel said "yes"?'

'Of course it was yes!' Dorothy interrupted. 'You've seen the pair of them together, haven't you? Like two lovebirds they are. Totally smitten. Aren't they, Ange?'

Angie, crouched down on her haunches, was rummaging around in her bag for her headscarf and merely grunted her agreement.

Dorothy looked over at Ange, who, she felt, didn't seem as excited about the news as she should be. After all, it wasn't every day someone they knew got engaged. They had both met Bel and Joe when they had taken baby Hope back to the Elliots' house just after she was born. When they'd walked home that evening they had gassed on for ages about 'how pretty Bel was' and how Joe looked the spit of Errol Flynn. And they had sighed at the thought of how wonderful it must feel to be so in love – and how Bel and Joe were clearly head over heels. You would have been blind not to see it.

'Hey, silent night, cat got your tongue?' Dorothy prodded Angie, who was wrapping her olive green scarf expertly round her head so that not a wisp of her strawberry blonde hair was let loose. As she jerked round to look at her friend, Dorothy immediately noticed a red mark on her right cheek.

'What've you done to your face?' Dorothy asked; her voice had now lost its joviality.

Angie put her hand to the offending blemish on her face and shrugged it off.

'Got a clout this morning from my da cos I forgot to gan to the shops yesterday. There was nowt to eat for breakfast. Ma's doing night shifts so everything's gone to pot.'

'God,' Dorothy was clearly furious. 'Has your "da" lost the use of both of his own legs? Hm? Or does he just enjoy a little mindless violence every now and again?'

Angie let out a short laugh. 'He's not violent, Dor.' As she spoke she quickly looked across at Gloria and recalled the state of her face the day after Vinnie had done a job on her. Now *that* was being violent.

'I think he just feels the need to put me in my place every now and again.'

Dorothy stomped across and started to scrutinise Angie's face. 'Maybe someone needs to put *him* in his place every now and again,' she muttered, pulling her bag from under the workbench and fishing around for her powder compact.

Angie just tutted and rolled her eyes.

'Yeh, Dor, all sixteen stone of him. I've seen him in a few punch-ups 'n he never so much as comes away with a scratch.'

Hearing the girls' chatter, Gloria had to swallow her tongue. Bloody men. Why couldn't they just keep their hands to themselves?

Dorothy was now covering Angie's red mark with a flurry of loose powder. 'There,' she said as she stood back, 'as good as new. I think me and you should go out tonight and you can stay over at mine – *bugger the shopping*!'

'All right, you lot,' Rosie said sternly in her put-on boss's voice. 'Let's get to it.'

And with that the horn sounded the start of their shift. Within seconds any kind of chatter was pointless, as the deafening din of the yard got into full swing, drowning out even the banging in Polly's head.

At twelve o'clock on the dot the klaxon sounded out once again and the yard fell silent, or as silent as a shipyard ever could be. Within minutes the women had freed themselves from their metal masks and pulled off their thick, over-sized work gloves. Within five more minutes they'd arrived at the canteen, beaten the other workers to the front of the queue, and were settled with their plates of hot steaming food at what had become known as the 'the lasses' table'.

'So, I'm guessing you're going to be the maid of hon-our?' Dorothy asked Polly, who was busy shovelling fork-fuls of mince and potato into her mouth. She was still looking as white as a sheet, but at least her head had stopped throbbing. She nodded her answer.

'And what about bridesmaids?' Dorothy probed some-what hopefully.

'I don't think godmothers can also be bridesmaids,' Gloria butted in, deadpan.

'Really?' Angie said, looking baffled.

'Ignore her, Ange, she's just being sarky and trying to wind me up,' Dorothy said.

Gloria tensed as she looked at Angie's marked face. The powder Dorothy had brushed on had worn off and Angie looked like she had put a blob of rouge on one cheek but had got distracted and forgotten about the other.

'I don't think Bel's going to have bridesmaids,' Polly butted in. 'I think they just want a small family affair. Probably registry office.'

'What is "registry office"?' Hannah piped up. She had Martha on her left and on her right was Olly, who looked as pleased as punch to be with the women on their table, and was listening intently to the conversation.

'It's an office where you get married,' Martha explained through a mouthful of mince pie.

'Ah.' Hannah looked up at her friend and smiled, but she didn't look any the wiser.

'You see, Hannah,' Polly explained, 'with this being Bel's second marriage, I don't think she felt it would be right to have a church wedding. She didn't say anything, but I know for a fact she wouldn't want to get married at St Ignatius because that's where she and Teddy were married.

'But,' she said, looking across at Dorothy who had seemed a little dejected since the mention of a 'small' and 'family' wedding, ' . . . just because it's not gonna be some great big hoo-ha of an affair, that doesn't mean you're all not invited.'

Dorothy's mouth immediately spread into a smile.

'So,' Angie said cheekily, 'do yer think this means we might be hearing the pitter-patter of little feet in the near future?'

Polly laughed. 'God, Angie, you sound like Pearl! That's not why they're getting married, if that's what you're meaning.'

'So, have they set a date yet?' Dorothy asked Polly, who was now looking slightly less hungover.

'Not yet,' Polly said, scraping the last bit of gravy and mash from her plate. 'But my guess is they won't hang about.'

'Was there any mention about what Bel is going to wear?' Rosie asked curiously.

The women all looked at Rosie, surprised that she, out of all the women, would be asking about such things.

Polly laughed. 'I think the smartest bit of clothing Bel has in her wardrobe is her clippie uniform. I'm sure she'll find something, though. Anyway, you know Bel, she would look good in a load of rags sewn together.'

'Mm, I might have an idea,' Rosie said thoughtfully, as she got ready to leave. The women stared at her, awaiting more information.

'That's all I'm going to say for the moment!' she said with a chuckle.

'Anyway, Glor,' Dorothy said, pushing her plate away, 'while we're on the subject of weddings and the like, you thought any more about Hope's christening?'

Gloria sighed loudly and dramatically. 'Give me time to breathe, won't yer.'

'Glor,' Dorothy put on her poshest voice, 'I am just carrying out my designated role as Hope's appointed godmother. And the rules are that *my* goddaughter needs to be christened – and sooner rather than later.'

Gloria shook her head from side to side in exasperation. 'There *will* be a christening – I promise, Dorothy, but first of all I've got a divorce to sort out.'

As the women enjoyed the last few minutes of their lunch break, they continued to chatter on about every aspect of Bel's wedding.

Polly sat back, and listened to the banter, her mind drifting to thoughts of Tommy, and idly wondered what kind of wedding they would have. She chuckled to herself as she imagined all her workmates kitted out in ivory white bridesmaids' dresses, traipsing down the aisle after her. It would certainly be a sight for sore eyes.

*

'How's that hangover doing?' Rosie asked Polly as they packed up and got ready to join the throng of dirt-smeared workers hurrying to the main gates.

'Oh, I feel loads better now, thanks, Rosie. A mound of shepherd's pie and a gallon of tea have helped no end. Sam's been back and forth like a yo-yo refilling my flask. Poor lad.'

Rosie chuckled at the thought of the yard's skinny little tea boy, his long metal pole of clanging tin cans swaying like a seesaw across his shoulders, being run ragged by Polly's need for tea.

'Do you fancy a quick trip into town before you head home?' she asked.

Polly looked more than a little surprised. Rosie was never one to hang around after work. Even when they went out for the occasional drink at the Admiral, she'd always be the first to leave.

'I'm intrigued,' Polly said. 'The reason being . . . ?'

Rosie laughed. 'Grab your gas mask and bag. I'll explain as we go.'

Polly did as she was told, adding, 'As long as it doesn't involve any kind of alcoholic beverage, that's fine by me.'

For a change Rosie and Polly didn't take the ferry across the river but jostled shoulder-to-shoulder with the horde of mainly male workers up the cobbled lane from the yard on North Sands to Dame Dorothy Road, where they ran and jumped on a tram just as it was pulling away.

Climbing to the top deck, Polly glanced to her left as they passed the lovely thirteenth-century St Peter's Church, one of the oldest churches in the whole of the north-east – possibly even in the country. Behind it she could just about see the necks of the huge metal cranes peeking above the embankment, ready to serve the ship-yards and engine works which lay on either side of the river.

'So, come on,' she said as they caught their breath, paid their fares, and found a seat, 'tell me what the mystery trip into town's all about. I'm itching to know.'

'Well,' Rosie said, 'when we were all chatting about the wedding, I was thinking how much it's going to cost Bel and Joe. Even if it's a small affair, like you say, it's still going to put them back a bit. And, let's face it, no one's exactly flush these days.'

Rosie paused as a group of shipwrights spilled on to the top deck, shouting and joking.

'So, I was thinking how I could help out.' Rosie glanced at Polly, before adding quietly, 'Especially after Agnes looked after me that night.'

Polly looked back at her boss and saw just how deep her gratitude was. None of them had ever spoken openly about the night Rosie had been attacked by her uncle – the night when Agnes had nursed Rosie through the most horrendous case of arc eye and tended to all the tiny burns she had suffered after having her face held over a live weld.

'Honestly, Rosie, you don't owe Agnes, or any of us, anything, we'll just be chuffed to have you there. You will be able to come, won't you?' Polly asked.

'God, yes, I wouldn't miss it for the world,' Rosie said. 'My own life is totally lacking in any kind of romance, so I might as well enjoy someone else's.'

Polly smiled, but felt sad for Rosie. She wanted to ask about her detective, but thought better of it. Whatever they'd had, it was now clearly over. 'So? You were think-ing . . . ' Polly prodded Rosie to continue.

Just then the brakes of the tram started to hiss.

'Our stop,' Rosie said, 'come on.'

They both jumped off at the bottom of Fawcett Street, where there was a huge cordoned-off bomb site where Binns – the 'Harrods' of Sunderland – had once stood. Turning right, they started walking up Holmeside. Only then did Rosie finally start to tell Polly of her idea.

'It's a bit of a long story, really,' she said, 'and I don't want to bore you with all the details, but early on this year I met an old schoolfriend of mine called Kate. She had fallen on some hard times and was begging in town.'

'That's awful,' Polly said quietly. She was listening attentively. It was rare for Rosie to disclose anything personal about herself, and never anything about her 'other life'.

'Anyway,' Rosie said, 'we got chatting and, well, the long and short of it is that Kate now lives at Lily's. But,' Rosie added quickly, 'not to work there as such . . . We . . . that's Lily and I, suggested that Kate stay in the spare room in exchange for being our cleaner. Like a live-in maid, really.'

Polly was so entranced by every word coming out of her boss's mouth that she didn't even notice the two smiling young soldiers who had taken off their caps and moved to the side of the pavement to let them pass.

'Then,' Rosie said, her face brightening, 'by chance we found out that Kate was a total genius with a needle and thread. Honestly, I swear she could be the next Coco Chanel – she even looks like her.'

'I think I might know where you're going with this,' Polly said.

As they passed Maynard's the confectioners, Rosie slowed her pace.

'So, Lily and I came up with an idea, which,' she said, coming to a halt, 'we've just managed to put into action.' She pointed to the shop sign above them.

'Welcome to Kate's very own little seamstress shop – soon-to-be boutique.'

Polly looked up at the new hand-painted sign which read 'Maison Nouvelle'.

'Wow!' Polly said, eyes wide. 'What does it say?'

'*Maison* is "house" and *nouvelle* is "new". We thought it sounded nice even if people don't know what it means. Plus Lily's obsessed with anything French.'

Rosie opened the glass front door, criss-crossed with tape to stop it shattering in the event of an air raid, and as she did so the little brass bell above them tinkled.

'Oh Rosie, how lovely to see you.' Kate hurried from behind her large wooden table on which was strewn a huge pattern, and a smattering of pincushions, needles and bobbins of thread. She gave Rosie a quick kiss on both cheeks.

Polly was standing looking around her in fascination. This was like an Aladdin's cave of all things fabric and fashion. There were rolls of different textiles, some plain, some patterned, stacked up against the wall or lying on the floor. There were ribbons and lengths of lace hanging from coat hangers and hooks, and boxes full to the brim with an assortment of buttons and all kinds of other haberdashery.

The shop's centrepiece was the huge table Kate had been working at, which had a long iron measuring tape embedded in its thick wooden top. To the side was a dressmaker's mannequin, partially dressed in swirls of rayon and laced with needles.

'So . . . Polly, this is Kate. Kate – Polly.' Polly forced her eyes back to the young woman who stood in front of her, her hand held out. Polly grabbed her hand and shook it energetically.

'This place is incredible,' she said, 'it really is. How long have you been open? I'm surprised Dorothy and Angie haven't been here.'

Kate beamed at Polly's compliments.

'Well,' Rosie interrupted, 'that's because it's not officially open yet.'

'Come and have a cup of tea out the back,' Kate beckoned, heading towards a thick curtained partition. Polly watched Kate walk towards the back of the shop and tried to imagine this pretty, well-dressed and perfectly coiffured young woman sitting on the streets with her hand stretched out begging for change, but couldn't.

When Polly ducked round the velvet door panel, she found herself in a tiny, but very warm and cosy back room. There was just enough space for a stove and a little square table.

Kate told Rosie and Polly to sit while she made the tea.

'It really is quite a wonderful place,' Polly said.

'Well,' Kate said, as she carefully poured the tea into three small china cups, 'it's *going to be* wonderful. I've got so many ideas – and hopes.' Her manner was timid but she held herself with confidence – a confidence that Lily had been trying her hardest to instil in her. Since her arrival at the bordello in March, Lily had taken it upon herself to transform Kate from the raggedy down-and-out street beggar she had once been, into a well-spoken and well-groomed young woman.

'I'm going to start off doing basic seamstress work, lots of make-do-and-mending, some tailoring, that kind of thing, you know. Since clothes rationing came into force, people are wanting curtains and all kinds of things made into dresses . . . and,' she added a little self-consciously, 'I hope to create my own designs – see if anyone likes them enough to buy them.'

'Which they will,' Rosie said, taking a big slurp of her tea. 'I've seen some of her designs,' she told Polly.

Rosie looked at both women seated opposite her before turning her attention to Kate.

'But, now for the reason we're here . . . Polly came into work this morning not only with a hangover . . . ' Kate giggled softly as Polly pulled a shocked face as if trying to deny the accusation. 'But,' Rosie continued, 'she also came with the marvellous news that her brother Joe has proposed to her sister-in-law Bel.'

Kate looked slightly puzzled.

Quickly, Rosie explained, 'Bel was married to Joe's brother, Teddy, but he was sadly killed out in North Africa at the end of last year.'

Kate was now looking even more puzzled.

'You see,' Polly butted in, 'Joe was injured and was shipped back home and it was Bel who nursed him. In a nutshell, the pair of them fell in love – and are now wanting to get married.'

'Which,' Rosie broke in, 'is where you come in . . . '

Kate's face lifted in comprehension.

'You see,' Rosie swung her gaze to Polly, 'I was thinking this afternoon about what to get Bel and Joe for their wedding present, and I was also wondering how Kate was getting on today setting up the shop – and that's when the idea struck me! If Bel is in agreement I'd love to bring her here and for Kate to design and make her a dress for her wedding. What do you think?' She looked at them both for their reaction.

'Oh my goodness, Rosie,' said Polly, genuinely taken aback. 'I think that is the most wonderful, kindest and most thoughtful present ever. Bel will be over the moon, but she's a proud one. I know she'll want to pay for it herself. She hates anything that smacks of charity.'

'Well,' Rosie said, 'you'll just have to tell her straight. It's a present – and people don't pay for their own presents. It's as simple as that.'

Rosie turned her attention to Kate.

'And this can be your first commission, Kate. You'll get paid the going rate, and if Bel is all right with it, you can put the dress in your window after the wedding to show customers just what you can do with those nimble hands of yours.'

Kate instinctively looked down at her hands, before quickly looking up again with excitement sparkling in her eyes.

'Oh, I would do it for nothing, Rosie, no one has to pay me,' she said, imploringly.

Polly had automatically followed Kate's gaze down to her hands and been shocked to see how gnarled they were for someone of her age. One of her fingers looked a little wonky, as if it had been broken and never healed properly, and there were old calluses on her knuckles. Her nails were also bitten so badly the tops of her fingers and thumbs looked swollen. Quickly Polly looked back up.

'This is just so exciting,' she said, looking at Kate and then Rosie. 'I can't wait to get back and tell Bel.'

'Tell her to come round tomorrow,' Kate said, 'if she gets a chance. We can chat through some ideas. I'll draft out a few sketches tonight.'

Rosie laughed. 'I know all you want to do now, Kate, is get back to Lily's and raid her collection of *Vogue*.'

Kate chuckled. Rosie had read her mind.

In a few minutes Polly and Rosie were back out on the street, with Polly saying her thank-yous and Rosie brushing them off.

The two women walked down Holmeside and on to Borough Road before going their separate ways – Polly back to Tatham Street, excited about telling Bel the news, and Rosie back to her flat where she was planning to have a quick wash down and change of clothes before heading out to Lily's for the evening.

Kate left the Maison Nouvelle at seven o'clock when darkness had fallen. After buttoning up her thick woollen coat and pulling out a jangle of keys from her pocket, she locked up. Then she stood back and looked at the shop – *her* shop.

As she did so, something caught the corner of her eye and she looked right, but with no street lights on she couldn't see much. She felt a shiver go down her back as her eyes fell on the darkened outline of the town's Museum and Winter Gardens with its two huge Romanesque pillars. She had spent countless nights freezing to death huddled at the top of the stone steps that led to the entrance, either starving hungry, or half-cut on cheap spirits.

Kate turned away from her memories and started walking up to Park Lane. She quickened her pace. It was dark and cold and she wanted to be shot of all reminders of her past life. As she reached the bus depot she broke into a jog in her eagerness to get back to Lily's, where it was warm, and there was laughter and music and joviality, and where she could get sketching out some ideas for Bel's wedding dress that were already floating across her mind's eye.

It was only by chance that he spotted Rosie and Polly coming out of a new shop called Maison Nouvelle. The two women had been so engrossed in their conversation that neither of them had spotted him on the other side of the road, nor had they paid heed to anyone else around them.

Seeing Rosie made him stop dead in his tracks in the middle of the pavement, causing a woman with her pram to run into the back of him. The woman apologised profusely, but he reassured her that the fault was all his.

As usual, whenever he saw Rosie or was in her company, or even when he just thought about her, his whole being became more alive, more alert, more energised. Seeing her now he instinctively wanted to rush over to her, to go and talk to her, but thankfully his head caught up with his galloping heart, and reminded him:

Rosie does not want you, Peter!

And not only did she not want him, but she had made it clear it would not be a good idea for them to simply be friends.

That had hurt, but he had known she was right. They could never be just friends. It would have been torment for him. But what was niggling him was that, for some inexplicable reason, he felt that it would be torment for her too.

Why?

Why did he feel that?

It made no sense.

Again his heart was speaking to him – and not his head.

Seeing Rosie had floored him, and instead of carrying on walking up to the police station in town, he found himself going into a little coffee shop across the road from the Maison Nouvelle, where he ordered a cup of tea and a sandwich. He told himself it would be a change to the canteen at the police station, but really he just wanted a little time on his own to gather his thoughts before starting the night shift he had volunteered for.

As he sat there, forcing down a dry corned beef sandwich, he kept thinking about Rosie.

Why couldn't he accept it was over? Why didn't it feel like it was really over between the two of them?

You just have to give up, Peter. She said she doesn't want you. Accept it.

After paying for his stale sandwich and weak tea, DS Miller left the café. As he did so he heard the tinkle of a shop bell and looked across the road to see a petite young woman locking the door to the Maison Nouvelle.

He was about to carry on to the station when the woman turned and looked down the road. She looked deep in thought. It was dark but he immediately recognised her, although, for the life of him, he couldn't remember where from. He continued on his way, racking his brains as to who the woman was. He hated it when his memory failed him.

As he turned to walk up Fawcett Street and passed the

badly bombed Binns department store, it suddenly came to him.

It was Kate, the beggar girl!

From what he remembered she had spent quite a few years on the streets. Strange, though, that she was now working in a shop. And in charge, by the looks of it.

And what a coincidence Rosie and Polly had been in the shop.

Five minutes later, DS Miller stepped through the swinging glass doors of the Sunderland Borough Police headquarters.

'Hello there, Pete.' The sergeant at the front desk had known DS Miller for years. 'You out with the Home Guard this evening?'

'Aye, I am, Neville.' DS Miller raised his black trilby hat; all the detectives in the force wore them. 'You keeping well?'

'Aye, aye, all good. Our Billy is back for a few days' leave next week so the missus is running round like a crazy woman, using up all our rations and cleaning the house from top to bottom.'

DS Miller smiled. He didn't envy parents the worry they went through if they had sons in the forces, but he did covet their being a part of a loving family unit. His own wife Sal had been taken from him before they had been able to have their own sons or daughters. Sometimes he railed against the injustice of it all – not only of losing his wife so young, and at the hand of such an evil illness, but of being deprived of the joy of having children. Other times, though, when he was feeling less sentimental, he thought it was probably just as well. How unfair for a child to be raised without a mother's love.

As DS Miller made his way down the nicotine-stained corridors to the changing rooms where he kept his Home Guard uniform and tin helmet, he passed the archive rooms. He stopped and looked at his watch. He still had half an hour before the crossover of shifts.

His curiosity had been piqued, seeing Kate. And Rosie. It just seemed so odd that Rosie knew Kate. And she must have known Kate as the shop had clearly not opened for business yet; from the way she and Polly had left the shop it was obvious by their body language that it was Rosie who had orchestrated the visit there – and not Polly, who had looked excited but also a little bewildered.

DS Miller put his hand on the brass knob of the door to the archive department.

Just to cure my curiosity, he told himself.

Chapter Twelve

Saturday 6 September 1941

'Thank heavens you're here, Mum. I thought you were never going to make it.' Helen was sitting, shoulders slumped, on the large plastic-covered armchair that was positioned next to the iron-framed hospital bed. Her normally sparkling emerald green eyes were bloodshot and there were dark bags underneath.

Miriam ignored her daughter and stared at her husband, lying flat on his back, looking like a corpse on a mortuary slab, his arms by his side and the outline of his slightly parted legs showing under the stiff starched sheets. The only visible movement came from the slight rise and fall of his chest as he breathed.

Miriam felt a wave of irritation. She had rushed here as quickly as she could when the hospital had called her, but from what she could see, Jack looked exactly the same as when she had been here the time before – and the time before that.

For the past ten days she'd been trooping to and from the Royal. And with each trip her resentment had grown. Why they couldn't have simply kept him at the hospital in County Mayo where they'd initially taken him was beyond her. He'd barely been there a fortnight when the doctors in their infinite wisdom had deemed him 'stable', and decided that it would be best to get Jack back home 'to those who loved and cared about him'.

'If Mr Crawford is to come out of this coma he's in . . . ' the neurologist had told Miriam, his broad Irish accent and the crackling on the phone line making his words barely comprehensible, ' . . . the chances are it will be in the next few weeks.'

Miriam had felt impatient as he started rambling on about 'two possible prognoses' for coma patients like her husband. The first being that he would gradually start to regain consciousness, but that usually happened within the first month. The second was that he would not wake up, but instead would 'progress into a minimally conscious state'. When Miriam had asked him what on earth he meant by that, the consultant had cleared his throat a little nervously. When Miriam heard the words 'vegetative state' she had immediately hung up.

'Sit up straight, Helen.' Miriam swung her gaze to her daughter. 'You look like the letter C!' Her words bore not a slither of humour or affection.

Helen automatically pulled herself up straight, like a puppet as its strings are tugged. Her mother's words were a familiar rebuke; one of her favourite and most frequently used recriminations. It didn't matter that her father was lying there, right in front of their very eyes, *totally comatose* – or that Helen had been more or less living at the hospital these past few weeks. Oh no, all that her mother was clearly bothered about was her daughter's goddamned posture.

'And, if I were you,' Miriam added, 'I'd go and splash your face with some cold water. You look like death warmed up.'

Helen glared at her mother, who stood there, perfectly made-up, hair expertly styled into victory rolls – her nails

French polished – and thought she had never hated her mum as much in her entire life.

'God, Mother, you're unbelievable! I thought you might be more interested in knowing how Father is doing, rather than making catty comments about my posture and appearance.'

For once Helen would have liked to just chat to her mother like normal mothers and daughters. But instead, she'd had to gear herself up for another bout of verbal sparring, and, if she was honest, that was the last thing she wanted to do at this moment. She had neither the energy nor the inclination, but she was damned if she was going to capitulate and let her mother get the better of her.

Looking at her mum's slightly victorious demeanour, she could swear that on some sick and twisted level she was actually enjoying seeing her daughter look as rough as a dog and totally done in while she stood there, fresh as a daisy, and still remarkably good-looking for a forty-odd-year-old woman.

Miriam sniffed. 'Of course, I want to know about your father, but from where I'm standing he looks exactly like he did when I was in the other day. The nurse on the phone told me that there'd been some improvement – but this is clearly not the case.'

Helen had to stop herself screaming at her mother. Hadn't she listened to anything the doctors had been telling them these past few weeks?

'There *has* been an improvement, Mother,' Helen said through gritted teeth. 'And if you'd been here more often you might have actually seen it.'

Miriam had walked to the end of the bed and was pretending to read her husband's medical chart. She hated the fact that Jack looked so weak and pathetic, lying there, mouth half open with a load of dribble coming out. She looked over at a steel trolley that had been pushed up against the wall and caught sight of a load of sterilised metal syringes and glass thermometers lying in an enamel kidney-shaped bowl; tucked underneath on the middle shelf was a porcelain bedpan. Quickly she looked away.

'So, then, pray tell, what is the great improvement that I am failing to see?'

Helen's mouth pursed. Part of her wanted to tell her mother to just 'get out and go home' – that she was the most heartless, cold-hearted bitch she had ever known. But she knew she couldn't. She might have let herself go these past few weeks, but she wasn't going to humiliate herself in public and act like some old fishwife, and in a hospital of all places.

'A few hours ago,' she said in a low, controlled voice, 'Father squeezed my hand, then he started to move his arm ever so slightly. I immediately shouted for the nurse.' Helen paused, remembering the drama. 'She came rushing in and started checking his pulse, and that's when he started to try and speak!'

'Well, what did he say?' Miriam demanded, hanging the medical chart back on the bottom of Jack's bed and walking over to the bedside cabinet to inspect a small glass vase of flowers that she presumed Helen must have brought in.

'Nothing that I could understand,' Helen said, more than a little exasperated by her mother's lack of any kind of excitement about what had happened. 'It was as if he was having a bad dream and trying to call out.'

'And then what?' Miriam snapped.

'Well, that was it,' Helen said, feeling like a schoolgirl who had not done as well as she should have in a test. 'He just went back to the way he was.'

'And that's what the doctors call *an improvement*?' Miriam's voice was starting to climb. 'I get my hopes up that I might finally get my husband back and not be left with some vegetable—'

Miriam's rant was just about to really get going when a loud cough at the doorway caused her to brake abruptly mid-flow. She looked round to see a middle-aged man wearing a starched white coat over a dark grey tweed suit. He had a stethoscope hanging around his neck and his hands were resting in the large pockets of his jacket.

'Ah, Mrs Crawford,' he said, 'so glad you could make it.'

Miriam looked him up and down.

'I was just saying, Dr . . . ?'

'Mr Gilbert,' the consultant said. 'Yes, I know what you were just saying and I wanted to explain to you what I have been telling your daughter, Miss Crawford, here.'

Mr Gilbert smiled at Helen. The poor girl looked shattered. She had been by her father's bed every time he had come to do his rounds, and whenever they had needed to carry out more tests.

'The fact that your husband has started to try and move his limbs and has attempted speech is actually a really good sign. Unfortunately, it's not like in the books when a patient simply wakes up out of a coma and starts chatting away as if they've just had a little snooze. I'm afraid, in reality, it's a far more long-drawn-out affair.'

Miriam sighed impatiently.

'People,' he continued, 'who are lucky enough to wake up from a coma – especially those like your husband, who not only suffered hypothermia, but whose brain was deprived of oxygen – well, they usually come round very gradually.' He paused. 'If at all . . . It really is a slow process, and very often, when a coma patient does start to regain consciousness, the chances are they may well be very agitated and extremely confused to begin with.'

Miriam was still standing by the bedside cabinet and was looking intently at the doctor.

Mr Gilbert pulled up one of the hospital's stackable chairs that was in the corner of the small square room.

'Why don't you sit down, Mrs Crawford? Or we could talk more in my office?' He looked at Helen. He hadn't wanted to say what he was about to say in front of the man's daughter.

'There's nothing wrong with my legs, Dr Gibbert,' said Miriam, deliberately mispronouncing the name. The consultant, however, wasn't going to split hairs. He was tired, had been working a twelve-hour shift and now he just needed to get home to his wife and two young children and get some shut-eye. He had not the least inclination or energy for getting into power games with this awful woman.

'That's fine, Mrs Crawford. Now that you are here, though, this might be a good time to have another chat. Your husband has been with us for well over a week—'

'Ten days,' Miriam interrupted.

'Yes, of course, it's now been ten days,' the doctor said and scratched his head in an attempt to hold back his irritation. 'And as I explained to you back then, every day is important, which is why this might be a good time to have another chat to you about your husband's prognosis.' The doctor paused and glanced at a worn-out-looking Helen, before asking, 'Would you like to go somewhere to chat privately?'

Miriam followed his gaze to Helen, who she noticed with irritation had started to slump again.

'No, you can say anything you want to in front of my daughter. She's a big girl now – too old to be mollycoddled.'

Mr Gilbert didn't think this woman's daughter would

have had a lot of – if any – 'mollycoddling' from her mother in the whole of her young life.

'Very well,' he said, 'but if you're not going to sit, then I think I will.'

He drew up the lightweight tubular steel-framed chair and sat down on its hard plywood seat. He leant forward, put his elbows on his legs and clasped his hands together as if in prayer. His narrow dark grey tie dangled down in front of him.

'Your husband's slight movement and attempts to speak today are positive signs, although we really don't know how it will go from now on. There is still the possibility that he may never wake up ... or he may wake up but have suffered damage to the brain, in which case he may well need round-the-clock care for the rest of his life.'

He paused and looked anxiously at the man's daughter as she digested the reality of what he was saying about her father.

'It's what we call being in a "vegetative state" ... Or, of course,' he added, trying to be more upbeat, 'that may well not be the case and Mr Crawford may come out of his coma and make a full recovery ... I'm afraid we just don't know. We don't have a crystal ball,' another pause, ' ... it really is a matter of waiting, and hoping, and praying for the best possible outcome.'

There was silence in the room. The doctor twisted his wrist round and sneaked a look at his watch. He was now into his thirteenth hour on duty. His head felt fuzzy and the scene in this little box room, with its pastel-painted green walls and the long blackout curtains drawn across the large sash windows had taken on a slightly surreal quality.

'Well then, doctor,' Miriam said. 'We'd better start

"hoping and praying" if that's really the best medical help you can offer.' She glared at him.

Mr Gilbert realised he was being rudely dismissed. He pushed himself up out of the chair with his hands on his legs. As he stood up he realised just how stiff he felt.

'Goodnight, Mrs Crawford . . . Miss Crawford, just call the nurse if you need anything. And, no doubt, I will probably see one, or both, of you tomorrow.'

And with that Mr Gilbert was gone.

In twenty minutes he would be climbing into bed and cuddling up to his wife's warm body, and tonight, in particular, he would be counting his blessings that he was married to a woman who not only loved him dearly, but who also loved to 'mollycoddle' their two young children, and would probably continue to mollycoddle them for as long as they allowed her to.

Miriam and Helen were quiet for a good few minutes after Mr Gilbert said his farewells. This was a situation neither of them had ever foreseen they would be in.

'Well,' Miriam eventually broke the silence, 'it's pointless the both of us being here. So you might as well get yourself back home and get some sleep and,' she sniped, 'tidy yourself up before you show your face back here tomorrow. Remember, you've got to keep up appearances. Your grandfather is one of the main benefactors of this hospital.'

A part of Helen wanted to stay by her father's side. A part of her believed that if she stayed with him it might somehow help him to come out of this coma. But she was tired, and she didn't think she had the energy to deal with her mother for a moment longer.

'All right, but you will ring me if he wakes up again,

won't you?' Helen hated the fact that she sounded like she was having to beg.

Miriam looked at her and gave her a smile that seemed genuine.

'Of course I will, darling. Now tootle along. I'll see you in the morning.'

And with that Helen got up and left without saying a word, giving her father one last hopeful look on the way out.

Shortly after she heard her daughter's footsteps reach the end of the corridor, Miriam sat down in the chair by the side of the bed; it was still warm from where her daughter had been sitting for such a long time.

As Miriam allowed herself to relax a little, she felt glad that she was alone. Time for her own thoughts. After a little while she stood up again and walked over to the door and quietly closed it, before sitting back down in the chair.

She took a deep breath and picked up her husband's hand and placed it on her own. She then leant forward and whispered in his ear.

'Now you listen to me, Jack Crawford.' Her voice was steady and stern.

'I've listened to that doctor – whatever his name is – and I have come to a conclusion.' She looked down at her hand in his. It was the first time she'd noticed he was not wearing his gold wedding band. She presumed the doctors must have taken it off for some medical reason.

'I have decided that there are only two options. You either wake up soon – and you wake up the person you were – *with all your mental faculties intact and physically able* . . . you wake up the husband that I want and need you to be, or,' she hesitated, '– and there is no in-between, I'm afraid, Jack – *or* . . . you damn well let go of this life and leave us be.'

Miriam took a breath. 'The choice is clear-cut. I'm simply not having you wake up handicapped . . . or as some half-wit. I simply won't have it.'

Now Miriam was practically hissing.

'*This was not the life I chose*. And I'm not going to be stuck with some mentally or physically disabled imbecile for the rest of my time.'

Miriam looked at Jack but there was no response.

She kept holding his hand, though, which felt surprisingly warm, and as she did so her mind wandered back to the time she first met Jack when he had been a lowly plater at the yard. She had known, despite his poor, working-class upbringing, that he was going to rise through the ranks, could tell he was ambitious – and that he worked as hard, if not harder than the next man.

But it wasn't his work ethic or ambition that had made her want Jack. She had quite simply fallen for him, hook, line and sinker. She had looked into those grey-blue eyes and fallen, as only the young can – without rhyme or reason, and without any thought for what the future might hold. He had been so dashing, with his mop of thick black hair, his manly physique, those broad shoulders, and the way he stomped rather than walked. His face had always looked older than his years, but that was also part of the attraction. He was, in her eyes, a real man. He was not one of these namby-pamby types her mother kept trying to match her up with. God, her darling mater had begged her to choose a husband who was her equal, but her mind had been made up from first setting eyes on Jack when she had gone to the launch of a ship at Thompson's. As soon as she had spotted him, she wangled an introduction and had insisted on shaking hands with him, despite his reluctance due to the dirt that was practically engraved into his skin. She knew then it was Jack she wanted.

And there had been no doubt that she would get what she wanted. Her whole life she had always got what she wanted, so it had come as a shock to her that it hadn't been as easy as she had anticipated. But she had been adamant: Jack was going to be hers – and no one else's. After all, who would not want her? She was gorgeous – and she was rich. What more could a man want?

She had gone on a few dates with Jack, but was shocked when he told her that he was back with his old girlfriend, Gloria. That they'd had a tiff but had made it up again. Miriam had been furious. How could he choose some poverty-stricken, uneducated half-wit from the slums over her? With all her breeding, her schooling, her looks – and her money? Miriam was mad, but she was wise enough not to show it. Strangely enough, it had actually made her want him all the more. Had made her even more determined to succeed. And she *had* succeeded. She had used all of her cunning and sexual know-how to lure Jack back to her parents' house one night when she knew they would be out. Once there, she had gone to work, teasing him, subtly refilling his glass with her father's very expensive whisky. And then she had seduced him. She had known it was unlikely their evening of passion would be enough to make her pregnant, but she had also been savvy enough to realise it would suffice to make Jack *believe* she was with child.

She had been pretty certain Jack would do what was expected in decent society, and she was right.

Jack broke off his relationship with Gloria and did the gentlemanly thing: he made Miriam his wife.

Shortly after tying the knot, Miriam had put on the performance of a lifetime, and with gut-wrenching sobs had told Jack that she had lost their baby. Her phoney pregnancy had been followed by a phoney miscarriage.

Of course, by this time it was too late for Jack. He had committed himself. He had married her. There was no going back. Miriam had got exactly what she wanted.

Within just a few years of marriage, though, Miriam learnt the hard way that sometimes you have to be careful what you wish for. She had not thought ahead, had not considered how life would be when there was such a class divide, but also, she had never thought of what it would be like to spend your life with someone who did not love you. And when Jack started to suspect that she had tricked him into marriage, she started to see pure hatred in his eyes.

Miriam arched her back and sat up straight in the chair. Still, she thought bitchily, if Jack saw Gloria now, he would be thanking her. When she had seen Gloria the other day in the shipyard, her eyes had nearly popped out. What a worn-out wreck.

And when Helen had told her later that Gloria had just had a baby, Miriam had literally gasped in disbelief. *Who on earth has a baby at her age?* She wished Jack would wake up just so she could show him Gloria – so he could see what a lucky escape he'd had all those years ago.

Miriam yawned. It was getting late, and it felt warm in this small, stuffy room.

As she looked down at Jack, her eyelids started to droop and her neck jerked as she started to doze off. 'Keep awake, woman,' she muttered to herself. They didn't need two of them sleeping and dribbling. Perhaps she should think about going home?

Her eyes were just starting to close again when she felt Jack's hand twitch. Her eyes shot back open. At first she thought it was her own hand, but when she looked down she saw Jack's hand move again.

Then his fingers started to curl around her hand and slowly start to squeeze. Miriam watched in what felt like slow motion as Jack's hand gripped hers tighter and tighter, squashing her fingers painfully until she cried out in panic.

'Jack! Jack! Wake up,' she demanded. Miriam tried to wrench her hand free, but Jack's grip was like a vice.

'Nurse! Nurse! Come quickly!' she shouted out, but as her head swung towards the door she realised she had shut it earlier on and the nurse was in a little room further down the corridor.

She might not even be there!

As Jack let out a huge heave of air, Miriam's head whipped back around to stare at him. It was as if he was trying to say something, but couldn't quite get his mouth around it.

'Orrr . . .' The word came out as an incomprehensible sound.

'Jack, wake up! For God's sake, just wake up. You're scaring me!' Miriam was becoming hysterical, half out of her seat and desperately trying to prise Jack's hand off her own.

'Orreeea . . . ' Jack tried to say again.

'Nurse!' Now Miriam was practically screaming, terrified by Jack's sudden awakening.

Finally she heard hurried footsteps tapping down the corridor before the door swung open. The young nurse rushed over to the far side of the bed and grabbed Jack's other hand to check his pulse.

'It's all right, Mr Crawford,' she said soothingly, 'you're going to be fine.'

Miriam looked at the nurse. *How could she be so calm!*

'Get him off me!' she shouted at the young ginger-haired girl, who was forcing open Jack's eyelids and shining some kind of small, pencil-like torch into his eyes.

The nurse looked across at Miriam and hurried back round to her side of the bed.

'Mrs Crawford, calm down,' she said sternly, as she took Jack's hand and slowly peeled back each finger, releasing Miriam from his grip. When she had done so, the nurse strode over to the open doorway, stuck her head out into the corridor and shouted out.

'Nurse Taylor, get Dr Parker – and quick!'

As she turned back and saw the look of horror on the man's wife's face, she took her by the arm and gently guided her out the door.

'Mrs Crawford, let us deal with your husband for now. Go and rest in the waiting room down the corridor – to the right.' The nurse manoeuvred Miriam out of the room, then immediately turned back and bustled over to Jack, who was now calm.

Within minutes Doctor Parker and the nurse were around Jack's bed, checking his heart rate, his blood pressure, and gently talking to him as they took a sample of blood with a large brass and glass syringe. They then prodded and poked him, before sitting him up and putting a stethoscope to his chest and to his back.

'He keeps trying to say something,' the nurse said. She was desperately listening to Jack who was now no longer shouting out, but simply muttering quietly to himself. She leant in closer and put her ear close to his mouth.

'I think he's saying "Gloria" . . . What's his wife's name?'

'Miriam,' Dr Parker said. 'She's one of the Havelocks.' The two nurses nodded. Everyone in the town knew of the Havelock family.

'Maybe Gloria's his daughter?' the nurse continued.

'No, she's called Helen.' Dr Parker knew this for certain as he had chatted to the man's daughter quite a lot since he had arrived here. She was a bit stuck-up – but she did seem to genuinely care for her father.

'It doesn't matter who he's calling for,' he said. 'He's woken up. That's the main thing. Now let's run some tests and see if we can tell if there's any serious damage. I want round-the-clock care from now on, with hourly observation notes brought to me on the dot. He's probably going to be in and out of consciousness for the next few hours.'

The doctor hung his stethoscope back around his neck and moved away from the side of the bed. 'Let me go and have a word with his wife and I'll be straight back.'

Dr Parker softly knocked on the door of the small restroom. He had met Miriam before, just the once, but it was enough to know exactly what kind of woman she was. He came from a fairly well-to-do family himself and his own mother had not been too dissimilar to Miriam – probably a fraction nicer, but only just. He knew that everything had to be focused on her and her well-being.

'Mrs Crawford? I'm Dr Parker. How are you feeling?'

Miriam looked up at the doctor and was relieved someone was finally asking how she was faring. It had been 'Jack, Jack, Jack' these past few weeks, and she thought she might scream if anyone else asked her how he was doing.

'Oh, I'm a little shaken, if I'm honest. It was like being in a living nightmare just then. He wouldn't let go of me,' she said and dabbed her eyes, although there were no tears forthcoming.

The young doctor bobbed down next to Miriam so he was at eye level with her.

'Often,' he started to explain, 'when patients start to come out of a coma, their muscles go into spasms, which may well explain why your husband was gripping so hard and for so long . . . ' His voice tailed off as he could see that the woman sitting in front of him was not interested in listening to him. She just wanted attention. And lots of it.

His aim now, he realised, was to get shot of her as fast as he could, with as least fuss as possible. If she hung around she would end up pestering the nurses and generally get in the way. He knew the sort.

'I think the best thing for you, Mrs Crawford, would be to go home, pour yourself a stiff drink, and try and get some sleep. There's nothing you can do for your husband tonight. He's in capable hands here, and we can ring you at home if you're needed. I'm guessing you have a telephone at home?'

Miriam nodded. The thought of a large gin and tonic geed her up no end. And quite frankly she couldn't stand being in this place of illness and death for a moment longer.

Immediately she stood up. The gin was now calling her and all she wanted to do was sit in front of her gas fire and drink herself into a stupor. As she made to leave, she turned. 'Does this mean he's going to be all right?'

The young doctor smiled reassuringly. 'It's looking very positive, Mrs Crawford. He'll probably sleep for a while now, but so far all the signs are good.'

He was lying, of course. He had no idea whether or not this woman's poor husband was going to be able to walk, talk, or even be able to feed himself again. But he knew there was no point in telling her this. Tonight they just needed rid of her. His patience – and, he knew, that of the two nurses who had been working back to back twelve-hour shifts – was just about out.

The little that was left most certainly wouldn't stretch to dealing with the likes of Mrs Crawford.

Chapter Thirteen

Thursday 11 September 1941

'I'm afraid she might be a bit tetchy today. She's been grizzly all night,' Gloria warned as Bel came hurrying down the hallway at Tatham Street. She always had the front door open on a morning ready for Gloria and Hope's arrival just before seven.

'Ah,' Bel cooed down at Hope, who was snuggled up and sleeping soundly in her pram. 'I had the same problem with Lucille when she was born. I don't think I got a decent night's sleep for the first year ... To be honest, she still wakes up a lot during the night now.'

Bel looked up as Gloria yawned. 'Not that that's what you want to hear.' Bel could see the extent of Gloria's sleep deprivation by the dark circles under her eyes.

'Oh, I almost forgot!' Gloria said, perking up. 'Congratulations on your engagement! Everyone's so happy for you both. We can't shut Dorothy and Angie up. They're man-mad at the best of times, and now, thanks to you two, they've gone into overdrive. I think they're desperate to follow you up the aisle as soon as humanly possible.'

Bel chuckled. She had met Dorothy and Angie a few times and thought they were a hoot. 'I can't see either of them settling down any time soon. They just want to have some fun. And I don't blame them.'

'That's true,' Gloria agreed. 'And at least I've managed to put them off babies for a while. They've seen it warts and all thanks to this little one deciding to be born in front of an audience in the middle of a shipyard.'

'Ah, but she's just so adorable,' Bel said, picking the sleeping baby up out of the pram and cradling her in her arms. Gloria saw Bel's look of pure adoration and love as she gazed down at Hope and knew that the realities of being a new mum might have put Dorothy and Angie off having families for some time, but had clearly not had the same effect on Bel.

As Gloria started to manoeuvre the Silver Cross pram she had bought from one of the second-hand shops in town, she spotted Joe hobbling down the street, his walking stick swinging forward and propelling him forward at a remarkably fast pace. Gloria turned to Bel in time to see a huge smile spread across her face as she spotted her fiancé looking ever so handsome in his smart Home Guard uniform. Gloria thought that the girls were right. Joe did look like Errol Flynn with his tall, slender build and slicked-back dark brown hair.

'Ah, the welcoming committee,' he said, taking off his cap. 'To be greeted by three gorgeous girls, what more could a man ask for?' he joked.

'Make that four,' a voice from behind them shouted out. It was Polly, a piece of toast in one hand, her holdall and gas mask dangling from the other.

'I think you'll find that's only *two* gorgeous girls,' Gloria spluttered, looking at Polly and Bel, 'and *one* very old and very worn-out mother, and a very grouchy baby girl ... Anyway,' she added, 'I was just congratulating Bel on your engagement. Everyone's dying to hear if you've set a date yet.'

Joe let out a hoot of laughter. 'It'd be tomorrow if I had my way.'

Bel tutted in mock annoyance.

'We're looking at November,' Polly butted in. She was

enjoying her role as self-appointed wedding organiser, which, she had told everyone, was what being a Maid of Honour really meant.

'Come on, Gloria,' she said, looking at her watch, 'we'd better be getting a move on, otherwise we'll be late.'

Joe stood to the side to let the two women past; they were dressed in identical oil-stained overalls, with head-scarves tied like turbans around their heads.

'Take care, the both of you,' he said with unusual seriousness. There hadn't been any bombs dropped on the town for the past month or so, but that didn't mean there wouldn't be more. It was no secret the Luftwaffe's prime target was the town's shipyards and engine works. Hitler wanted them gone. There was a part of him that hated the fact that women were working in the yards, especially as one of those women was his sister, but he knew that, if they didn't, the shipyards would grind to a halt, which could only mean one thing – the war would undoubtedly be lost.

As Gloria and Polly hurried down the street, joining the rest of the workers all heading in the direction of the south docks, Gloria turned to have one last look at her baby girl and caught Joe, his head dipped down, kissing Bel's upturned face. Hope was snuggled between the two of them – now quiet as a mouse.

As the two women made their way along Tatham Street, past Jennings foundry, right at Borough Road, and then left down to Panns Bank, where they jostled to get their place on the old steam-paddled boat, they chatted away about work, the wedding, baby Hope, and, of course, Jack.

Polly, like the rest of the women, knew Gloria relied on work to keep her mind off her worries about her lover, but she also knew it was something that was always there and couldn't be ignored.

'I'm guessing there's no more news?' Polly asked as they walked up to the yard's huge iron gates. There was no need for Polly to say Jack's name.

'No.' Gloria shook her head, but her look told Polly that she was worried sick.

Half an hour later the two women, along with Rosie, Dorothy, Angie and Martha, were engrossed in their work, their masked faces immersed in a constant shower of sparkling molten metal. Occasionally, their arms would drop to rest for a second or two before their rods re-engaged with metal and their fountain of glitter was reignited.

When lunchtime came, they all packed up quickly and made their way over to the canteen. Normally, with such a clear blue sky and the sun out, the women would have sat out and enjoyed their packed lunches by the side of the dock, but Dorothy and Angie were on the prowl, and so the women had been cajoled into eating in the canteen.

Rosie had made her excuses and was heading over to chat to Basil about some welding concerns he had with one of the new ship designs he and his team were working on. On top of which she had promised Martha she would wrench Hannah away from Olly and send her over for lunch – without her new 'friend' in tow.

As Rosie neared the drawing offices, she saw Hannah's excited little face pressed up against the window that looked on to the yard. As soon as she spotted Rosie, she came hurrying out, followed by an equally ardent-looking Olly.

'What's up? You two looked full of the joys,' Rosie asked as soon as she reached them both.

Hannah waved her hand, beckoning Rosie to follow her

to the side of the building so they could speak without anyone overhearing them.

'It's good news,' Hannah said, 'I think.'

Rosie looked at Hannah and then at Olly.

'It's Jack,' Hannah whispered, *'he's woken up.'*

'That's fantastic news!' Rosie said. Her face lit up. 'How did you find out?'

'Olly, here,' Hannah turned slightly to her friend standing behind her. 'He overheard one of the managers, Harold I think his name is, talking to Basil in his office. Olly was standing outside with some drawings Mr Basil had asked for, waiting to go in.'

Rosie swung her gaze to Olly, whose face looked so serious that anyone would believe they were involved in some kind of top secret espionage.

'Did you hear which hospital he was in, Olly?' Rosie asked, her eyes glued to Hannah's friend, desperate for an answer.

'Yes, I think I heard them say something about the Royal,' Olly whispered.

'And did you hear anything else?' Now Rosie's own voice had dropped to a near whisper.

Olly shook his head. 'I'm afraid not.'

'All right,' Rosie said, her voice returning to its normal volume.

'I want you to go to the canteen, Hannah. Have a quiet word with Gloria and tell her to get her stuff and meet me at the gates – but don't say why. Quick as you can!'

Hannah nodded, rushing off, leaving Olly looking after her dolefully like an abandoned puppy.

Five minutes later Gloria came bustling out of the canteen's main entrance, shrugging on her coat and swinging her gas mask and holdall over her shoulders. She strode quickly over to Rosie, who was just coming out of the time-keeper's cabin. As soon as Gloria reached her, Rosie took her to the side of the main gates.

'He's woken up, Gloria! Jack's woken up!'

Gloria took one long look at her boss as if registering the information, then suddenly put her hands to her face and started sobbing uncontrollably. Rosie immediately put her arms around her workmate and could feel her body juddering as she cried tears of sheer relief. It was as if months of pent-up emotions had suddenly been released.

'Oh, thank God. Thank God . . . ' Rosie heard Gloria's muffled words of gratitude between deep intakes of breath. Gloria stepped back, wiping the tears from her wet, dirt-smeared face. Rosie had never seen her friend so emotional and upset.

'Is he all right? I'm guessing it's good news if he's woken up?' Gloria asked.

'I think so,' Rosie said a little uncertainly, 'but I don't know much more than he's out of the coma and he's at the Royal . . . which is why,' she added, 'I think you should go up there this afternoon.' Gloria looked at her boss and then up at the timekeeper's cabin.

As if reading her thoughts, Rosie said, 'Don't worry, I've had a word with Alfie, and he's said he'll turn a blind eye. I've told him it's a family emergency. So, get yourself home, get cleaned up and get yourself up there. I'm pretty sure Miriam and Helen are both meant to be coming in this afternoon for a meeting with the head honchos, so this might be the perfect opportunity.'

Gloria's face was suddenly awash with panic. Finally, she was going to be reunited with her lover. With the father of her child. She had waited nine months for this moment and had seriously doubted that it would happen at all. Now that time had come, though, she felt terrified.

'Go on, Gloria,' Rosie said, her voice excited for her friend. 'Go and see Jack. Tell him he's got the most beautiful baby girl ever!'

'Yes, of course. Yes,' Gloria said, adding, 'Thank you, Rosie.'

'Nothing to thank me for,' Rosie said. 'Now go!'

Rosie watched as Gloria walked out of the main gates in a daze and disappeared up the embankment. Rosie wished she or one of the other women could have gone with her, but questions would have been asked, and besides, Rosie knew this was something Gloria had to do on her own.

Chapter Fourteen

Gloria's mind was spinning with a multitude of thoughts and feelings as she took a tram and then a bus back home. But it was the memory of the final moments of Hope's birth that kept being pinged back into her consciousness: The vision she'd had of Jack's smiling face. *It had felt as if he had really been there with her.*

When Gloria arrived home, she had a quick wash and changed out of her overalls and into a skirt and blouse. Only then did the news that Jack had woken from his coma start to sink in. And as it did so, an overwhelming wave of euphoria washed over her and Gloria found herself standing in the middle of her bedroom, smiling and crying tears of joy.

She was going to have her happy ending. *Jack was alive – awake!* Hope was finally going to meet her father. They could all be together. One happy family. Sod everyone else. Nothing could part them now!

Spurred on by imagining Jack's face when they saw each other, Gloria opened her dresser drawer and put on a little mascara and some lipstick. She even dabbed a smudge of rouge on her cheeks. She took off her headscarf and brushed out her shoulder-length hair that had become even thicker and glossier since her pregnancy. She then pushed her feet into a pair of flat leather pumps and headed out the door. She hurried to the bus stop, just managing to catch a bus into town.

Ten minutes later she was walking through the grand, stone-porched entrance of the Royal Infirmary.

'Calm down,' Gloria told herself. Her heart felt it was going to burst out of her chest. She was breathless with excitement.

'Hello,' Gloria said and smiled politely at the young receptionist behind a mahogany counter. 'Can you tell me what ward Mr Jack Crawford's on, please?'

There were a few seconds' silence as the girl, who couldn't have been more than seventeen, quickly scanned through a long admissions list.

'Here we are,' she said. 'Ward 17 on the first floor. You'll just catch the end of visiting hours.'

Good, Gloria thought. *If any family have been in, they should be gone by now.*

Hurrying up the stairs Gloria had to stop herself from running. All of a sudden she couldn't wait a moment longer. She had to see Jack, kiss him, feel his arms around her, tell him all about Hope and just how wonderful and perfect and gorgeous the child they had created was.

Two more minutes and Gloria was pushing open the two heavy swing doors to Ward 17.

The nurse at the desk by the door smiled at Gloria and asked who she had come to see.

'Jack Crawford,' Gloria told her, all the while her eyes searching the ward. She took two steps forward as she heard the nurse's voice telling her, 'Bed number six, just on your left there.' But Gloria had already spotted him. Her heart was in her mouth. She had to restrain herself from shouting out his name, and instead hurried over to his bed. He was looking the other way, as if watching something further down the ward.

As she approached, Gloria softly called 'Jack.' It took a moment for him to turn to see who was calling his name.

Gloria stopped in her tracks when she saw her lover's weather-beaten face turn towards her. She knew every nuance of that face; every wrinkle and every scar from his years spent building ships. His face was pale and gaunt and it was clear, at just a glance, that he had lost an awful lot of weight. She walked towards the bed, looking into his grey-blue eyes.

'Jack,' she said, her own eyes lighting up in anticipation of finally being reunited with the man she loved so very much. But when Jack looked back at her, there was nothing.

No smile. No change in his facial expression. Not even a flicker of recognition in his eyes.

She hurried the last few steps to his bedside. 'Jack, it's me . . . Gloria.'

But still Jack just looked at her blankly.

'I'm sorry, do I know you?' Jack's voice sounded frail and his eyes squinted as if the light from the overhead fluorescent tubes was too much for him. He looked exhausted, as if the effort to speak was almost too much.

'Of course you do, Jack. It's me, Gloria. Remember?'

Now Gloria was beginning to become fraught. What the hell was going on? Did he really not know who she was?

She wanted to grab hold of Jack and shake him, scream at him that it was her. *Gloria*. The woman he had not wanted to leave. The woman who told him he *had* to leave – to do his bit for the war and go to America to help with the new Liberty ships. The woman who had waited for him – thought about him all day, every day. Worried about him. Cried herself to sleep at night with thoughts that she might never see him again.

Was this some sick joke? No. Her Jack would never do something so perverse.

But how come he didn't know who she was?

Perhaps it was a bad dream. A nightmare she just needed to wake up from.

'Excuse me?'

Gloria jumped, turning around to see a young man, a doctor in a white coat, his hands clasped together in front of him, a pair of horn-rimmed spectacles on his head.

'I'm sorry, madam. I didn't mean to give you a shock,' the doctor said with sincerity. 'Do you mind me asking what relation you are to Mr Crawford?'

Gloria looked at the very young, very nicely spoken doctor.

'I'm,' she hesitated, 'I'm . . . ' another pause. 'I'm an old friend.' She managed to get the words out.

'Do you mind telling me your name?' the doctor persisted.

'Mrs Armstrong . . . but please just call me Gloria . . . '

As she said her name, Gloria could have sworn she saw a look of recognition pass across the young man's face. She looked at his coat and could see the surname 'Parker' on a badge half-hidden by his lapel.

'Ah, Mrs Armstrong, would you mind if we go somewhere for a private chat.'

Gloria's head swung back to Jack, as if he might have suddenly remembered who she was, ending this nightmare into which she had been propelled.

But still there was nothing. No recognition. Just a polite smile – the kind strangers give to one another as they pass on the street.

Bewildered, Gloria allowed herself to be guided by the doctor into a little side room. There was a metal desk covered with stacks of files and papers. The doctor stretched out his arm to indicate that Gloria should sit down in the empty seat. As he did so, he swiftly pulled out his own chair from behind the desk and placed it within arm's reach of Gloria.

'I'm afraid your friend's had a rough old time out of it.' The doctor started talking, as Gloria stared at him blankly.

'His body's been through quite a lot of trauma these past few weeks . . . '

Gloria was looking at the doctor's almost juvenile and, as yet, unblemished face, and for a second she thought of her own boys, who must be around the same age.

'He suffered hypothermia after being in the water for so long, coupled with the fact that he nearly drowned. His body basically shut down.'

He looked at this woman – the woman his patient had called out for. The one he was sure was Mr Crawford's mistress. But he had to admit to himself that she looked nothing like he had imagined. Sitting there in her slightly frayed tweed skirt and a blouse that was more than a little outdated, she did not look like your stereotypical 'fancy piece'. If anything this woman looked more like the frumpy wife – and Mrs Crawford the mistress. The pair of them were like polar opposites. Unlike Mrs Crawford, who was as thin as a pin, and perfectly coiffured and manicured, Mr Crawford's 'friend' was carrying more than a little extra weight. She had obviously made an effort to appear her best as she was wearing make-up, but it looked as if it had been put on in a dash. If he hadn't known better he would have said this was a bedraggled working mum who had a young family to look after, although, judging by her age, any children she might have had would probably be grown up now.

'It's incredible he's regained consciousness.' The doctor searched Gloria's face, trying to see if she was taking in what he was saying. 'To be honest,' he continued, 'we were worried he was past the point of no return. It's really surprising that he's pulled through. Not many patients come round after the four-week marker. But what is particularly great news,' the doctor pressed on, ' . . . is the fact that he's made a massive improvement over the past five days since he woke up. He's talking now, and can sit up – and he's even managed to walk around the ward a few times.'

The doctor smiled at Gloria, but he was still concerned that she didn't seem to comprehend what he was telling her. She looked confused.

'He's a strong chap,' Dr Parker lifted his voice, 'made of hardy stuff, I can tell you!'

And it was true. He'd been totally gobsmacked that his patient had regained consciousness in the first place.

'I would go so far as to say that this is almost a miracle,' he said, speaking more slowly and genuinely wanting to stress the positives – before he dropped the bombshell. '*But*,' he added, taking a breath, 'I'm afraid Mr Crawford didn't come out of all of this totally unscathed . . . There has been a price to pay.'

He took another deep breath.

Gloria, sitting rigidly, was now clearly concentrating on every word coming out of the doctor's mouth.

'When Jack was drowning,' Dr Parker explained, 'his brain was deprived of oxygen, although we don't know for how long . . . It would seem that the lack of oxygen caused some damage to a part of the brain which affects memory.'

Finally he saw a look of realisation begin to pass across the woman's face.

'Mr Crawford would appear to be suffering from something we call in the profession "retrograde amnesia". In other words, he appears to have lost his memory.'

Gloria looked shocked.

'That's why he doesn't recognise me . . . ' It was a statement rather than a question.

Dr Parker nodded solemnly. 'You and just about everyone else he has ever known . . . The mind's a very complex organ,' the doctor continued, now confident that what he had been telling her was being processed.

'So, although Mr Crawford might not be able to really remember who he is, he still knows how to walk, talk, and basically how to behave and function. And it's likely he will be able to remember things from now on in. In fact, we're pretty certain he can. He has remembered who I am, for instance – and the nurses. So, it's really just his past that he's presently missing.

'Which is why,' he stressed slowly, 'even if someone was very important to him before, he will not be able to remember them now.'

The last words were said in as professional, but comforting, a manner as he could muster. He felt sorry for this woman who sat opposite him now. He could tell that she had not had an easy life.

'Does that mean Jack'll never get his memory back, Dr Parker?' Gloria was now finding her voice, forcing herself to get with it. This was important.

'I'm afraid only time will tell on that score. There is the possibility that he *will* get his memory back in full, but,' he paused, 'there is also the possibility that he will remain an amnesiac for the rest of his life.'

Gloria sat silent for a moment, letting the doctor's words sink in.

She looked up at his face, and for the first time noticed he looked tired, and his eyes were bloodshot. She stood up to leave. She knew there was nothing else that he could really tell her.

'Thank you, Dr Parker,' Gloria said, holding her hand out. 'Thank you for your time – and for explaining everything to me.'

The young doctor shook Gloria's hand. He knew he wouldn't see her here again. He was pretty sure his suspicions were right. She had taken quite a chance coming here today. The man's wife and daughter had left only about ten minutes before she had arrived. She must have been pretty desperate to take such a risk.

'You're welcome, Mrs Armstrong,' he said, before adding, 'here's hoping.'

As Gloria left the consultation room she took one last look at Jack. He looked pale and was half dozing, propped up by pillows in his bed. Her whole being yearned to go over to him, to wrap him gently in her arms and hold him, to kiss him, to make him better. Make him remember. But she knew she couldn't. She had to leave, even if every cell in her body pleaded with her to stay and never leave her lover's side.

As she forced herself to turn away, she caught sight of a photograph that had been placed on his bedside table. It was a black and white photograph of Jack and Miriam on their wedding day. They were covered in confetti and laughing.

Gloria managed to make it out of the hospital before she burst into heaving sobs. She staggered to a little alleyway down the side of the main stone-pillared entrance so no one could see her in such a state, and with her back leaning against the wall, she allowed heartbreak to pour out of her untamed as she bent over double. Her tears blinded her and stung as her mascara ran into her eyes; her nose streamed and she felt the urge to vomit.

She loved this man, had borne him a child just a month previously, and yet she had no rights to him. It was Miriam's right to be there – even though she had no love for Jack.

It was Miriam who was the wife and, therefore, it was *she* who would look after Jack.

The frustration ripped through her. Her powerlessness. The total injustice of it. One simple photograph placed on a bedside table had said it all: Jack was Miriam's. And as long as his memory remained at the bottom of the Atlantic Ocean, he always would be.

Both Gloria and Hope would be erased from his life for ever.

'You all right, pet?' asked a young woman walking past the hospital's entrance, who had spotted her in the alleyway.

'Yes, I'm fine, thanks for asking.' Gloria straightened herself up, wiping her eyes with the back of her hand.

The concerned passer-by continued on her way, while Gloria forced herself to leave the shade of the narrow passageway and go back out on to the street. Her legs walked her to the bus stop and her mouth spoke the words that told the bus conductor where she wanted to go, and her hands found the appropriate change in her purse and handed it over – but her mind was in turmoil, unable to take on board what had happened these past couple of hours.

Just over an hour ago, as she had sat, possibly on this very same bus, on her way to see Jack, she had been almost drunk with happiness and expectation. The gratitude she felt that her lover had been spared – that he was awake and alive – and by all accounts well – was overwhelming.

But then, within minutes of entering the hospital, it was as if her heart had been bludgeoned to a pulp. The physical pain in her chest actually felt real. The crushing hurt and confusion she had felt when Jack had looked at her as though she was a stranger had made her feel as if she was having the life slowly squeezed out of her.

As Gloria got off at her stop and walked back to her house, she wondered if perhaps this was her punishment.

She had been brought up to believe in good and evil, in saving yourself for marriage, and that it was a sin to commit adultery. Was she getting her just deserts?

If she was, it could be no crueller. Jack, the man she had loved twice over in her life, who she had lost once already when she was just a young woman, was now lost to her again. She didn't think she could bear it. Her whole being felt battered, as if she had finally been given one hurt too many and it had pushed her down on to her knees and she did not have the strength or the will to stand up.

Her heart had been torn apart yet again and this time she doubted she would ever be able to piece it back together.

Chapter Fifteen

That evening there was just Bel, Polly, and Arthur sitting round the kitchen table drinking tea, while Agnes pottered about getting the supper ready. Arthur had brought a big bundle of broad beans back from his friend Albert's allotment and Agnes was cooking them up into a stew, made with some bacon bits, black pudding and dumplings. Joe was out with the Home Guard, Pearl was working in the Tatham, and little Lucille had been nagged into submission and was now finally fast sleep in her cot.

'Poor Gloria,' Bel said, fetching the cutlery and the plates and setting the table. They had all listened in disbelief as Polly had told them about the shocking events of the day: how Hannah had told Rosie that Jack was out of his coma, and how Gloria had rushed off to the hospital to see him, only to return to work a few hours later looking like she'd had the stuffing knocked out of her.

'She looked heartbroken. When she told us what had happened, none of us knew what to do or say,' Polly said.

'That's so awful,' Bel repeated.

'But there's always a chance Jack'll get his memory back, isn't there?' Arthur said, his face full of concern.

'Mm,' Polly said, but neither she nor Bel seemed convinced of a happy ending to this particular love story. 'She's been through so much. It makes you wonder how much more she can take,' Bel spoke her thoughts aloud as she finished setting the table. 'She's as tough as old boots, but even old boots wear out eventually when they've been scuffed too many times.'

'I know,' Polly agreed, bending down to give Tramp and the puppy a stroke. The two dogs were positioned under the table in the hope that they might get some titbits once supper had been served.

Bel sat down next to Arthur. 'You knew Gloria and Jack in younger days,' she asked, looking at the old man's sad face, ' . . . when they were a couple, didn't you?'

Arthur nodded. 'Aye, I did.'

'What were they like?' Bel asked, curious to know more. Arthur puffed out air, and thought for a moment.

'That was quite some time ago,' he said, 'must be well over twenty years ago, more . . . ' he paused, collecting his memories of that time.

'I knew Jack much better than I knew Gloria because I worked so closely with Jack in the yard – but Gloria always struck me as a nice girl. They just seemed like a normal, happy courting couple. Flo always said she thought they made a good match.'

'Which is why,' Polly chipped in, 'I can't understand why Jack was lured away by Miriam.'

'Well,' Arthur said, 'you know, Miriam is a very determined and a very complex woman.'

Agnes came into the kitchen from the scullery and opened the heavy lead door of the range, letting out a waft of hot air and delicious smells. Lifting the pot out of the oven, she placed it carefully on a mat in the middle of the table.

'In what way?' Bel demanded, as she went to get a ladle so that she could start doling out the piping hot stew.

'Well, she's from a different world to us,' Arthur said. 'Born with a silver spoon in her mouth, always getting what she wanted. She could've had her pick of rich, eligible young men, but she had her mind set on Jack.'

'Like mother, like daughter, then,' Polly chipped in bitterly, thinking how Helen had spread a load of malicious lies to try and break her and Tommy up. And what's more, had nearly succeeded.

'Aye,' Arthur said, 'but believe you me, Helen's not a patch on her ma – luckily for her she's a pale imitation of Miriam.'

Agnes was now sitting at the head of the table looking puzzled. 'What did this Miriam do?' she asked, curious.

Bel and Polly looked at each other.

'You tell her, Pol,' Bel said.

'Well, to put it in a nutshell, Ma, Miriam seduced Jack one night after he'd had a tiff with Gloria,' Polly explained.

Agnes looked shocked and tutted hard to show her disapproval.

'But worst of all,' Polly continued, 'she made out that she was in the family way, so Jack had to marry her.'

'And was she?' Agnes asked. 'In the family way?'

'No,' Polly said, 'that's the point, she'd made it all up, but by the time Jack walked her down the aisle it was too late.'

'But worse still,' Bel butted in, 'she made out she'd had a miscarriage and said she had lost the baby.'

'And what about poor Gloria?' Agnes asked, aghast.

'She met and married some beastly guy called Vinnie. She had two boys with him and has spent her life in misery – coupled with bouts of being used as a punchbag,' Polly said.

'Until she met Jack again.' Bel brought Gloria's story up to date.

'I don't know,' Agnes said a little wearily. 'People's lives seem so complicated these days.'

Arthur nodded. Both he and Agnes had only ever loved and married the one person. When they had been taken away from them, they had accepted their lot, and made the most of being on their own, bringing up their children – or in Arthur's case, his grandson – the best way they could.

'I really feel it for Gloria – and for little Hope,' Bel said. She had become quite attached to the child since becoming her daytime carer.

'By the sounds of it she's going to grow up without ever knowing her dad. Or him ever knowing her.'

Hearing a noise they all turned to see Pearl standing in the doorway of the kitchen. She had finished work earlier than normal and had been standing in the semi-darkness listening to their chatter. She had not meant to earwig in on the conversation, but hadn't been able to stop herself.

'Well, that won't be the end of the world, will it, pet?' Pearl said, stepping into the room and dumping her gas mask on the sideboard. 'There's plenty of bairns grow up just fine without a father about. Look at you, Bel – and you, Polly. You two didn't fare too badly, did you?'

Bel huffed her exasperation, while everyone else suddenly became extremely interested in their bowls of stew.

'You know, Ma,' Bel said, looking at her mother, now grappling around her bag for her packet of fags, 'a little bit of compassion every now and again wouldn't kill you.'

Chapter Sixteen

King's Cross Station, London

June 1913

When Pearl walked under the huge stone arches that made up the main thoroughfare in and out of King's Cross station, there was still no respite from the melee she had just left behind her. She continued to be pushed along in a choppy sea of people, all seemingly headed in different directions, some laughing, some shouting, and some crying as they said their farewells to loved ones.

Looking down, Pearl saw an old bearded man seated against one of the station's colossal pillars, begging. Further along, Pearl saw other beggars, women with their babies swaddled in rags, and young children running alongside those they perceived to be wealthy – flailing flat caps in their way, using their eyes and unwashed, innocent faces to plead for pennies.

When Pearl was spat out on to the main stretch of pavement in front of the railway station, she was confronted with a barrier of hansom cabs, automobiles, and horse-drawn carriages, all either waiting to pick up their fares or in the process of unloading luggage. Behind them in the distance Pearl could see a few trams, the odd double-decker bus, and a number of horses and carts trundling up and down the wide dirt road.

As she breathed in the air, she coughed a little. It felt dry and dusty. She stopped in her tracks but was forced forward by another wave of people being emitted from the station. She staggered to get her footing. Trying to escape the river of passengers, she stepped behind one of the pillars and, without the disturbance of pushing and shoving, started rummaging in her bag.

A few moments later she pulled out what she had been searching for.

A magazine.

The magazine which had been handed to her as she'd walked past the workhouse along Church Walk in Hendon a few weeks previously, when a plain but friendly-looking woman with a black bonnet tied round her head, and wearing a black cloak and long black skirt, had given it to her. Pearl had noticed an unusual red brooch, shaped like a shield, pinned to the woman's chest. At the time Pearl had no idea why the woman with the long brown hair and pinched but kindly face had handed the magazine to her – even now she didn't really know why – but Pearl had never been one to turn down any kind of gift, even if it was just a few sheets of paper stuck together, so she had taken it from the woman's outstretched hand and muttered 'thank you', before hurrying off in case the woman wanted something in return. If nothing else, Pearl had argued to herself, it could always come in handy for starting the fire.

In fact, that was what had nearly happened to the magazine, for that night Pearl had been about to start tearing it up into strips to scrunch up and shove between the little sticks of kindling she had collected for the evening fire when her attention had been caught by the picture on the front. There were four black and white photographs, the largest showing a group of nurses stood on the front steps of an imposing house; the other smaller images showed a nurse holding a baby, a baby swaddled up in a mass of blankets in a cot, and a slightly balding older man who was smiling for the camera. The magazine had the words 'The Deliverer' emblazoned on the front. She had no idea what – or who – *The Deliverer* was, but after scrutinising the photographs she had become intrigued and had started to read – or read as best she could – the words inside. Words which had offered her salvation. Or, at the very least, an answer to her problem.

Now, as she stood in the shelter of the arches of London's finest railway station, Pearl thumbed through the magazine until she came to the page she needed. Slinging her bag over her shoulder and holding the magazine open so it was easy to read, she stepped back out into the clamour of King's Cross Road and scanned the immediate vicinity. When she spotted a young porter standing about, looking around for his next tip, she marched over to him.

'Excuse me,' Pearl said with as much volume and confidence as she could muster. 'How do I get here?' She showed the magazine to the skinny lad with the bowler haircut. He squinted and mouthed the address Pearl was pointing to.

'Hackney,' he said aloud. 'Here—' he grabbed her skinny shoulder and pulled her round and pointed to a double-decker bus. 'Get on the number three to Dalston. Then change to the number fourteen to Hackney.' As soon as the words were out of his mouth, he was off, having spotted an elderly gentleman climbing out of a grand-looking chauffeur-driven black car.

Pearl hurried to the number three bus. The conductor pulled her on to the platform and pointed to the spiral stairs leading to the top deck. Pearl thought she had never felt so pushed and pulled about in all her life.

When she was settled on the front seat of the top deck, she took a deep intake of breath. Her heart was hammering, and she was still gripping the magazine as if her life depended on it.

As the bus began its journey Pearl looked about her at the sights of London – the people, the traffic, the array of buildings that were higher than any she had ever seen before. She inhaled the fumes, and the overpowering smells of open gutters and horse manure, and thought, *Well, the streets aren't paved with gold, that's for sure.*

Three quarters of an hour later Pearl's snaking start-stop bus journey came to an end and she once again found herself on a busy street, trying to catch someone's attention to ask for directions. Her first few attempts to ask the way were ignored by smartly dressed, harried-looking men and women who pretended not to see her. Eventually, a young man with slicked-back hair and a narrow face, smoking a rolled-up cigarette, stopped, and after giving her the once-over, told her what she needed to know.

A quarter of an hour later Pearl was walking down Hackney's Mare Street, her eyes searching for the house pictured on the front of the magazine. It didn't take her long before she found the very posh-looking four-storey Georgian mansion, and it was only then that she was hit by a flurry of nerves and uncertainty. She watched for a few minutes from her spot on the grass verge as people – mainly women – came and went. Every now and again a couple of nurses, dressed in long, starched blue and white uniforms and stiff white caps, hurried in and out of the building.

Well, you've made it, Pearl said to herself. *You're here. What you gonna do, stand here and gawk all day?*

But, despite her self-recriminations, Pearl remained rooted to the spot. Her bravado would not propel her up the steps and into the building she knew to be called Ivy House.

'Can I help you?' A voice came from behind her and as Pearl turned her head she saw an older woman standing to her side.

Pearl suddenly found herself unusually speechless. In place of words, she delved once more into her bag and pulled out the now dog-eared copy of *The Deliverer*.

'Ah,' the softly spoken woman said. 'You've come to the right place. Come in so we can have a chat.'

Chapter Seventeen

Tuesday 30 September 1941

'Rosie, don't forget, Maisie – our new girl – should be here within the next hour.' Lily bustled about the large front room, plumping up tapestry cushions that didn't need plumping up, and running her hand over polished surfaces to check for non-existent dust.

'Lily,' Rosie said, sitting down at her plush cherry wood desk in what was now the bordello's official office where bills were paid and business was conducted, 'I don't think you'll find even a speck of dirt anywhere in the house after the way you've had Milly at it all week.' Milly was the bordello's cloakroom girl, who now doubled up as a cleaner. The young girl had earned a good sum this week as she had spent just about every waking moment sweeping and scrubbing floors, shaking rugs out, and washing and mopping the whole house from top to bottom – and everything in it. Every single nook and cranny of the three-storey house was spotless.

'And,' Rosie added, suppressing a smile, 'I don't think I need reminding that Maisie is the "new girl". I honestly feel like I know her already with the amount you've talked about her. It'll be like greeting an old friend when she walks through those doors.'

Rosie looked at Lily, who had gone all out this evening to look the personification of fashionable chic with her Coco Chanel little black dress and elegant slingbacks.

'You'll make yourself available?' Lily looked worried. 'No making excuses and hiding away with your face stuck in those wretched ledgers all night?'

It was true that Rosie had become quite obsessed with the bookkeeping and accounts since she had finally drawn a line under her romance with Peter. Now, when she went to bed at night, she saw numbers and calculations, and only very occasionally did thoughts of Peter manage to barge their way through.

'Those "wretched ledgers" as you put it, Lily, are what keep us in business.' As she spoke Rosie opened up one of her drawers and took out the main red leather-bound accounts book.

'Oh, leave it for tonight.' Lily tottered over to the desk in her heels, waving the offending book away with hands that were heavy with gem-studded rings and thick gold bracelets; picking up the decanter of brandy she poured a splash into the two large cut crystal glasses placed next to it on the front of the desk.

Rosie frowned. 'I try and save that for clients,' she reprimanded Lily, but realising she was not going to get any work done with Lily in the mood she was in, she gave up, put the ledger back in the drawer and took the Rémy Martin from Lily's outstretched hand. She noticed Lily's nails were freshly manicured and painted in a crimson gloss.

'You would think we had royalty coming to visit,' Rosie said, taking a sip of her drink.

Lily ignored Rosie's comment. Her mind was already galloping ahead to the arrival of the new addition to their workforce.

'George has gone to pick her up from the station. He said it was because his beloved MG needs a run out, although heaven knows how he manages to get in it these days with his leg the way it is – never mind drive the thing.

'I'm not sure if he's just an old man trying to impress a pretty young filly, or if he is as excited as I am about our *new venture*.' Lily looked at Rosie for a reaction, and was pleased when she leant forward, her interest clearly tweaked.

'Well, first of all I don't think it's some young filly George is trying to impress,' Rosie said, with a playful smile on her face. Lily ignored the implication in Rosie's tone of voice, but couldn't stop a slight flush from appearing on her face.

'And secondly,' Rosie continued, sensing Lily's disquiet, 'this is the first I've heard of any "new venture", so tell me more.'

Lily's face became animated as she perched herself on the edge of the burgundy rococo-style chair directly in front of Rosie's desk.

'I've wanted to chat to you all this week about our "vision" for the future. For the future of the business – providing Mr Hitler doesn't end up running the country,' Lily said, checking the sides and back of the elaborate hairdo that Vivian had artfully crafted into a number of victory rolls, which were now balancing very stylishly on the top of Lily's head.

'Your hair's fine,' Rosie said a little impatiently, 'it's been sprayed with so much lacquer I'd say it would probably survive a walk through a force ten gale.'

Lily purposely ignored her comments and continued.

'Maisie isn't going to work with the other girls as such,' Lily said, her attention now focused entirely on Rosie, 'because George and I want her to be front of house for a . . . ' she paused for dramatic effect, ' . . . a new *exclusive* Gentlemen's Club,' she said, sitting up straight and looking rather pleased with herself.

Rosie sat back. 'This is the first time you've mentioned this.'

Lily took a quick sip of brandy. 'I didn't want to say any-thing before I had really thrashed the idea out with George – or, of course, before we knew Maisie was defi-nitely going to leave London and come here.'

'So,' Rosie said, 'you're going into business with George?' Now she was really interested. She had suspected the pair of them were up to something the evening they had told her about pooling their resources to buy the house next door, but she hadn't thought too much more about it as her mind had still been reeling after bumping into Peter.

'Ah,' Rosie said, putting all the pieces together and understanding what Lily and George had planned. 'You want to run the "exclusive" Gentlemen's Club from next door?' Rosie sat back. 'Well, I have to admit, that sounds like a brilliant idea.'

'And, *ma chère* –' Lily was clearly relieved that Rosie seemed to be very accepting of the idea '– what's more is that it may be a way for the business to gradually become legitimate.'

Rosie was now leaning forward with her arms on the desk, both hands cupping her glass tumbler. 'Oh, that *would* be good,' she said.

'It'll take time,' Lily said. 'As I said, at the moment, it is a "vision", but I'm convinced it can become reality. And,' she added with a twinkle in her eye, 'your excellent head for figures is going to help us no end.'

Rosie was just about to ask Lily more about the com-plexities of running a club and how they could start to con-vert the bordello into a business that was legal and above board, when they heard the heavy wooden front door swing open, followed by the chattering sound of two voices.

One belonged to George.

The other, Rosie guessed, belonged to Maisie.

Rosie didn't think she had seen Lily move so quickly in her life. In seconds she was out of her chair, across the room and out into the hallway without being slowed down in the least by her high heels and tight dress.

'Oh, *mon Dieu, bonsoir*,' Rosie heard Lily gush. 'How lovely to see you, Maisie. How was your journey up here?'

Rosie listened to Maisie telling Lily that her trip had been 'quite heavenly'. That first class was really 'the only way to travel these days', and that she too was 'absolutely charmed' to finally be here.

Rosie then heard Lily usher Maisie into the Louis IV themed reception room, where all the girls were waiting in anticipation of the start of the welcome party.

Rosie's mind was tossing around what Lily had told her and at the same time she was listening to Lily's faux French accent as she introduced Maisie to the girls and a few of their regulars who had also been invited to this evening's little soirée. The women's voices sounded excited and there were short bursts of laughter as the party got under way.

A few minutes later, Lily's head appeared around the doorway.

'Well. Come on! Chop chop!'

Rosie took a final sip of her brandy and got up.

'Honestly, you'd think I was asking you to walk the bleedin' plank.' Lily's exasperation at Rosie's lack of enthusiasm had made her cockney roots reveal themselves.

Rosie straightened her blouse and brushed down her slacks with her hands, before walking past Lily and deliberately winding her up by pulling a forced smile across her face.

As soon as Rosie entered the party she spotted the back of a slender, petite young woman, dressed in a classy designer box suit. From behind Rosie could see her hair had been cut into a shoulder-length bob which gave a modicum of order to a mass of tight chestnut brown curls. Most of the girls were standing around Maisie in a circle, looking entranced while the newcomer held court.

George was at his usual place, perched on the stool of the baby grand, tinkling a perky piano rendition of 'All the Nice Girls Love a Sailor'. There were also the couple of regulars Lily had invited smoking and chatting to their escorts for the evening.

'Maisie, *ma chère*,' Lily called out as she followed Rosie into the room. 'There's someone I want you to meet.'

Rosie watched as Maisie turned round. She had a cocktail glass in one hand and a long ebony cigarette holder in the other. When she spotted Rosie her eyes widened and a smile spread across her face.

'Ah, Rosie,' she gushed, stepping forward and putting her glass down on the little art deco glass coffee table near to one of the leather armchairs.

Rosie fought hard to beat down her shock and surprise. She managed to catch it before it found its way to her face. Rosie could see why the girls were so entranced, for Maisie was absolutely stunning. Her wayward tousled bob framed a perfectly sculpted face, high cheekbones, and full, sensuous lips.

But, what had startled Rosie more than anything was Maisie's mixed heritage; her skin was a light sun-kissed brown, as if she had just returned from an exotic holiday in some far-flung country.

If Maisie had picked up on how taken aback Rosie was about her ethnicity, she did not show it.

'How wonderful to meet you at long last,' she said and gently touched Rosie on the arm and kissed her lightly on each cheek. As she did so Rosie noticed a slight smattering of freckles that could just be seen across her nose and the tops of her cheeks.

'I've heard so much about you.' Maisie spoke in an almost whisper that created an immediate intimacy.

'And I have heard so much about you too,' Rosie said, noticing for the first time Maisie's captivating almond-shaped eyes that were light brown, flecked with hazel.

Now she understood Lily's excitement. This woman could have men – and women – eating out of the palm of her hand. She was, as Lily had described, 'exquisite'.

'So, please tell me, Maisie, what has inspired you to leave the bright lights of London for the north-east of England? Don't tell me it's because of the Blitz, because if it is, I hate to tell you, we're getting pretty hammered here as well. London may be the capital, but we've got a lot of industry up here that is attracting a fair amount of attention from the Luftwaffe.'

Maisie gave a little laugh. 'No, no, there are a few reasons I've wanted to come up. For starters, I've got family here that I haven't seen in a very long time and who I'm just dying to catch up with . . . '

Rosie was about to ask her what part of the town her family were from, but Maisie continued on without a pause.

'And I'm also rather excited about this new Gentlemen's Club Lily and George want to start up. I think it could be quite the success. There's nothing else like it in the town, by all accounts. And there certainly won't be a shortage of those wanting to become members – not with RAF Usworth nearby, and, of course, you've got the members-only cricket and social club literally across the road. They'll be fighting to get through the door.'

Maisie took the smallest of sips from the cocktail that

she had gracefully retrieved from where she had left it. 'But, enough about me. I want to hear about you.' She leant in closer and said in a conspiratorial voice, 'I have to admit to being totally fascinated by the fact that you also work as a welder. And in a shipyard, at that.'

Maisie would have said this had it been the last thing on earth she wanted to hear about, but in this case she did really mean it. The woman standing opposite to her now, with the scarred but very attractive face, and who was now jointly running the bordello with Lily, fascinated her.

In fact, the bordello had far exceeded her expectations, and she had been pleasantly surprised that Lily's description of the place had not been exaggerated. A part of her had been dreading leaving London with its cosmopolitan way of living, and exciting night life. She had resigned herself to the fact that she had to come here, to this poor northern town, full of factories, shipyards and industry, to do what she needed to do. But, from what she had seen already, it looked like she might also be able to have some fun.

'Well, Thompson's is certainly quite a change from this place,' Rosie said, turning to look around her to see if any of the chairs were free. Spotting a couple of their regulars getting up to leave with two of the girls, Rosie motioned for Maisie to join her and they sat down.

'Ah, that's nice,' Rosie said, relaxing in the warmth and comfort of the cushioned chair. 'I love my job, but it does take it out on the old pins.'

As the two women sat chatting, Lily kept a discreet eye on them as she stood by the fireplace talking to George, who had gently taken hold of her hand, although his show of affection could not be seen by others.

George could tell Lily's mind was not on what he was talking about, but he didn't mind as she had gently squeezed his hand. He knew Lily always had half an eye on what was going on around her, even if she looked totally engrossed in conversation. He had to smile to himself, though, as Lily was clearly cock-a-hoop that Maisie and Rosie seemed to be getting on. Not that he doubted Maisie's ability to get on with anyone. That girl could charm the birds right out of the trees, but she would have her work cut out with Rosie as she wasn't always the easiest of people to get onside. He knew from experience that if Rosie took a dislike to someone, she wouldn't give them the time of day.

George had known that Lily had been nervous about Maisie's first encounter with Rosie, which wasn't surprising as they were both strong, no-nonsense women. There could well be a personality clash and he and Lily needed the two of them to get on if they were to make a success of this new business.

Seeing that Rosie didn't have a drink in her hand and that Maisie had almost finished her cocktail, Lily pressed close to George for a brief moment and looked over to the two women.

'George,' she spoke gently into his ear, 'can you be a dear and get them both a drink? Something with bubbles in, please.'

A few minutes later George was playing waiter and handing a champagne cocktail to each of the two women, who were now happily chatting away. When he returned to Lily, she whispered conspiratorially, 'So, what were they talking about?'

George laughed, but didn't answer; instead he walked off to fetch Lily her drink.

'Darling,' he said on his return, 'I'm not your spy as well as everything else –' he downed the rest of his whisky '– but if you must know, they were talking about,' he paused for dramatic effect, ' . . . the shipyards.'

'Bleedin' typical,' Lily gasped. 'Rosie's favourite subject. Bet you she's waffling on about those new Liberty ships the yard's become so famous for.'

'Actually,' George said, 'if I heard right, they were chatting about Rosie's team of women welders. Maisie seemed genuinely interested.'

'Hm,' Lily said, taking a quick swig of her drink, 'Maisie's the kind of girl who could feign interest in drying paint if she had to.' But her words were said with a clear sense of relief that it did, in fact, look like the two women's acquaintance had got off to a good start.

Finally Lily could begin to relax and enjoy her drink with George. She was secretly congratulating herself on how well everything was going when, filtering through the chitter-chatter of the party, she heard the mournful wail of the air raid siren start up.

Within seconds the room had fallen silent.

'All right, everyone,' Lily said. 'You know the drill.'

She looked around at the faces staring at her, before adding, 'And don't forget the house motto, which is . . . '

Vivian, who had made herself the unofficial head of the girls, stepped forward so that she was positioned in the centre of the room.

' . . . Keep calm and party on!' she declared with her drink raised as if giving a toast.

Then turning on her heel and looking like a glamorous female Pied Piper, she shouted, 'Follow me, everyone!' and led them all out of the large reception room and down the hallway.

As they ambled out of the room, Maisie sidled up to Rosie. 'I see what you meant about the Luftwaffe having a particular liking for your little town!'

Opening the small wooden door to the cellar at the side of the main staircase, Vivian made a great show of pulling on the light that illuminated half a dozen stone steps leading down into the cellar.

Maisie's eyes widened in wonder. 'Well, it beats being stuck in the London Underground for hours on end,' she said as she peered down into the cellar at a fully stocked drinks cabinet, a record player, and a beautiful chaise longue that had been upholstered in a delicate golden silk fabric.

'Ah, is that rosewood?' she asked as she climbed down into the cellar and made a beeline for the antique couch.

'You've got a good eye, *ma chère*,' Lily said following her down the steps and over to the chaise longue. 'I may love all things *français*, but I do have rather a particular penchant for our very own Regency furniture.'

Maisie trailed her smooth, caramel-coloured hand along the hand-carved scroll-shaped arms and back of the chaise lounge, before sitting down on it gently so as not to damage it.

Rosie again noticed Maisie's hands, which did not look like they had done a day's hard labour in their life – unlike most of the other girls here, who often wore laced fingerless gloves to disguise their former lives.

By now everyone had made it down into the cellar, and Vivian was lighting candles and carefully placing a record on to the deck of the old portable gramophone. It was, as expected, the music to 'I'm No Angel' and it was Vivian's showpiece at the start of any air raid.

As she cleared her throat, everyone fell silent. The distant sound of the sirens could just about be heard.

'Before you start, Vivian, has anyone seen Kate?' Lily looked about the small gathering, but there was no Kate.

'Oh, she's a little minx, that one,' Lily said anxiously. 'I bet you she's working on Bel's dress and won't tear herself away from it.'

One of the regulars, an older man called Charles, a brigadier in the Durham Light Infantry who visited Lily's whenever he was on leave, called out, 'I'll go and get her.'

But Lily shook her head. 'That's very kind of you, Charles, but I'll send George here.'

Lily made it sound as if she couldn't possibly have one of her clients running about on chores, but in reality it was because she made a point of never allowing the bordello's punters to have any dealings whatsoever with Kate. Her *'petit enfant'*, as she often called her in private, might live at Lily's, but she had made it known that Kate should have no contact with any of the men who visited.

George didn't need asking twice, and as Vivian started singing the first verse of 'I'm No Angel' in a convincing American drawl, he could be seen disappearing back into the house.

By the time Vivian was finishing the second verse, swaying her womanly hips suggestively along to the lyrics, 'Love me, honey, love me till I just don't care, I'm no angel', Kate and George were both safely ensconced in the cellar.

Maisie watched curiously as Kate made a beeline for Lily, who then put a protective arm around the young girl's skinny shoulders. She saw Rosie go over for a quick chat. As Rosie turned away, Maisie managed to catch her eye, and patted the seat next to her, beckoning her to come and sit down.

'If ever Mae West needs a double,' Maisie said in awe of Vivian who was now in full flow and had everyone entranced and swaying to the music, 'she need look no further.'

'If you tell Vivian that, you'll make yourself a friend for life. I'm sure she's convinced she should be Mae West and is actually more like Mae West than Mae West herself.'

The two women chuckled and when Vivian finished

with a sultry 'I can make it heaven where the shades are drawn . . . I'm no angel', Maisie got up and, gently clapping her hands, trilled out, 'Encore, encore.'

Lily tottered over to Rosie and took the place where Maisie had been sitting; they both watched as Maisie chatted away to Vivian and the rest of the girls and their clients. Rosie thought everyone looked completely taken with Lily's 'new girl'.

'What do you think, then?' Lily asked.

'Well,' Rosie said, turning to look at Lily, 'you've certainly found yourself a little gem there, haven't you?' Lily glowed, revelling in the praise.

Rosie continued to watch Maisie.

'She's certainly . . . how did you describe her before . . . "exquisite",' Rosie said, adding thoughtfully, although more to herself than Lily, 'Almost too good to be true.'

Chapter Eighteen

The next day, as the people of Sunderland traipsed to work after just a few hours' sleep, having spent most of the night cooped up in shelters, the talk, as expected, was dominated by the previous evening's air raid attack.

'Aye, a whole family was taken out – four bairns 'n all,' Polly overheard one of the shipwrights tell his mate as she stood on the early morning ferry. She felt her stomach sink. She had heard that the bombs had dropped in Southwick on the north bank of the River Wear. It was likely their aim had been the shipyards, but, as usual, they had only succeeded in destroying homes and killing the innocent.

No wonder so many of the townsfolk were packing their children off to go and live with strangers out of harm's way. Polly had chatted to Bel about sending Lucille away, but she'd been adamant. Lucille was to stay at home.

As Polly was jostled off the ferry, she threw Stan, the old ferryman, a sombre look, before being carried along with the mass of other shipyard workers up to the main gates. After collecting her card from the timekeeper's cabin, Polly hurried over to the welders' area, and was relieved to see all the women were there. None of them lived in Southwick, but they could have easily been visiting friends or relatives.

'Morning, Pol,' Rosie said as Polly reached the five-gallon barrel fire they were stood around. The temperature was dropping and the mornings had graduated from chilly to cold. 'You and yours all right?' she asked.

'Yes, thanks,' Polly said, pulling out her Thermos from her holdall and pouring herself a cuppa.

'None of the hospitals were hit, were they?' Gloria asked quietly as they all stood around the fire, warming their hands and drinking steaming hot tea.

Rosie glanced over at Gloria. She looked dead on her feet, and the dark shadows under her eyes showed she was getting next to no sleep.

'Sounds like it was just Southwick,' Dorothy said, looking to Angie to elaborate.

'That's what I heard,' Angie agreed. She was also thinking that Gloria looked shattered even though they hadn't even started their day's work yet.

'Some of my da's family are from Southwick – the Marley Potts estate. They weren't hurt, but their friends who lived on Shakespeare Street, well, let's just say they haven't got a home now . . . Four houses,' she continued, 'totally demolished. Sixteen damaged beyond repair. And the gas and water mains. Broken.'

Martha let out a heavy sigh. No one said anything.

'Come on then,' Rosie said, geeing everyone up. 'Let's get on with building *Brutus*, eh? We're making good progress. Let's keep the momentum going.'

At ten o'clock, Rosie declared a tea break. No one needed telling twice and soon they were all huddled round their makeshift metal fire. The seagulls were screeching above them. Today they seemed particularly loquacious; their shrill cries could even be heard above the noise of the workers and their machinery.

'Something's got their goat,' Dorothy said, as her neck craned to look at the large white and grey flecked birds with their Pinocchio-yellow beaks as they swooped down around them.

As Dorothy brought her eyes back to ground level she spotted a small group of smartly dressed men coming out of the main admin building.

'What're the suits doing here?' she wondered aloud, before letting out an audible gasp as she saw a man and a woman step out of the doorway.

It was Jack and Miriam.

'Oh, no,' she said.

The other women welders automatically turned to see what had given Dorothy such a shock. There was a collective intake of breath.

'It's Jack,' Martha said bluntly.

'And Miriam,' Rosie added.

The women's eyes swivelled from Jack and Miriam back round to Gloria.

No one said anything. No one knew what to say. Gloria went to walk away, but Rosie grabbed her by the arm.

'Stay,' she said to her quietly. She didn't want them to wonder why Gloria had suddenly scarpered, especially if the young doctor who had been so nice to Gloria had said anything about her impromptu visit.

'Bloody Nora,' Angie said, her eyes fixed on the small group, 'they're coming over here.'

'Don't stare, Ange,' Dorothy told her friend, as she looked across at Gloria, who had the dazzled look of a rabbit caught in the beam of a car's headlights.

'And here we have the yard's very special group of women welders . . . ' Harold's voice boomed out as they approached ' . . . who, I have to say, are doing a grand job here. I think they've surprised everyone.'

Rosie immediately stood forward and went to shake Jack's hand.

'Hello, Jack,' she said, squeezing his hand firmly and looking straight into his eyes. 'It's great to have you back.'

Jack smiled back at her, but there was not one iota of recognition on his face.

'Jack . . . ' Miriam stepped forward to stand by her husband's side, ' . . . has been having a few problems with his memory since he came back to us.' She looked at the women's expectant faces, but made a point of completely ignoring Gloria.

'So, we're giving him a tour of his workplace,' Miriam explained. 'Hopefully, he'll be back at work soon – and back to normal.'

This was the first time Polly, Dorothy, Angie and Martha had met Miriam. They had spotted her in the past from afar – once at a laying of the keel ceremony, and very occasionally when she popped in to the main offices, but this was the nearest they had physically ever got to her. They knew she wasn't one to mix with the hoi polloi. And if they hadn't gathered already, from looking at her now and hearing her tone of voice, they'd have no doubt Helen was her exact replica – only younger.

Rosie moved to Jack's other side so that she was standing by him, facing the women. As she did so the smile vanished from Miriam's face.

'Well, Jack,' Rosie said, 'it'll be great to have you back. But in the meantime let me reintroduce you to my squad . . . This is Dorothy,' she said, stretching her arm out towards an unusually dumbstruck Dorothy. 'She's our best – and fastest – welder. And this is Angie, who used to work the cranes . . . and Martha who has a work output of twice the average man . . . ' Martha's chest puffed out with pride. 'And Polly,' she said, looking back at Jack, ' . . . who you might recall is engaged to be married to Tommy Watts, Arthur's grandson?' Rosie paused, but on seeing Jack's blank look, continued. 'And last, but not least . . . this is Gloria.'

There was a moment's silence as Gloria looked at Jack. Her heart was in her mouth. Would Jack remember her from the hospital? Her mind raced.

How would she explain herself if he mentioned she had been in to visit him?

Jack looked serious for a moment, before breaking into an apologetic smile.

'I'm so sorry, I don't remember you all. But I'm telling this brain of mine to get itself into gear and to start working properly. Pronto.' His words were spoken with a genuine smile.

It was so like Jack, Gloria thought as she desperately fought back the urge to grab him and hold him in her arms.

'Well, that's quite the "re-introduction", Miss Thornton. I'm sure *Mr Crawford* will be seeing you all about soon.' As Miriam spoke she cast Rosie a look of reproof, knowing she was well aware that calling her husband by his Christian name was a pet hate of hers. She did think, though, that the women didn't seem all that surprised by Jack's memory loss. If she hadn't known better, she would have said they already knew.

As Miriam took Jack's arm and guided him away from the welders' area and over to the platers' shed, Polly sidled up to Gloria and asked, 'Are you all right?'

Gloria nodded, but her lip was trembling and they could all see she was struggling to keep her emotions in check. Dorothy went over to her and gently squeezed her arm.

'Don't be nice to me, Dor,' Gloria whispered, 'otherwise I'll be a total mess.' But Dorothy ignored her friend's command and gave her a quick cuddle.

As Gloria and the women switched on their machines, they didn't see Jack turn away for a few moments from Miriam and her entourage.

Nor did they notice, as he stood and stared at them all, the slightly perplexed look on his face.

As Jack sat down for his evening meal with his wife and daughter in the dining room of their beautiful end-of-terrace house that had been built at the turn of the century for one of the town's shipyard owners, his mind kept running over the events of the day, and, in particular, the conducted tour of Thompson's.

It had felt good walking around the yard, surrounded by the clashing and banging of machinery, the gruff voices of the men trying to make themselves heard above the din, and the incessant squawking of the hungry, low-flying seagulls. It was the first time he had felt happy – and at home – since he had woken from his coma. Everything had felt strangely familiar, but at the same time he couldn't remember having been there before. It just didn't make sense. It was like having a word on the tip of your tongue and not being able to recall it.

He had listened to Miriam and the yard's managers as they told him how he had gone over to America to join the yard's owner, Cyril Thompson, and a few other bigwigs as part of the British Shipbuilding Mission that had been set up by Churchill. The ships the Yanks were building were based on the designs of the SS *Empire Liberty*. The difference between the two was that the British Liberty ships were all-riveted, and coal-fired, built piecemeal from the keel up. The Yanks were keeping the same simplified hull design, but were constructing prefabricated, all-welded, oil-fired ships with two deckhouses instead of four. The reason being that it would speed up production. At least then there would be ships available to replace the crippling numbers being lost to the German U-boats.

Jack had no recollection of his trip to America, but he

seemed to have an innate understanding of what they had talked about. Dr Parker at the hospital had explained to him that often a patient in his condition could still remember old habits – and perform everyday functions – but could not remember people, or past events. Which would explain why he could remember the workings of the yard, and the intricacies of how ships were built, but not any of his family or friends.

The doctor had said the brain was 'a complex organ' about which the medical profession still knew very little, especially when it came to understanding 'the effects of trauma on the brain'. He had told him that what was remembered – and what was forgotten – could be somewhat random, depending on what part of the brain had been damaged.

'More peas, darling?' Miriam's almost melodic voice spoke over his thoughts.

Jack put his hand up to show he'd had enough and as he looked back at his wife's perfectly made-up face, he wished he could remember her from before he had gone away.

But there was nothing.

He could see why he had married her. She was a stunning woman, who clearly looked after herself. Yet for some reason he didn't feel attracted to her. But perhaps this was just another side effect of his amnesia? Jack finished his food and sat back in his chair and yawned.

'Dad, you look shattered,' Helen said, her voice full of genuine concern. 'Remember what the doctors told you? You're going to feel very tired to start with and should have plenty of rest. To quote the very nice Dr Parker, "Take life at an easy pace to start with – it'll take a while to adjust".'

Jack looked at his daughter and although he had no real recollection of her, there was that 'almost there' feel – as if he was just on the verge of knowing her.

'Doesn't he, Mum?' Helen persisted. 'I think he should rest now. He's had such a busy day.'

Jack smiled at Helen. He must have done something right as a father, as the girl clearly loved and cared deeply for him. The doctor had told him she'd hardly left his side when he was in the coma.

'Yes, Helen's right, Jack. I think you need to rest,' Miriam said, smiling across the table at her husband.

'Come on, let's go upstairs,' she said. She pushed back the dining room chair and made her way round the oval table to put her hand gently on Jack's shoulder. He put his hand on top of hers and looked up to her. This woman was so kind and considerate. And lovely-looking. So, why didn't he *feel* anything for her? Had he forgotten how to love, on top of everything else?

When they climbed the stairs to the first floor Jack automatically started heading for the spare bedroom at the back of the house.

'Darling,' Miriam gently coaxed Jack away from the small back room. 'I can't understand why you keep veering off to the spare bedroom. You've always hated sleeping on your own.'

'Sorry,' Jack said, confused.

'We've always shared the same bed. Always,' Miriam said, leading him into the large marital bedroom at the front of the house that overlooked the corner of Roker Park. From here the sea was just about visible through the leafless trees.

'We've barely spent a night apart in all the years we've been married.'

Helen's mouth dropped open in disbelief as she earwigged on her mother and father's conversation as she stood quietly in the large mosaic hallway at the bottom of the stairs. Her mother was lying through her teeth. Helen had never heard so much codswallop in her entire life. She couldn't even remember the last time her mother and father had so much as held hands – never mind shared a bed. For years now her father had slept in the spare room, which in her younger days Helen had thought was normal – that this was what all mothers and fathers did. But, of course, as she had got older, she'd realised that, although not exactly unheard of, this was not the norm. Now she was nineteen, and far from innocent of the ways of the world, she was pretty sure her parents' marriage had been dead in the water for a very long time. Passion certainly no longer played a part in it.

As she heard her mother shut the bedroom door, Helen tiptoed in her bare feet down the cold tiled hallway, through to the breakfast room, already set for the morning, and into the warmth of the kitchen where the cook was up to her arms in pots and pans.

'We're all done in the dining room now, Mrs Westley,' she said. Helen never thought to tell the cook that the food had been nice, or to thank her for her trouble. Instead she pinched a cheese scone from the parlour and headed back out of the kitchen. Her departure was followed by the sound of Mrs Westley tutting loudly, and saying, 'Mrs Crawford won't like it.'

Helen knew the cook was right. Her mother was always telling her to watch what she ate as she needed to keep her figure.

As she trailed crumbs on the floor and headed up the stairs to her own bedroom on the second floor, Helen really did have to hand it to her mother – when she wanted something, boy, did she make damn sure she got it.

Jack watched his wife as she sat at her dressing table in front of her vanity mirror and rubbed a variety of creams and potions on to her face, neck and hands. She was humming a song he didn't recognise, but it sounded light and happy. He really was a lucky man to have all this – a lovely wife and daughter, a great job, and to be so wealthy. The house they lived in was more like a mansion than an end-of-terrace. You could get lost in it. Miriam had sat him down the other night with some old photographs and told him how they had lived here for the past twenty years. She'd given him a short summary of his life and how he had worked his way up from being a young apprentice to yard manager – one of the top, and most important, positions in the shipyard.

Miriam had told him, with tears in her eyes, 'Darling, I wish you could remember just how young and in love we were. Nothing could keep us apart. We were inseparable. Even if Father had threatened to disinherit me, I wouldn't have given two jots.' Then she had cuddled up to him on the sofa and chuckled as she had recalled, 'I used to say we were like Romeo and Juliet, because we both vowed that nothing would stop us being together.'

Jack had held his wife in his arms, but their physical closeness felt so alien. He hated to admit it, even to himself, but it had seemed in some way unnatural. Why did he feel this way? *This was his wife*. The love of his life. And yet he felt awkward just holding her.

Lying now in the comfort of the soft double bed that had been warmed with hot-water bottles, and seemed to envelop him, he started to drift off. As Miriam continued humming her tune, screwing the lids back on to her small round jars, Jack struggled to keep his eyes open. It had been more than three weeks since he had woken from his coma but still every time he went to sleep he was hit by a terrible anxiety that he would not wake up again.

Tonight, though, he was too tired to care, and, besides,

there was something else troubling him. Something he couldn't work out. Something he felt he should keep to himself. At least for the time being.

When he'd been introduced to the women welders at the yard he had recognised the woman called Gloria – not from his life 'before', but from the hospital. He had been about to say that he remembered her coming to see him a few days after he had woken up, but a voice inside his head told him to hang fire and not to mention it. Throughout the day he had kept thinking about the woman. Why hadn't she said anything? When they were introduced in the yard she had acted like she didn't know him. Yet she had come to see him at the Royal? It just didn't make sense. You wouldn't visit someone in hospital if you didn't know or care about them.

He had glanced at Miriam, but she hadn't even looked at this Gloria, never mind acknowledged her. She clearly didn't know her, or she would have said something, surely?

As Jack fell asleep he forced himself to recall the woman welder's face. She had a nice-looking face, although she looked tired, which wasn't surprising considering the kind of work she was doing. But he thought he'd seen a sadness in her eyes.

The more he thought about her, the more she intrigued him, and as sleep finally overpowered him, he took the strangely comforting vision of this woman welder with him.

'Jack,' Miriam whispered across the bedroom, 'are you asleep?'

There was a short silence before the air was filled with the sound of Jack's snoring, which Miriam knew would grow in volume the deeper he fell into sleep. She had never realised he was such a loud snorer. She had never been able to hear him before in the back room – sometimes she hadn't even known if he was there.

Happy that her husband was now fast asleep, Miriam swivelled back to face her three-way vanity mirror and leant down to slide open the bottom drawer of her French dresser. Rummaging through some underwear and silk stockings she pulled out a quarter-bottle of Gordon's gin. She poured a good measure into the glass tumbler she always kept next to her hairbrush and creams.

Her hands trembled ever so slightly as she raised the glass to her lips and took a large gulp.

God, I needed that, Miriam said to herself. She had not allowed herself to have a drink until Jack was asleep. She didn't want him to have any reminders of their past life together, and her gin drinking was very much a part of that former life – and one that had led to more than a few alcohol-fuelled arguments.

As she sat back now, relishing the feel of the gin as it started to do its work, Miriam knew that her daily tipples had become her friend – her comfort – and were now something she could not do without. Not that she wanted to, anyway. She enjoyed a drink, but at the moment she wanted Jack to see her as nigh on perfect. A wife he would thank his lucky stars he had woken up to.

Miriam pulled her long silk nightgown around her and tied the belt tight. As she took another sip, she grimaced a little. She needed some ice and a little tonic water. She stood up and looked at Jack sleeping peacefully in their bed. A bed he had not graced with his presence for so many years she had lost count.

Carefully opening her bedroom door, she slipped out on to the wide landing and made her way quietly down to the kitchen. The place was quiet as Mrs Westley had cleared up and gone home and Miriam felt herself relax for the first time all day.

The kitchen was still warm from the heat of the Aga and after tottering into the larder for a bottle of tonic, Miriam sat herself down on the bench that ran alongside the long wooden table, and drank her gin.

Well, Miriam, she congratulated herself, *you're doing a pretty good job, even if I say so myself.*

She raised the glass to herself and took another drink.

Let's just hope to God Jack doesn't ever get his memory back.

As Miriam sat and sipped her drink, she mulled over the past week since Jack had been discharged from hospital. She had worked hard, had carried out her plan with almost military precision. Photographs had been placed around the house of the two of them together, which had been no easy task – she'd struggled to find any recent ones. She'd also put a picture of them both on the desk in his office after going in there the other week and finding not a single one of her. She'd been livid.

Still, she couldn't get too angry as everything was going to plan rather perfectly – all things considered. Especially as just a few weeks ago she was looking at the very real prospect of becoming a widow or, worse still, the wife of a handicapped husband.

Miriam took another sip, savouring the slightly bitter flavour of the gin and tonic.

As things had turned out, she actually couldn't have wished for a better scenario. She'd been given a blank canvas on which she could draw whatever picture she desired. She could create the perfect husband and enjoy the perfect marriage.

At long last she was going to get what she wanted. The husband she had always wanted. The life she had always wanted.

She could reclaim her dream. The one she'd had all those

years ago. This time she could make him into the husband she had always wanted; the one he had refused to be.

Over the years she had thought of divorcing Jack and finding herself another, more suitable husband – one that went to dinner parties with her, one that actually *liked* her, never mind *loved* her; but she knew she couldn't bring that kind of shame on herself, never mind her family. She had rebelled enough by marrying Jack in the first place. The last thing she needed was any 'I told you so's, or 'that's what happens when you marry below yourself'. Words that would never be said to her face, but that she knew would be said behind her back.

Now she had her second shot at having the husband she had always wanted and she wasn't about to blow it.

She just had to make sure no one rocked the boat and – more than anything – that no one jogged his memory and in doing so brought the old Jack back.

It had worried her when they were at the yard today that their visit might trigger thoughts from the past, especially when he'd met Rosie and her women welders, and, of course, Gloria. Thankfully, judging by the blank look on his face, there hadn't been even a flicker of recognition. And the longer he didn't remember anything, according to what the doctor had said, the more likely it was that he would never get his memory back.

Miriam continued her musings as she wandered into the dining room and opened up the drinks cabinet. Finding a half-empty bottle of gin, she uncapped it and poured herself another measure.

'My problem now,' she ruminated, 'is how to keep Jack out of the yard.'

This was going to prove difficult because Jack's bosses had made it clear that he could come back to work whenever he felt ready, and they would accommodate his needs. In their eyes Jack was a hero. He had risked travelling all the way to America in the middle of a world war, spent months teaching the Yanks how best to produce this new ship – and in doing so established the reputation of the Thompson yard as one of the best in the world.

As she finished off her drink, a thought suddenly jumped into her head.

'Those bloody Liberty ships may well end up doing me a favour,' Miriam said aloud to the room.

The new ships had raised Jack's reputation in the whole of the shipyard community, never mind just at Thompson's. Any of the yards would welcome him with open arms.

She felt a rush of excitement as her idea started to take shape. Hadn't she recently heard a whisper that Cyril Thompson was contemplating buying Jackie Crown's shipyard?

Miriam stood up, a little unsteadily as the gin had more than hit its mark, and teetered over to the phone at the far end of the room.

A leather-bound address book was lying next to the black Bakelite phone, but she didn't need it. She knew the number she needed to call.

Miriam dialled and waited for the person at the other end to pick up. It had just gone ten o'clock.

After several rings she heard a click on the slightly crackling line and then the sound of a familiar voice.

'Hello, Father,' Miriam said softly, ' . . . sorry to call so late, but there's something I need to chat to you about.'

There was a pause while Miriam listened to her aged father, who had started waffling down the phone about something she had no interest in. Miriam continued to listen as he asked her how Jack was doing. Her father had been a hard-nosed businessman in his time, but, unlike her mother, he had never tried to stop her marrying Jack.

'Yes,' Miriam answered his question, 'Jack's doing very well. Better than expected, actually.'

There was another pause, as yet more questions were asked.

'Yes,' Miriam said, trying to disguise her irritation. She was sick to the back teeth of people asking about Jack. 'Yes, he's putting the weight back on . . . looking more like his old self.'

Her father started coughing and she impatiently tapped her manicured nails on the side table. When he had finally got his breath back, she got to the point of her phone call.

'Father,' she said gently, 'I've got a favour to ask . . . '

Chapter Nineteen

The Ford Estate, Sunderland

As Miriam quietly sneaked back into bed, four miles across the river on the south side Gloria was not only still wide awake, but also not far off becoming completely demented as she tried in vain to subdue a colicky Hope.

From the moment she had bumped the pram up and over her front doorstep, her daughter had not stopped crying. It didn't matter what Gloria did, nothing would soothe her baby. Hope's cries had turned into screams and then the screams had become interspersed with bouts of coughing and snot. Her little girl's face had become as red as a beetroot, and she had clenched her hands into fists so tightly that Gloria reckoned she wouldn't have been able to prise them open even if she tried. Now Hope was arching her back as if trying some contortionist trick to free herself from her mother's arms.

Gloria had started to worry that there was something seriously wrong with her baby, and had considered taking Hope to the Royal, until she'd reminded herself that her eldest son had also been like this when he was just a few months old.

Thoughts of the hospital, however, had brought images of Jack back into Gloria's consciousness – how he had looked at her with blank, unknowing eyes as if she was a total stranger, and that, in turn, had brought another crushing wave of despair down on her.

When Gloria had given Hope her name she really did have 'hope'; now she felt like slapping herself. She had been living in cloud cuckoo land. Reality had come back to bite her on the backside – and had done so with a vengeance. Jack may have returned, but he was lost to her, as were all her dreams that they would be together and live a happy, loving life with their little girl. Today's events at the yard had spelt it out to her in black and white: Jack was under the control of Miriam – like he always had been.

When Gloria and Jack had started meeting up in secret, Jack had confided in her about his life with Miriam and how their marriage had been dead for many years. She had been shocked to the core when he had told her that later on in their marriage – when he had really got to know the true depths of his wife's manipulative nature – he had become convinced she had faked her pregnancy. The look of sadness and regret in Jack's eyes had been easy to read and neither of them had needed to say what they'd both been thinking: if Miriam had not claimed to have been pregnant, Jack would have chosen to be with Gloria and their lives would have been very different.

Now that Jack had no memory of his past life, Gloria was damn sure Miriam, true to form, would be moulding and shaping him into exactly the husband she wanted. Today had proved that to her beyond any kind of doubt. Just seeing the way Miriam had been with Jack, Gloria knew that she had been beaten yet again. Miriam had won. Just like she had when they had all been young and she had snatched the man she loved away from under her nose. And now, over twenty years later, she had done the same again. The only difference this time was that Miriam was unaware that she was taking Jack from her. As far as Miriam knew, Jack had not spoken to Gloria for years – *never mind had a child with her.*

As Gloria started to shake Hope's bottle of milk, the top suddenly came off and she unwittingly sprayed milk all around her little kitchen.

'Oh no!' Gloria's cry of anger and frustration almost blotted out Hope's wailing. The neighbour on her left started banging on the wall, and in temper Gloria banged the half-emptied bottle of milk down on the side.

'Yer weren't so quick to complain when I was having seven bells beaten out of me, were ya!' Gloria shouted as she hammered on the kitchen wall with her fist so hard she thought she could see slight indentations in the plaster. The pain it caused her knuckles though was worth the sense of release the outburst had given her, but it also had the effect of draining her of all her energy and she grabbed the bottle of milk and traipsed into the living room with Hope still screaming and coughing in her ear.

As an act of rebellion she sat down in 'Vinnie's chair' and almost wished he were here now to see her sitting on *his throne* so she could make him experience the full force of Hope's lungs. She'd give him a piece of her mind, with Hope as her backing vocals. He would surely rue the day if he knocked on the front door now. Would probably run a mile rather than try to batter his way in.

After a few moments, though, her anger became sorrow and tears started cascading down her cheeks. She was a terrible mother. She was too old, and past it. She was a wreck now at this age. God knew what she would be like when Hope was older. The poor girl was going to feel like she was being brought up by her granny. She would be much better off being raised by someone like Bel. Young and happy and full of life. She'd bet her boots that Bel wouldn't be bashing on walls and shouting like some nutter at her neighbours.

Taking a deep breath, Gloria once again tried to placate

her little girl by putting her over her shoulder and rocking her gently. But the screaming continued, and Gloria swapped Hope over to her other side to even out the assault on her ears.

The more Hope screamed, the more Gloria's thoughts of being an incompetent mother steamrolled on – how she thought her daughter would be much happier at the Elliots' than here with her, and that Hope was never like this when she was with Bel.

Gloria gently took Hope's little squirming body and placed her on her lap; as she did so she remembered how sometimes it had calmed both her boys if she rubbed their stomach in circular motions.

As she gently touched Hope's tummy she could feel how tense her poor little girl was. Gloria started speaking in as soft a voice as she could muster as she rubbed her baby's belly like it was a genie's bottle.

'Twinkle twinkle little star . . . how I wonder what you are . . . '

Gloria closed her eyes as she half spoke, half sang the soothing lullaby despite being deafened by the high-pitched volume of her daughter's screams. Still, when Gloria reached the end of the verse, the sound of her daughter's bloodcurdling cries had dropped down a notch. Driven on by the success of the nursery rhyme, Gloria started singing it again. Her heart lifted as Hope's crying started to stutter and there were gaps between the bawling.

By the time Gloria had *'wondered what you are'* half a dozen times, Hope was crying intermittently.

Gradually, like a car running out of fuel, the crying spluttered to a halt, her daughter's Cupid's bow mouth emitting a trail of short, shuddering barks. Gloria felt her body heave the most monumental sigh of relief as, finally, Hope started to drift off to sleep.

Terrified of waking her up again, Gloria decided to remain sitting in Vinnie's armchair with her little girl cradled in her arms. She managed to reach over and pull the thick woollen throw off the back of the sofa and delicately place it over them both so at least they could stay warm.

For the next hour Gloria sat there, looking at her mantelpiece with the photos of her two sons on it, as well as the stack of letters they wrote to her. She kept them to hand as she often liked to sit with a cup of tea and reread them. She wondered what they would think of their little sister. If they saw her now they would surely fall instantly in love.

Gloria knew it would be a shock for them when they found out that their mother had not only had a baby, but that the baby was not their father's. By the time they came home the truth would surely be out, that much she knew. But she didn't care – as long as they came back safe, and in one piece, it wouldn't matter what they said or thought.

As her mind drifted, she wondered how on earth she was going to keep her eyes open tomorrow at work. She couldn't recall the last time she'd had a decent night's sleep. If Hope wasn't keeping her up, the voice in her own head was. She worried that she had made a mistake by going back to work so soon, or indeed, if she should even be working at all. But then again, she argued with herself, financially she needed to.

As the clock struck midnight Gloria started to drop off to sleep, but the respite from her constant stream of thoughts and worries and resentments didn't last for long; every half hour or so she would wake up and her mind would start whirring once more, working overtime.

By three o'clock she had lost all ability to be even the tiniest bit positive about her life. Like the pitch black night outside, she could only see doom and gloom. And lots of it. She even began to doubt Jack's love for her before he'd left for America.

How, in all seriousness, she asked herself bitterly, *could she have believed Jack would be hers after all these years?*

Now she doubted whether – even if Jack had returned with his memory intact – he would have chosen to be with her and Hope. The night they had said their goodbyes, and Jack had sworn his love to her in the porchway of St Peter's Church, she had felt nothing would ever stop them being together.

Now she wasn't at all sure.

Would he really have given up his good, secure, and wealthy life with Miriam to be with a very dowdy, very poor – and now a very plump – Gloria?

When she finally fell into a deep sleep at around four, Gloria's dreams brought her no comfort. She found herself running around the shipyard unable to find what she was looking for, and the faster she tried to run, the slower she got, as if her limbs were sinking into quicksand. Disjointed images of Vinnie's snarling, hate-filled face kept coming and going, mixed with the image of Miriam and Jack covered in confetti and laughing at her as she cradled her baby.

When Hope stirred at around six o'clock, Gloria was quite relieved to be woken from her dreams and she found herself sweating, even though the house was now cold.

Looking down at her baby girl as her eyes scrunched up and she enjoyed the biggest yawn for such a small mouth, Gloria had to smile. The little mite now snuggling happily in her arms bore no resemblance to the screaming terror of the previous night.

'You want to go and see your aunty Bel now, don't you? And I just *know* you're going to be as good as gold for her.'

Gloria eased herself up out of the chair and carried Hope through to the kitchen to get her some milk.

This time, though, she made sure the top was tightly screwed on.

Chapter Twenty

The following day Gloria congratulated herself on making it through the shift without either falling asleep on her feet or dropping through exhaustion. There'd been a rush on to get a 400-ton coastal collier back to work delivering coal from the area's mines to London's power stations on the Thames Estuary. Most of the welding had been overhead and her arms now felt like lead weights.

At five thirty she said goodbye to the women who were staying late. It had been agreed that Gloria would be exempt from overtime because she had to pick Hope up before six, but also because she simply didn't have the energy to do even a few minutes' extra work – never mind a few hours.

'Wait for me,' Rosie shouted over as she grabbed her bags and gas mask and joined Gloria as she left for the main gates.

'How you feeling?' Rosie asked.

'My brain feels like a merry-go-round, only there's nothing merry going on in it, but it keeps going round and round,' Gloria said with a tight smile.

'While it's been going around,' Rosie continued the analogy, 'has it thought any more about Jack? Or what to do about Vinnie?' Rosie couldn't help but worry about what Vinnie might do next. She knew that Vinnie was chomping at the bit to see the baby girl he believed was his. And, worst of all, she knew that the more Gloria refused to let him see her, the more wound up he would be. Men like Vinnie did not like anyone, let alone a woman, to tell them what to do.

'Well, I think about Jack all the time,' Gloria said. 'I was up all night with Hope . . .' her voice sounded sad and hopeless, ' . . . and I kept thinking about what I should – or shouldn't – do. And I realised I've got to *do* something . . . I can't *do* anything about Jack getting his memory back. And,' she added, her voice hardening, 'I can't *do* anything about Vinnie being a vile and violent man. And at the moment I can't come clean about who Hope's father really is. But I know one thing – I want to be free of Vinnie. And I can *do* something about that.'

Rosie looked at Gloria, and asked, 'Get divorced?'

Gloria nodded. 'I'm working full-time, so I can probably just about afford it.'

'Shall I ask George to sort out someone decent who won't swindle you?' Rosie asked. 'He knows just about all the solicitors in town. He probably went to school with most of them,' she said, as they reached the ferry crossing and paid their fare.

Gloria looked at Rosie.

'You really are a star, you know? That'd help me out no end. It'll be one thing I don't have to worry about . . . And it'll be nice to meet George,' Gloria hesitated for fear of overstepping the mark, ' . . . and perhaps Lily as well, one day.'

Rosie looked at Gloria, and laughed. 'Goodness, I don't know if you'll be so keen when you do meet them. George is a dear, but Lily is – how should I say it? – a bit of a character.'

As they reached the other side of the river and headed up the bank, Rosie gently touched Gloria's arm.

'I know you want to tell Vinnie that he isn't Hope's father. But I'd hang on for a while longer if I were you. Let things calm down. Perhaps wait until your divorce is through. Give you some time to play with.'

201

Gloria sighed as they reached the corner of the street where they went their separate ways – Rosie to her home further up the Borough Road, and Gloria to Tatham Street. She wanted to tell Rosie that more than anything she just needed to get it all out in the open. To hell with the consequences – that she was tired of feeling trapped. Of living a lie.

Instead, though, she gave Rosie a sad smile and nodded her agreement, for she knew her workmate was right.

Gloria got home just before seven o'clock, and there was a loud knock on the door within minutes of her dragging Hope's pram over the threshold.

Gloria knew it was Vinnie – knew he'd be around again.

Quickly putting Hope in her cot, Gloria hurried to the front window. When she peeked through the curtains her suspicions were proved right. It was Vinnie. Thankfully, he looked relatively sober. If he had been at work, then the chances were he was on his way to the pub and, therefore, hadn't had the chance to get tanked up.

Gloria turned away from the window, checked on Hope, who was sleeping soundly, before marching out of the living room, making sure to close the door behind her.

'What do you want, Vinnie!' Gloria shouted through the door. Sod it, she'd been quiet for too long. It was time her voice was heard.

'Is that you, Glor?' Vinnie sounded a little confused.

'Yes, Vinnie, who else is it going to be?' Gloria said impatiently. 'What do you want?'

Now it was Vinnie's turn to sound irritated and angry.

'I want to see my bloody daughter, that's what!' he snarled back at the door.

'Well, you can't,' Gloria said defiantly. 'She's sound asleep and I'll be damned if anything is going to wake her.

I've had no sleep myself for God knows how long, so just bugger off. You're not wanted here. And like I told you before, I'm not having you anywhere near my daughter – whether she is asleep or wide awake.'

Gloria jumped out of her skin as Vinnie smashed a fist against the front door. Her body started to shake involuntarily. She was sick to death of feeling this fear course through her body whenever Vinnie was around.

'I've just about had enough of you – and your fists, Vinnie. If you bash on this door once more, or try to get in, I swear to God I'll get the police on to you. One of my mates across the road is going to send her nipper down the station if you kick off again, and mark my words her bairn can run like a whippet, so you're best off leaving – now.'

Gloria, of course, was lying, but Vinnie wasn't to know that.

There was silence on the other side of the door, before another great thump caused it to judder.

'You're gonna have to let me see my bairn, Glor. Whether you like it or not.'

Gloria could tell he was backing down, but, as always, he had to get the last word in.

'She's my flesh and blood.' His face was so close to the front door, his lips were practically touching it. 'There's no getting around that,' he spat the words out, angry beyond belief that he couldn't just smash his way in and give her a good slap. The beating he'd taken from the man in the balaclava, though, darted across his mind, and he backed off.

Gloria forced herself to keep quiet. How she wished she could scream at him, *She's not yours, Vinnie!*

But she didn't. The words would just have to be screamed in her own head. For now, anyway. But it was getting harder to keep shtum. She wasn't sure whether it was sleep deprivation that was making her feel like she couldn't care less, but she was getting to a stage where she simply didn't give a damn any more. The only reason she was just about managing to hold back was to ensure the safety of her little girl sleeping in the next room.

For her sake, she would keep a lid on it.

For now, Vinnie could have the last word.

Chapter Twenty-One

Grindon, Sunderland

When Vinnie got back from his abortive attempt to see the baby he believed to be his, he was bursting at the seams with pure fury.

'It's just not right!' he said, stomping back and forth within the claustrophobic confines of the small flat which was now his home, and had been for almost a year.

'I should be able to at least *see* my own bairn!' His voice was increasing in volume, along with his ire.

'It's like every man and his dog has *seen* my own bairn, apart from me – her soddin' father! I wouldn't know her from Adam if she was right in front of me. Talk about being made to look like a complete and utter idiot!'

Sarah lit another cigarette and crossed her legs. She was sitting on her two-seater settee, looking up at Vinnie as he prowled around the perimeter of the room like a caged tiger. Ever since he had taken a beating that night outside of the pub a few months back, he'd become tetchier. He was drinking more, and that meant he was more prone to sparking up at the slightest opportunity.

'Vinnie, you're beginning to sound like a broken record,' she said with a smile, trying to joke him out of his bad mood. 'Come and sit down and have a fag,' she told him, 'you're gonna give yourself a wobbler if you keep on going like this.'

Vinnie's head turned sharply. He stepped over to the

little coffee table, pulled a cigarette out of the half-empty packet and rammed it into his mouth.

Sarah held her lighter out and sparked it up as Vinnie bobbed his head down and puffed hard on his cigarette. Bellows of smoke filled the room. No words of thanks were uttered.

'It's that *soddin' cow* who's gonna give me a bloody heart attack,' he snarled.

Sarah's mood always lifted a little whenever Vinnie slated his ex – or rather his soon-to-be ex-wife. She just wished Vinnie would get his act together and sort out a divorce, like he'd promised he'd do, so that the two of them could get married. It would be nice to finally be his 'missus' in name. She was sick of being his 'mistress' – couldn't wait to have a ring on her finger so she could stick it up at all those on the estate who looked down their noses at her. And it wasn't as if getting a divorce was like it used to be – just for the well-to-do snobs of this world. People like her mate's sister from work were getting divorces. Nowadays people could start afresh, with someone new – someone they loved, not hated. And Vinnie certainly did hate Gloria now. Before he had been indifferent towards her, but since the baby had come along, his anger had well and truly spilled over.

As Sarah kept a close eye on Vinnie while he continued to stalk around the room, sucking in smoke and almost spitting it back out, she felt annoyed at him being so obsessed with this bloody baby.

Why did he care so much? From what she knew of him before they'd got it together he'd never exactly been the doting dad. He was like most men she knew: he'd done the business – given Gloria two kids, and that was it. That was him done. The rest was up to the woman.

'She'll come round,' Sarah said, taking a drag on her

cigarette, disguising a long sigh as she blew out a slow wispy grey stream of smog up towards the ceiling.

'Aye,' Vinnie fumed. 'She'll come around when the baby's all grown up. It'll be too late then. I want to see my daughter now! I've a right to! I should just go there and take the bairn off her. It's my right as her father, for God's sake!'

In the middle of his rant, Vinnie suddenly stopped in his tracks as if he had been struck by a brilliant idea.

'Come to think about it,' he said, his voice sounding happier, more hopeful. 'What's to stop me doing just that? I've got as much right to that baby as she has. Probably more. I'm the *father*.'

Sarah looked at Vinnie and felt her heart plummet. A little thread of panic started to weave its way into her mind. She knew Vinnie and she knew that when he got an idea in his head he was always loath to let go of it. The last thing she wanted was to be stuck with some screaming baby. And she would bet her bottom dollar that it would be her who got landed with looking after the wee thing. There was no way, not in a million years, that Vinnie would look after the bairn himself. He might *want* the baby, but he certainly wouldn't want to actually *look after* her. Of that much she was sure.

It'll be muggins here, she thought, taking another drag and expelling smoke. She would be the one left to do all the work, the one to have to get up in the middle of the night, the one to feed it – all the time up to the elbows in dirty nappies, and never having the time nor the money to be able to just saunter out whenever she felt like it, or whenever she wanted to go out for a booze-up, which, if she was honest, was most nights.

Didn't Vinnie realise that her years of babies and child-rearing were well behind her? She was done with all of that. There was no way she wanted a re-run – especially with someone else's baby.

She had to use her noddle.

'Listen, Vin –' Sarah always shortened her lover's name when she was trying to be nice, or to turn him round to her way of thinking.

'The bab's not going to know whether you're there or not at the moment. Wait until all the hard work is done and then go round and play daddy when she's walking and talking and being as cute as pie.'

She took another drag on her cigarette.

'Just wait a little while and see what happens. Chances are Gloria'll be round here, knocking on our door, begging you to have her in a few months' time when she's had enough of its squalling.'

She wanted to add that he should be counting his blessings that Gloria wasn't round here already, shoving the damn baby in their faces, demanding money for its upkeep. Most men would be only too happy at being let off the hook. But, oh no, not Vinnie.

He just couldn't stand the thought of a woman getting one over on him. Of him not being the one to call the shots or being the big man. God forbid he'd feel like he was being dictated to by a woman.

Vinnie stopped pacing. He took another draw on his fag and ash fell onto the newly cleaned carpet.

Sarah watched as it dropped and stopped herself from saying anything. She knew Vinnie was on the cusp – and if she started nagging him or saying anything to upset him, he'd spark off.

'Why don't we go to the pub and have a chat about it there?' she said, stubbing out her cigarette in the ashtray and getting up off the sofa.

Vinnie immediately started to calm down, placated by

the thought of a nice frothy ale going down his throat. 'Aye, sounds like a plan to me,' he said, grabbing his coat from the back of the chair and pulling out his comb from the inside pocket.

As he looked at his reflection in the mirror above the mantelpiece and slicked back his few remaining strands of hair, he made a vow to himself.

He wouldn't let Gloria get her own way.

Who the hell did she think she was, telling him what he could and couldn't do?

She was still his bloody wife.

He was in control. Always had been. Not *her*.

And if he wanted to see his bairn, he damn well was going to. No one was going to stop him – especially not a woman.

Chapter Twenty-Two

DS Miller walked down Holmeside, a route he took almost every day to the police station. Over the past few weeks he had seen the Maison Nouvelle take shape, although it still looked like it would be a while before it was ready to officially open.

He had tried to push what he had discovered from his visit to the police archives to the back of his mind, but it was no good. It was keeping him awake at night, his mind churning over everything he had learnt – and everything he had yet to learn. Part of him wished he hadn't. It certainly had not cured his curiosity as he'd hoped it would, but had further antagonised it.

He had been right, though. Kate and Rosie did know each other. As soon as he'd looked into Kate's background and seen she had been born and brought up in Whitburn, and was the same age as Rosie, he knew they must have been schoolfriends.

He'd found out that Kate's mother had died suddenly, and, as her father had been killed in the First World War, and no other relatives had come forward, Kate had been placed under the care of the Poor Sisters of Nazareth. Judging by the date of her first vagrancy offence she must have left Nazareth House and more or less gone straight on to the streets.

It would seem unlikely that Kate and Rosie had stayed friends during that time. Had they only recently got to know each other again? And how was it that Kate had managed all of a sudden to turn her life around?

And where was she living now, if not bedding down in some shop doorway?

But it was what he had found out about Rosie that had really thrown him. Both Rosie's parents had been killed in a hit and run accident just before her sixteenth birthday – the police at the time had made a half-hearted attempt at finding the culprit who had knocked them both over and left them for dead, but no one had even been questioned, never mind arrested for causing the couple's death.

Why hadn't Rosie told him about this? Was it too painful for her?

And what was really odd was that she hadn't even mentioned she had a younger sister called Charlotte, who was eight at the time her parents were killed, which would make her about fourteen now. He had no idea where she was, though, as she wasn't registered as living in Sunderland, or, indeed, anywhere in the county.

Why hadn't she mentioned her sister? Perhaps Charlotte had been sent away to live in another part of the country and they had lost contact?

Somehow that didn't seem like something Rosie would let happen. She was such a loyal friend to her women welders – had been there for them whenever they needed her, so it didn't make sense that she would simply forget she had a sister.

The more he thought about Rosie, the more he realised just how little he really knew about her.

He had thought they trusted each other, but the more he thought about it, the more he realised that Rosie had only really ever talked about what was happening in the present.

As he walked past the Maison Nouvelle on the opposite

side of the road, he looked over at the shopfront. He had never seen anyone coming or going since the day he had seen Rosie and Polly there, but this evening he spotted Kate locking up. He slowed down and watched as she slung a big patchwork cloth bag over her shoulder, and hurried up the street.

DS Miller hesitated for a moment. The question he had asked himself repeatedly over the past few weeks, sprang back to him:

I wonder where she lives now?

His curiosity got the better of him and he found himself following her up Holmeside, past the Park Lane bus depot, and then along Grange Terrace. He wondered if perhaps Kate was living in the same tenement in which Rosie had been living last year – where he had first gone to see her to inform her of her uncle's drowning. But, no, Kate hurried past the boarding house without even a second glance.

Unable to stop himself, he followed Kate all the way along Briary Vale Road until it turned into West Lawn. Only then did she slow down.

Intrigued, he watched from a distance and saw her slow her pace as she approached a magnificent three-storey Victorian terrace. The house had a wonderful brick balcony which overlooked the Ashbrooke Social Club, which he himself had frequented on quite a number of occasions as a few of his work colleagues were keen cricket players.

He watched as she opened the bottom gate and walked up the long pathway, up the stone steps, before letting herself in the front door.

Well, that was a turn-up for the books.

Kate really had gone from rags to riches.

That in itself was intriguing – but what he still just couldn't work out was the puzzle of how Kate and Rosie were connected now. Why hadn't Rosie mentioned Kate to him?

If Rosie hadn't been open with him about what he had learnt recently, it strengthened his argument that she had also not been honest about the way she felt about him – and that she did, in fact, have feelings for him.

Which could only mean that there was something stopping her from being with him.

But what?

God, why was it every time he tried to find out some answers, he was left with more questions?

Chapter Twenty-Three

The next day

'Yay! They've set a date!' Dorothy shouted out as she hurried over to the welders' work area, leaving Polly and Gloria, who she'd bumped into at the timekeeper's cabin, lagging behind.

Dorothy might have met Bel only a few times, but she felt she knew her. Polly had chatted a lot about her sister-in-law over the past year, especially after Teddy had been killed, but she hadn't really got to know her until the day they'd all turned up after Hope was born.

Hearing Dorothy's jubilant voice ring out, Rosie, Angie, Martha and Hannah all looked up from their spot around their fire.

'That is wonderful news!' Hannah chirped.

Martha, who was standing next to her little friend, looked at her and asked, slightly confused, 'Who's set a "date"?'

'*The wedding*, Martha,' Dorothy almost sang the words. 'The wedding! What other date *is* there? This is *the* event of the year.' She rolled her eyes dramatically as she put her bag and gas mask down next to her welding machine.

'Anyway . . .' Dorothy asked, directing her gaze at Hannah, 'what brings our "little bird" back to the flock? We're not normally graced with your presence this early on in the day. And without young Olly hanging on to your coat tails.'

Hannah looked a little guilty and shot Martha a quick

look. 'Perhaps it is because I wanted to see my friends,' she said, enunciating each word clearly. Martha looked down at her beloved mate and smiled, showing the big gap between her two front teeth.

Angie looked at Dorothy and raised her eyebrows. Someone, probably Rosie, must have had a quiet word in Hannah's ear about Martha, and how their workmate had been mooching about lately and was obviously missing her friend.

'So,' Angie piped up, 'when is it?'

'The eighth of November,' Dorothy declared.

'Blimey,' Angie said, 'that's in four weeks' time.' She chuckled. 'Hey, Pol, you sure there's not a bun in the oven?'

Polly frowned and opened her mouth to speak, but was beaten to it by Dorothy.

'Bel's not like that, Ange! They're in love. You've seen the pair of them. Anyway, what's the point in waiting when you *know* you want to be with someone for the rest of your life?'

Dorothy looked over a little guiltily at Gloria, suddenly aware that all this chatter about romance and marriage and being together for ever was probably the last thing she wanted to hear, but when she saw her friend, standing, sipping her tea by the fire, a glazed look on her face, she realised she was miles away.

'So, bet you it's a madhouse at yours?' Rosie said to Polly as she cleared the workbench of bits of scrap metal and used rods.

Polly laughed. 'You could say that. Ma and Bel are like two queen bees working nineteen to the dozen to get everything ready – but what's a real turn-up for the books is that even Pearl seems to be getting into the spirit of it all. The plan is to have the reception in the Tatham, so, Pearl's chuffed to pieces because that's her domain.'

'I suppose she is "the mother of the bride",' Rosie said, thinking of her own mum for a fleeting moment. She had been dead now for ten years but she still missed her.

'Well, I know Bel would much prefer Agnes. Ma's been more of a mam to Bel than Pearl ever has,' Polly said truthfully, 'but, you know, blood's thicker than water and all that.'

'And,' Hannah started speaking and paused for a moment before asking, a little uncertainly, 'who is going to, how do you say it, hand the bride over?'

'Give the bride away,' Dorothy corrected.

'I don't think they're going to have anyone as such,' Polly said, not wanting to elaborate. It didn't feel right talking about Bel's father – or rather her lack of one – in front of everyone.

'And what about the dress?' Angie asked. She and Dorothy had been intrigued to hear that it was Rosie's old schoolfriend who was making it, and that she actually *lived* at Lily's. The pair of them would have given anything to have a good neb around the bordello.

'Oh, the dress,' Polly said, looking over to Rosie, 'is going to be fantastic, although to be honest I have no idea what it looks like. Bel's tried to explain, but I haven't got a clue, other than it's a pastel pink colour.'

Rosie laughed. 'It's got to be amazing, the amount of time Kate's spending on it. I've hardly seen her lately. She's totally obsessed.'

'Oh goodness,' Polly suddenly perked up, 'I almost forgot—'

Everyone looked at Polly as she hurried over to her bag and pulled out a dozen small envelopes.

'Ta-da!' she said dramatically. 'The wedding invites.'

Dorothy gave a little jump of excitement and clapped

her hands. 'Oh, this is sooo exciting,' she said, putting her hand out as Polly handed them all their individual cards.

'Bel's got lovely handwriting, hasn't she?' Hannah said, admiring the swirling lettering on the front of the card.

'Cor, we get to bring someone with us 'n all,' Angie said, astounded.

Dorothy shot her best friend a mischievous look. 'Are you thinking what I'm thinking, Ange?'

Angie nodded with a big grin on her face.

Martha was looking at them both, the card still unopened in her hand. 'Not another "double date!"' she said with a slightly disapproving look on her face.

There was a joint howl of laughter just as the klaxon sounded for the start of their shift.

'Eee, I remember the day when Martha didn't know of such things,' Gloria said, casting a reproving look at Dorothy and Angie. 'You two are a bad influence.'

'See you all in the canteen at lunch,' Hannah said. 'And, Polly,' she added, 'can you tell Bel "thank you". It will be my first British wedding. And I am very excited.'

Dorothy chuckled as she watched Hannah, trotting back across the yard.

'No guessing who Hannah'll be inviting,' she said. ' . . . And it won't be her aunty Rina, that's for sure.'

Rosie slipped her invite into her top pocket and wished more than anything that she too could get excited about who she would bring to the wedding.

'Come on then, you lot,' she said, waving her hand for them to follow her. 'Get your gear. I need you over with the platers this morning.'

When they arrived at the platers' shed, the men were just starting up the huge metal rolling machine. When the women were trainees, they had all said the same thing – it reminded them of a mammoth-sized mangle – only instead of laundry coming out of its rollers, there were huge sheets of metal.

'I'll see you all in a little while,' Rosie told the women as she branched off and headed towards the main office buildings.

Harold had asked to have a quick word when he'd spotted her coming through the main gates this morning. She just hoped Miriam wasn't going to be there. She was not in the mood today. Hopefully, it was some good news about Jack. He had looked well when he'd visited with Miriam.

When she reached the main offices, she took the stairs up two at a time, knocking before she went into Jack's office. When she heard Harold's 'Come in!' and stepped into the small office, she was glad to see that he was on his own.

'Morning, Rosie,' Harold said. He was sitting behind Jack's desk with his elbows resting on the steel top, where, Rosie noticed, a photograph of Jack and Miriam had been put on show.

'Have a seat –' He indicated the wooden chair in front of the desk.

'I'm all right standing, Harold. What's up?' Rosie asked.

'I just wanted to let you know . . . ' Harold got out a cigarette and lit it. 'Jack's not coming back to the yard,' he told her as he blew smoke out. 'He's been moved to Crown's.'

Rosie was shocked. 'Why's that?' she replied, her voice not hiding her disbelief.

Harold coughed nervously. He hated dealing with women when it came to work or business – he was never quite sure how hard or soft to be with them. Thankfully, it was something he didn't have to deal with very often.

'It's what Mrs Crawford wants,' he explained, trying hard to keep his face deadpan.

'I don't understand,' Rosie said, trying to rein in her annoyance, 'I don't see the point of moving Jack to another yard. I don't see why or what good that will do. Surely he needs to be in a familiar place. Somewhere full of memories. Somewhere he has spent most of his life?'

Secretly Harold couldn't have agreed with Rosie more. Thompson's had been Jack's home for his entire life. It made more sense to keep him here.

'It's out of my hands,' he said with a defeated shrug of his shoulders.

Rosie let out a deep huff. 'Well, I think it's a terrible idea and I don't care whether that gets back to Mrs Crawford or not.' She pushed a straggle of blonde hair back from her face. She wasn't about to give up – for Gloria's sake, above all else.

'Is there no way you can change Miriam's – I mean Mrs Crawford's mind? No offence, but she doesn't even work here.' Rosie knew she was pushing the boundaries that someone of her position – and gender – was supposed to keep within.

'Yes, Rosie, but she is *his wife*,' Harold said, 'and more importantly she is the daughter of Mr Havelock. And it is Mr Havelock who is sanctioning the move to Crown's.'

'But,' Rosie persisted, desperate to keep Jack at the yard, 'Crown's is a smaller yard, and no one there really knows him.'

'The argument is that Mr Thompson may well be looking at buying out Crown's – *if* we win this bloody war, that is – so if that is the case it might make sense for us to have Jack there to help with the transition.'

Rosie listened and knew she was beat. She also knew Jack's move to another shipyard had nothing whatsoever to do with any kind of amalgamation.

Miriam was far from stupid.

Chapter Twenty-Four

Maison Nouvelle, Holmeside, Sunderland

Two weeks later

'Eee Bel, you look stunning. Our Joe's not going to know what's hit him when he sees you.' Polly was still in her overalls, having come straight from work, and she was seated on top of one of the cutting tables that had been pushed against the wall to make more room in the middle of the small shop, her legs dangling just inches from the wooden floor.

Bel was in the middle of the Maison Nouvelle with her arms slightly elevated, like a small bird just about to try to flap its wings to take off. She looked embarrassed at Polly's words and was standing stock-still in order to prevent herself from disturbing Kate, who was busying around her, taking pins out and putting more in.

'Oh, Polly . . . ' Kate said, tugging her measuring tape from around her neck and checking the distance from underneath Bel's armpit to her waist, ' . . . this is nothing. It's nowhere near ready. If you think Bel looks stunning now, just you wait until I've finished.'

Just then the little bell above the door to the shop tinkled and Agnes stepped in from the rain and fog outside.

Bel's face lit up with a big smile. 'You made it!' she said. But when Agnes held the door open and Pearl came traipsing in behind her, her enthusiasm ebbed. 'Oh,' Bel's voice dropped a notch, 'Ma, you've come too. I wasn't expecting you.'

'Well,' Pearl said, her eyes widening as she looked about the shop, 'you could sound a little more pleased to see me, Isabelle. I'm only your mother, after all.' But Pearl didn't sound at all upset by Bel's tepid greeting. Like the rain she was shaking from her overcoat, for Pearl, it was water off a duck's back.

'You've got yourself a great place here, haven't yer, pet,' she said to Kate, her eyes scanning the shop. 'Makes a change from shop doorways, I'll bet?'

'Ma!' Bel's mouth had dropped open in shock.

Polly looked at Kate, but other than a slight flush to her cheeks, she looked unperturbed by Pearl's comments.

'I'm only joshing, hinny,' Pearl said with a chuckle. 'Looks like you've done well for yerself. Good on ya!' She looked at Kate. 'I don't suppose you could sort me out with something for the big day – me being the mother of the bride 'n all?'

'I think Kate's got her hands full as it is, Ma,' Bel sniped.

Agnes and Polly exchanged weary looks. It was always the same when Pearl and Bel were in the same room. It was as if they had accepted each other's presence in their lives, but they were still not entirely happy about it, and were not too concerned about whether it showed.

'Mrs . . . ?' Kate started to say to Pearl.

'Just Pearl, pet. I have had the good fortune never to have been married.' Pearl straightened her shoulders a little defensively.

'Pearl,' Kate said, 'I would be more than happy to help you with your dress for your daughter's wedding. Like you say, you are the bride's mother. It's very important.'

Bel marvelled at this young woman who was creating for her a dress worthy of the fashion pages of *Vogue* and was amazed she could be so courteous to someone who had just been so down-and-out rude.

'Eee, that's kind of you, pet,' Pearl couldn't keep the surprise out of her voice. 'I've actually got a dress that just needs a little stitch, and a nip and a tuck here and there.'

'You have to pay her, Ma,' Bel butted in. 'Kate doesn't do this for the love of it, you know?'

Kate, who had been pinning the back of Bel's coral-coloured silk dress, popped her head around so that her narrow, slightly peaky face was looking through Bel's arm.

'Oh, *but I do*,' she said, taking a pin from her mouth, 'I *do* just do it for the love of it. So please no mention of money. This is my gift.'

'Thanks, petal,' Pearl said, jumping at the offer and sounding more than a little taken aback. 'I'll come back with the dress tomorrow if that's all right? Providing little Miss Muffet here doesn't need your services?'

Kate smiled. 'Yes, come tomorrow. We're running out of time. Only a few weeks to go to the big day!'

Pearl looked uncannily chirpy as she turned to leave the shop. 'Well, I'd better get off now. Can't be late for work –' she opened the door '– see you tomorrow, *Katie!*'

Kate waved a free hand and felt her heart miss a beat; her mother had been the only one to call her 'Katie'. After she had died it had been too painful to hear anyone else call her that, and she had made a point of telling people it was 'Kate' and not 'Katie'. But Pearl had gone by the time Kate had the chance to correct her.

Kate thought that Pearl looked like a right character, and she had a feeling that Bel's ma had probably slept in a few doorways herself in her time. Perhaps, Kate thought, she would make an exception for her.

Within minutes of Pearl leaving there was another jingle of the doorbell.

'Kate, darling . . . ' It was Maisie.

'Oh, I'm so sorry. I didn't realise you had clients,' she apologised.

Kate, who had been bending down pinning Bel's hem, stood up and straightened her back. 'No worries, Maisie. They're not really clients as such . . . This is Polly who works with Rosie at the yard . . . '

Polly jumped off the table so that she was standing with her back against the side, and smiled over to Maisie.

' . . . and her mum Agnes,' she added, ' . . . and, of course, the bride-to-be – Bel.'

Kate stood back so everyone could say their hellos.

'Oh, how wonderful to meet you all,' Maisie said, stepping forward and putting her hand out to Bel.

Bel laughed as she arched her arm so as not to prick herself.

'You too, Maisie. Gosh, I feel like a pincushion here.'

'We haven't met before, have we?' Bel asked, but when the words were out of her mouth she immediately regretted them. If she had met Maisie before, she would have remembered. She couldn't recall ever even speaking to anyone who was 'coloured', even during her time on the buses, let alone someone who looked like Maisie.

But still there was something strangely familiar about her.

'I don't believe so,' Maisie said with a curious smile. 'I've only just moved up here from London . . . Anyway, this was just a quick call,' she went on, looking at Kate.

'Lily's asked if you could bring a few diamanté beads back. She has an idea for the hat she might wear to the wedding.'

Polly raised her eyebrows at Bel. Now, this was news to them all. Rosie hadn't told them she'd invited Lily as her guest. This was going to cause great excitement amongst the women.

'Nice to meet you all,' Maisie said. 'And have a wonder-ful wedding!'

Bel, Polly and Agnes watched a little bewitched as Maisie gave them the most dazzling of smiles, showing off perfectly straight, white teeth, before she glided out of the shop door.

None of them said anything after Maisie had left, but each of them knew what the others were thinking.

It wasn't just Maisie's outstanding beauty that had taken them all aback, but the colour of her skin.

Chapter Twenty-Five

Ivy House, London

June 1913

The moment Pearl walked through the doors of Ivy House, she felt she had stepped into another world. A better, cleaner, more caring world than the harsh, dirty and poverty-stricken one she had inhabited up until now.

She had learnt that this new world had been created by an organisation called 'The Salvation Army', and that the woman in black who had given her the magazine called *The Deliverer* was a member of this strange 'army' – which was not an army, but a charity.

The woman who had greeted her that first day was one of their 'soldiers' – only she wasn't a real soldier, but a midwife called Evelina.

On that first day Pearl had felt well and truly disorientated as she had tried to take in everything that Evelina told her. She had struggled to concentrate. She had been starving, having not eaten all day. Her attention kept wandering to the large oil portrait hanging on the office wall that Evelina had explained was of a man called William Booth, who was some kind of preacher, and it was he who had founded this charitable army.

Pearl had felt as though she was dreaming when Evelina walked her along the corridor, down some steps and into a small canteen, where she'd asked the cook, who'd been busy preparing the nurses' supper, to make a sandwich for Pearl. Then Evelina had showed her to a bed in a dormitory and Pearl had slept solidly until six o'clock the next morning when the other women started to stir and get ready for the day ahead.

After a heavenly bowl of hot porridge – made with milk – Pearl had again found herself in the same office as the previous day, where Evelina told her that the building was rented by the charity for use as a refuge and hospital for unmarried mothers.

'It is also,' Evelina explained, 'a training school for midwives. There are six wards here and a total of twenty-two beds and twelve cots. With two private wards for married women.' She stood up. 'I'll give you the grand tour.'

As Evelina showed her around, she tentatively asked Pearl a little about her present situation, and Pearl had been quite open about the fact that no one she knew was aware of her condition.

'My ma and da would thrash me from here to kingdom come,' she said in such a way that Evelina had been in no doubt that they would have done so in the blink of an eye. In her time at Ivy House she had seen such marks of anger and disgust punched or belted on to the faces and bodies of other pretty young girls who had found themselves in the family way. Pearl had been wise not to say anything to anyone, and wiser still to come to Ivy House for help, even if she'd had to travel the length of the country to get there.

It was only when Evelina probed a little about the baby's father that Pearl became more wary, although she seemed happy to tell Evelina that the father was a sailor, who'd had no idea when he'd left for foreign shores that Pearl was pregnant.

'Mind you, neither did I,' Pearl admitted.

When they had got to the second floor and Evelina

stopped outside a large door which she explained was 'the Matron's bedsitting room' and asked Pearl to wait outside, Pearl was terrified she had said or done something wrong, and that she would be kicked back out on to the streets. But five minutes later when Evelina re-emerged from the room, she was all smiles and Pearl immediately relaxed.

'Good news, Pearl,' she said, as they made their way back down the stairs. 'The Matron agrees with me that it wouldn't be right for us to tell you to come back when you are due – and that we'd be happy to have you stay with us for the duration of your pregnancy. We've got a few places here for what we call "waiting cases", for women like yourself . . . But, in return for staying here, you are required to help out with the daily domestic duties.'

Pearl could hardly get her words out quick enough.

'Ah, thank you, Miss Evelina. Thank you so much.' She had never wanted to thank someone so much for anything in her life.

At first it had taken Pearl a little while to get used to all the rules and regulations, but as the weeks wore on, she had to admit she liked the set routines and enjoyed her cleaning and domestic chores. More than anything, though, she enjoyed the simplicity of the life at Ivy House. She didn't have to worry about anyone kicking off, like she'd had to back home – the worst that ever happened at Ivy House was a squabble, or some catty words from the other girls.

Within weeks of her arrival, Pearl's bump seemed to blossom – as if it sensed it was now safe to come out and show itself. And as her bump grew, so did Pearl's feelings for the baby growing inside her. Lying awake at night, looking out at the London skies through the high windows in her dormitory she would chat away to her unborn baby. Not out loud, of course, but in her head.

Some of the other girls had told her that they were going to keep their babies, but Pearl thought they were just saying it. How could any of the girls here look after a baby? None of them had two pennies to rub together – they could barely afford to look after themselves, never mind a baby as well.

As Pearl's pregnancy progressed Evelina had talked to her about what would happen when the baby came.

'There aren't any laws for adopting out,' Evelina had explained, 'but here we do draw up our own contract which we call a "document of conveyance". It just makes it more official and helps us to keep a record.'

It didn't mean much to Pearl. As long as the baby was looked after by a couple who were kind and had a bit of money – someone who would give her child a better life than she could – then that was all right by her.

Towards the seventh month of her pregnancy Pearl started to experience the odd twinge; sometimes she felt her baby kick and she would feel her stomach and be convinced she could make out the outline of her child's tiny foot, pushing against her belly as if it was trying to stretch out.

After she had hit the eighth month, Pearl had to stop work. She was just too big. She felt as wide as she was tall, and joked with the other girls that if she toppled over she'd just roll away. But as her girth grew, so did her closeness to the child inside. She would have great lengthy conversations in her mind with her baby, chatting away about this and that, telling her about her home town, and about her brothers and sisters, and her ma and da.

Sometimes she even talked about the baby's father, but these were very private conversations, and even though they were conducted in her head, they were still whispered, as if she was fearful someone might read her thoughts.

Sometimes, Pearl allowed herself to dream about keeping her baby girl – for she was sure it was going to be a girl. It would be just them two against the world. They would survive. But in the clear light of day, Pearl would chastise herself for even allowing herself to think of such lunacy. How could she, a girl of just fourteen, bring up a child without a roof over her head, with no money in her pocket, and without much hope of even feeding herself – never mind the child?

But, still, she kept having these daydreams, and the bigger she got the more she thought about how she could possibly keep this baby growing inside of her.

When Pearl went into labour she was terrified. She had always prided herself on being tough, but the agony of childbirth was like nothing she had ever experienced before. Her labour was long, agonisingly painful, and very bloody.

But, when her little girl was born, and it *was* a little girl as she had always known, all the pain and suffering were forgotten in an instant, and in their place was a most overwhelming sense of love.

'You're beautiful,' Pearl said to the tiny baby, cradled against her. Its little arms were positioned as if it was about to start boxing; even the miniature fists were balled up as if ready for the next round. Pearl's white hand looked like a giant's as it gently stroked her baby's mop of black hair.

Pearl couldn't stop gazing at her daughter, who looked so happy and contented, all curled up, warm and cosy – her little mouth moving around as if she was chatting away to herself. But Pearl's bubble of love was soon burst when Evelina reached down to take her baby off her.

'Your baby will have a proper home,' she said. Evelina was trying to be gentle. To speak in a reassuring way. She hated doing this, but there was no other choice.

As she reached down to scoop the baby up, she saw the look in Pearl's eyes and knew this was not going to be easy.

'No, please!' Pearl started to beg. 'I've changed my mind. I'm gonna keep her! She's mine! I love her!' The words spilled out of her mouth. All those words which had been bouncing around in her head for months now, just escaped in one go.

Evelina looked at Pearl and saw tears welling up in her marine blue eyes. Not for the first time she had thought how pretty Pearl was and that in her life she would attract a lot of male attention – wanted or otherwise.

'Pearl,' she said, pulling up a wooden chair from the side of the room and placing it by the bed and sitting down. 'You can't. You know you can't. Perhaps if circumstances had been different,' she said looking down at the robust little girl who was already staring about her with the most beautiful eyes and incredibly long dark eyelashes. Every child was gorgeous, but this one was truly the epitome of beauty.

'I think I may know of just the family for your special little girl,' Evelina said. 'They're a nice couple. They'll give your baby girl a good home.'

Pearl did not look convinced – was still clutching her child, unwilling to give her up.

Evelina's voice became harder. 'This baby needs a mother and father. A *good* home. As we discussed when you first came here.'

Evelina remembered the conversation she'd had with Pearl, how she had struggled to understand her strong north-east accent. At the time she had believed that Pearl would be a fairly straightforward case. Pearl had told her that she would be relieved to get shot of her baby. Had tried unsuccessfully herself. The only reason she hadn't gone to some backstreet abortionist was because of all the horror stories she'd heard.

She had watched Pearl as she had settled in at the home and had seen her change as the weeks and months passed. Evelina had been prepared for a possible change of heart. It was far from uncommon. Looking down at Pearl and her baby girl, though, she knew that this young, unmarried mother did not have the luxury of choice.

Quietly Evelina told the other nurse who had helped with the delivery to give them a little time on their own.

'Pearl,' Evelina said, touching her arm. 'You know you can't keep her, don't you?'

Pearl flashed her a look. Her eyes had gone from being filled with love for her child, to angry and protective as she looked at Evelina, who was demanding her attention.

'I can only imagine what you are feeling, but you have to be strong – for the baby's sake.'

Pearl's gaze was drawn back to her baby.

Evelina persevered. 'The couple I know will be absolutely perfect for your baby.'

Pearl continued to ignore Evelina.

'They are well off and come from respectable families. Which is exactly what your child needs. She will be brought up properly – and she will be *accepted*. Do you understand what I am saying?'

Pearl continued to cuddle her baby. She gave her a gentle kiss on her forehead, and brushed a little wisp of dark hair away to the side.

'Your baby will not want for anything,' Evelina said, touching the newborn's soft skin.

Pearl looked at the baby in her arms; her little face looked happy and contented, as if that was all she wanted – just to be there.

If Pearl could have held that moment for eternity she would have.

She had never felt a love or happiness like this. And she doubted she ever would again – for she knew the words that Evelina was speaking were the truth. That she could not keep her child, no matter how much love she felt, no matter how wrong it felt to give her up.

Pearl knew there was no choice.

As Evelina got up, she squeezed Pearl's arm. 'I will leave you for a moment, Pearl. But when I come back I'm going to take the baby. Say goodbye to your little girl. But do so knowing you are doing the right thing. Trust me,' Evelina said, 'by giving up your baby, you are giving your daughter a life.'

And it was then Pearl realised that if she really loved this child in her arms, which she did – with every bone in her body – then she had to let her go. She had to give her a chance. A chance at life that she would not have if she stayed with her mother.

And with that knowledge Pearl's heart broke.

As she lay there cuddling her baby and whispering the only words she knew she would ever get to say to her daughter, she understood that, from this moment onwards, her life would never be the same.

Chapter Twenty-Six

Ashbrooke, Sunderland

Thursday 30 October 1941

There was no getting away from it. His instinct was telling him – no, screaming out at him – that Rosie had not ended their relationship because she had simply had a change of heart. He was convinced there was more to it. And if he found out what it was, then there might well be a chance they could be together.

He was now convinced there was something stopping her from allowing herself to have love in her life.

Was it something to do with her parents' death?

Or her sister?

And he kept thinking about her uncle Raymond. She said she had not really known him. But had she been telling the truth? Had he hurt her? Like he had hurt those other women?

Whatever the reason, she was not going to tell him. It was up to him to find out.

He had tried to force himself to let go and get on with his life, but he couldn't. And he was actually glad he hadn't just walked away and ignored his gut feeling. He was glad he had gone through the archives that day. That he had followed Kate back to the house in Ashbrooke.

And now, he was glad he was here tonight. Rosie hadn't

been able to tell him the truth, so he would find out for himself.

Then perhaps they could be together.

For he was convinced that was what they both wanted.

Something told him that Rosie had been instrumental in getting Kate off the streets, but he had no idea how. Nor how she was connected to the Maison Nouvelle, or the house on West Lawn.

Which was why he was here now, waiting on the corner of this street.

He had no idea what he was expecting to find out – perhaps nothing.

As DS Miller started walking up the road without the aid of a torch, he could barely make out where he was going, but the advantage was that he could easily see someone else who was using one. Natural darkness was perfect for covert work, as was his dark three-piece suit and overcoat.

As he turned the street corner, he slowed down and stopped. It was a few minutes before seven – if his guess was right, he wouldn't have to wait long. The streets were empty. Anyone with any sense would be at home, in front of a warm fire, or in their local, supping a pint with their mates.

A few minutes passed and then he saw a weak tunnel of yellow light shining down on the pavement. It swung from left to right as the person holding the torch walked briskly along the street. Hearing the faint click-clack of heeled shoes, DS Miller knew it was a woman. As the sound grew louder, DS Miller dropped behind a lamp post that had not been lit since the start of this war. He took shallow breaths so as not to give away his presence by creating a cold mist of air, not that the woman who had now turned on to West Lawn would have noticed. She was in a hurry and seemed set on her destination, keeping her head down, and her eyes glued to the pathway the light from the torch was creating.

As the woman turned to open the little gate, DS Miller caught her profile.

And as he did so, his heart seemed to slow and thud heavily, resounding in his ears, making him feel a little queasy.

His suspicions were right. He knew the woman's face. Had looked at it many times over countless cups of tea.

Had imagined it at night when he'd lain in bed and thought about her.

It was Rosie.

As Rosie shut the little wooden gate behind her and hurried up the narrow gravel pathway of the bordello that was speckled with leaves, proving that autumn was well under way, she had no idea she was being watched.

As she turned off her torch, and started rummaging around in her handbag for the key to the front door, her mind was full to the brim of thoughts about weddings, divorces – and now christenings, thanks to Dorothy's insistence that baby Hope be baptised 'as soon as possible'.

How strange, she thought, that all these beginnings and endings and celebrations of love and life were happening at more or less the same time.

Rosie skipped up the half-dozen steps which led to the black gloss front door and continued the fruitless search for her keys. Realising that she must have left them back at her flat, Rosie reached for the large brass knocker and gave the cursory three loud knocks that signalled it was friend rather than foe who wanted to be let in. She would have done the same had she entered the property from the back, although the rear entrance had the added benefit of a spy-hole to double-check the validity of the visitor.

A few seconds later, Rosie heard the loud, sing-song 'Comiiinnnng'. It was Lily and she sounded in high spirits. Had indeed been in high spirits since the arrival of Maisie.

'I'm guessing that's you, Rosie?' she sang through the door.

'Yes, Lily, it's me, now open the door, it's freezing out here,' Rosie replied, moving from one foot to the other to keep herself warm.

The large door swung open and the yellow light of the hallway shone out, illuminating the women as they embraced and gave each other the usual pecks on both cheeks.

As Rosie stepped across the threshold she eyed Lily's newly dyed hair, which was now more orange than auburn.

'I'm surprised you let Vivian loose on your hair!' Rosie said incredulously. Vivian was branching out and was now not just cutting the girls' hair, but also colouring it.

Watching Lily shut the door and put the safety catch on, Rosie couldn't help but think that it was just typical that Lily was looking even more eccentric than usual at a time when she would have preferred her to have looked a little more normal – even if it was just until after the wedding.

Rosie had thought long and hard about inviting Lily to Bel and Joe's wedding. She had still been umming and ahing until George had come up with the idea of offering the use of his MG in place of hiring a wedding car, something he knew the happy couple would not have the budget for. As George had also suggested he take on the role of chauffeur for the day, it had left Rosie without much of an option other than to invite Lily as her 'plus one'.

With all the talk about the wedding, and the incessant chatter between Dorothy and Angie debating who they should invite, Rosie had fought hard to stop thoughts of Peter forcing their way into her mind, but still the devil inside had teased her with images of what it would be like to have Peter by her side for the day – and the night.

After her final meeting with the detective, she had cried herself to sleep, but after that, she had resolved – no more. No more. It was time to move on. Get on with life. She had forced the shutters down. But now, with all this talk about love and romance, it was like they were being levered open again.

'Come into the back parlour,' Lily enticed Rosie. 'The bookkeeping can wait for the time being.'

Following Lily into the large scullery she walked into a hub of excited chit-chat: Maisie stood with her back to the Aga, and Vivian was positioned behind Kate, who was sitting ramrod straight on the kitchen chair. Vivian's hands were busy curling Kate's hair into small rolls and carefully pinning them into place.

Rosie looked at the three women and then across to Lily who had gone over to the large wooden kitchen table and was pouring two cups of tea out for them both.

'I think Vivian here is going to leave us and start work as a hairdresser,' Rosie said mischievously.

Vivian let out a loud, gusty laugh, as she picked up the lacquer and sprayed vigorously around Kate's head, causing her to cover her mouth and suppress a cough.

'You've got to be joking,' Vivian said, smiling across at Rosie. 'Not unless I want to be a pauper all my life! I'm quite happy here thank you very much – earning the money I do.'

Vivian put her hands on Kate's slender shoulders. 'Not like this one here, who would work for next to nothing as long as it meant she had a bit of fabric and a needle and thread to hand.'

Rosie looked at Kate as she blushed; something she always did when the attention was on her, no matter how briefly.

'So, Kate, how's *the* dress coming along?' Rosie asked as she sat down with Lily and pulled her cup of steaming tea towards her. There was no need to say whose dress – there was only one dress at this moment in time that was of any importance.

'Oh,' Kate said, putting her hand up nervously to her hair, which had now been successfully piled on top of her head. 'It's coming along really nicely . . . Well,' she added, nervously, 'I think so . . . I just hope Bel thinks so too when she sees it at the next fitting.'

'Oh, there's no question she's going to adore it.' Maisie moved from the warmth of the Aga and sat down at the head of the kitchen table. 'She's lucky to have you making her such a fantastic dress – in fact she's very lucky to have all her family and friends around her, making her wedding so special.'

Rosie looked at Maisie and wondered if she had been to see *her* family – the family she had claimed were the main reason for coming up north. She was sceptical. Rosie, like Lily, had her doubts about the veracity of Maisie's claims to have relatives up here. Both women had agreed that they were more inclined to surmise that Maisie had wanted to leave London for reasons other than seeking out her kin.

'Oh, I do like a good wedding,' Vivian chirped up, sashaying around Kate and inspecting her workmanship.

'Now, don't forget, Rosie,' she added, 'next time you see Polly or Bel, tell them I'd be more than happy to do Bel's hair for her if she wants. I can come to the shop when she's getting ready and do it. And I won't charge a penny.'

Lily laughed before taking a sip of her tea. '*Ma chère*, you are *so* transparent. One free hairdo does not earn you a ticket to the ball you know?'

Vivian haughtily turned her heavily made-up face, complete with large fake eyelashes and a cherry red pout, away from Lily and focused on Rosie. Looking like butter wouldn't melt, she said, 'And, Rosie, you must not forget that if Lily here can't accompany you to the ball, for whatever reason, I will be more than willing to step in for her – at a moment's notice.'

Rosie smiled and shook her head from side to side. 'Honestly, I feel like I'm in a real-life version of *Cinderella*. If you weren't so gorgeous, Vivian, I'd say you fitted the part of one of the Ugly Sisters perfectly.'

They all looked at Kate, who, it was obvious, would have made the perfect Cinders.

Speaking their thoughts, Maisie chirped up.

'And, Kate, pray tell us, what are you going to wear for the ball? As the chief seamstress I'm guessing that you *have* been invited?'

Kate nodded.

'And wouldn't you know it,' Vivian butted in, 'but Fairy Godmother Lily here has given Kate one of her designer dresses from her younger days to tinker with.'

Everyone looked at Lily, who nodded. And by the smile on her face she clearly had no objections to being assigned the role of the good angel.

Maisie pushed a cigarette into the long ebony holder that had become her trademark. She was just about to light it, but asked first, 'And the mother of the bride? Has she a dress to go to the ball?'

Kate blushed again. 'Well, I'm doing a few alterations for her.'

'I'd say our Kate here is doing far more than a few alterations,' Vivian blustered. 'When I popped into the shop the

239

other day, I copped a look at the most wonderful "mother of the bride" dress I've ever seen.'

'Who is the mother of the bride, again?' Maisie asked.

'Pearl,' Kate said.

'Well, *Pearl* is one very lucky woman,' said Maisie. 'Not only is her daughter marrying a war hero – a daughter who also has what some would see as the encumbrance of a young child – but she is also having a specially designed dress for the occasion . . . in times when we're all doing a Scarlett O'Hara and having to make clothes out of old curtains!'

Rosie looked at Maisie. Her velvet voice was complemented by the most beguiling smile, yet she had managed to ever so subtly demean both Bel and Pearl in the same breath. By intimating first of all that Bel had done well for herself in finding another husband in spite of having a child in tow, and then that Pearl was equally fortunate in having her own personal dressmaker to hand. Was there a touch of jealousy there?

No one really knew much at all about Maisie's personal circumstances, about her own parentage, or even if she had any siblings. Lily's 'new girl' kept quite a closed shop. Naturally, there had been idle chatter amongst the rest of the girls about Maisie – and her life before she came to Lily's. And, of course, they were all more than curious about her ancestry. But no one, so far, had felt it appropriate to ask her outright.

Lily had confided in Rosie the little she knew about Maisie – that her mother had been fair-skinned and that her father's lineage was South African, although they were both from America and had emigrated to England at the beginning of the century and settled in London. Lily had intimated that her family had been quite well off, which Rosie thought seemed to fit with Maisie's soft hands and more educated way of speaking. But that was about all Lily had managed to glean about Maisie's past, and she had confessed to Rosie that she was curious herself as to how Maisie had drifted into her chosen line of work.

'Ah, George,' Maisie's voice lifted in genuine pleasure as the door to the kitchen swung open. Rosie turned to see George hobble into the room, his walking stick clattering against the doorway. He looked like he was in a rush.

'Good evening, ladies.' George doffed an imaginary hat.

'If you're after the Chablis or Rémy, it's in the larder – top shelf,' Lily instructed.

'No, my dear, I'm afraid I'm after Maisie, if you ladies can spare her, please?' He took a deep breath, then went on. 'We have some potential members of the Gentlemen's Club in reception and I wanted Maisie to show them around next door, give them a guided tour of the place . . . and describe to them what it'll be like when we're ready to open.'

Maisie stood up, put her cigarette holder down in the cut-crystal ashtray in the middle of the table and straightened out her cream embroidered silk evening dress. She needn't have worried about creases, for even if there were any, Maisie had the ability to carry off any slight imperfections, with her gracefulness and faultless femininity.

'D'accord, mon cher,' Lily said, putting her teacup down, 'business before pleasure. Always.'

'Oh George,' Rosie said as he turned to leave, 'you won't forget about your appointment tomorrow with Gloria, will you? I've given her the morning off. I think she's a little apprehensive about it all.'

George lifted his stick in the air as if it were almost an extension of his arm and nodded his head energetically. 'Of course, my dear. It has not been forgotten. I will be there and will endeavour to do my best to make the whole process as easy and as painless as possible.'

Rosie caught Vivian and Maisie giving each other a questioning look, but both knew not to probe about the mystery appointment. Rosie was always friendly with all the girls, but she kept her distance as well. Like Maisie, she had never really disclosed anything too personal about herself to the girls at the bordello, nor did she talk much about her women welders at the yard.

As George and Maisie left the room, Rosie poured another cup of tea.

'None for me, *ma chère*,' Lily said, tottering over to the larder and retrieving the brandy. 'I think I'll just have a little tipple to set me up for the evening. Anyone care to join me?'

The question was really just a courtesy, as Lily knew Rosie would be itching to get back to her beloved books and ledger, and Vivian would be due to start work soon and rarely allowed herself a drink until later on in the evening.

And Kate, she was sure, wouldn't have as much as a drop of any kind of alcohol. Nor would Lily allow her. The first week she had come to live with them, after Rosie had found her begging in town, she had gone through the most awful withdrawal, complete with sweats, nausea and the tremors. Lily had seen it before in her long and varied life and had done what she could to help. Thankfully her new charge had been more resilient than she looked and had come through to the other side in one piece.

'I'm going to get on with Pearl's dress,' Kate said, standing up and self-consciously touching her hair. Rosie and Lily knew that as soon as she got to her own room on the third floor, the first thing she would do would be to release her tresses from the confines of Vivian's hairpins.

'Yes, and I've got the brigadier in soon, so I better shake a leg,' Vivian said.

After they both left, Rosie and Lily sat in comfortable silence for a few minutes, before Lily broached the subject of DS Miller.

'So, that's it with your detective then?' she asked warily. 'No more rendezvous or tea and cake dates?' She took a sip of the Rémy Martin.

'Goodness, Lily, absolutely not, he's a distant memory now. I've almost forgotten who he is,' Rosie said, pushing her chair out and getting ready to go back to her office.

Lily looked at Rosie and knew she might be telling the truth about not seeing the copper any more, but she was lying through her teeth when it came to claiming he was a 'distant memory'. All this excitement about the wedding must be pulling at her heartstrings.

Unlike Maisie and Vivian, who appeared all sweetness and light on the outside but were actually as hard as nails on the inside, Rosie was the reverse. She gave a good impression of being a steely, no-nonsense woman, but inside she had a soft centre and Lily knew it had hurt her terribly to end her love affair.

'All right,' Lily said, turning to watch Rosie leave the parlour, 'I'll be in to see you later to talk through all the *boring* financial details about this new Gentlemen's Club. The official paperwork has come through from the Corporation allowing us to use next door as a place of business, although they have made a few stipulations about noise and the like.'

Rosie nodded as she left, but she wasn't really listening. Her thoughts had been dragged like a magnet back to Peter. She wished Lily hadn't mentioned him. She was trying hard to forget about him, to keep the shutters well and truly closed. On the whole, she was succeeding, especially as she was so busy, but sometimes, like now, when his name cropped up or thoughts of him crept through her defences, then it was as if a dark cloak enfolded her and she was suddenly weighed down with a heavy sadness and a feeling of being totally bereft.

She missed him. Really missed him.

And it was that which made her heart ache the most.

As DS Miller sat crushed up in the small police cabin near to the Sea Lock along the south dock, he tried to look interested in what the two other police officers were saying – that there had just been a shipment of beef and lamb carcasses into the docks and there'd been whisperings that a known gang was going to try and steal them. He hated to admit it to himself, but his heart just wasn't in this particular potential collar. His lack of enthusiasm perturbed him. He had always been so passionate about his job. Had been driven by a need for justice for as long as he could remember – and for once the law was coming down hard on these black marketeers who were raiding supply depots and docks up and down the country for precious produce; there had even been talk of increasing the maximum jail sentence from two to five years, as well as heftier fines for those caught dealing in illicit goods. All of this should have been music to DS Miller's ears – after all, he was always lamenting the numerous loopholes in the law which allowed too many villains to get off scot-free.

Tonight, though, his mind wasn't focused on getting the bad guys, but on solving the mystery that was Rosie, especially after everything he had seen this evening.

His instinct had been right. Rosie was somehow connected to the Ashbrooke house.

He might have put her visit tonight down to her simply visiting her friend Kate, had he not seen the very eccentric-looking woman who had opened the door to Rosie and embraced her. He wasn't sure if it was the effect of the light, but it looked like she had orange hair. It was all very odd.

But what troubled him the most – and try as he might he hadn't been able to shrug it off – was the feeling that there was something dodgy about the house.

And then a half hour later three men, all old enough to have seen a good few years' service in the First War, came out of the house, accompanied by a stunning dark-skinned woman, who certainly didn't look like she came from these parts. The four of them had walked down the garden path, turned left and then let themselves in to the house next door.

He'd waited until nine o'clock but Rosie had not come out again and he had been forced to leave his spot under the lamp post to come back to the docks and start the graveyard shift.

'Who wants to patrol up the south pier?' Arnold, one of the older detectives, asked.

'That'll be me.' DS Miller couldn't volunteer quick enough. 'I need to wake up and stretch my legs.' Neither was true as he had been on his feet and out in the cold all day, but he needed to let his mind sort through what he had learnt tonight.

DS Miller knotted his muffler round his neck, pulled his overcoat off the back of the door and headed out of the cabin.

As he walked in the pitch black, following the curved outline of the quayside towards the harbour entrance, DS Miller's mind kept asking the same question:

Who was this woman who had captured his heart?

There was no doubt in his mind now that Rosie was harbouring a secret. Or *secrets*. Otherwise why hadn't she mentioned her friendship with Kate? Or her sister Charlotte? Or her parents' tragic death? Or her visits to the Ashbrooke house?

Whatever her secret was, every fibre of his being told him that the answer could be found in the unusual goings-on in the house in Ashbrooke.

So why did his heart feel heavy?

Up until tonight he had thought that once he had found out the real reason for Rosie's rebuttal, they would be able to talk about it, and start afresh.

Surely nothing could be that bad?

Or could it?

Chapter Twenty-Seven

Gourley & Sons, John Street, Sunderland

Friday 31 October 1941

The following morning, at ten minutes before nine o'clock, Gloria was waiting at the bottom of the stone steps leading up to Gourley & Sons, solicitors. The wide, cobbled street was lined with grand Georgian houses, most of which were inhabited by the town's shipyard owners and important Wearside businessmen and their families. Some, however, like Mr Gourley & Sons had converted the three-storey town houses into sumptuous offices. There was no mistaking that the street was the embodiment of middle-class respectability, which was exactly why Gloria was standing feeling terribly self-conscious and like a fish out of water.

It was now the back end of October and this morning was particularly bitter. Gloria was shuffling from one foot to the other and banging her gloved hands together partly to keep warm, but also because her nerves were making her feel jittery.

She had arrived early as she was worried about being late, but now regretted getting here quite so prematurely as she felt she was sticking out like a sore thumb. Everyone she had seen so far, mainly men, coming in and out of the various houses and offices, looked very dapper, verging on aristocratic. It was obvious by the looks she'd got from a few passers-by that they were wondering what on earth she was doing here.

With each minute, her resolve to be the strong and independent woman she was determined to be seemed to dwindle and dissolve. Talking about divorcing Vinnie and taking control of her own life was so much easier said than done – she was beginning to feel like just giving up now – and she hadn't as much as set foot inside the solicitor's office.

'Gloria!'

Gloria turned to see the man she guessed was George hurrying towards her. His gait was uneven due to his bad leg, but his speed was aided by an extremely ornate walking stick.

'At least . . . it is Gloria, I assume? Have you been waiting long?' As he spoke trails of vapour streamed from his mouth. 'Honestly, you should have gone in, you'll catch your death out here.'

Gloria smiled nervously. 'Ah, I don't feel the cold now – not after working in the shipyards for the past year.'

George could see that not only did Gloria look frozen to the bone, but she was also very nervous. He was glad Rosie had suggested he come along for moral support.

'Anyway,' he said, stretching out his hand, 'as I'm sure you've deduced, I'm Rosie's friend George. It's a pleasure to meet you, Gloria.'

Gloria took his hand. 'And you too, George.' She hesitated a moment before adding, 'And I have to say thank you so much for sorting this out for me – and for taking the time out to come here today.'

George waved his hand as if to dismiss Gloria's comments. 'Not at all, you've done me a favour. I haven't seen old Rupert for ages. It'll give us a chance to catch up over a little snifter after you've had your appointment with him.'

He turned to the steps, and said, 'Let's get in there then, before we both freeze to death.' And like a true gentleman, he extended his arm to allow Gloria to take the lead and walk ahead of him up the steps.

Gloria hesitated for a second. She was not used to being treated so courteously. It had been a long time since a man had been so chivalrous with her. She was more used to being pushed and shoved in a scrum of burly men all determined to get to the yard gates in time for the half-seven blower, than being treated like the woman she was.

'So,' Rupert explained, leaning forward across his solid mahogany desk, an action which was hindered by his quite substantial belly, 'without wanting to sound in any way flippant, there has never been a better time to get divorced. If you had been sitting here four years ago, we would be having a very different conversation and you would be looking at a far more difficult and complicated scenario . . . I won't, however,' he added, taking a sip of water from a glass on his desk, ' . . . bore you with all the ins and outs of the history of legislation regarding the ending of a marriage.'

Gloria nodded even though she was not really taking on board much of what Rupert was telling her.

'So,' he continued, 'to keep my waffling short and to the point, there was a change in the law in 1937, which was about time as the law regarding divorce hadn't really changed much since 1857.' He chuckled and opened up a wooden box of cigars. Picking one out, he continued.

'So, Gloria, the way the law stands at the moment in this country, you can divorce your husband on any of the following grounds . . . ' He smelt the cigar, and continued: 'Adultery – cruelty – incurable insanity – and desertion – although this would have to be for a period of at least three years. These are termed "matrimonial offences".'

'Well,' Gloria said, 'I could tick three out of the four boxes.'

Rupert let out a deep laugh. He liked this woman's feistiness and sense of humour.

'Of course, we could always see if we could get him committed to the local madhouse,' he chuckled. George had given him the low-down on this woman's husband and by the sounds of it he deserved to be strapped up in a straitjacket, if it were only to force him to keep his hands to himself.

'But failing that –' he puffed on his cigar and the room was immediately filled with a sweet, oaky aroma '– we would be looking at petitioning for a divorce on the grounds of either adultery or cruelty.

'This means, however, that we would have to have proof of either said adultery or cruelty.'

Rupert cast a glance at his old friend, George, who had been sitting quietly in a chair next to Gloria.

'Well,' George coughed nervously, 'I'm sorry to have to bring this up, Gloria,' he looked back at Rupert, 'but as I have mentioned to you before, Rups, and it pains me to say such an awful thing, but the man was far from averse to using his fists on Gloria – and on a fairly frequent basis, I hasten to add.'

Gloria felt herself go bright red. Even now the shame of what Vinnie had done to her was still there, right at the surface.

Rupert waited a moment, before saying, 'I'm afraid it pains me even more, though, to say that the law is far from sympathetic when it comes to spousal abuse of any description. For our purposes we would need medical reports on any harm inflicted, or a report from the local constabulary which would prove the actions of this despicable man . . . And, I'm assuming that, as in the case of most women who have found themselves in this position, such physical violence has not been documented in any form.'

Gloria nodded in agreement.

'So,' Rupert continued, 'if you don't mind, Gloria, would you tell me a little more about your circumstances – and in particular, about your husband's adultery?'

'Well, my husband has been living with his mistress now for over nine months. Since the day he left the family home,' Gloria admitted.

Rupert's face immediately lit up and he took another puff on his cigar.

'Excellent!' The word was emitted with a swirl of grey smoke. 'Then this should be a lot easier than I had first thought . . . '

Over the next half hour or so Gloria remembered why she had never really liked school, and why she enjoyed working outdoors, even if the weather was arctic. Despite making a good show of looking like she was taking in what Rupert was saying, and nodding in what she hoped were the right places, the solicitor's words about 'decrees nisi' and 'absolute' went over her head.

The only bits she took notice of were when it came to discussing financial arrangements between her and Vinnie, to which Gloria said outright that she did not want a penny from her estranged husband, and that even if she did, there wouldn't be a cat in hell's chance of getting anything, as any money Vinnie had always ended up being poured down his neck.

When Rupert had gone on to talk about Hope, Gloria was all ears.

'Thankfully, any issues relating to your child will not form part of the divorce proceedings,' Rupert explained. 'If, by chance, there were any kind of disagreement over you having sole care and custody of your daughter, then that would be dealt with separately.'

Gloria had never considered that Vinnie would want to have Hope. He might want to see her, and occasionally play the role of doting dad, but have responsibility for her? No. He wouldn't. Would he?

'So,' Rupert said, 'I think that will do for today . . .'

Gloria straightened herself in her chair. The open fire in the room had made her feel a little sleepy.

'I'm not sure exactly how this works,' she said, uncertainly. She was clutching her handbag, in which she had all her savings, should they need the payment in full up front.

'But do I pay you now, or . . . ?'

'No, no, my dear,' Rupert said, balancing his half-smoked cigar on the side of the glass ashtray on his desk.

'Sorry, Gloria,' George interrupted. 'I should have explained earlier.' He turned on his chair so he was looking at her. 'You won't be needing to pay anything. I should have said before. This is on Lily and me.'

Gloria looked at George, not quite understanding what he was saying.

'You're not paying a penny for this wretched divorce,' George explained. 'I'll be sorting the money side of things out with Rupert here, who owes me more than a few favours anyway.'

'Oh, George, no,' Gloria interrupted, her pride bristling at the suggestion, 'I can't have you and Lily paying for all this. I just can't. It's as simple as that.'

George laughed, and took Gloria's hand, which was still clutching her handbag that had been sitting in her lap the whole time.

'My dear, I hate to say this, but this is one battle you *are* going to lose. And that is the end of the matter.'

But Gloria was insistent. 'George, I can afford this, I

have the money, here,' she said, lifting her bag up to show she meant what she said.

'Well, that may well be,' George said, looking a little incredulously at the bag and realising why Gloria had been holding on to it as if her life depended on it, 'but it makes no odds. I will be settling up with Rupert here when the time comes and you are no longer bound by matrimony to your husband ... And,' he said, looking over to his old school chum, before turning his attention back to Gloria and dropping his voice as he spoke.

'This is Lily's and my way of saying "thank you" for helping Rosie out when she really needed it.'

He leant forward and rested his hand on the ivory hand-carved handle of his walking stick.

'If it hadn't been for you and the rest of your gang, Lily and I would be without someone who is so very dear to us, and who we love very much. No amount of money could have made up for that.'

George and Lily had always felt indebted – and incredibly thankful – to Rosie's squad of women welders. If they had not gone back to find their boss that night, and saved her from her uncle's murderous intentions, there was no doubting that the woman George and Lily loved like a daughter would not still be with them now.

Gloria saw that George meant every word he said, and that just the thought of what had happened to Rosie that night had caused tears to well in his eyes. 'It is Lily and I,' he said, *who owe you.'*

'So,' George said, his voice returning to its normal volume, 'I'm not going to enter into any more of a discussion with you.'

Gloria smiled at George. Never before had she received such kindness or generosity. And she knew there was no point arguing. George and Lily had made their minds up.

'And, if I were you,' he added as they both stood up to leave, 'I'd jolly well get those savings in a bank *tout suite* – to borrow one of Lily's well-worn phrases. It makes me ill just thinking of you walking around with all your hard-earned money in your bag.'

Gloria laughed. George's accent reminded her of how male actors talked in the films that Dorothy was always trying to drag them all off to see.

'I think that's a good idea, George. I shall go right there now . . . And,' she added, *'thank you.'*

Rupert managed to lift his immense bulk on to his feet and lean over to shake Gloria's hand.

'So, I'll sort out all the nitty-gritty, as it were, but, as I said, unfortunately these things do take time, several months I'm afraid – but we will get there – and I'll be see-ing you in the interim to sign those forms we talked about.'

Gloria shook hands with both men and left the room. As she walked down the steps, she felt quite overwhelmed. The past hour had drained her more than an entire day welding. Her head was full to bursting. She knew her divorce would bring with it a real stigma and she would be wearing the label of a 'divorcee' for the rest of her life, but as she turned the corner to walk along Toward Road, she realised that she really didn't give a fig. She had taken the first step, and it had felt like a humongous step at that. She had put her words into action and she had seen the lawyer. The ball was rolling. She had done it. For the first time in a long time she felt proud of herself.

As she walked round to Fawcett Street and up towards Lloyds Bank, she knew it was time for her second step.

It was time for her to get a bank account.

Chapter Twenty-Eight

'Yay! She's back!' Dorothy pushed her helmet back and stood up so quickly that she bashed into the back of Martha, who, of course, didn't budge an inch. They were with *Brutus* again, helping the riveters to flesh out her huge metal ribs with sheets of metal.

On seeing Gloria, the rest of the women welders all stopped what they were doing to greet their workmate. They knew she had been really nervous about her meeting with the solicitor that morning.

'How'd it go?' Dorothy had to practically shout to be heard above the sound of the drillers working nearby. Rosie pointed at an imaginary watch on her wrist and then put up both hands to signify ten minutes to go before lunch.

Knowing chatter would have been fruitless due to the noise, they all went back to work, but as soon as the horn sounded out their break for lunch, they were quick to down tools in their eagerness to hear how Gloria's important appointment had gone.

After they clambered their way out of the dry basin, they hurried across the yard to the canteen. Today it was too cold to eat outside and the skies had darkened over the course of the morning and rain had begun to spit down. Once in the warmth of the canteen, Gloria gave them a brief résumé of what Rupert had told her, which was short and to the point as much of what had been said had gone over her head. All Gloria really knew was that the process of divorcing Vinnie had now begun.

'Well done, Gloria!' Rosie said, as they joined the queue. 'It must have been really nerve-racking. I find those kinds of places really intimidating.'

Gloria agreed, but knew it was highly unlikely Rosie would feel belittled in such circumstances. Her boss had seen and experienced all levels of society, from the top to the bottom, and she doubted she would have been unnerved by a visit to a lawyer.

As they reached the front of the queue, Dorothy couldn't wait to ask the question that she and Angie had been dying to ask.

'And George? What was George like?' she asked as she sidled up to Gloria. Angie managed to push her way in front of Martha, who didn't seem to mind.

'You lot all want pies and peas?' Muriel the dinner lady interrupted. ''Cause there's nowt else on offer if you don't,' she cackled.

'Not that there ever is!' Angie snapped back. She didn't like Muriel. Angie knew Muriel, who lived down the road from her and was known as a real gossip – a 'right stirrer' was how her ma described her, 'always sticking her nose in other folk's business'.

After they had all been served, paid their dues, and sat down at their table, Dorothy asked again, 'So then? George? What was he like?'

'Well, you all might find out for yourselves soon,' Polly butted in, sensing Gloria's discomfort, and taking a big bite of her mince and onion pie.

'Have I missed anything?' Hannah's voice sang out behind them as she arrived at the table, squashing herself between Martha and Polly. Martha checked if Hannah had anyone with her and on seeing that Olly was nowhere in sight, allowed herself a self-satisfied smile; she put her thick arm around her little friend and gave her a squeeze.

'Well,' Polly explained to five enrapt faces, 'George's lovely little MG is going to be the wedding car – and George is going to be chauffeur for the day.'

Dorothy and Angie squealed with excitement, causing the table of older men next to them to turn their heads and look.

Rosie had to purse her lips so as not to laugh. This wedding was going to be quite a day. From what Polly had told her, Bel and Joe had wanted it to be a small affair, but Pearl had commandeered the use of the pub for the reception. All of a sudden there was room for many more guests, and the invitation list had grown to fill the space.

As the women started to chatter about the wedding, Rosie felt a jab of anxiety that it would be the first time her two normally very separate worlds would merge. A part of her was apprehensive – the other pleased. It was certainly something she'd never thought would ever happen. But these were times of change. You just needed to look at Gloria; or at all the women, for that matter. They had all changed.

'Oh,' Rosie chirped up, 'and I forgot to tell you.' A mischievous twinkle had come into her eyes. 'You'll also get to meet my friend Lily. She's going to be my guest for the wedding.'

Dorothy and Angie looked as if they were going to explode with excitement. They stared speechless at each other. Eyes on stalks.

'Ohh, this just gets better and better!' Dorothy exclaimed.

Rosie looked down at Dorothy's untouched pie. 'Well, you *better* get some food down you or you'll not have the energy for any wedding, never mind any welding.'

'Anyway,' Polly looked at Dorothy and Angie, 'you two, you haven't told us much about who you're bringing along?'

'We're not sure,' Angie answered, as Dorothy now had a mouthful of pie and could only mumble.

'We did have a couple of blokes in mind, but then you told us that Joe's got some of his Home Guard brigade coming along and there's a couple of farmers from out Hetton-le-Hole way going . . . So, we might just come our two selves.'

Polly rolled her eyes and Martha chuckled.

'And how's your mother coping with all the organisation?' Hannah asked. 'I know my mama would be . . . what is the word? Frantic . . . That's it. She would be quite frantic about preparing her child's wedding.'

'*Frantic*, Hannah, is spot on,' Polly said. 'Ma's running round like a headless chicken. But she's a happy headless chicken. And, of course, Lucille is getting more excited by the day. Even the two dogs seem to be getting under everyone's feet more than usual.'

Hannah sighed. 'It sounds wonderful.'

Martha looked at Hannah's sad face and gave her friend another surprisingly gentle hug; they all knew Hannah would give anything to be in the warm, hectic hub of her own family, but that she now knew with increasing certainty, due to the news reports being drip-fed to the nation, that the situation with the Jews in Europe – and now in Russia – was going from bad to worse.

'And,' Dorothy forced down the last of her pie, 'what about the honeymoon? Have they got anything planned?'

'Ah, funny you should ask,' Polly said a little mysteriously, 'but I've got something up my sleeve for them . . . I'm hoping to get them a suite in the Grand for the night.'

'Wow!' Angie looked as if she thought Polly had said she was going to send the couple to the moon and back. 'That's amazing!'

'It will be, if I can get it sorted,' Polly said.

As they all stacked up their plates and cutlery and made to leave their table, Rosie suddenly butted in. 'I keep forgetting to say to you, Polly, but one of the girls, Vivian her name is, well, she's a dab hand at hairdressing. She's offered to do Bel's hair, but please don't feel you have to invite her to the wedding if you take her up on the offer.'

Polly told Rosie to thank Vivian for the kind offer and that she would relay the message to Bel.

As they walked out of the canteen, Rosie looked up at the administration office and caught sight of Helen, her jet black hair wavy and loose, walking away from the window. Rosie automatically looked at Gloria, who thankfully hadn't noticed that their nemesis was back. Her return was a reminder that Miriam had got her own way. Helen was back doing Jack's job which had only been meant to be temporary until his return. Jack had now clearly been sent to work at Crown's.

As the women slowly made their way back to the dry dock, Dorothy sidled up to Gloria. 'How you feeling about Jack?' she asked quietly.

'Honestly?' Gloria asked. There was no sharpness in her voice, but there was an overriding sense of despair.

'Honestly,' Dorothy repeated, looking at her friend's face and seeing a real sadness there.

'I really don't know any more,' Gloria said, forcing a smile. 'I really don't know . . . '

'Well,' Dorothy said, lifting her voice and giving Gloria's arm a reassuring squeeze, 'don't you think that just because everyone's wrapped up in this wedding malarkey that I've forgotten about little Hope's christening. Because I haven't!'

Gloria smiled. This time it was genuine.

'Eee, I don't know, Dorothy. Yer never give up, do ya? When am I gonna get time to even think about it, never mind organise it – as if working here, looking after a two-month-old baby, and sorting out a divorce, aren't enough to cope with!' she exclaimed in mock exasperation.

'But,' she added, giving Dorothy a friendly nudge as they reached their work area, 'if I do somehow miraculously find the time to sort it, then don't *you* forget about that "great big cake" you promised me.'

Dorothy's face broke into a wide smile.

'At last! A glimmer of hope.'

Chapter Twenty-Nine

'So, I'll bet Isabelle and Pearl are getting quite excited about the big day?' Maisie quizzed Kate. The two women were seated in Kate's bedroom-cum-dressmaker's-studio on the third floor at Lily's. The room was surprisingly big considering it was an attic room; even the low slanted ceiling was actually quite high, and Kate had made sure she had utilised every square inch of the room. A mass of fabrics lay around on the floor, designs were pinned to the walls, and baskets overflowed with a bounty of different coloured threads and ribbons. In the midst of it all was a small table, on top of which was Lily's donated black and gold Singer, a dressmaker's dummy, and, of course, Kate's bed.

Kate had felt like she had won the pools when she'd been taken in by Lily. She still had to pinch herself every now and again to check that this was real, and often when she woke during the night she had a moment's panic that she was back on the streets, until she felt the softness of the feather down pillow under her head. Despite what the nuns at Nazareth House had put her through, Kate still believed in God, and every morning she woke and found herself in this room she offered up a prayer of thanks.

'I think Bel likes to be called Bel, not Isabelle,' Kate said quietly, 'only her ma calls her Isabelle.'

Maisie shifted a little uncomfortably on Kate's lumpy

mattress and started picking out bits of ribbon from a basket next to the bed.

'Oh, does she now? That's nice. They must be close, the two of them?' she probed.

'Mmm,' Kate was non-committal in her answer. She was not one for gossip and besides she felt a strange kind of loyalty to Pearl. She didn't feel it was right to start and tell a complete stranger the ins and outs of their mother–daughter relationship, especially as Bel and Pearl were about as far from 'close' as you could get, and there was most definitely a love–hate relationship going on between the pair of them, with a rather larger dose of 'hate' than 'love'.

'Well, that's the way it should be on a girl's wedding day, isn't it?' Maisie persevered. 'Mother and daughter enjoying the excitement of dresses, and planning and organising and chatting about it all until the cows come home. Vivian says they even live in the same house in the east end! Sounds very cosy. What do they call families like that – close-knit?'

Kate didn't answer so Maisie continued.

'The only person who seems to be missing is Isabelle's father. Is Pearl a war widow? I've not heard a peep about him. Surely Isabelle would want her father to give her away?'

'I don't think her da's about,' Kate said. 'Not heard anyone mention him anyway.'

Maisie stood up and peered over Kate's shoulder as she inspected a line of stitching on the fascinator she was making for Bel.

'Oh Kate,' Maisie said, 'you really are something special, you know? That is just so beautiful.'

Kate's chest puffed out a little with pride. The fascinator was a new venture for her and she had tried to make it different by using a rather eclectic mix of beads, crystals, feathers, and there was even a touch of velvet on it.

'I'm guessing this is in place of the veil?' Maisie said, bending over and gently touching the ostrich feather in the centre of the headpiece.

Kate had to stop herself from slapping Maisie's hand. She wished she would go now. Wasn't sure why she had come up in the first place. Usually she was left in peace when she was up here. Only Vivian and Lily really bothered her, and then only when they were desperate for something to be repaired, or to show her a design they'd fallen in love with.

'Was there anything in particular you were after, Maisie?' Kate said, trying not to sound like she wanted rid of her. She was never impolite to anyone under Lily's roof, but she struggled with Maisie. She had never really taken to her from when she'd first arrived.

'Actually, there was, but there's no rush, it was just something I wondered whether you could run up for me – once all this wedding's out of the way, of course.'

Maisie dug into the pocket of her cashmere cardigan and pulled out a creased-up page from a magazine. She unfolded it to show Kate the dress she wanted her to replicate.

'I'll pay you, of course,' she said.

Katie took the picture and scrutinised it. 'This is actually quite a straightforward design. It's quite twenties with its dropped waist,' she mused.

'I'll leave you in peace, then,' Maisie said, getting up and stepping across pieces of tweed, silk and cotton to get to the open doorway. 'And thanks, you know,' she paused, 'for the chat. And for agreeing to make my dress.'

As soon as Maisie had gone, Kate got back to work. She still had lots to do and the wedding was now only four days away. She would probably be up most of the night finishing this fascinator, but it was going to be worth it.

'Oh, Rosie,' Maisie said, 'you're here late.'

Rosie was coming out of the front office and was putting on her coat ready to go home. She had heard Maisie come down from the third floor.

'You been to see Kate?' she asked.

'Yes . . . you know . . . the usual beg for her skills,' Maisie smiled. 'But not until after the wedding, of course,' she added.

Rosie looked into Maisie's incredible hazel and brown speckled eyes. Her words seemed true and her voice sounded genuine but her eyes told another story. Why did Rosie always feel a little uncomfortable around her? It was as if she didn't quite trust her and she had no idea why she felt like that. After all, Maisie seemed nice enough. And she was certainly working all hours to get the Gentlemen's Club up and running.

'I think there's going to be a bit of a backlog for Kate after the wedding's been and gone. I think she's going to need an extra pair of hands,' Rosie said. She felt compelled to return Maisie's friendliness; besides which, Lily hadn't said as much, but she knew it was important they both got on. Maisie would be managing the club and Rosie the bordello and there might well be a few crossovers.

'Ah, well I'd best get off home. I don't know where the time goes,' Rosie said, turning to undo the latch on the front door.

'I'll lock up behind you,' Maisie said, walking over to the thick wooden front door, now ajar. Maisie wasn't wearing her usual heels, but was barefoot and Rosie suddenly realised just how small she was. Under the bright hallway light Rosie also noticed how much light-coloured foundation and powder Maisie used.

'Thanks,' Rosie said, stepping outside into the cold, dark night, 'see you tomorrow.'

'*Bonne nuit*,' Maisie said with a chuckle. Rosie forced a laugh out as she made her way down the steps.

'Lily will be pleased!' she shouted back over her shoulder. 'She'll have you fluent before you know it.'

As Rosie pulled out her small torch and started walking down the road, she chided herself. Maisie seemed like a lovely person, so then, why did she feel so uneasy around her?

As Maisie perched on the little wooden stool in front of her dresser, and carefully wiped her make-up off with a damp ball of cotton wool, she slowly revealed the natural brown colouring of her skin. Maisie had spent a lot of money on cosmetics over the years trying to make her skin as pale as possible. Now she had got her mix of foundations and powders down to an art and knew what she could get away with. She knew how light she could go without it looking obvious.

But it didn't matter how skilful a beautician she was, she knew she would never pass as 'white'. She would never be able to disguise the fact that she was of mixed race.

Maisie believed the colour of her skin had blighted her life from the moment she had been born. It was responsible for the life she'd had foisted on her and all the awfulness that went with it. For many years it had been an anchor around her neck, dragging her down, trying to drown her. But, she had survived. In spite of her colour. In spite of what life had chucked at her. For she had turned the way she looked to her advantage. Made it work for her, rather than against her. She had learnt to be chameleon-like, in both looks and personality, in order to get what she wanted.

As Maisie inspected her face in the mirror, she traced the line of freckles that ran across the bridge of her nose, and as she did so she let her mind trail over the outline of a plan. When she had decided to come up north, she had known exactly *what* she wanted to achieve, but hadn't really worked out *how* she was going to achieve it. But that was just her way. She wasn't exactly impulsive, but at the same time she wasn't one of life's great planners.

At first, it had simply been enough for her to move up here, with a job that paid well and somewhere to stay. She had been more than pleasantly surprised when she had arrived here at Lily's. The place was as magnificent as Lily had described, and was very like some of the beautiful and opulent houses she had been invited to in Belsize Park and Hampstead in north London.

Then she'd had another stroke of luck and been introduced to Rosie, and found out all about her squad of women welders.

And now – the icing on the cake. This wedding . . .

If she was a gambler, she'd be at the tables now. She was having a good run. It was as if a plan of action was being laid out right in front of her, showing her exactly what to do – like one of those dot to dot drawings she had loved doing when she was a child. The picture was drawn for you. All you had to do was draw your lines and then colour it in.

Thoughts of her childhood, however, made Maisie naturally tense up. She realised she was clenching her teeth, so she blew out air and forced herself to relax.

Memories of the years as a young girl, left alone and unloved, being passed from pillar to post, being either reviled or loved in a way she did not want to be loved, flashed across her mind and the anger she felt for the person she held responsible rose like bile to the back of her throat.

At least now, finally, she was going to get her revenge for the loss of her childhood. The person who was ultimately responsible for ruining her life was going to get her just deserts. One way or another.

'Maisie, my dear,' she told the reflection in the mirror. 'You will have your retribution. At long bloody last. And you're going to enjoy every moment of it.'

Chapter Thirty

Ivy House, Hackney, London

September 1913

When Evelina found Pearl's bed empty, there was a part of her that wasn't at all surprised. She could understand why she had wanted to leave as soon as possible – but it would just have been nice to say a proper goodbye, check that she was all right, and see if she was going back up north. These girls that came through their doors were so young – many of them, like Pearl, were just children, really. Some left with a sense of relief that they didn't have the burden of another life to care for; others, like Pearl, were deeply affected by being parted from their newborn.

Evelina should have seen how attached Pearl had become to her unborn baby, but life had been so hectic these past few months; Ivy House was no longer big enough to cope with the number of young girls knocking at their door, so they were moving into a larger purpose-built maternity home on Lower Clapton Road. It wasn't until she had seen Pearl cradling her baby daughter that Evelina had seen it – that fierce motherly love. Like a lioness with her cub. She had worried that Pearl would not forsake her baby; but there were no two ways about it – *she had to*. There was no other option for Pearl.

Perhaps it's for the better, Evelina mused as she pulled the sheets off Pearl's bed and bundled them up ready to take to the laundry; the couple were coming today to sign the adoption papers and take their new baby home with them. Having witnessed the strength of Pearl's maternal pull towards her baby girl, it might well have caused problems if she'd been about when her daughter's new parents arrived. And Evelina didn't want to let anything get in the way of this particular adoption.

For, if Evelina hadn't got to know this couple, she was under no misapprehension, it would have been nigh on impossible to have found even a halfway decent home for Pearl's unique little girl.

Mr and Mrs Washington arrived a little before they were expected. Evelina could tell that underneath their show of calm, they were both nervous and incredibly excited. As soon as they clapped eyes on their new daughter, they looked totally smitten. Mrs Washington even shed a few silent tears as she bent down to the cot and picked up her baby for the first time.

Evelina just wished Pearl could see what a lovely family her daughter was going to, and also that they were more than well off. Pearl was getting her wish: her daughter would not be brought up in the kind of poverty she'd had to endure. Far from it.

Apart from this, Pearl had asked Evelina if she could do one more thing for her. Pearl had never asked for anything in the all the time she had been at Ivy House – had always seemed eternally grateful they had simply taken her in – so Evelina had listened carefully as Pearl told her that she had chosen a name for her baby, and could Evelina persuade her baby's new parents to keep the name? It was a nice name and Evelina said she would try her hardest, so when she took Mr and Mrs Washington into the office to fill out the official documentation, she told the couple about Pearl's request and repeated the name Pearl had chosen.

Evelina was pleasantly surprised when both Mr and Mrs Washington's faces lit up; they seemed to genuinely like the name, and happily agreed to give their child the name the birth mother had chosen.

Evelina wished she could have told Pearl that she had managed to do this one thing for her. It might have been some consolation – even if it was just a very small one.

When Pearl reached King's Cross station shortly after midnight she was in a state. She had been crying on and off since giving birth to her baby girl. For the last few months of her pregnancy, the love she had for the little being growing inside of her had become all-consuming. She had thought of endless ways in which she could keep her baby. Her brain had actually ached on a daily basis with her relentless questions and meanderings as to how she could bring up her child, but she had realised there was no magic solution. There was no option other than to let her baby go. Evelina was right – she had to give her baby the chance of a life. And the only way she could do that was by giving her to someone else.

As Pearl sat huddled up under one of the stone arches in the main entrance of the station she almost welcomed the bitter cold that was creeping into every part of her body. *Please let me freeze to death*, Pearl had silently prayed. *Please let me drift off to sleep and never wake up*. The pain was too much and it wasn't the physical pain she felt from having just given birth, nor the aches in her limbs from having walked miles to get here from Hackney. That pain she could suffer, but the searing heartache, the constriction in her chest, she simply could not bear. Never before had she experienced pain that had made her want to leave this life for good.

As the tears started to roll down her face once again, a down-and-out came to sit next to her. Pearl didn't care that he smelt, nor that he was chatting on inanely about something that made no sense; there was even a part of her that wished the bag of bones sidling up to her had murder in mind. At least then this terrible torment she was going through would come to an end.

Pearl felt the tramp nudge her and she looked at him through a blur of tears as he raised his arm. In the semi-darkness she thought he was going to punch her, but then she saw he was holding a bottle in his hand and that he was actually offering her a drink.

Pearl's mouth was dry; only her lips were salty and wet with the tears she was still shedding and which seemed to know no end.

She watched as she raised her arm and took the dirty bottle from his hand. She took a drink – two big mouthfuls – and swallowed. A harsh burning sensation filled her mouth and her throat, and, for a moment, the pain distracted her from the agony in her heart. The moment's relief was welcome.

For the rest of the night Pearl and the tramp sat together. He chatted on unintelligibly while she cried quietly to herself. They both drank from the bottle and as Pearl supped the burning liquor, the terrible sorrow and grief she felt slowly started to fade – until finally she had her wish. She was numb. She had managed to escape her heartache.

For a few hours, at least.

Chapter Thirty-One

The day before the wedding

Friday 7 November 1941

'Pearl, have you sorted everything out at the Tatham?'
Agnes sounded fraught.

'Aggie,' Pearl said giving a deep, dramatic sigh, 'stop
getting your knickers in a twist. Everything's sorted at the
pub. I'm just off there now to do a couple of hours and to
remind Bill and the two young lasses he's got working
there that they've all got to be on their best behaviour
tomorrow – and that the place has got to be spic and
span . . . Oh, and of course, that they're well stocked up!'
she cackled. 'Can't be having them run out of booze, can
we? If you can't have a skinful on a wedding day, when
can ya?'

Bel looked over at her mother and, not for the first time
these past few weeks, had to pinch herself. The change in
her was incredible. Of course, she was still the same old
Pearl – totally self-obsessed, completely devoid of any
kind of empathy, and with a razor sharp tongue she
enjoyed inflicting on anyone and everyone. But what had
amazed Bel the most was that her ma had positively
thrown herself into the preparations for the wedding with
gusto. Bel had expected her mum to be sloping around,
drinking and smoking, and generally being unhelpful and
negative in the run-up to her nuptials with Joe. But,

incredibly, quite the reverse had happened – Pearl had actually offered to help out. In fact, it was thanks to her mother that they were going to have a proper wedding reception at the Tatham, instead of everyone simply cramming into the house and having a few drinks and sandwiches. It had made the whole event so much more celebratory – more of an actual party.

'That's all well and good, Ma,' Bel said, 'but that doesn't mean you can get bladdered, you know.' Bel was suddenly hit by an awful and embarrassing image of her mother, slurring and staggering about, as was her way when she had too much. Fortunately, since she had shown up out of the blue back in February after Teddy had been killed, she seemed to be better at knowing her limits, or at least, if she was away with the mixer, she was more adept at hiding it.

'Ah, dinnit worry, petal. I'll be as good as gold, cross my heart and hope to die and all of that.' She let out another cackle that morphed into a cough.

'Sounds like you need another fag, Ma. You've not had one for at least, ooh, ten minutes?' Bel verbally prodded her ma, but nothing was going to get the better of Pearl's obvious good mood and unusually high spirits.

Bel had a sneaking suspicion that her mother's growing excitement for her wedding had gained momentum after Kate had very kindly offered to alter her dress. Why anyone would want to do her ma any favours Bel had no idea, especially as Pearl had initially been so rude, but Kate had seemed to take to her mum and, strangely enough, her mum seemed to have taken to 'her Katie', as she now called her.

'Aye, I think you might be right there, Isabelle,' Pearl said, purposely ignoring her daughter's incendiary comments, and instead pulling her bag up from under the kitchen table and rummaging around for her packet of

Winston's. 'I'll just go and have a smoke and check that Ronald's all set for the big day.' And with that Pearl hurried out the back door, and after pausing to spark up her cigarette, she could be heard clomping down the backyard and out the back gate. Bel had given up telling her mother that Ronald wasn't allowed at family dos and get-togethers as Pearl always ignored her and did what she wanted anyway. Besides, Joe and Arthur appeared to enjoy the man's company. He seemed an all right bloke, which made Bel wonder why he seemed so enamoured of her mother. Bel knew her ma, and although Pearl might like the bloke, she was sure her affection for him was more to do with his limitless supply of cigarettes and whisky.

'Well, I would never have thought I'd see the day,' Agnes said as she hurried over to the range, wearing her oven gloves and pulling out another loaf from the stove. 'Your ma seems genuinely excited about your wedding. I would have bet money on her being more of a hindrance than a help.'

'I know,' Bel agreed, as she heaved the wicker laundry basket on to the large wooden kitchen table.

'Not like—' Bel stopped herself mid-sentence. She had been going to say how different Pearl had been when she had got married to Teddy, and that they hadn't even been certain she was actually going to show up, never mind be sober. Yet it wasn't these thoughts that caused Bel to suck back her words, but the feeling of guilt she had about Teddy. This wedding was going to be completely different to her first wedding day – in all ways – but she still couldn't stop herself thinking about it, or Teddy.

Agnes looked at Bel, and knew what she was thinking – and feeling. She herself had not been able to suppress thoughts about Bel's first marriage, to her other son, and because of that she knew Bel would be finding it hard to

274

deal with her own conflicting emotions about her love for her dead husband and the love she hadn't been able to deny for his twin brother.

'Bel,' she said, putting the hot loaf on to the side in the scullery and coming back into the kitchen. She took hold of Bel's hands as she sat down on the kitchen chair, making her daughter-in-law follow suit. She continued to hold her hands in her own as she spoke.

'I've been wanting to say this to you for a while now, but there hasn't seemed to be the right time, so I'm just going to say it now.'

Bel looked at Agnes and could see a sorrow in her eyes that seemed to reflect her own.

'It is only natural you're going to think about our Teddy,' Agnes said, forcing herself to hold back the tears which still seemed to come freely whenever she spoke about her son. 'He'll always be a part of your life. You have Lucille, after all. And there's a part of you that will never stop loving him, or thinking about him.'

Bel could feel her emotions forge their way to the surface, and her blue eyes immediately filled with tears.

'Oh, Agnes,' Bel's voice quavered, 'I swear you can read my mind.'

Agnes squeezed her daughter-in-law's hands. 'Well,' she said, 'I do feel like I know you as well as if you were my own flesh and blood.'

She took a deep breath. 'I would never want you – or any of us – to forget Teddy, or try to forget him. He's in all our hearts and minds and always will be. But,' she said, leaning towards Bel, 'tomorrow is about you and Joe. I don't want any tears, or any feelings of guilt. It's to be a happy, joyful day. Your wedding is about love and life – there's to be no room or time given over to any thoughts or feelings of sadness and death, do you hear me?'

Bel nodded, tears now trickling down her face.

'So,' Agnes said, 'those tears . . . ' she put her hand up to Bel's face and wiped her cheek with her thumb, 'are the last for now, you understand?'

Bel nodded but started sobbing all the same. Agnes scraped her chair forward and put her arms around the young woman who had not only been like a daughter to her, but was about to become her daughter-in-law for the second time.

'I know . . . ' Bel said between sobs, 'I know you're right . . . And I know Teddy would be happy for me and Lucille – and Joe. But sometimes I can't help but feel battered down with guilt and grief.'

Agnes listened, and continued to hold Bel until she had expended her tears and they were all out.

'All right,' she said, taking Bel by her shoulders and looking her straight in the eye. 'That's your lot. I mean it,' and Bel nodded and wiped her face dry with her hands.

They heard the front door open and close, and the familiar shuffle of Arthur as he made his way down the hallway and into the kitchen. As he entered the room he saw Bel's tear-stained face and his gaze swung to Agnes, who gave him a sad smile.

'Ah, Arthur,' Bel said, turning to look at the old man. 'You've caught us being all maudlin and weepy.' But as soon as she saw what Arthur was holding in his hand, her face lit up.

'Oh my goodness, Arthur. Are they what I think they are?' Bel wiped her nose with the back of her hand as she looked at the wonderful array of flowers Arthur was clutching.

'Aye, they most certainly are, pet,' Arthur said. As Bel stood up, he handed her a large and very colourful bunch of wild flowers. 'Albert and I thought we'd get you everything we could find and then you could use yer womanly ways to make it into a bouquet of yer choosing.'

Arthur was clearly chuffed to pieces with Bel's overjoyed reaction.

'Where did you find them all?' she asked, taking the flowers into the scullery and putting them straight into a big jar of water.

'Well, Albert's been growing a few flowers in his allotment, both intentionally and otherwise,' he chuckled.

'There may be a few weeds in there, but at least they're pretty weeds . . . ' Albert paused as he eased himself down into the chair Bel had been sat on. 'We got some of the flowers from having a good walk around the Town Moor – and the rest we got from swapping some of our homegrown veg with the florist in Villette Road.'

'There's loads here,' Bel shouted over her shoulder, a smile now wide across her face. 'There'll be plenty left over for a little display to put in the pub.' She came back into the kitchen carrying a large glass vase in which she had put the flowers. Carefully she put it on the table, then put her arms around Arthur and gave him a hug and a big kiss on the cheek.

'Thank you, Arthur. They mean the world to me,' Bel told him.

Arthur blushed. 'Now don't go and embarrass an old man.' He got up out of his chair. 'It's the very least I could do. A wedding gift of sorts.'

'Actually, Arthur, there's something I wanted to ask you,' Bel said as Arthur made his way into the scullery to wash his hands.

'Anything for you, pet,' he answered, turning on the tap and scrubbing his gnarled hands of any remaining dirt and soil.

'I know this isn't a church wedding,' Bel said, 'but I wondered if you would give me away?'

Arthur was taken aback. He turned off the tap and reached for the towel hanging from a hook in the wall.

'Pet, that's the nicest thing anyone has ever asked me to do. I'd be honoured.'

Seeing Arthur's pale blue eyes start to shine and water ever so slightly, Agnes said sternly, 'Now, I'm not having any more tears in this house tonight. There's been enough of that already this evening. So Arthur, you go and get your suit, and we'll give it a good shake out and a press.'

Arthur obeyed orders, but as he made his way up the stairs to fetch his morning suit from his room, he couldn't stave off the few sad tears that pricked the backs of his eyes as he recalled giving his own daughter away many years ago, and how, three years later, he was following her coffin down the very same aisle, in the very same church.

Reaching the top step, Arthur tried to push his own 'maudlin' thoughts away, but as he opened his bedroom door and went over to his small wardrobe, he realised that this was the first time he had actually felt sadness – rather than anger – when he'd thought about his daughter. About her death. About the taking of her own life after her husband's life had been snatched away from her in the final few weeks of the First World War.

His anger had told him she had been thinking only about herself, and not the child she'd made; a child she'd had a duty to stay around and care for. In his mind, leaving his grandson to grow up without a mother's love had been unforgivable.

As he pulled out his suit and turned to go back out of the room, Arthur suddenly felt tired with the burden of that anger and resentment. Perhaps now, he thought, it was finally time to forgive.

Perhaps now it was time to let go and feel the sadness his anger had been keeping at bay for so long.

On his way back down the stairs with his old, slightly faded suit that was frayed at the cuffs, he heard a loud knock on the front door, followed by the sound of it swinging open and Beryl's voice sounding out.

'Only me,' she hollered down the hall. 'Just returning this little girl.'

By the time Arthur walked back into the kitchen with his suit, it was mayhem. Lucille was running around chasing the dogs; Bel was chastising her daughter to 'calm down' while setting up the ironing board; and Beryl, he could hear, was in the scullery chatting to Agnes about the cake. Arthur knew that Beryl had made a two-tier fruit cake, and that Maud and Mavis, who ran the sweet shop across the road, were busy doing their best to decorate it. Beryl had been determined that the cake topping was not going to be a cardboard cover lookalike, and she had persuaded just about everyone she knew to give up their sweet rations so that Bel and Joe would have the best iced and decorated wedding cake possible – in spite of wartime restrictions.

'I'm home!' Polly's voice could just about be heard over the excitement and chatter in the kitchen.

'You're late,' Bel said, putting the iron down on the side of the board to give her sister-in-law a quick hug.

'No rest for the wicked,' Polly said, distractedly, as she looked around at the chaos. 'Right, what can I do to help?' she asked Bel.

Bel pressed down hard on Arthur's suit, causing a cloud of steam to fill the room.

'You couldn't try and get this little monster calmed down and in bed, could you?' Bel grimaced as she threw a look over to Lucille who was carrying the pup in both her hands and practically dragging the poor thing backwards towards its bedding, which was made up of a few old cushions and lined with an old yellow pinafore dress that had once belonged to Lucille.

Polly chuckled. 'I'll give it a go.'

By half past nine, a modicum of calm had descended on the Elliot household. Lucille had been cajoled into bed but Polly had had to read two storybooks before her niece finally dropped off. Arthur was half snoozing in the wooden armchair by the fire, his wireless quietly playing next to him. Agnes had finished making enough sandwiches to feed an army, and Polly had surprised them all by creating a rather beautiful wild flower bouquet with Arthur and Albert's foraging, as well as half a dozen small but sweet buttonholes made from lilac and cream coloured freesias.

The kitchen now resembled a dry cleaner's with Arthur's suit, Joe's army uniform, Agnes's little black dress, and the only decent skirt Polly possessed, hanging from the picture rails on the walls.

'And last but not least,' Bel said, putting a pretty little lemon-coloured dress on to a clothes hanger and reaching up to hook it to the curtain pole, ' . . . is Lucille's new dress.'

'It's a good job you didn't show that to her tonight,' Polly said, 'she'd be so excited, I'd still be in there now, trying to get her to sleep.'

Everyone chuckled. Much as Lucille had been ecstatic when they had all come back that day and found Tramp had had her puppies, she had not been best pleased the dog had chosen her favourite frock to have them on. Bel had persuaded her daughter that the dress was past redemption and had been getting too small for her anyway, and had promised she would find her another.

Bel had been able to save up all her clothes coupons and

had bought a lovely replica pinafore from Blacketts department store.

'It really is adorable,' Agnes said, pouring herself a cup of tea and easing her exhausted body down into the chair next to Polly. 'She's going to look pretty as a picture.'

'Just like her ma!'

Agnes, Polly and Bel turned around, and Arthur roused himself from his snooze, to see the groom-to-be, Joe, walk into the room.

Bel blushed. Seeing Joe always had the same effect on her. She might live in the same house as him, and had known him all her life, but since they had fallen in love with each other, whenever she saw him she felt like a teenager.

'Joe!' she said, going over to give him a quick kiss, feeling her engagement ring self-consciously as she did so. She had worn it every day, only taking it off before she had her hands in a load of soapy suds.

'Don't worry,' Joe said, looking around in awe at the conversion the kitchen had undergone. 'I'm only here to pick up my uniform and then I'll be off to Major Black's. I promise to abide by the traditions of marriage and not clap eyes on my bride from now on until the ceremony.'

Bel got his uniform down and was just handing it over to him when the clock struck ten. At almost that exact moment, they heard the dreaded sound of the air raid siren start its long rising wail across the town.

'I don't believe it!' Agnes said, putting her hand on her forehead in despair.

'Bloody typical,' Arthur murmured. 'Jerry gets one sniff of a bit of fun and he has to try and blast it away.' He pushed himself out of his chair. 'I'll get the little 'un up.'

Bel looked around her at all the laundered and freshly pressed wedding attire, and then at the mound of freshly made sandwiches in the scullery that Agnes had covered with a sheet of greaseproof paper, and she clenched her hands into a fist.

'You just dare land on this house – and I'll, I'll . . . '

Joe took her fist and kissed it. 'Come on, we can blaspheme as much as we want in the shelter.'

Ten minutes later Joe was shepherding the Elliot household into the air raid shelter round the corner in Tavistock Place. He was just about to climb down the steps into the basement of the large mansion when he heard Pearl shouting his name in less than dulcet tones.

'Joe, Joe!' Pearl was breathless by the time she reached the open wooden trapdoor. Behind her followed Bill, the landlord, the two barmaids, and trailing behind them was Ronald, who Joe noticed was carrying Pearl's bag. By the way his shoulder was sagging, the bag looked like it was weighed down with a ton of bricks.

'Two bottles,' Ronald wheezed. 'She forced me to bring them in case the pub got bombed.'

Joe had to suppress a smile.

Even in a time of crisis his future mother-in-law was determined not to go short.

For more than two hours now they had been in the cold, dank basement. It was virtually pitch black, apart from a few flickers of light given off by some candles that had been left there from the last air raid. Not that Joe minded the dark, as it meant he could hold Bel close to him and give her the occasional kiss that no one could see.

They had heard the distant sound of bombs exploding, but Joe guessed that they were over the other side. Roker and Fulwell had really got a hammering this past year, punishment for being on the north side of the Wear and on the doorstep of most of the town's shipyards, as well as its colliery. He would sacrifice their wedding tomorrow for the bombs not to have taken lives, but he doubted that would happen. The Luftwaffe might not be hitting their intended targets, but they had still managed to kill plenty of the townsfolk while trying.

Joe looked over to check on Lucille and saw that she was cuddled up between her grandmothers, Pearl and Agnes – two women who couldn't have been more different if they tried. They did, however, share common ground when it came to Lucille, as they both adored their little grand-daughter, which was surprising in Pearl's case as she had never shown any kind of motherliness in all the time he had known her – and he had known her for most of his life.

But, if Pearl hadn't been such an awful mother, Polly wouldn't have found Bel alone and crying when they were little, having being abandoned by Pearl, who had disap-peared with one of her fancy men and not come back. Bel wouldn't then have been brought back to their home and taken into Agnes's care. And he would not now have the love of his life wrapped in his arms.

As if sensing Joe was thinking about her, Bel shuffled a little and murmured, 'We're not meant to be with each other tonight.' Her voice was croaky. 'It's bad luck, you know,' she said, before her breathing started to labour and she fell back into sleep's embrace.

Joe didn't believe in any kind of superstition. Nothing would spoil their day tomorrow. As long as the Registry Office was still standing and the Registrar there to marry them, that was all he cared about.

'Hey, Joe.' It was Polly. She had sidled up to him quietly so as not to disturb Bel. 'How you feeling about your big day?'

Joe looked at Polly and was amazed at her energy. She'd had a full day at the yard, had come back and helped out with the wedding preparations – it was now gone midnight – and she still looked bright as a button.

'Can't wait,' Joe whispered back. He looked at Polly and knew her excitement must be tinged with a little sadness that it wasn't her wedding tomorrow. Thank goodness she'd just had a letter from Tommy, which always buoyed her up.

'You're not too disappointed you're not going to have a honeymoon?' Polly asked quietly, as she pulled her knees up to her chest. She was still wearing her work overalls and had wrapped her overcoat around herself to keep warm.

'Nah,' Joe said. 'All I'm bothered about is getting married. That's all I want. We can always go on a honeymoon when this war's won.'

'It's not ideal, though,' Polly persisted, 'is it? Living in separate rooms, with both your ma and your mother-in-law under the same roof?'

'We'll sort something out,' Joe said, looking down at Bel. She was now fast asleep and had the jacket of Joe's uniform over her in place of a blanket.

'Sleeping beauty,' Polly laughed, as she put her hands on both knees and pushed herself up. 'Let's hope we get out of here soon or we'll all be needing matchsticks to keep our eyes open tomorrow.'

Joe chuckled as he watched Polly go over to Agnes and the two start to chat. He wasn't sure if it was the light playing tricks, or if Polly and his ma were casting slightly conspiratorial looks over in his and Bel's direction.

Chapter Thirty-Two

The cellar at Lily's was full. The air raid siren had gone off at the worst possible time when the house was pretty much bursting at the seams. They had all had to cram down in the cellar, and, as usual, Vivian had taken charge, although tonight she was skipping her Mae West tribute and instead was playing back-to-back records on the gramophone.

The mood was light and jocular and the call to 'keep calm and party on' had been made, but it had not escaped Maisie's notice that those going to the wedding were far from happy about having to spend a good part of the night before cooped up in the basement.

Rosie was never the chattiest of people, but she wasn't even bothering to make any effort to socialise, and Maisie could tell by the dour look on her face that she was worried about the bombs putting a stop to Bel and Joe's nuptials.

Lily and George had tried their hardest to keep the jovial atmosphere going, but even they had wilted after half an hour or so and were now seated quietly chatting in the corner. Maisie would bet money on there being something other than a mere friendship going on between the two, but would never voice her suspicions.

Kate, unbelievably, had brought Bel's fascinator down with her and looked like a woman possessed. When Maisie had asked her how the finishing touches were going, she'd barely muttered an answer and had just kept on unpicking some stitches on the headpiece.

'I wish you were coming as well tomorrow,' Vivian,

squashed up next to Maisie on the chaise longue, whispered into her ear, all the while keeping her eye on a couple of the girls and their clients slow dancing to the sound of the Glenn Miller band.

'So do I,' Maisie whispered back, putting her hand across her mouth to prevent others from hearing what they were talking about. Maisie and Vivian had become firm friends. Both had been surprised that they were so alike, and, fortunately, their natural competitiveness hadn't caused them to clash as their work at Lily's was separate, with Vivian now the official 'head girl', and Maisie manageress of the Gentlemen's Club.

But although the pair had become close, Vivian had no idea just how much Maisie wanted to go to the wedding, and would never have guessed she had been racking her brains to work out how she could wangle herself a last-minute invite.

'I'm going to feel like a right gooseberry going with Lily and George,' Vivian said, looking across at 'the two oldies' as she liked to jokingly call them, although she would never have dared say that to their faces. 'They've been getting a bit too cosy for my liking lately,' she added. 'I think George's practically moved in next door. I don't think he's been back to his own flat for about a week now.'

'I think you might be right there,' Maisie agreed. She and George had been working pretty much flat out getting the Gentlemen's Club ready for the opening, and George had taken over one of the top rooms and more or less made it his own.

'Do you know how you're going to do Isabelle's hair?' Maisie asked.

When Polly had conveyed Vivian's offer of a free hairstyle to a harried Bel one night, she had jumped at the chance. As she was no expert herself, and with everything else that needed to be done, it was one less thing to worry about. When Bel's acceptance of the offer, complete with an invite to the wedding, had been relayed to Vivian, she had practically jumped for joy. Since then she had been practising a variety of elaborate 'updos' on a couple of the girls whose hair was a similar length to Bel's.

'I think I'm going to go with something classic but with a modern twist,' Vivian said, 'although I'm a little limited with the fascinator. A veil would have been easier, although I think Bel did right in going for something less traditional – this being her second wedding, and all.'

Maisie smiled automatically as one of the clients came over and offered Vivian his hand for a dance.

'Won't be long,' Vivian mouthed before she turned to her partner and the pair started to do a very slow waltz.

Maisie put on a convincing show of looking as if she was admiring those who were dancing and was forcing herself to sway to the music, but behind her serene-looking veneer she was far from happy, and had been glad of a few moments when she could be left in peace to think her own thoughts. It had been increasingly difficult to disguise the jealousy that was rising up in her, which was unusual for Maisie, as one of her strong points, apart from her looks, of course, was that she was a master of deceit when it came to showing, or rather *not showing*, her emotions.

Lately, though, she just couldn't stop thinking about Bel and how bloody lucky the woman was. She'd had a blessed life, marrying her childhood sweetheart, having a gorgeous daughter, and, yes, fair enough, it must have been heart-breaking when her husband was killed – but then his brother had come back, and hey, like some happy-ever-after ending, they'd fallen in love and were now getting hitched.

And, on top of everything else, Bel was not only close to her own mother, but by all counts, her mother-in-law too.

And they all lived together – one big happy family.

Maisie felt her whole body fill with bitterness and resentment. Her own life had been one big mess-up from the very start. And she knew exactly whose fault that was. There was only one person to blame – only one person who had ruined her life from the off, before it had even started.

And, by God, was she going to get her comeuppance.

Come hell or high water, she would make sure of that.

Chapter Thirty-Three

When the all-clear finally sounded out at just after two in the morning, the news quickly circulated that, as suspected, it had been the north side which had been hit. The centre of town and – more importantly – the Registry Office in John Street were still standing.

Everyone sheltering at the Tavistock House basement emerged tired and bleary-eyed. Joe went to stay the rest of the night with his Home Guard zone commander Major Black in Frederick Street, and everyone else headed back to Tatham Street.

As soon as Pearl had got through the front door she declared she was 'knackered' and had gone straight up the stairs and climbed into her bed. These past few weeks had been full on and she hadn't had a minute to spare. All her time had been spent either working at the Tatham, or helping organise Isabelle's wedding.

Lying in her narrow little bed she tried to close her eyes, but her mind insisted on staying wide awake. As she lay there, willing sleep to come, she could hear Arthur's loud snoring start up and reverberate through the walls from his bedroom next door, and downstairs she heard Agnes still clattering about.

Pearl would never admit it, but during their epic four hours in that bloody basement, she had felt sick as a dog thinking that the bombs might end up ruining the wedding. Thank goodness the south side of the town had escaped unscathed, and, moreover, that Kate's little shop hadn't been hit. The thought didn't bear thinking about. If her dress had got ruined she might well have stomped her way across Europe herself to strangle that horrible little man with her own bare hands.

As Pearl pulled the blankets around her neck it suddenly occurred to her that she was happy – happier, in fact, than she had been her entire life. She liked living here – had even grown to quite like Agnes. The woman might be a bit bossy, but she kept the place in order, and she was a bloody good cook; lately, even Polly and the dogs didn't get on her nerves half as much as they used to.

Of course, there would always be friction between her and Isabelle, it was just the way it was with the pair of them, but at least now she didn't feel like they hated each other's guts, and these past few months they had even managed to rub along without too many fall-outs.

As Pearl started to nod off, she was aware of Agnes trooping up the stairs and going into her bedroom next door, and the creak of the metal bedstead as Agnes finally put her head down.

Tomorrow, Pearl thought, was going to be a special day. It felt important. Like it was the start of something new. Not just for Bel and Joe, but for herself too. Her daughter's wedding and her part in it had made her feel she had finally come in from the cold – where she had been for so long now – and that, as mother of the bride, she was at last becoming part of a proper family.

As Pearl slowly slipped into a deep sleep, she heard the voice.

The same voice she often heard when she drifted off and her subconscious took over.

'Well done, Pearl, you've done really well.'

The voice was soft and gentle, reassuring. She *had* done

well. She couldn't see the baby in her arms, but she could feel her. Knew she was perfect and healthy and very beautiful. If she had been able to see the woman whose voice it was, she knew she would see the face of Evelina. Her kind Evelina. Her caring Evelina.

But then she heard the voice again. Only this time it was different. It was harsh. Coarse. Unkind. 'Eee, well then, yer did well there, pet . . . *like you've done it all before.*'

In her dream the voice cackled like a witch. A croaky, heartless witch who was mocking her, knowing that she had, in fact, done this all before.

Pearl looked down but she didn't see any baby – only blood. Pools of blood. A frightened voice sounded out. 'What's happening? Why's there all this blood?'

It took a few moments to realise that the voice was her own. It sounded childish, but she was not a child. She was a young woman now. Still, she sounded as fearful as a young, vulnerable child.

And then the pain came. She could feel the terrible stabbing pain. The dark figure of a witch woman seemed to block out all the light. She was doing something. Down there. And it hurt.

Pearl screamed but no sound came out. The stabbing pain kept on. And on.

And during it all she was aware of a baby, only her baby was no longer in her arms, but just out of reach to her side. And the little bairn was crying, whimpering. She reached out to take the child but the woman with the witch's voice was suddenly there again and she wouldn't give her it.

'Yer can't have her! We're not done yet!' The voice was loud and the words were banging against her throbbing head.

Suddenly Pearl was aware that she was dreaming, but she couldn't wake herself up and the dream continued: on and on with pain and blood and soundless screams. Until finally the pain ended. The screaming stopped and she was given her baby.

'This'll be your first and yer last, *bonny lass*' – all of a sudden the witch had changed into the old fishwife she used to see by the beach.

'I'm sorry to tell yer, petal, but there'll be no more babs fer yer,' she said.

Pearl could hear the sadness in her voice.

'Perhaps that's not a bad thing, eh?' The voice was almost soothing. The woman gave her something in a tin can.

'Drink it. It'll make yer feel better,' the woman commanded. The cold liquid tasted bitter, but within minutes the pain started to ebb away.

She could hear the baby near her. Crying. Then she felt the baby in her arms, and she looked down.

But when she looked she got a shock.

This wasn't her baby. Was it? No, this was someone else's baby! It had ivory skin and big blue eyes. Where was *her* other baby? The 'special' baby. The one they said she couldn't keep.

Pearl looked down again at the baby in her arms. It was beautiful. It even had a veil of thin blonde hair. It looked like her. It must be hers. So, why didn't she feel it was hers? No, this wasn't right.

'Where have you taken my baby?!' Again Pearl cried out. But again there was no sound. No one could hear her.

When Pearl woke she was sweating and her bedsheets were on the floor. She sat up and grabbed the sheets and pulled them back around her. She told herself it was only a dream, but of course, she knew it wasn't.

Chapter Thirty-Four

When Bel opened her eyes just after half past six she felt an immediate rush of nerves and excitement.

This was her wedding day!

She still couldn't quite believe it. The war had brought a sense of surrealism to her life. To everyone's lives. Sometimes she doubted her own reality. If someone had told her two years ago that her husband would march off to war and not come back and that, as a result, she would harbour dark thoughts of joining him – only to find love again with her brother-in-law, she would never have believed them in a million years.

But, here she was, and in just a few hours she was going to be Mrs Elliot for the second time in her life. As thoughts of Teddy started to sneak through to her consciousness she pushed them back. Agnes had been right yesterday when she had said that there was to be no room for sorrow or sadness today, nor any guilt-ridden thoughts about Teddy.

This day was to be a joyful one. Last night's air raid had proved more than anything just how short and unpredictable life was. Today was going to be a chance for everyone they knew to have a little fun, let their hair down and have a party. Everyone certainly needed it, and if her wedding to Joe was a chance for them to do that, then that pleased Bel no end.

As she quietly swung her legs out of the bed, Lucille started to stir in her cot. Her sea blue eyes squinted open, and on seeing her mum getting up, she stretched her arms out for a morning cuddle. Bel stood up and reached down to pick up her daughter.

'Dooeeey. Where Dooey?' They were always the first words uttered by Lucille on waking up. Normally Bel would give in to her daughter's demands and take her next door to have a good-morning hug from Joe.

'Sweetheart, he's not here this morning.' Bel heaved her daughter on to her hip and carried her out of the room. 'We'll be seeing him later on ... but,' she added, giving Lucille a kiss on her little rosy cheek, 'because it's a special day, you've got a special present.'

On hearing the word 'present', Lucille immediately sprang to life. And as her mother carried her into the kitchen and she spotted her brand new yellow dress hanging from the curtain rail, she let out a squeal of pure joy that successfully woke up the rest of the Elliot household – and in doing so heralded the start of her mother's wedding day.

By ten o'clock the Elliot house was mayhem. Agnes and Pearl were toing and froing from the Tatham Arms, which, thankfully, was just two minutes' walk away; both were wearing curlers and carrying large trays of sandwiches and other nibbles. Pearl had a fag hanging from her lip and left a trail of smoke behind her as she tottered across the tramlines to the other side of the road.

Inside the pub the two barmaids were sweeping up the wooden floor from the night before and Bill was arranging the tables and chairs and assembling an old rectangular decorating table that he was intending to cover with a long white tablecloth ready for the wedding buffet.

Polly had already been over to the pub to take the large vase of flowers she had arranged last night and Bill had given them prime position in the middle of the bar. Polly had returned to clear up the breakfast bowls, although very little of the big pan of porridge Agnes had made had been consumed. Copious amounts of tea, however, were being drunk and Polly was busy making another fresh pot, while keeping half an eye on an excited Lucille playing chase with Tramp and the pup.

Arthur was upstairs, staying out of the way, listening to his wireless as he got himself ready. In his head he was going through his duties as stand-in father of the bride.

'Cooee!' Beryl's voice sounded down the hallway. Polly hurried out of the kitchen to find their next-door neighbour looking flushed and excited.

'Agnes over the pub?' she asked.

Polly nodded and asked, 'Everything all right?'

'Aye, hinny,' Beryl said, 'I just wanted to tell yer ma that I've just been to see Mavis and Maud and the cake looks *fantastic*!'

'Ah, Beryl, you are the best neighbour anyone could ask for . . . ' Beryl and Polly looked round as Bel came out of her room. ' . . . and Polly, you're the best sister-in-law.' Her words were said with the utmost sincerity and her voice warbled a little with emotion. The two women looked at the bride-to-be with her hair pinned back so that it showed off her perfectly made-up heart-shaped face.

'Wow,' Polly said. 'Honestly, I hope my brother realises just how lucky he is!'

Beryl smiled as she looked at Bel, who she had known since she was a child. 'Eee, lass, you look like one of them movie stars – only better!'

Bel blushed, and waved away their compliments.

'I've got awful butterflies,' she admitted, putting out her hand and showing it was trembling a little.

Beryl let out a loud belly laugh. 'Yer know what yer want for that? A bit of brandy in yer tea. That'll sort yer out.'

'Good idea, Beryl,' Polly said. 'And there's a pot just brewed.'

Chapter Thirty-Five

'Oh dear me. I'm running late!' Kate was panicking as she gathered up Bel's dress, as well as her own wedding outfit.

'Here, let me give you a hand,' Maisie said as she idled through Kate's open door and into her bedroom. Kate had to bite her lip. She would have preferred to have been left on her own. She had a dozen and one things on her mind and just needed some space to think and make sure she didn't forget anything. But, she couldn't be rude, and Maisie was only trying to be helpful, after all. She really did feel like Cinders going off to a ball that everyone else wanted an invite to.

As Kate turned to throw a few more 'just in case' bits and bobs into her big tapestry bag – and look around for her own small clasp bag which matched her outfit – Maisie watched her like a hawk.

Then, as Kate bent over the top of her little sewing table and started to push around strands of ribbons and threads and pincushions in an effort to find her favourite thimble, Maisie very stealthily slipped her hand through the slit of the large cotton garment bag that was being used to transport the wedding outfits, and unhooked Bel's custom-made fascinator from the coat hanger.

Carefully she placed it on the floor, then pushed it under Kate's narrow bed with her bare foot.

'*I'm ready when you are!*' George's voice sounded out from the bottom of the stairs. It was his job to round everyone up and get them to their chosen destinations on time; at present his cherished MG was parked up outside the house, ready to take Kate and Vivian to the Maison Nouvelle where they were to dress and coiffure the bride and the mother of the bride for the big day. He was thankful he hadn't used up all his petrol rations so there was no chance of him conking out on the way to the Registry Office.

'Blimey, George,' Lily said turning away from the front door, which had been left ajar. 'You could eat your dinner off the bonnet it looks so clean.'

'Well, it's not every day the old gal gets to chauffeur a bride on her wedding day,' he said, puffing his chest out with pride. 'I'll be putting a ribbon on her when I come back from dropping Kate and Vivian off . . . The plan,' he added, looking at his gold fob watch, 'is I come back for you, my dear, transport you to the wedding, then go and pick Bel up – do a lap round the town so she can be a few minutes late, as is the tradition – before delivering her to the Registry Office.'

'I'm sure, *mon cher*,' Lily said, 'that you've got it all timed to military perfection . . . Now, I'm going off to try and disguise the ravages of time and look the best a woman of my age can look.'

George was going to say something in response, but instead smiled and watched as Lily turned and sashayed her way up the stairs. As she did so, Vivian came hurrying down and was just about to run down the last flight when she was stopped in her tracks.

'*Arrête!* It's bad luck to cross on the stairs, Vivian,' Lily scowled at her. 'You do want to get married one day, *don't you*?'

'Sorry, Lily,' Vivian said, forgetting that one of Lily's many superstitious beliefs stipulated that anyone crossing on a flight of stairs would never walk down the aisle.

'I'm in a bit of a tizzy this morning,' she added while she waited for Lily to reach the landing. Vivian had been run ragged all morning, doing everyone's hair – her own, Lily's, Kate's – she'd even been asked by George for a quick short back and sides.

As Lily continued on her way up to her boudoir on the second floor, Kate appeared from her room on the third floor, her skinny arms wrapped round the bulging cotton garment bag. In seconds she was squeezing past Lily in her rush to get to the shop.

Lily stood still, dramatically rolling her eyes.

'Nobody takes a bit of notice of me,' she mumbled to herself, before carrying on up the stairs and disappearing into her room.

Two minutes later after a chorus of 'See you there!', Kate and Vivian clambered into the MG and were driven away by George, who was clearly enjoying his role of taxi driver for the day.

Lily, meanwhile, was settling herself down at her dressing table to make good her promise to George.

And Maisie was quietly tiptoeing into Kate's bedroom and stealthily retrieving the fascinator from where she had hidden it, before sneaking back into her own room – where she, too, started to get ready for the ball.

On the other side of town Polly was hurrying towards the five-storey Queen Anne-style Grand Hotel on Bridge Street in the town centre. She had her boxed gas mask slung across her shoulder and an overnight bag in one hand; the other had a tight grip on her little handbag as it contained an entire week's wages, plus overtime. As she stepped through the hotel's huge entrance with its folded-back oak doors, she spotted Dorothy and Angie. They were waiting by a mahogany partitioned wall under one of the stained-glass windows that had stripes of brown tape across it. Both were dolled up to the nines and looked exactly like two young women on their way to a wedding. A couple of uniformed Admiralty officers, who had been billeted at the hotel, passed them and touched their caps as they passed.

'Goodness,' Polly said, seeing the officers' approving looks, 'it's so strange to see you both in something other than your overalls. You look gorgeous.'

Dorothy and Angie self-consciously smoothed down their figure-hugging fishtail party dresses that looked almost identical, except that Dorothy's was red and Angie's blue. Polly's compliment caused two big smiles to appear on their faces.

'Ta, Pol,' Angie said, 'yer dinnit look too bad yerself.'

Polly knew Angie was being kind, but she also knew that she looked a little plain next to her two friends.

'Come on, then,' she said mischievously, *let's do this.*'

The three women all took a deep breath and approached the front desk where Polly pinged the brass bell on the counter.

Seconds later a grumpy-looking old man, dressed in what looked like a butler's outfit, came bustling through from the back office. Polly spoke in the poshest voice she could muster.

'Good morning, sir, we've come about the honeymoon suite for Mr and Mrs Elliot.'

Dorothy and Angie nudged each other and suppressed a giggle as they held their shoulder bags, which seemed to be abnormally bulky, down by their sides.

As Maisie finished rubbing a translucent face cream into her face, she leant forward and inspected her reflection in the oval-shaped mirror on her small vanity table. Normally, if she was going out – or even if she wasn't – she would have carefully and very artfully applied a light foundation to her skin. Today, however, she was more than happy for her true skin colour to be exposed for all and sundry to see.

For today was all about revelations.

Maisie moved her chair back and stood up, pushing her bobbed hair up with both hands and enjoying the feel of her soft, tight curls, as well as the way her shiny, chestnut brown hair enhanced her look. Then she walked over to her wardrobe and slipped into an ivory, floral crêpe tea dress which hung perfectly on her slender frame, the V-shape of the neckline showing off just a hint of her modest breasts. The dress looked casual but elegant and contrasted perfectly with her olive-brown skin.

Checking herself in the narrow full-length mirror on the inside of the closet door, she then glanced at her delicate gold wristwatch and knew it was time.

As she picked up the fascinator from her bedside table, she took one final look in the mirror and walked purposefully out of her room.

Standing on the landing she could hear the chink of a crystal decanter stopper and knew Lily was having a sneaky splash of brandy. She knew that her boss, in spite of her brash outward appearance, felt nervous when it came to mixing with what she called 'the general public'. Maisie understood that feeling – but, like Lily, she too had learnt to hide it well.

As she started walking down the stairs, Maisie sucked in air and reminded herself what a convincing actress she had been for just about all of her life. She could do this.

'Oh my goodness!'

Maisie shouted down the stairs as she began her performance.

'Lily, look!' She hurried down the two flights of stairs and reached the bottom just as Lily came rushing out of the front office, a large bulbous brandy glass in her hand.

'*Ma chère*, what *is* the matter?' she asked, her face all concern.

'It's Isabelle's fascinator. I've just found it on the stairs. Kate must have dropped it on her way out.'

Lily looked at Maisie and then down at her hand which was holding the beautiful coral pink fascinator. 'Oh gawd,' she said, reverting to her native tongue and putting her drink down on the little hallway table. 'Kate'll be in a right state. She's put blood, sweat and tears into that thing.'

Lily looked around her, as if she would find the answer there.

'Bloody typical! George said he had to do some kind of errand after dropping them off at the shop, so he's not going to be back for a little while.'

She looked at Maisie.

'Could you be a real darlin' and take it to Kate? I think it'll break her heart if Bel gets married without it.'

Maisie didn't miss a beat. 'Of course I can, Lily. Let me just get my coat. I can be there in fifteen minutes if I hurry – and quicker still if I manage to hail a cab.'

'Oh, you are a treasure,' Lily said, hurrying back into the front office to fetch some cash. When she came back out, Maisie was pulling on her fur coat which had been hanging from the stand by the door.

'Here,' Lily said, pushing a small purse full of coins into Maisie's hand. 'For the fare. It's Saturday so you might get lucky.'

And with that Maisie slipped out the front door and was gone. She didn't want to waste any time in case George returned earlier than expected and took the headpiece to the shop himself.

So far, so good, she thought as she hurried down the path and out on to the street.

Chapter Thirty-Six

Maison Nouvelle, Holmeside, Sunderland

'What do you think?' Kate asked Pearl as she tilted the full length cheval mirror at an angle so that Pearl could see how she looked in her new dress.

Vivian and Bel were also staring in admiration at Kate's wonderful creation. For once Pearl did not look like mutton dressed as lamb, but, to everyone's amazement, like a very attractive older woman. Kate had nipped the deep blue velvet dress in at the waist, but let it taper down to mid-calf length. In doing so, it had enhanced Pearl's figure, making her look more slimline than scrawny.

Vivian had contributed to the transformation by working her magic on Pearl's hair, twisting and pinning the dyed blonde locks into rolls around the side of her face, teasing out loose curls so that they fell down the nape of her neck.

'Eee, Katie,' Pearl said, her eyes glued to the apparition staring back at her in the mirror. 'I feel like royalty.'

Bel looked at her mother and was surprised to see that her eyes looked wet. Never before had she seen her mother so genuinely happy and emotional. Out of habit, Bel nearly said something sarcastic, but she stopped herself. Today was about love. Not just her and Joe's love, but the love they all had for each other. So, instead, Bel simply looked at her ma and smiled.

'You've done a fantastic job, Kate, and you too, Vivian,'

Bel said, before adding a little awkwardly, ' . . . and Ma . . . you look really nice.'

Pearl's head swung around to look at her daughter. She had never once said anything even remotely complimentary to her at all – ever.

Kate moved away from the mirror and looked outside. The weather wasn't particularly wedding-like, but it was November, after all. There were some dark clouds looming, but most important of all, it wasn't raining.

'All right, Pearl. I would get yourself away now – just in case it starts to spit. I don't want that velvet getting as much as a drop of water on it.'

'Good idea, pet. I'll see you all there.' Pearl looked across at her daughter. She wanted to say something, but couldn't think of any words.

The little bell tinkled as Kate opened the door for Pearl.

As she walked out, Pearl turned. 'Eee, Katie,' she said, grabbing her hand and giving it a quick squeeze. *Thanks so much.*'

And as she stepped out on to the pavement and started the quarter of a mile or so to the Registry Office, Pearl really did feel like she was Queen for the day.

'And now for the bride,' Kate exclaimed as she shut the door and turned to Bel, who was sitting on a high wooden stool by the large oblong sewing table. Vivian, standing behind her, had already got to work, rolling and pinning sections of Bel's hair up on top of her head.

'Let's get the bride into her dress!' Kate commanded. She hurried over to a metal rail at the side of the shop and pulled out the most beautiful ivory pink silk dress from the clothes carrier.

Bel felt a thrill of nerves as she got up from the stool, and both Kate and Vivian carefully held the dress above her head.

As Bel put her arms up and the dress just seemed to float down on to and around her, Bel felt all her nerves – and all her fleeting thoughts of the past and the future – disappear; the dress momentarily dissolving everything – apart from the here and now.

Kate then carefully pulled up the zip she had sewn into the side so that it was almost invisible, which had the effect of keeping the fall of the dress undisturbed. A subtle nip and tuck of fabric at the waist and a pussy bow neckline had the effect of showing off Bel's full bosom, but without drawing too much attention to it.

Bel bent down and slipped on a pair of cream slingback shoes she had borrowed from Rosie. Then she straightened up, and stood forward.

'Go on, give us a twirl,' Vivian begged. She was mesmerised by the sight of this beautiful woman who could easily give the likes of Lana Turner and Bette Davis a run for their money.

Responding to Vivian's plea Bel stepped into the middle of the small shop and did a little twirl. The movement caused the lower part of the dress, with its irregular hem, to move around her legs like gentle waves.

Bel looked stunning. The pastel pink of the fabric perfectly complemented her pale skin. She looked classy, yet demure. Bride-like, but also a little seductive.

'Excellent,' Kate said, scrutinising every square inch of fabric.

Bel sat back down on the stool to allow Vivian to finish her hair. She had already created a row of loose, victory rolls, positioning them so that they sat on the top of her head; now she carefully eased out two thick strands of curly blonde hair so that they framed Bel's face, and in doing so created a slightly wanton effect.

'And . . . ' Kate said, turning to the garment bag hanging

from the rail, 'to copy one of Lily's favourite expressions . . . for *la pièce de résistance*.'

As she parted the opening of the cotton bag, she reached up to retrieve the fascinator which should have been hanging from the middle of one of the hangers – but it wasn't there. Thinking it must have dropped to the bottom of the bag, she bent her head down to look.

Not finding it, Kate presumed it must have become entangled in her own wedding outfit, so she pulled her dress out, shook it gently – then more violently.

'Oh, no –' Kate's face went ashen. 'I don't believe it!'

She flung her dress on the sewing table and patted it down, praying that it was there. 'I don't believe it!' she repeated, as she started scrabbling around in the dress bag.

'What's wrong, Kate?' Vivian asked. She had her lacquer out and was creating a mist around both Bel and herself.

'The fascinator. It's not here! I must have left it . . . or dropped it. Oh my God. This is a disaster!'

Bel stood up and went over to a panic-stricken Kate. She had never seen her in such a state. 'Hey, Kate, don't worry. It's not the end of the world. I can get married without it.'

'No, you can't! The dress is incomplete without it,' Kate said, tears starting to build up in her eyes. There was no arguing with her. 'I can run back and get it.'

Kate sounded desperate as she looked up at the clock on the wall. But it was now nearly quarter to one. George was due at any moment. The Registry Office was booked for one.

'There's not enough time, Kate,' Bel said. 'Please, don't get upset. Look at this amazing dress.' She looked down at the most sublimely beautiful dress she had ever seen – never mind worn.

Vivian was quiet. She knew how much time, energy and

effort Kate had put into the headpiece, and so she knew, more than anyone, just how totally gutted Kate was feeling.

Kate started to look frantically around the shop, knowing deep down that it was not there but forcing herself to believe that it might somehow suddenly reappear.

Just then the little brass bell tinkled as the door opened. It was Maisie.

And in her raised hand she was holding the coral pink fascinator.

'I think you forgot something, Kate!' she said, purposely sounding breathless as if she had run all the way from West Lawn, when in fact she had managed to catch a taxi as soon as she'd turned on to Tunstall Vale. After being dropped off halfway down Holmeside, she had waited a little while in one of the shop doorways across the road from the Maison Nouvelle. She had seen Pearl leave – and had then given it a good five minutes before blustering into the shop.

Kate stood stock-still and raised her hands to her cheeks.

'Oh my! Maisie! Thank goodness! Where did you find it?' The words of gratitude spilled out.

'On the stairs,' Maisie told her, her breath now sounding more normal, 'you must have dropped it on your way out.'

'Oh Lord! Thank goodness you saw it!' Kate was beside herself. 'Thank you thank you thank you thank you! You've saved the day. Gosh, you must have practically sprinted here to get it to us on time. I can't thank you enough.'

'Oh, you've nothing to thank me for, Kate.' Maisie looked across at Vivian, who smiled back at her friend. 'I knew how much this meant to you.'

Vivian let out a huge sigh of relief. She felt almost as elated as Kate. The whole bordello knew just about every stitch of the fascinator now held aloft in Maisie's hand. If Bel hadn't got married with it adorning her very pretty head, she honestly thought Kate would have gone into some kind of designer mourning.

'Can I do the honours?' Maisie asked Kate as she walked across to Bel and raised the fascinator like a crown ready to be placed on the head of the bride-to-be.

'Oh, yes, please do!' Kate would have agreed to anything at that moment, so ecstatic was she about the reappearance of the headpiece.

Maisie smiled at Bel as she carefully placed it on top of her golden locks, making sure not to spoil Vivian's handiwork.

As Maisie adjusted the fascinator Bel realised that she and Maisie were more or less the same height. It was the first time Bel had seen Maisie up close and she realised not just how striking she really was, but also how brown her skin was – much more than it had seemed when they had been introduced in the shop a few weeks ago.

As Maisie stood back to check the headpiece, Kate clapped her hands together lightly, and declared, 'Perfect!'

Bel turned to look at herself in the mirror and it was then she understood why her ma was feeling like royalty – for Bel had to admit that she felt like a princess. Her wedding day was really starting to feel rather magical.

'Kate, you'd better get your dress on,' Vivian cajoled her. 'George'll be here any minute.'

The words were barely out of her mouth when the door opened, the bell rang out, and George entered.

Quickly Kate whipped her dress off the sewing table, where it had been tossed and patted down in their desperate search, before darting behind the curtain panel and into the back room to get changed.

'Thank goodness, you made it, Maisie,' George said. 'Lily's been worried sick you wouldn't get here in time to give Bel her tiara.' George looked at Bel and smiled.

'It's not a *tiara*, George,' Vivian reprimanded. 'It's called a *fascinator*.'

George guffawed. 'Well, whatever it is,' he paused, 'it looks wonderful.' Then, making a show of being totally bowled over by the vision of the bride in front of him, he added, 'Or should I say that it is *Bel* – the bride-to-be – that looks rather stunning.'

Bel blushed. She had never met George before, but he was just as she had imagined.

'Right,' he said, putting his stern voice on, 'your carriage awaits, and . . . ' he looked at Kate and smiled as she slipped back through into the shop, now wearing the black dress that he knew had once been Lily's, 'the rest of you need to get to the Registry Office – pronto!'

'Oh, I'm not going, George,' Maisie said, quickly making her way to the door as if to leave.

'Oh, no, please don't!' Bel pleaded. Her voice had gone a little shaky with nerves. 'Won't you come to the wedding? The ceremony itself won't be long, and there'll be a little party afterwards at our local – a buffet and a fair amount of alcohol?'

'I'd love to!' Maisie said with a wide smile. She looked at Vivian, whose face had instantly lit up at the prospect of her best mate accompanying her.

'All good,' George said, looking anxiously at his fob watch. 'Now, you young fillies need to shake a leg. Go – be gone!' he said, opening the door and shepherding them out. As he did so Kate pressed the key to the shop into his hand and was about to say something, but was beaten to it.

'Yes, my dear,' George sighed, 'don't worry. I will make sure the shop's all secure. Now go, the lot of you. Scram!'

As Kate, Vivian and Maisie started hurrying down the street, Bel waited on the pavement while George locked up.

She watched the women and smiled.

She was just walking over to the MG, which had been parked outside the shop and was decorated with a thick white ribbon, when Maisie turned back and shouted up the street.

'Oh . . . and "Happy Wedding Day", Isabelle!'

Bel felt herself stiffen. She hated being called by her full name. Only her mother called her Isabelle and that was only because she knew it was guaranteed to wind her up.

As George opened the car door, giving Bel his hand so she could carefully climb in, she suddenly felt a little perturbed by Maisie's impromptu appearance, which was stupid as she had saved the day and brought the fascinator.

George manoeuvred himself into the driving seat, placing his walking stick on the back seat, and revved the engine. As he started to pull away the first few spots of rain started to fall from the darkening clouds.

'Good job the old gal's not an open-top,' he said, as he began his detour around the town centre making sure Bel would be fashionably late by just five minutes.

Chapter Thirty-Seven

The Registry Office, John Street, Sunderland

'Oh look, there's Hannah ... and *surprise, surprise*, Olly's with her,' Dorothy said cheekily to Angie and Polly. The three women were feeling particularly pleased with themselves as they'd done what they'd needed to do at the Grand Hotel and were now outside the Registry Office at the bottom end of John Street, just up from the wine and spirit merchants J.W. Cameron & Co. They were waiting for the rest of their workmates to arrive, as they had all arranged to meet up before going in.

Rosie had arrived earlier with Lily, and had bobbed out to tell them she was keeping Lily company inside. When Dorothy and Angie had seen she was wearing a pair of grey slacks their eyes nearly popped out. Although when their boss had disappeared back into the warmth of the stately Georgian building, they had admitted she carried them off really well.

'Hi Hannah ... hi *Oliver*,' Dorothy said as their 'little bird' and her 'friend' reached them. They all proceeded to 'ooh' and 'ah' about what the others were wearing, apart from Olly, of course, who seemed more than happy to take a back seat as long as that back seat meant he was by Hannah's side.

When they spotted Gloria pushing baby Hope across the Borough Road in her large Silver Cross pram, they all waved to her. Just as she was starting up John Street,

Martha suddenly appeared from around the corner, and, on seeing Gloria, bellowed out her name and stomped to catch up with her, nearly knocking over a well-dressed man coming the other way.

As Gloria and Martha joined the women, Polly glanced up to the darkening skies. 'Those clouds look a bit heavy to me,' she said. 'I reckon we all get in and get settled.'

'Yes, I agree,' Dorothy trilled, looking at her watch. 'Anyway, it's nearly time!' Her voice had climbed an octave. 'The bride should be here soon!'

'I'm guessing the groom is here already?' Gloria asked Polly, who laughed. 'Oh, yes, he got here with the Major before anyone else. Talk about eager! Although he is looking ever so nervous.'

'Speak of the devil,' Gloria said, seeing Joe come out of the front door with a couple of younger lads, who looked very smart and handsome in their khaki Home Guard uniforms and caps.

Dorothy nudged Angie and whispered in her ear, 'I reckon they're the farmer boys Pol told us about.'

Angie gave them a quick once-over and nodded her head. 'Agreed,' she said, in all earnestness. 'They've got the look.'

As soon as Joe spotted Gloria he hurried down the steps. 'How's our little Hope doing today?' he asked, taking hold of the top end of the pram, while the two 'farmer boys' took charge of the other end.

'This is Bert and this is Hector,' Joe introduced the young men to Gloria, as they hauled the pram up the short flight of stone steps, taking care not to rock the carriage and wake the baby.

As they manoeuvred the Silver Cross in, putting it at the side of the wide, tiled hallway, Gloria reached down and carefully lifted Hope out, gently cradling her in her arms.

'Thanks, lads,' she said, quickly adding, 'Joe, you'd better get yourself in there, she'll be due any minute now.' Gloria had to stifle a little chuckle as Joe did in fact look as nervous as hell as he hurried off into the large oak-panelled Registry Office, where all the guests were now gathered.

Gloria followed him through the open doorway and was immediately immersed in a hum of happy chatter and an air of anticipation.

'Budge up, girls,' she said as Dorothy, Angie, Martha, Hannah and Olly were fussing about which seats they should be in.

Dorothy patted the seat next to her, and as Gloria sat down in a chair by the aisle, Dorothy took a peek at her beloved goddaughter, who was all swaddled up in a blanket in her mother's arms.

'Fingers crossed she stays like this,' Gloria said.

Just then, Angie grabbed Dorothy's hand and squeezed it hard. 'Dor, look!' she whispered. 'There's *Lily!*'

If Dorothy could have screeched she would have. Instead she squeezed Angie's hand back – but even harder.

'Ow, that hurts!' Angie hissed into Dorothy's ear, but her eyes were glued to the back of Lily's head. Some strands of her peachy, orange-coloured hair had already broken free from the confines of her carefully coiffured bun. Dorothy and Angie stared at her profile as she turned her head to chat to Rosie.

'Blimey, I'd love to raid her make-up bag,' Dorothy said, eyeing Lily's perfectly made-up face which, for a change, had been done very subtly.

'I'd love to raid her jewellery box,' Angie said, just as Lily raised her hand to check her hair and in doing so flashed a hand covered in diamond and gold rings and a heavy gold bracelet.

The women welders all shuffled around in their seats,

trying to disguise the fact that they were having a good gawk at the other guests.

Hannah was looking at Agnes, who was in the front row. She was saying something to Arthur, who then got up and made his way down the aisle to wait for Bel.

Martha was looking at Joe's best man, Major Black, who was at the front in his wheelchair. They all knew he was a First World War veteran, and that he and Joe had become close since Joe had joined the Home Guard. She watched with interest as the Major turned his wheelchair around to check on the other six Home Guard soldiers. He seemed pleased that they were all sitting bolt upright and looking straight ahead of them.

Gloria, meanwhile, was transfixed by the sight of Pearl in her blue velvet dress as she walked around the Registrar's table, trying to keep an over-excited Lucille occupied.

'Blimey, Pearl looks good,' Gloria said to Polly. She couldn't keep the surprise out of her voice.

'I know,' Polly agreed in a loud whisper, 'I was quite taken aback myself when I saw her earlier on when she arrived. I thought that Kate was just doing a few alterations, but I think she must have binned the dress Pearl originally gave her and started afresh. Although where she managed to get hold of that velvet I have no idea.'

'Who's the bloke sitting on the other side, in front of the Home Guard?' Angie leant forward and asked. 'He looks a bit dodgy.'

Polly chuckled. 'Ah, that's Ronald. He's Pearl's *male friend*.'

'What?' Dorothy butted in. 'Like Hannah here's *Boy Friend*?' Hannah cast Dorothy a death stare and Olly turned a bright shade of red.

'Sort of,' Polly said quietly, 'although I think their friendship is based more on cigarettes and alcohol than anything else . . . He's all right, though. Joe and Arthur get on with him, so he can't be all bad.'

'And what about that old bloke – the other one who looks as ancient as Arthur?' Angie asked.

'That's Albert,' Polly said, 'Arthur's friend. The one with the allotment.'

Just then Beryl and her two girls, Audrey and Iris, bustled in and sat in front of the women welders. Beryl turned round. 'All right, you lot?'

Polly, Gloria, Dorothy, Angie, Martha, Hannah and Olly all smiled and nodded that they were. Beryl nudged her two teenage daughters and said, 'My two – Iris and Audrey.' On hearing their names both girls turned round and said a shy 'hello'.

Beryl then swivelled back around and leant across an empty chair in front of her to prod Agnes in the back. When she turned round Agnes's face lit up and the two old friends started nattering way.

The chatter in the room seemed to grow in volume for a few more minutes before a loud cough sounded out from the doorway. Fifteen heads turned as the Registrar, carrying a large, leather-bound book, entered the room. Everyone stopped talking as the middle-aged, smartly dressed town official entered. He smiled at the upturned faces as he walked down to the large wooden table at the front. He quickly surveyed the room, and was thankful there was just the one baby; newborns always seemed to pick the most inopportune moment to wake up and give their lungs a good workout.

'Ah, Mr Elliot,' the Registrar said, stretching out his hand to Joe. The gentle murmur of chatter started up again as Joe introduced the man to those in the front row.

One of the Registry Office employees, an older woman dressed from head to toe in brown, struggled into the room carrying a portable gramophone, which she placed on a small table at the back. She scuttled out of the room, returning seconds later with a record, just as Kate, Vivian and Maisie slipped into the back row.

'Blimey,' Kate whispered across to Vivian and Maisie, 'we're just in the nick of time.'

Maisie, however, couldn't have been more pleased with what she considered to be their perfect timing. Her plan was going better than she could ever have expected. There was no way she wanted to be introduced to any of the other guests – let alone the mother of the bride – at least, not until everyone was gathered at the wedding reception.

A few seconds later a slightly breathless George hurried through the entrance and sat himself in the seat next to Kate.

'Gosh, you'd think it was my daughter getting married,' he said quietly to Kate, who allowed herself a quiet chuckle.

Just then there was a crackle and then an instrumental version of 'Here Comes the Bride' filled the air. The whole room fell into an expectant silence as all the guests swivelled around.

Within seconds Bel entered the room, clutching her bouquet and walking arm in arm with a very proud-looking Arthur.

Bel's eyes immediately sought out Joe, standing straight, his walking stick barely visible in his left hand.

There was an immediate intake of breath as the guests took in the vision of this radiant bride who was wearing the most stunning silk dress, along with an incredibly elegant fascinator.

Joe looked mesmerised by the woman slowly making her way towards him.

Agnes looked at her daughter-in-law and then at her son and swallowed hard, determined not to cry.

When Bel reached Joe, the music stopped. The room was so quiet you could hear a pin drop.

The silence was broken by the clear, confident voice of the Registrar as he began the ceremony with a short statement on marriage.

'Bel looks pretty amazing, doesn't she?' Vivian's whispered question was directed to Kate on her right and Maisie on her left. Kate nodded. She felt both elated and exhausted. Her thumbs and fingers were as sore as hell, but it had been worth every pinprick – worth every minute she had spent hunched over her sewing machine to see the end result now, and on such a perfect model.

Maisie also nodded agreement, but as she did so she had to physically bite her bottom lip to prevent the envy and spite that had been building up in her from breaking free. She knew she had to keep it all in – for the moment, anyway.

'And now,' the Registrar said, 'for the wedding vows.'

He turned to look at Joe. 'Please repeat after me . . . "I, Joe Harold Elliot, take you . . . "'

Everyone looked on as Joe and Bel promised to love each other 'for better or for worse, for richer, for poorer, in sickness and in health . . . '

There were more than a few watery eyes – from both the women and the men – by the time the Registrar asked Major Black for the ring.

As Joe slid the small gold band that he had bought on tick from Blacklock the jewellers in town on to Bel's hand, the Registrar said, 'I hereby declare you man and wife . . . You may kiss the bride.'

Dorothy and Angie didn't move a muscle as they gawped at the newly-marrieds, who were, in their eyes, akin to a Hollywood couple. As Joe took Bel's upturned face into his hands and kissed her ever so gently on the lips, Dorothy let out a loud sigh, causing Iris and Audrey to giggle.

There was a spontaneous round of applause, before another record, 'Night and Day' by Cole Porter, was played, and Bel and Joe signed the marriage register, with Agnes and Pearl stepping forward to add their signatures as witnesses.

By now everyone had started shuffling around in their seats and chattering to each other. Polly turned round and introduced the women welders to Kate, Vivian and Maisie. There was fascination in both camps, who were equally intrigued by the work the other did. Hannah congratulated Kate on her 'magnificent dress' and Dorothy asked Vivian how she had created Bel's hairdo.

As they chatted, Maisie feigned interest but all the while she kept surreptitiously looking at Pearl and Bel at the front of the room, watching their every move.

As Bel and Joe came out of the Registry Office, Major Black wheeled himself towards them, stopping them on their way out.

'Congratulations! Happiness and health!' he declared.

'Ah, Major,' Bel said, bending forward to take his proffered hand and shaking it vigorously. 'I've heard so much about you. It's lovely to finally meet you – to put a face to a name.'

As she spoke Bel sensed a flurry of movement behind them and felt a gust of cold air as the front door of the Registry Office opened and closed.

'Ah, but it is even more lovely for me to meet you – and to see that Joe was not exaggerating when he spoke of you.' Major Black beamed at Bel and then at Joe. 'And I have to say, Mrs Elliot,' he paused, his attention flickered to the doorway behind them, ' . . . that you have got yourself a very honourable man here.'

Joe shuffled uneasily. He always hated any kind of praise.

'Well, we'd better get off to the Tatham, have a little knees-up . . . although,' Joe chuckled, tapping his gammy leg with his walking stick, 'that might be hard for the both of us.'

The Major let out a loud laugh. 'Aye, that may well be, but, you know, I was never much of a dancer – even before,' and he looked down at his missing limbs. 'The women all used to complain I had two left feet,' he said and chuckled.

When someone coughed loudly behind Bel and Joe, Major Black edged his wheelchair forward and spoke to the man who stood a few yards away.

'All ready, Private?' His voice had lost its conviviality and was now unmistakably sergeant-majorly.

'Yes, sir,' Hector replied, saluting the Major, then looking at Joe and Bel. He was standing to attention, with one arm holding open the front door of the Registry Office.

Joe looked questioningly at his best man.

'Private Elliot,' the Major commanded. 'Time to escort your wife out of the building.'

Joe put his arm out and Bel, smiling, hooked her arm into his, unsure what was going on but so blissfully happy that she didn't care.

As they walked out the front door, they saw what had been orchestrated behind their backs while the Major had been keeping them talking. The half-dozen Home Guard soldiers from Joe's squad were lining the steps of the Registry Office, and had created a V-shaped canopy of long rifles under which the newly-marrieds were to take their first walk as man and wife.

Joe felt pride well up as he and Bel made their way down the stone steps.

'Hip hip hurrah!' the crowd of wedding guests, all now positioned on the pavement, shouted out.

As the couple neared the last step a shower of confetti and rice rained down on them, amidst shouts and claps, and whistles from the men.

A spindly, grey-haired photographer called Clement Humphreys, who had his shop just a few doors down from the Elliots, had agreed to take the wedding photos for a small fee, but due to the wartime shortage of film, he was limited to just two photographs. He had chanced it and snapped a lovely, natural shot of the bride and groom walking down the steps, full of smiles and laughter.

'Just a quick group shot of everyone together, please,' Clement requested, looking up at the sky. Dark clouds overhead intimated that it wouldn't be long before the heavens opened. Luckily everyone quickly squeezed together.

'Cheese!' Clement shouted out the time-worn signal to smile. He managed to get the whole wedding party in – everyone, that was, apart from Maisie, who had left the wedding just before the end, telling Kate and Vivian that she was nipping to Joseph's department store to get a little present for the newly-weds.

In reality, she was keeping to her well-thought-out plan, and didn't want to risk meeting any of the other guests until they were all happily ensconced in the Tatham.

As Clement hurried back to his studio to develop the two photographs, George took over and started to usher the happy couple into the wedding car, which he had left parked up right outside the Registry Office.

Bel was just about to get into the car when she realised she had forgotten something.

'The bouquet!' she shouted out. 'I haven't thrown the bouquet!'

George stepped forward. 'Look out, there's a lovely bouquet of flowers about to head someone's way.'

As he spoke Bel turned her back on her wedding guests and threw the bouquet into the air. It went higher than she had meant it to go. Some of the crowd were still chatting, others like Vivian, Dorothy and Angie were watching with eagle eyes as the colourful bouquet of wild flowers dropped down – and straight on to the balding head of one of the Home Guard soldiers who was engrossed in conversation with Lily.

The bouquet proceeded to bounce off him – and landed straight on Lily's ample bosom.

Lily jumped in shock, instinctively catching the bouquet before it dropped to the ground.

Everyone cheered and Lily looked mortified, turning and desperately trying to give it away to one of the younger girls – but with no joy. No one would take it off her. It was against tradition, after all.

As George closed the passenger doors and made his way around to the driver's side, he looked over to Lily who stood, looking more than a little flushed, still awkwardly holding the wedding bouquet. As he caught her eye he gave her a smile and a wink.

It was a good omen.

As Joe and Bel sat with their arms wrapped round each other in the back of George's MG, Bel could feel her heart hammering. She looked up at Joe and thought how attractive he was, and how it amazed her that she hadn't noticed how handsome he was until recently – despite knowing him just about all of her life.

Of course, that was probably because she had only ever

had eyes for Teddy. She had never even looked at another man once they'd started courting. For the briefest of moments Bel's mind slipped back to her previous life, and she allowed it – but just for a second.

As the car turned into Frederick Street, Joe bowed his head to Bel and kissed her, before sitting back and sighing.

'Ah, my first proper kiss as a married man,' he smiled. 'I think I'm going to enjoy this marriage malarkey.'

Bel looked at her husband and let out a gasp of mock outrage, before lifting her face up to his and kissing him back. She then sat back and sighed equally dramatically.

'You know what? I think I am too,' she said with a cheeky smile.

Joe chuckled and put his arm round his new wife and held her close.

'So then, George –' he turned his attention to their chauffeur for the day '– what did you think of the ceremony. Short and sweet, eh?'

George kept his eyes on the road, but let out a loud laugh. 'Absolutely perfect, I'd say!'

'And now for the good part,' Joe joked, as they pulled up outside the Tatham Arms. Bel nudged him playfully.

'You can say that again . . . ' George said, clambering out of the car and opening the door for Bel. 'I don't know about you two – but I'm parched!'

Joe hauled himself out the other side with the help of his stick and as he hobbled round the back of the car he noticed the 'Just married' sign that had been strapped to the boot, along with three long strings of cans, which they had heard clanging behind them during their short journey.

'Right,' George commanded. 'You two lovebirds get yourself inside, while I go and pick up a few more guests. I do believe Pearl and Agnes – being the bride and groom's mothers – are top priority and, of course, Lily, as it'll be a complete shock to her system to actually have to walk anywhere.'

He was still laughing to himself when he got back into the driving seat and sped off. As he did so some of the cans broke free and were left rolling in the middle of the road.

Watching the car drive away, Bel and Joe looked at each other, knowing this would probably be the only part of the day they would get to be totally on their own.

'I never thought I would feel this kind of love,' Joe said in all seriousness. 'Thank you for giving me that.'

Bel put her arms round her husband's neck and kissed him. She didn't need to tell him that she too had never expected to feel this kind of love again, and that she loved him even more for it. They knew that what they had was very special and that – in these uncertain times – they were a very lucky couple.

As they stood for a moment and gently kissed each other, Bel felt it really was the start of a new life.

Their quiet moment together, however, lasted just a few minutes before it was broken by the sound of the pub door banging open and Bill's gruff voice telling them to 'Get yerselves in here – there'll be plenty of time fer smooching later on!'

Chapter Thirty-Eight

The Tatham Arms, Tatham Street, Sunderland

Half an hour later the bar was heaving with the guests from the wedding and other friends and neighbours from around the doors. Mavis and Maud had brought the wedding cake over and it had taken pride of place in the middle of the buffet and been admired by just about all the guests, who were equally keen to sample a slice.

Dorothy and Angie were chatting to Lily and Vivian while George bobbed about, replenishing their glasses. He brought a plate of sandwiches and napkins over to them, but all four women shook their heads; they were far more interested in having a good chinwag. Hearing that the conversation was still on all things fashion and hair, George veered off with his plate of food to introduce himself to Ronald and some of the neighbours.

'I don't know where Maisie's got to,' Vivian said. She looked towards the entrance of the bar. 'Surely it doesn't take that long to get a wedding present?'

'Perhaps she had a change of heart about coming,' Lily suggested. She knew that she herself had certainly thought of a few excuses to back out of the wedding, although she was glad she had summoned the courage to brave the real world; she was actually fitting in better than she would have thought. If the north-east accents around her were to be replaced by cockney she would feel like she was back on her home turf.

On the other side of the room Bel stood chatting to some of her old workmates from the Corporation, as well as her old boss, Howard, but her mind was only half on the conversation as she had been watching her ma and Kate chatting away while they looked after Lucille. The two of them had really bonded these past couple of weeks in the run-up to the wedding.

As Kate caught a giggling Lucille as she raced around their legs, and hauled her up into the air, Bel looked at her ma, who had a large Scotch in her hand. Bel was relieved to see that she didn't look too far gone, but she knew there was still plenty of time for her to get plastered.

Bel's eyes strayed, looking for her new husband, and she found Joe behind a hazy blanket of cigar smoke, at one of the small pub tables, chatting with Major Black and a couple of the other soldiers. Bert, the younger of the two farmer boys, was spluttering as he half choked on a cigar that the Major had just given him.

Seeing the small group of uniformed men, Bel remembered the day Joe had returned home after joining the Home Guard, and how she had stupidly thought he had re-enlisted with the army, in spite of his medical discharge. She had nearly been in tears. Looking back, it was then she had started to have feelings for Joe, although she hadn't realised it until much later.

'Order! Order!' Major Black had moved his wheelchair away from the table and was chinking the side of his glass with a knife he had borrowed from the buffet table.

'Before everyone starts to enjoy themselves too much, I think it is time to formally toast the happy couple.'

There was a murmur of agreement and everyone picked up their glasses, as Joe stood up and looked around to find his wife. On seeing her, he strode over to where she was;

his gait lopsided due to his reliance on his walking stick, but strong and determined nonetheless.

'To a long and happy married life together. Joe and Bel,' the Major said simply.

Everyone raised their glasses and there was a general shout of, 'Hear! Hear!' as everyone took a sip of their drinks.

'Speech!' Hector shouted out. His demand was seconded by various other guests.

'Come on, Joe! It's not like you to be shy!' Polly shouted.

Bel chuckled to herself as she knew Joe was dreading having to make a speech, but it was clear he wouldn't be able to get away without giving one.

'All right … all right,' Joe said, leaning a little on his walking stick and taking Bel's hand with the other.

The chatter in the room dwindled as everyone looked towards the groom.

'As you all know, I'm not the best talker ever … '

His words met with a few jeers from the Home Guard, who knew Joe could be as verbose as the next person when he wanted.

'I think you all know just how happy and how lucky I feel … how lucky *I am* … having persuaded Bel to marry me.'

There were a few quiet 'ahs' from the women.

'I never thought in a million years,' Joe continued, 'that I would be stood here now – having wed the woman of my dreams … '

Heads turned to Bel, who blushed and smiled back at Joe.

'There is only one other wish I have now – and I'm sure you will all agree with me – and that is that this damnable war is won, and that there is not another single life lost.'

'Hear! Hear!' The whole room agreed with fervour.

Just as everyone raised their glasses in another toast, Maisie slipped into the bar. She had been standing quietly in the narrow hallway by the entrance to the bar, listening intently, waiting for the right moment. On hearing the start of the toasts, she had quietly opened the glass partition door and slipped into the room, which was now clouded with a mixture of cigarette and cigar smoke.

'Where've you been?' Vivian hurried over to her friend as soon as she spotted her sidle into the bar. She looked down and saw that Maisie was empty-handed.

'And where's the present?'

'Long story,' Maisie said. 'I'll tell you later.'

The room was starting to fill with the sound of chatter, when Joe spoke up again.

'Sorry, everyone –' he had to raise his voice to be heard, 'there is one more thing I want to say . . . and that is a big "thank you" for everyone who has come today to help us celebrate – and for everyone's hard work in making it happen . . . and for all your lovely presents . . . Mavis and Maud and Beryl for the wonderful cake . . . Bill, for allowing us to run riot in his pub . . . and Rosie,' Joe looked over a few heads so he could speak directly to Polly's boss. 'You have been so kind. It's thanks to you – and Kate, of course – that my wife – and my new *mother-in-law*,' Joe looked over to Pearl who stood up straight as the spotlight fell on her momentarily, ' . . . are wearing dresses that not only look amazing, but,' he added, looking back at Bel, 'have made this day even more special for them both.'

As he spoke a resolute-looking Maisie stared at Bel, then her angry-looking eyes sought out Pearl.

'And,' Bel chirped up, squeezing Joe's hand, 'Polly has just told me that she has done something which she really *shouldn't* have done – something that is over-generous and totally exorbitant – *she has booked us into the honeymoon suite at the Grand Hotel.'* Bel's voice rose with excitement. She really could not believe her sister-in-law had done that.

The expression on Joe's face showed just how taken aback he was. He had certainly not expected this. He looked over to his sister, who he knew must have spent every penny she had to afford such an extravagance, and mouthed *thank you.*

Bel turned to Joe and gave him a quick kiss. Her wedding day was turning out so much better than she could ever have wished for. She had never imagined she could be so happy.

As everyone started to chatter once again amongst themselves and make their way over to the buffet to replenish their plates, Maisie's refined voice could be heard as she weaved through the guests to reach the newly-married couple.

'Excuse me,' her polite voice sounded out. She was smaller than most and so could not be seen.

It wasn't until Maisie came into view at the front of the line of guests that Pearl saw her for the first time – and when she did she took a sharp intake of breath.

Kate turned her head sharply to look at Pearl and saw that she was as white as a ghost. Lucille also immediately sensed the change in her grandmother and started tugging at her arm for reassurance. But Pearl was as still as a statue – unresponsive to either Kate's concerned look or the demands of her perplexed granddaughter.

'Sorry, excuse me,' Maisie repeated as she finally made it through the crowd and stepped forward.

Bel looked at her, wondering why this woman, who she had met only very briefly twice before, was making a beeline for them both.

'*Isabelle,*' Maisie said with the most winning smile.

Bel couldn't help but flinch for the second time that day at the use of her full name, and again was reminded of the unease she'd felt earlier on when Maisie had wished her a 'Happy Wedding Day'.

Maisie looked around her; she knew how to work a crowd and how to ensure she had everyone's attention.

Towards the back of the room, Lily was standing stock-still, her drink halfway to her mouth, wondering what on earth Maisie was about to do. Vivian, too, was staring at her friend with a puzzled look on her face. Maisie didn't really know Bel or Joe, so why was she approaching them now – in front of the entire wedding party?

'You're all probably wondering what I am doing here,' Maisie's voice sang out as she gave another enchanting smile, scanning the room until finally she found who she was looking for.

Pearl.

For a fleeting moment the two stared at each other before Maisie turned her attention back to the bride and groom.

'Well,' she said with a deliberate hint of mystery, 'I have rather a special – or should I say a somewhat *unusual* – gift for the happy couple – and for the bride, in particular.'

Bel was looking at Maisie, her face questioning. Alarm bells had started to ring in her head. Something wasn't right.

The pub was completely quiet. You could hear a pin drop.

Bel tried to smile. 'This all sounds ever so intriguing, *Maisie*,' she said, looking up at Joe, who appeared equally baffled.

Everyone's eyes were totally focused on Bel and Maisie as they now stood facing each other.

No one saw the look of shock and total disbelief on Pearl's face – nor did they notice her grab one of the chairs as her legs gave way on hearing the name:

Maisie.

328

Chapter Thirty-Nine

'*Isabelle*, my wedding present to you . . . ' Maisie said, ' . . . *is me*.

'I present *myself* to you . . . ' As Maisie spoke there was the hint of a tremor in her voice, evidence of her underlying nerves.

' . . . *as your long-lost sister.*'

Bel looked at Maisie and didn't say anything. She was speechless. She opened her mouth to speak but nothing came out.

'Oh, I'm so sorry, Isabelle,' Maisie feigned an apology, looking about her with doe eyes. 'I should have really waited until later . . . But I just couldn't put it off any longer . . . I've wanted to tell you for so long now . . . I've just been unsure when the right time was.'

The pub was at a silent standstill, everybody captivated by the most shocking and totally unexpected wedding scene being played out in front of them.

An appalled Lily turned to George and hissed in a whisper. '*Really?! And this was the right time?*'

Polly was looking aghast as she watched Bel and Maisie. The unsaid question on everyone's lips was, '*How could this be?*'

'When I saw you today, I knew I just had to tell you . . . You've not just gained a husband today – *but also a sister.*'

Maisie took Bel's hand in her own. Bel was too dumbstruck to snatch it away.

Finally she found her voice, and stuttered, 'I don't understand!'

Bel was struggling to comprehend what Maisie was saying to her. For a moment it flashed through her mind that it was some kind of sick joke.

'You are my *sister*?' Bel asked incredulously, her voice shaking. Her disbelief more than evident.

'Yes, *I am*,' Maisie said, moving even closer to Bel.

'Well, technically –' she touched her cheek self-consciously with her free hand '– you are my *half*-sister . . . We both clearly have different fathers, but . . . ' she added as she turned her gaze away from Bel and once again sought out Pearl.

'*We most certainly have the same mother.*'

All Pearl could do was stare at her daughter. Her baby girl. The one she had loved with all her being. The one she had given away.

She was aware that Kate was saying something; there was a worried look on her pretty, elf-like face, but all Pearl could hear was a strange roaring in her ears. Like the angry waves of the sea on a bitter, cold winter day. For a moment she was back on the coal-speckled beach in Hendon, her stomach burning with hunger, her eyes on the pregnant belly of the girl, knowing that this too was the fate which awaited her.

Pearl sat in shock. The faces around her were painted with a mixture of astonishment and curiosity. It was as though life had suddenly changed tempo so that everything and everyone was now moving in slow motion.

In the corner of her eye she saw a yellow blur of a little girl in a pretty pinafore dress who was running around.

Pearl's vision, however, was glued to her daughter.

Her Maisie.

They kept the name, was all she could think.

And as she continued to stare she took in her daughter's look.

She marvelled at how stunning *her* daughter was.

The colour of her skin was just like it had been as a baby. A beautiful brown. And those eyes. Eyes that had made her fall in love. Eyes that had broken her heart.

Pearl watched as Maisie turned slightly away from her to look at Bel.

Her two daughters. Together.

Only then did Pearl find her voice.

'*Maisie*,' she said.

It was the first time she had uttered that name aloud since the day Maisie had been born.

'*Maisie*,' Pearl repeated as she stood up. 'Is it really you?' She could still not quite believe that her daughter was here. Now. That what she was seeing with her own eyes was true.

Pearl stepped towards her daughter. The daughter she had thought she would never see again.

The daughter that she had thought about every day since the moment she had given her up.

But as Pearl walked towards her Maisie – her baby girl – the roaring in her ears became louder. Then, all of the strength in her body deserted her and her legs buckled. The floor rushed towards her – and Pearl's world went black.

Chapter Forty

'Oh, my God, Ma!' Bel went to catch her mother as she crashed to the floor but it was too late – she landed hard, her head cracking on the wooden floorboards. Bel and Joe instinctively went to Pearl's aid, while Hector, who had been chatting to Dorothy, pushed through the crowd of stunned wedding guests, and, crouching down next to her, scooped her up in his thick muscular arms as if she was a sleeping child.

'In the snug, son.' It was Bill, red-faced and looking worried, pointing the way to the back room.

Lucille started whimpering, 'Nana! Nana!' Kate grabbed her and hoiked her on to her hip, shushing her and telling her it would be all right. Polly started to head towards Bel, but then stopped. Joe was there for her sister-in-law.

Everyone watched in shocked silence as Joe, Bel and Maisie followed Hector as he carried a limp, unconscious Pearl through to the adjacent room.

The snug was, thankfully, empty as everyone had been in the main bar, enjoying the wedding and the food and drink. As Pearl started to come round, Hector carefully put her down on to one of the cushioned chairs by the small coal fire that was burning in the corner. Bill hurried in with a large glass of brandy and put it down on the table in front of her.

'Do you think she's ganna be all right? Do ya think I need to fetch a doctor?' he asked Bel, all the time his eyes darting back to Pearl, the woman who had become just as much a friend as an employee these past few months.

Bel perched herself on a stool next to her mother and moved a thick strand of dyed-blonde hair away from her forehead to inspect the damage. Pearl had a tiny cut on her forehead, and her velvet dress had some dirt on it from the wooden floor, but otherwise she appeared unhurt.

'No, Bill, I think she's going to be fine. Thanks anyway,' Bel said, giving a concerned-looking Bill a tight smile before she shot a look at Maisie, who had sat down on the chair next to Pearl.

Bel glanced up at Joe who was leaning on his walking stick in the middle of the snug, a look of grave concern on his face.

'Joe, can you let everyone know that Ma's all right and to carry on with the party.'

Joe nodded solemnly and walked out of the room, followed by Hector and Bill. This, they all knew, was a family affair. As the door to the snug was pulled to, Bel heard Joe carrying out her wishes, then Bill's voice offering everyone a free drink at the bar.

'Maisie . . .' Pearl was now fully conscious, although her speech was a little slurred, as if she had just woken up.

'Maisie?' she repeated. She had so many questions; she didn't know where to start.

'Yes, *Mother?*' Maisie said, staring at Pearl. This was the first time she had seen her mother at such close proximity. Since she had moved up from London, she had only observed Pearl from afar. She looked more worn than she had expected, for a woman in her early forties, but Maisie could tell she had once been very attractive.

'Or should I call you "Ma" like your other daughter?' Maisie asked with more than a hint of vitriol in her voice.

Bel looked at Pearl and then back to Maisie. 'Can one of you at least tell me what the hell's going on?' Bel asked. Anger was starting to find its way through the shock.

Maisie's head turned slowly towards Bel.

'*Isabelle* . . . ' Maisie's tone was now filled with condescension, ' . . . it doesn't take a genius to work it out, *does it*?'

Bel stared back at her new-found sister and fought the urge to slap her hard around the face.

'Your "ma",' Maisie continued, her eyes shooting daggers at Bel and then at Pearl, 'quite frankly, didn't want me . . . so, she simply gave me away.' Her words dripped bitterness and anger.

' . . . That's "*what the hell is going on*", dear sister. No ifs or buts. Our mother . . . ' a disingenuous smile spread across Maisie's pretty face, 'for reasons that are clear for anyone but a blind man to see, decided to keep you. But me? Well, she decided to simply toss me away – hand me over to complete strangers – and then toddle off to happily get on with her own life . . . unburdened by some bawling half-caste brat.'

Pearl looked thunderstruck and opened her mouth to object, to tell her how wrong she was, but Maisie beat her to it and continued.

'So, when I found out who my mother was – and where she was – I thought it would be nice for us all to be together. To finally meet each other – after all of these years apart.'

Bel looked at her mother who now had tears in her eyes and a look on her face that Bel had never seen before in her entire life. If she didn't know better, she'd think her ma was broken-hearted.

'*Maisie*,' Pearl pleaded. She hadn't been able to take her eyes off her daughter. She looked so like her father it was untrue. The young boy she had loved, even if it had just been for a short while.

'Maisie, yer dinnit understand,' Pearl's voice was breaking with emotion. 'I didn't just "toss ya away". I didn't just "hand yer over" willy-nilly. I had no choice. You *have to* believe me. Yer *have* to understand . . . '

'No, I don't *understand*!' Maisie spat back sharply. 'You seem to have a perfectly good life here. With all your family around you. You even live with your daughter, for heaven's sake! You don't get much cosier than that, do you?'

Bel looked at Maisie in disbelief. *How wrong could someone be?*

'Oh, Maisie, you really have *no idea* . . . ' she started to say, but neither Maisie nor Pearl were paying her any heed.

'Maisie,' Pearl was now begging, 'yer *have* to believe me. I wanted to keep ya. *Would have done anything to keep ya*. But there was no way I *could* keep yer . . . I was so young . . . still a child, really . . . times were different then . . . '

But Maisie wasn't listening. She could only feel her own hurt – her own intense resentment and fury that *she* had been the forsaken child. The one who was not wanted.

'I *loved* you!' Pearl implored.

Bel stared at her mother; never once in her own life had her ma told her that she loved her.

'Well,' Maisie said, her eyes narrowing, staring intensely at Pearl, 'that's a strange way of showing someone you love them – *giving them away*.'

Pearl was leaning forward, straining to get as near as she could to her child. She tried to take her hand, but Maisie snatched it away before Pearl managed to touch her. The hurt stabbed at her. Her heart, broken when she had given her baby away all those years ago, was being ripped apart once again. Her baby. Her child. Her daughter. The one being she had loved as she had not loved anyone else since *hated* her. Truly and deeply. She could see it in her daughter's face – hear it as clear as day in her voice.

Bel meanwhile was astounded by what was happening in front of her very eyes. She had never seen so much

335

hatred and bitterness, nor so much hurt and heartache, exchanged between two people. Her ma's face was deathly white, while Maisie's seemed to be radiating pure animosity.

Bel watched, feeling like a spectator in a terrible tragic drama as Pearl pushed herself out of her cushioned chair and glared at Maisie.

Maisie mimicked her mother's actions and as she got to her feet, their faces were only inches apart.

'Well, if you *loved* me, *Ma*, then I can tell you for a fact that I have *hated* you my entire life. There has not been a day in my life when I haven't thought about you – and detested every bone in your body. It's just such a relief to finally tell you to your face.'

Bel was shocked at the ferociousness of Maisie's tone. She herself might sometimes have felt that she too hated her mother – might have even told her a few times in a fit of anger – but that was nothing compared to this.

For a moment Bel thought her ma was going to swing for Maisie, but instead Pearl clenched both hands into fists and held them firmly by her side. She glared at Maisie. Her mouth opened, but she seemed unable to speak the words piling up inside her that wanted – needed – to get out.

Instead her mother did something Bel had never seen before – she started to cry. Tears began to spill unguarded down her face.

Bel stared in disbelief. She had never in her whole life seen her ma this way.

'I . . . ' Pearl stuttered, her voice cracking up with emotion, '*loved yer* . . . I *loved yer* like I have never loved anyone since. I *loved yer* for the nine months you were in my belly, and I loved yer even more when I gave birth to ya. I didn't think it was possible to love another human being the way I loved you . . . '

Tears were streaming down Pearl's face. Her mascara was running down her cheeks in dark rivulets. Bel was stunned.

'The day I gave birth to you,' Pearl heaved in air, 'was the best day in my entire life – and also the worst. That day I felt what *real* love was,' Pearl sucked in another breath – 'but when they took you from me I thought I would die right there . . . '

She looked down at the untouched brandy on the table and reached for it, then knocked it back in one. The sting of brandy seemed to quell the tears.

Maisie's look was still one of venom. Her mother's words had not so much as touched her, and she told her so.

'Words are easy to say, Mother. But what's the expression, "Actions speak louder than words"? If you had really wanted me, you would have kept me.'

Pearl looked at her daughter and saw only the deep-seated hatred. The lack of desire for any kind of reconciliation.

'But Maisie, I *did* want you . . . wanted yer more than anything in the whole wide world . . . Don't you see, *I gave yer up because I loved yer too much to keep ya?*'

Pearl then turned her attention momentarily to Bel and a softness crept into her eyes as she stared at her daughter, who looked so pretty in her pink wedding dress.

'And when Isabelle here came along a few years later,' she told Maisie, 'I . . . ' Pearl flashed another look at Bel, this one tinged with guilt, ' . . . I felt nothing . . . I tried. Really tried. It was like I gave you all the love I had and I just didn't have any more left in me . . . ' Pearl looked bereft as she regarded Bel with true remorse.

'But. Aye. Yer right,' Pearl snapped, her tone hardening as she swung her gaze towards Maisie. 'I kept Isabelle, because I was older . . . because I could.'

Maisie's delicate features formed an ugly sneer as she glowered at her mother before she spat out her retort.

'So, let's get this right, *Ma*. You loved me *so* much you gave me away – and the daughter you claim not to have loved, you kept. Makes a lot of sense, that.'

Maisie shook her head from side to side.

'You know what, *Ma*, I didn't think it was possible for me to hate you any more than I did already, but I can honestly say that after finally meeting you, *I do*.'

There was a deathly silence.

There were no more words.

Enough had been said already.

Pearl stared at Maisie, before slowly turning and walking out of the snug, and out of the pub. And, once again, out of her daughter's life.

Chapter Forty-One

As Bel and Maisie watched their mother walk away, neither of them seemed able to move.

After what felt like an eternity Bel finally stood up and faced her sister. She was still in shock, but she was also very angry.

'Well, *thanks*, Maisie,' Bel uttered her words with a tight mouth. 'I hope that little reunion went just the way you wanted – just the way you planned it.

'Actually, you really do deserve a round of applause, because – let's face it – your timing couldn't have been better. I mean, you got to kill two birds with one stone, didn't you?

'You told my ma – sorry, I mean, *our ma* – exactly what you thought of her – got it all off your chest, didn't you? But as an added extra you got to ruin my wedding into the bargain.

'It wasn't enough to knock the stuffing out of your long-lost ma and humiliate her in front of everyone she knows – not that she'd give two hoots about that, to be honest – but you got your icing on the cake by making me suffer as well.

'By spoiling my special day. Ruining what should have been a happy occasion . . . I realised just then, sat back, watching your perfectly planned revenge, that it wasn't just Ma who had to suffer, but me as well. Am I right? It wasn't just Ma you wanted to get back at, but me too . . . because, of course, I've had such a gilded life, haven't I?

I've been such a lucky little mummy's girl, eh? The one she kept? The one she didn't toss away? Am I right?'

Bel manoeuvred her way around the small bar table that separated her and Maisie.

'Well, bravo, Maisie. I hope you're feeling really pleased with yourself now. You succeeded perfectly in what you very clearly set out to do.'

Bel turned her back on Maisie and took a few steps towards the snug door, before hesitating and turning back round again.

'But, *sister* – sorry, *"half-sister"* – when you're ready to come out of that fantasy world of yours and hear the truth about what it was really like growing up with *our mother*, then please do come and see me, and we can have a nice cup of tea and a good natter,' Bel was now spitting nails, 'and then I can tell you just how perfectly wonderful our life together really was . . . '

Bel's head swung round and she cast a look through the frosted glass of the snug door.

'As can most of the people out there,' she pointed her finger at the door: 'friends and neighbours who used to see her staggering around the place, half-cut, or with some dodgy no-good bloke – but that, of course, was only when she decided to grace us with her presence.

'Oh, and one more thing before I go back and join my guests at my wedding reception, you might as well know – as you are my sister, after all – everyone calls me "Bel". I hate being called "Isabelle" so, please, don't ever call me "Isabelle" again otherwise I might not be as polite as I am being now.'

And with that Bel stomped towards the door, swung it open, and walked out of the snug, leaving Maisie standing on her own in the middle of the room.

*

'Are you all right? We can go home if you want?' Joe asked Bel as soon as she emerged from the snug. He had watched Pearl leave and had anxiously waited for Bel to resurface.

'What?' Bel forced an unconvincing smile. 'And miss my own wedding reception?' Her words came out with a large breath. Her heart was hammering, and she felt like she'd just done a hundred yard dash.

Joe put his arm round her and gave her a quick hug.

'And we're not going home,' Bel added, 'that's for sure. My wonderful sister-in-law ... ' she spoke up as Polly came hurrying over, ' . . . has got us a room in the best hotel in town.'

'Are you all right?' Polly asked, her face etched with concern.

Bel let out a slightly embittered laugh.

'You know my family, Pol, as well as I do. Always full of surprises.'

It hadn't escaped Bel's notice that she might only just have met Maisie and had spent barely half an hour in her company, but she was clearly every inch her mother's daughter; born with an inherent need to be the centre of attention, whether that be for good or bad.

'If you want I can go to the Grand and see if they can change the reservation to another night?' Polly asked, tentatively, glancing at Joe to gauge his reaction.

'No way!' Bel said. 'You've got to be joking. Wild horses couldn't stop me going there tonight. I haven't even been inside the foyer, never mind stayed in one of the rooms there. I'm fine,' she told Polly. 'Honestly, I am.

'Now, come on,' she added, taking hold of Joe's hand, 'let's go and see what that little girl of mine is up to.'

As Bel walked on, Polly threw her brother a concerned look. He smiled sadly at his sister. They both knew that it didn't matter how hard Bel tried, Maisie had succeeded in chucking a great big pan of cold water over this special day. They also knew, however, that Bel would put on a show for the remainder of her wedding reception, and would only sit back and lick her wounds in private.

Chapter Forty-Two

Lily was furious with Maisie and had been keeping an eagle eye on the snug door waiting for her most recent employee to come out. She felt more than a little guilty that this debacle they had all just witnessed on poor Bel's wedding day was, to a certain extent, her fault as she had been the person to bring Maisie into contact with the Elliots. And what was making her even angrier was that it looked like Maisie had used her – and Rosie – to get close to Bel and Pearl, thus enabling her to carry out her timely revenge.

'The ironic thing is,' George said quietly to Lily, 'that Maisie did actually tell us she had come up north to get –"reacquainted", I think was the word she used – with some of her relatives.'

'Hmm,' Lily said, her lips pursed shut, her eyes still glued to the snug.

As Maisie emerged, she put her head down and started to walk quickly to the saloon door leading out into the hallway – but there was no way that Lily was going to let her sneak out without giving her a piece of her mind.

'I want words with you when I get back, young lady,' Lily said, grabbing Maisie's slender arm and stopping her in her tracks.

'What you just did there was totally unforgivable,' Lily hissed in her ear. 'So, don't think you're going to get away with this lightly. And don't even think about doing a moonlight flit, because I will find you – and then you really will be sorry.'

When Maisie looked up at her boss, she saw she had crossed the wrong person. She hadn't really thought through the full consequences of her actions – had just been so focused on her plans and how she wanted to confront her mother. She had heard Lily could be vicious when she needed to be – had heard plenty of stories from the other girls – but Maisie had foolishly thought she might somehow be immune to it. Clearly this was not the case. And as for doing a midnight bunk, well, the thought had gone through her head, but she was a realist – she had nowhere else to go.

'I'm sorry, Lily,' Maisie said, trying to smooth the way for later on. She looked at Lily and then down to the ground. 'I'll wait up.' Maisie wasn't stupid. She knew what side her bread was buttered, and she knew she was going to have to work hard at placating Lily and making amends in order to get her and George back onside.

Lily loosened her grip on Maisie's arm just as Vivian came hurrying over, her normally animated face looking poker serious. She had been chatting to one of the Home Guards, who, it turned out, was actually a schoolteacher and was quite funny, but when she'd spotted Maisie being caught in Lily's vice-like grip, she had quickly made her excuses and gone to her friend's aid.

'You going?' she asked Maisie, her eyes flicking to Lily's stony face.

'Yes, she is, Vivian,' Lily said, releasing Maisie.

'And Vivian,' Lily said, as both women turned to leave, 'I'd better not find out you had anything to do with any of this.'

Vivian shook her head vehemently.

As Vivian and Maisie slipped out of the bar, their departure was not missed by Kate, now playing peek-a-boo with Lucille. Her comic façade belied the outrage boiling up inside her. Maisie had spoilt the wedding – not just for Bel, but for Pearl too. And worse still, she was seriously wondering if Maisie had actually been devious enough to have held the fascinator back so that she could orchestrate her impromptu invite to the wedding.

'My dear, are you all right?' It was George, returning to Lily's side. He had quickly nipped over to the newly-marrieds to see if they wanted to be taken to the hotel now rather than later. When Bel had told him it was a very kind offer, but they were going to stay and enjoy the party, he'd seen dogged determination on her face. She was not going to let this ruin her wedding day. For the first time George saw that behind Bel's sweet persona there was a very resilient woman. Joe had chosen well.

'No, George, I'm not all right.' Lily's voice was harsh but quiet; she did not want to give away the fury building up inside her. 'That girl's used us like a good 'un,' she said, taking a swig of her whisky, 'but worst of all, she's tarnished us.'

George looked at Lily and knew how much being invited here today had meant to her. It was the first social event she had been asked to in a long while. And now it had been ruined by one of her girls.

'God knows how Rosie's feeling. She's going to rue the day she even told us all about the wedding, never mind got us involved.' As Lily spoke, she and George automatically looked around to find Rosie, who was sitting chatting to Gloria.

'Don't say that,' George said. It hurt him even to think Rosie was in any way ashamed of them. 'There's only one person to blame for what has happened – and that's Maisie. No one's going to blame you – or Rosie. You're not responsible for the actions of others.

'Come on,' George cajoled the woman who had become such an important part of his life for the past few years.

'Let's try and enjoy the rest of the party. If the bride and groom can do it –' they both looked over to see Bel and Joe, now chatting away to Hannah, Olly and Martha, '– then we jolly well can. So, chin up,' he said, taking Lily's arm, 'it looks to me as if you need a refill . . . I certainly do.'

But as George guided Lily towards the bar he had to mask his own, slightly selfish concerns that Maisie might have also spoilt what was meant to be his own very 'special day'.

If any of the other guests saw Maisie leave they pretended not to notice. What had happened between Pearl and Bel and this 'coloured' woman called Maisie had clearly caused great upset, but this was a wedding – it was meant to be a happy occasion, and so that's exactly what they would try and make it.

Bill was doing a grand job of keeping the mood upbeat, playing the role of the loud and cheerful landlord, laughing and joking at the bar.

Dorothy and Angie were naturally lightening the heavy atmosphere with their youthful exuberance, captivating all the young men with their vivaciousness. It was also obvious Dorothy was more than a little keen on Hector, who, in her eyes, had been the hero of the hour.

Bel, naturally, was playing the perfect host, chatting away to her guests as if nothing had happened; inwardly, though, she was finding it hard to ignore the myriad of thoughts that kept finding their way back to the forefront of her mind.

She had a sister!

Her mother had had another child!

Bel had so many questions swimming around in her head, but she had to push them back, knowing that, at the moment, they would have to remain unanswered. She tried to keep a convincing smile on her face, but it wasn't easy, and on top of everything else she had an uneasy feeling in the pit of her stomach about her ma. She would have felt more at ease if her mother had come back to the party.

Bill was also concerned about Pearl – he knew how much today had meant to her and how much work she had put into it. If truth be told, it hadn't surprised him that Pearl had had another child, who she'd put up for adoption. It was far from unusual, especially for someone like Pearl who had been brought up in the slums down by the south docks. No one who came from that poverty-stricken part of town had had an easy upbringing.

But what *was* unusual was that the child she'd given up had grown up, journeyed all the way from the Big Smoke to track her down – and then declared herself in such a dramatic fashion. Bill could only surmise that this Maisie woman had wanted to shame Pearl, to humiliate her – not only for having an illegitimate baby, but for the fact that Pearl had been with a black man.

As Bill pulled himself a pint, he mused that such a public confrontation would have brought terrible shame to most women, but not Pearl. She really was a rare one; a right tough nut. Bill knew her well enough now to be sure she wouldn't have given a monkey's chuff what anyone thought of her. But, he also knew that seeing the baby she had given away had shocked her to the core. That much was clear for all to see.

'Poor Bel, eh?' It was one of the barmaids. 'Fancy having that happen on your wedding day.'

Bill nodded his head.

'Aye, that Maisie couldn't have picked a worse time to do something like this. Or better. Depending on your perspective . . . ' Bill's words tailed off as the beer frothed and spat out of the pipe, telling him he needed to change the barrel.

Most of the other guests' sympathies also lay firmly

with Bel; no one more so than Rosie, who, like Lily, felt responsible.

'Rosie, it's not your fault,' Bel had told her when she'd apologised. 'It's not anyone's fault. Honestly, I mean that. The biggest sin you've committed is being too kind.' Bel had spoken in earnest. 'Look at this gorgeous dress you gave me as my wedding present –' she had gently taken hold of her silk dress '– I could never have dreamed about being married in such a fabulous dress.'

The women welders had all been shocked by what they had witnessed. Hannah was particularly taken aback. The world she'd inhabited before the war had been a sheltered one. Martha too had been affected, although for different reasons, for she knew her mother and father were not her so-called 'real' parents, although it had never occurred to her – nor had she the desire – to find the woman who had given birth to her.

When the party was back in full swing, Joe and Bel jointly cut the cake, amidst much cheering and applause. Watching her son and daughter-in-law, Agnes's heart felt heavy. She wished that, just for once, a celebratory event could be just that – a happy occasion, with no upset or drama. God knew, they'd had enough this past year to last them a lifetime. But, it seemed, whenever Pearl was part of the equation there was invariably some kind of trouble, or scene. Bel's ma may have been easier to tolerate of late, but she still had an innate knack of bringing turmoil into the lives she touched – whether intentionally or otherwise. And, it looked like this Maisie was a chip off the old block.

They would all get through the day the best they could, but Agnes knew this was not the end of it. Far from it. She was under no illusion: what had occurred this afternoon would have wide-reaching repercussions.

*

By early evening, the older guests, including Mavis and Maud and some of the elderly neighbours, headed home, and were replaced by some of the regulars who slipped in to join the revelry. The buffet had been reduced to crumbs and Bill and Ronald had tidied up and moved the make-shift table out the back to make space so that the party-goers could have a little room to dance.

Beryl had cajoled Joe and Bel into having the first dance, and Joe had done the best slow waltz he could manage without the aid of his walking stick; everyone had chuckled when Lucille had interrupted them by tugging on Joe's trousers and demanding to join in.

Albert had been particularly moved by the sight of Bel, with her daughter on her hip, dancing with her new hus-band, who was now, much to Lucille's glee, the father she had been determined to have since first clapping eyes on him.

Bill kept the music going as the other wedding guests took to their feet, Dorothy being one of the first up with Hector, then Angie and Bert, followed by a blushing Hannah as Olly took her hand and gently tugged her on to the makeshift dance floor. Even George eventually per-suaded Lily to 'give me the pleasure of a dance'. But by nine o'clock Bel was starting to tire. Reading her thoughts, Joe asked, 'You ready now?' Bel nodded and the pair of them went round their guests and said their thank-yous and goodbyes.

On seeing them preparing to leave, George switched back into his chauffeur mode and ushered the newly-marrieds out of the pub and into the MG for the final trip of their wedding day.

'Honestly, George, we could walk from here,' Bel objected, but George wasn't having any of it.

'No, no, you're actually doing me a favour,' he said, 'I

need to clear my head for something . . . Need my wits about me – so *you're* doing *me* a favour.'

After George dropped them off at the Grand, he stayed a moment and watched them as they hurried through the impressive hotel entrance. He hoped what had happened earlier on wouldn't spoil their first night together as man and wife.

Checking his inside pocket for the umpteenth time that evening, he put the car into first gear, and headed back to the pub.

Chapter Forty-Three

The Grand Hotel, Bridge Street, Sunderland

Bel might have been able to put on a plausible show for her wedding guests, but Joe knew that behind his wife's happy exterior there was a troubled woman. As they waved George off and stepped across the threshold of the Grand Hotel, Joe could see his new wife wilt, but she still managed to smile sweetly at the concierge who gave Joe the key to their room and congratulated them on their nuptials.

As they walked up the Axminster-carpeted stairs to the second floor and along the corridor to their room, Joe put his arm around her waist and squeezed her gently.

'I can read you like a book, Mrs Elliot,' he said, as he put the key in the lock. Before he opened the door, he turned to look at her.

'You've been waiting for this moment all night,' he said, adding with a slight self-deprecating chuckle, 'and it's not because you're swooning at the thought of finally getting your new husband on his own.'

Bel smiled up at Joe a little sadly, and kissed him lightly on the lips. She then bent down and took off her slingback shoes.

'Ah, that's better,' she said, letting them dangle from her hand.

When Joe opened the door and switched the light on, they both took an intake of breath. The oak-panelled room, with its thick tapestry curtains and huge king-sized bed, was like nothing either of them had ever seen before. And to add to the opulence of their honeymoon suite, Polly, Dorothy and Angie had covered the bed with a sea of confetti and rose petals. Bel also spotted an overnight bag by the tall mahogany wardrobe, and a candle and box of matches on each bedside table, alongside a miniature bottle of brandy.

'Oh,' Bel said, stepping into the room and looking around in amazement. 'It's wonderful . . . ' She looked up at Joe. 'You know . . . I'm a very lucky woman.'

Joe looked down at his bride and thought only Bel could say that after all that had happened today.

'Well, if you're lucky I don't know what that makes me,' he said, then pulled her close and kissed her.

'Now, Mrs Elliot,' Joe said, sitting his wife down on one of the two armchairs next to a little coffee table by the huge sash window, 'tell me how you're *really* feeling?'

Joe knew that tonight would not be the night of their dreams when they fell into each other's arms and made love without a care in the world. Too much had happened and Joe knew Bel well enough to know that deep down she was in bits and needed to talk. There would be plenty of other nights ahead of them when they could consummate their marriage.

Joe hobbled over to the bedside tables and got the little bottles of brandy and poured them into two glasses. He gave one to Bel, who took a sip and leant back into the comfort of the cushioned leather chair. She had purposely not had much to drink at the reception as she wouldn't have trusted herself if she'd become a little tipsy.

'Oh Joe,' she said, tears starting to fill her eyes. 'It was awful. I don't know if you heard anything when you were stood outside the snug?'

Joe shook his head, easing himself into the chair with the help of his stick.

'Tell me,' he said.

As Bel unburdened herself, Joe listened, occasionally asking a question.

To many, Joe knew, this might have been a disastrous start to married life, but the fact that they were sitting here together, being open with each other, and supportive, said to him their marriage was going to be a good one. They would deal with whatever life chucked at them – and they would do it together. Like they were doing now.

'And . . . ' Bel said, her voice croaky from tiredness, and emotion, as well as the brandy she had now finished, 'I hate to admit it, but I feel really worried about Ma.'

Joe leant forward and gently squeezed her hand. He had known there was something else that was troubling Bel.

'I know that Ma's gone off before – God knows she used to disappear enough when I was younger – but she's been different lately . . . Dare I say it – nicer? There was just something about the way she left the pub that's worried me.'

Joe knew it would be pointless telling Bel that everything would be all right. You never knew where Pearl was concerned. And Bel was right, Pearl had had an odd look about her when she'd left. But, as Joe also knew, there was nothing either of them could do about it tonight. Even if they had gone out looking for her, they wouldn't know where to look and it would have been hopeless in the blackout.

'I'll bet you as soon as we get back tomorrow, she'll be there, out the backyard, a cuppa in one hand, a fag in the other.' Joe smiled and Bel allowed herself a bittersweet laugh. That was her ma to a T.

'Come on,' Joe said, 'let's get into bed.' He looked at Bel and saw a slightly nervous look cross her face.

'It may not be the most red-blooded suggestion for a man to put to his new wife on his wedding night, but, you know what I want more than all the tea in China?' he asked, before answering his own question. 'To simply spend the entire night with my arms wrapped around the woman I love more than anybody or anything in the whole wide world.'

Joe saw Bel's face relax, and although he might have been telling a little white lie, cuddling up to his new wife was going to be the next best thing.

Chapter Forty-Four

Lily took another sip of her whisky and shuffled to get comfortable on the high wooden stool at the end of the bar. She looked around her and mused on the unexpected events of the day. It had certainly been a wedding to remember – although memorable for all the wrong reasons.

Allowing herself an end-of-evening smoke, Lily got out her packet of Gauloises and lit a cigarette. She was feeling a tad relieved as she had just had a quick word with Agnes before she'd left. She'd apologised for having introduced Maisie to the Elliot family – albeit unintentionally. She knew just how protective Agnes was of Bel, having more or less brought her up as one of her own, and because of this Lily had been more than a little concerned that Agnes might well be angry with anyone associated with the woman who had ruined her son and daughter-in-law's wedding day.

Thankfully, Agnes had dismissed her words with a wave of the hand, showing that she in no way harboured any ill feeling towards Lily, and making no bones about the fact that there was 'always some kind of drama' wherever Pearl was concerned.

Their brief chat had also given Lily the opportunity to thank Agnes for caring for Rosie the night she'd been attacked by her uncle. Something she had wanted to do for the past year.

'Anyone,' Agnes had said to Lily, 'would have done the same.'

Lily had smiled; she knew that this was not necessarily

true, and not everyone would have taken in a complete stranger, nursed them all night, and not asked any questions. Lily liked Agnes. Perhaps in time they could become friends of sorts.

She had also been introduced to Gloria, who had thanked her profusely for paying the solicitor's fees for her divorce. Lily had told her that all that 'financial nonsense' was George's domain, and that it was she who should be thanking Gloria and the rest of the women welders for helping Rosie.

When Lily had said, '*No amount of money could have made up for that*' Gloria had chuckled and said George had used more or less the same words.

'That's what happens when you spend so much time with the same person,' Lily had laughed. 'You end up thinking the same, never mind speaking the same!'

Gloria had introduced Lily to Hope, but shortly afterwards the baby announced that it was time to go home by bawling her adorable little eyes out.

As Lily sat pensively in a swirling cloud of smoke, George crept up behind her and whispered in her ear, 'A penny for your thoughts, my dear?' He was back from dropping off the newly-weds.

Lily stubbed her cigarette out, turned around and laughed, 'It'll cost you more than that!'

George grabbed a bar stool. Propping against it the ornate ivory walking stick that Lily had bought for him earlier on in the year, he seated himself.

'I was actually thinking,' Lily admitted, 'that it's been rather an eventful day.'

George looked at Lily's manicured hand, which was wrapped round a glass of single malt. He thought how pristine she still looked in the beautifully tailored vibrant green dress that he'd been repeatedly told was designed by royal couturier Norman Hartnell.

'Eventful?' George let out a laugh, 'it's certainly been that.'

Lily looked at George and thought he seemed a little distracted.

'Lord knows,' she said, 'what we're going to do with Maisie.' As Lily spoke she looked across at Rosie, who was sitting with the big woman from her squad, the little Jewish girl, and some strange-looking skinny lad wearing bottle top glasses. Rosie was sipping on a port, and looked relaxed.

'It's been nice to see Rosie let her hair down a little today,' Lily said. 'She's even had a dance with one of the soldiers.'

George choked on a large glug of whisky. 'I wouldn't read much into that,' he chuckled. 'That soldier was at least as old as me . . . ancient . . . If you ask me, I still think Rosie's holding a candle for that detective of hers.'

'Oh don't, George,' Lily said, reaching for another cigarette.

'I really hope not . . . but –' Lily lit her Gauloise '– I've got a horrible feeling you might be right. She's not said anything about him of late, but I think she might secretly be mooning after him.'

She took a deep drag. 'Love, eh? Or should I say *unrequited* love.'

'Mmm,' George agreed.

Lily again thought George seemed unusually thoughtful – even a little on edge. 'You all right?' she asked. 'You're not worried about Rosie – or the Maisie situation, are you?'

'No, no, my dear, probably just getting a bit tired now. Can't party like I used to, you know?'

Lily laughed. 'Well, you give it a good try. Come on, then,' she said stubbing out her half-smoked cigarette, 'let's leave the young 'uns to it.'

357

George and Lily said their goodnights to everyone, and walked out of the pub and into the cold night air. It was pitch black, but the sky was clear.

When they reached the MG, George looked up to the inky darkness, speckled with stars and a half-moon, and declared, 'You don't get a more perfect sky at night than that.'

He waved his walking stick into the air.

Lily looked up to the heavens. 'Perfect these days means no searchlights and no Luftwaffe!' she declared. But as she dragged her vision away from the peaceful skies and glanced round, she took a surprised step back – George was bent down on one knee on the pavement.

'You lost something, George?' Lily scanned the ground.

'No, no, my dear,' George chuckled a little nervously, adding somewhat cryptically, 'although some may say I have *lost* my mind.'

Lily watched puzzled as he proceeded to rummage around in the inside pocket of his jacket. 'I know . . . ' he said, ' . . . that you have been embarrassed enough for one day . . . what with the wedding bouquet and all.'

Lily laughed out loud. 'Mortified, never mind embarrassed.'

'But,' George added with a mysterious smile on his face, 'there may well have been a reason why it was *you* who ended up with the bride's bouquet.'

Lily looked at George as if he really had lost his mind.

Until she saw it.

The magnificent diamond ring he was holding between his forefinger and thumb.

It looked like it cost a small fortune, and, knowing George, it probably did.

Lily stared in total disbelief. Her mouth was half open. She started to say something, but George got in first.

'No, Lily, I'm not ready for the loony bin, nor have I

had one whisky too many, if that's what you're thinking. I have wanted to do this for quite some time ... Have waited far too long, in my opinion ... So, I decided today would be the perfect opportunity to ask you ... ' He paused and took a deep breath.

' ... to ask you if you would do me the greatest honour in agreeing to become my wife?'

Lily's face lit up. She was about to speak but stopped herself – then her face broke into a cheeky smile.

'If I say "no" can I still keep the ring?'

George looked at Lily, like a headmaster about to reprimand his pupil.

'Lily,' he said sternly, ' ... you are not allowed to use your normal diversionary tactics with me. You have to give me a "yes" or a "no". And I'm going to stay here until you do.'

Lily knew she was not going to joke her way out of this. She was cornered. She stared hard at George and knew he meant what he said – he would stay there until she made her decision.

'George,' she said, her face softening and a smile playing on her lips, 'that's a very difficult question to answer ... so many things to consider ... '

George was still on his knee, his hand on the top of his walking stick keeping him steady.

'For instance,' Lily said, dropping her voice, 'what about the bordello and the new club?'

George let out a loud laugh.

'God, Lily, always the businesswoman. Of course, it goes without saying that what's yours, stays yours, and what's mine ... *is both of ours*.'

Lily looked at the huge diamond ring glinting in George's hand.

'Well,' she said, slowly, a genuine smile spreading across

her face, 'I think that may have just tipped the balance. My answer,' her voice was soft and her eyes shone with a rare display of tenderness, 'is . . . yes. Yes. George Hartley, I would *love* to marry you.'

George let out a huge, theatrical sigh of relief.

'Thank goodness for that.' He pushed himself back to a standing position, then took Lily's hand and put the ring on her engagement finger.

After he had done so, Lily stood, her arm outstretched in front of her, staring at the glittering diamond.

'Oh, George,' she said, 'I do love you, you know?'

She looked straight into the eyes of the man she had just agreed to marry. The person who had brought such happiness to her at an age when she had never expected to find love.

'And that's not just because of this beautiful ring.'

Neither of them said anything for a moment. Then they stepped towards each other and George put his hand around the back of Lily's head, gently pulled her face to his and the pair shared a long kiss.

As they stood there, kissing under the blanket of the night sky, Rosie came out of the pub, but stopped in her tracks when she saw the two people she loved dearly sharing this very intimate and romantic moment.

She was a little shocked, but not that surprised. She had always wondered about Lily and George.

Now she knew.

Chapter Forty-Five

When Gloria got home shortly after seven, she was jiggered. Thankfully, so was Hope, who was now sleeping soundly in her crib upstairs next to Gloria's bed.

'What a day,' Gloria said aloud to her empty home. A home she was glad was empty. There was only one other person she would have wanted here this evening, and that was Jack.

But that was obviously an impossible dream.

Rosie had told her that Jack had started work at Crown's, and she had heard Miriam was dragging him along to every dinner date and function going. Jack seemed to be physically well, but was showing no signs of getting his memory back.

It was now time for Gloria to face facts.

Jack was not going to be a part of their lives.

As Gloria put the kettle on, she got out the piece of wedding cake she had wrapped in a napkin and brought home with her. Dorothy, bless her, had forsaken her own slice to give to her.

Dorothy's right, Gloria said quietly to herself. *It's about time I got Hope christened.*

After she'd made herself a pot of tea, she poured a cup and put her slice of precious fruit cake on a plate, and trundled through to the lounge where she switched on the wireless for her favourite programmes. Tonight, though, they didn't give her the usual escapism from her own thoughts and concerns, and she kept thinking about

Maisie, and how her life had clearly been shaped by the fact that she had never known either of her parents.

When it came to her own situation, Gloria knew that she had to be honest – for Hope's sake. Of that she was now one hundred per cent certain.

She just had to choose the right time to break the news to Vinnie that Hope was not his. And when she did so, she would be doing it on her own. There would be no knight in shining armour galloping back into town to rescue her. It was time Gloria faced facts:

She was going to have to save herself.

Chapter Forty-Six

As Joe and Bel lay in each other's arms in the huge, confetti-littered bed, they chatted into the early morning before they both finally fell asleep. Bel's sleep was sporadic, though. She couldn't stop thinking about the fact that she had a sister. When she'd been a young girl, she had dreamed of having a sister to play with, to confide in – to simply keep her company during her ma's absences. When Agnes had taken her in, she had got her wish to a certain extent, as Polly had become like a sister to her.

Now, after all these years, she had found out that, all along, she did have a sister. But it was fair to say that Maisie was by no means anything like the sister she had dreamed of having as a child. Quite the reverse.

As her mind refused to rest, Bel thought back to snippets of information that Kate had told her during her dress fittings. Maisie had come up from London to help start up a 'Gentlemen's Club', whatever that was, but nothing had been known about Maisie's childhood and the life she had led since then.

What had happened to her to make her so bitter and so angry? She had wanted retribution, but the way she had done it told Bel she also wanted attention. And love.

Well, if she did, she had gone about it the wrong way.

As Bel fell in and out of slumber, she kept thinking the same thoughts over and over. Finding a long-lost relative should be wonderful, shouldn't it? Like in the films, where they hug and kiss each other and talk for hours and everyone lives happily-ever-after.

Why, Bel asked herself, *had she been so unlucky when it came to her family?* She had said to Joe this evening that she was a 'lucky woman', and in so many ways she was incredibly fortunate – but she couldn't escape the reality that she had picked the short straw when it came to her nearest and dearest: Her long-lost sister was a pretty horrible and vindictive person. And Bel didn't even know who her own father was.

But worst of all was that her mother – the only family she'd ever known – had never loved her.

When Bel had been growing up all she had really wanted was her mother's love and care. It wasn't until she herself had become a mum that she'd finally realised that her ma would never love her like a normal mother loves a daughter.

She had believed that this was just the way her mother was. That she wasn't capable of giving a mother's love. That she was missing some kind of natural maternalness. But she'd been proved wrong. She had seen it with Maisie the moment her ma opened her eyes in the snug at the Tatham and saw the daughter she had given up.

The realisation that her ma could give of a mother's love had shocked Bel. And, much as she had tried to reason with herself that she was a lucky woman, who had the love of a wonderful man as well as the love of Agnes, the hurt cut deep.

When she had heard her mother admitting that she had never been able to love her as a mother should, she had felt like a child again. Alone. Unloved. Worthless. In that instant, her mother's confession had catapulted her back to her childhood and all the wretchedness that had gone along with growing up. She had sensed her mother's innate inability to love her from when she was just a small girl. She had been able to tell, even when her mother gave her the occasional hug or tried to show some kind of affection, that it was forced, that it was not genuine, even if her mother had wanted it to be.

Hearing it today, with her own ears, coming from her mother's own mouth – well, that was another matter entirely.

She couldn't un-hear those words, or push them away. She could no longer try to convince herself that her mother had really loved her. The words had been said, and what's more, they had been meant. Her mother had been brutally honest.

Now Bel had to be face facts. Feel the hurt that had always been smarting just under the surface. *Her own mother had never loved her.*

But as Bel turned over and snuggled into Joe, who was now snoring lightly, a thought came to her that provided a slight smear of balm for her hurt. There was actually one consolation she could take from her mother's heartbreaking revelation today – that her ma had *wanted* to love her. She had *tried*. That much was clear. She had seen it in her guilt-ridden eyes and heard it in her voice. *Was that in itself not a kind of love?*

In the quietness of the room, with Joe's warm body pressed close to her own, try as she might, Bel couldn't shift the feeling of deep concern she had about her ma. Where had she gone? Was she back at the house now? In her own bed?

She had a gut feeling that her mother's bed was untouched, and that her ma was dealing with what had happened in the only way she knew how. With drink.

Bel had never seen her so upset. Never seen her – ever – so emotionally raw. She hadn't got a good feeling about the way her mother had left so abruptly. There was something about it that had felt very final.

As though her mother had no intention of coming back.

Chapter Forty-Seven

'Welcome home, Mr and Mrs Elliot!'

Polly had been playing with Lucille in the front bed-room before she was due to do an afternoon of overtime. Thompson's, like every other yard in the whole of the country, was going full steam ahead to get ships repaired, built and launched. Overtime was no longer a choice, but expected – even on a Sunday.

On seeing her brother and sister-in-law through the window Polly had grabbed Lucille and hurried to open the door for them.

'Mammy . . . Doey . . . *Daddy*!' Lucille stretched her arms out towards Bel and Joe as they stepped into the house. It was freezing outside and Joe put their overnight bag and gas masks down on the ground, rubbing his hands together before taking his niece – now his stepdaughter – from Polly.

Joe looked across at Bel. They had not discussed whether or not Lucille would be allowed to call him 'daddy'. Bel gave Joe a resigned look.

'Well, cheeky Charlie,' she said, turning her attention to her daughter and squeezing her little button nose gently, making her giggle. 'Your ma has to thank Aunty Polly here for the best wedding present ever.'

Bel looked at her sister-in-law. 'God, Pol, it was amaz-ing. How the other half live, eh?'

Polly laughed. 'I know. You should have seen Dorothy's and Angie's faces when we went into the room. Their eyes were out on stalks. As were mine,' she chuckled as she thought how the three of them had stood in the room just gawping, before they'd got to work, sprinkling the confetti about and setting out the candles and miniatures of brandy.

'Well, it was gorgeous, Pol. Out of this world. Joe and I can't ever thank you enough.' Bel gave her sister-in-law a big hug.

'I hope what happened yesterday didn't spoil it for you,' Polly mumbled quietly.

Joe stepped forward. 'Never in a million years,' he reassured his sister, giving her another hug and whispering, 'Thank you, little sis.'

Bel took Lucille from Joe. 'Best go and find Nana then?' But as soon as the words were out of her mouth, she could see by Polly's face that something was up.

'Erm,' Polly said, 'let's all get a nice cuppa down us, eh?'

In the kitchen they found Agnes seated by the range, supping her tea from her saucer with Ronald perched next to her on a stool, warming his hands in front of the fire.

'Ma not in?' Bel asked as she put Lucille down, who immediately toddled off in search of Tramp and the pup.

'Come and sit yourself down, pet,' Agnes said as Ronald got up and gave her his place by the fire.

Bel sat down and looked at Agnes.

'What's happened?'

'Nothing's happened,' Agnes said, trying to keep her voice upbeat. 'It's just that your ma didn't come back last night.'

Bel looked at Ronald, who looked downcast.

Polly and Joe sat down at the kitchen table and poured out three cups of tea and handed one to Bel.

'You know your ma,' Joe said, 'she's probably been on a bit of a bender and gone off with some bloke.' He looked at Ronald, 'Sorry mate, no offence meant.'

Ronald didn't look put out by Joe's comments. He knew

Pearl; knew what kind of woman she was. Joe might well be right. In a strange way he hoped he was, but he knew that Pearl had really been laying off the booze lately. And – as far as he was aware – men too. Last night he presumed that Pearl had simply gone off and got legless after Maisie had pulled her stunt at the pub, but when he'd come round here this morning and she wasn't out the back, chain-smoking and nursing a raging hangover, alarm bells had started to ring in his head.

'I thought I'd do a recce of her favourite haunts when they're open,' Ronald said. 'I'll bring her straight back if I find her.' Ronald tried to sound upbeat. He looked at the clock. 'I might as well get cracking then.' He stood up, and grabbed his coat and muffler off the back of one of the kitchen chairs. 'I'll start at the Tatham. Bill'll be getting ready to open up. You never know, he might have already heard something.'

'Thanks, Ronald,' Bel said.

'And come round for a bit to eat when you're done,' Agnes added, getting up from her chair by the range. 'I'm making a stew so there'll be plenty to go around.' It was Agnes's way of showing her appreciation. She too was getting a little tetchy about Pearl's whereabouts. She had checked Pearl's bedroom early this morning and it was obvious she hadn't been back; everything was exactly as it had been when they'd all left for the wedding: curlers and make-up everywhere, the bed still half made – but what had really given her cause for concern was that the few clothes that Pearl possessed were still hanging in her wardrobe. That meant only one thing – she must still be wearing her blue velvet dress.

'She didn't come back to get changed, then?' Bel asked, as if reading her mother-in-law's thoughts.

Agnes shook her head.

They all knew how much Pearl loved her mother-of-

368

the-bride dress – that she had not only been overjoyed to be wearing it yesterday, but was chuffed to pieces that Kate was planning on displaying it in her shop window alongside Bel's wedding dress. The least Pearl would have done, even if she was going on an all-nighter, was to come back and get changed.

'She's never stayed out all night since she got here.' Bel spoke her thoughts aloud.

Joe took hold of Bel's hand. 'Ronald'll probably find her propping up one of the bars in town this afternoon and drag her back home.'

Bel took another slug of her tea. The niggling worry she'd had in the pit of her stomach since yesterday was now developing into an ache.

'You know what,' she said, trying to disguise the growing sense of unease she was feeling, 'I think I'll nip and see Kate in the shop . . . go and thank her . . . ' She put her cup of tea down on the kitchen table.

'Agnes, can I leave Lucille here with you?'

Bel's mother-in-law gave her a quick hug. 'Of course you can, pet. I'll be nipping next door to see Beryl, so I'll take her with me. She'll get spoilt rotten like she always does there.'

'I need to get off and see the Major about a few things,' Joe chipped in, taking a final sup of his tea and standing up to leave.

Just then Arthur came down the stairs and popped his head round the kitchen door. He was wearing his flat cap, scarf and coat.

'And I'm guessing Arthur's out gallivanting as well,' Polly said as she spotted the old man.

Arthur smiled.

'You off up the allotment?' Joe asked.

'Aye, I thought I'd go and get some more veg and see

Albert while I'm at it.' Albert looked across to Bel and then at Joe. 'Lovely wedding, you two. Brought a tear to my eye, it did – and I don't mind admitting it.'

Bel smiled back. 'Ah thanks, Arthur, and *thank you* for the lovely flowers . . . and for giving me away.' Her voice warbled with emotion.

'It's me that's the thankful one,' Arthur said, tipping his cap. 'Now I'll get myself off,' he said, turning to make his way down the hallway.

As everyone shouted their farewells, Joe turned to Bel and gave her a kiss. 'I'll get away now as well. I'll see you later on. And,' he added sternly, 'no worrying, all right? Your ma'll be fine. That woman's as hard as nails.'

Bel nodded her compliance and kissed her new husband back.

'I'll follow you out, Joe,' Polly said, grabbing her bag and gas mask. 'I volunteered for the afternoon shift, so I better get a move on.'

A few minutes later, after Bel had put her overnight bag in her room, and taken out her dress and put it on a hanger so it wouldn't crease, she said her goodbyes to Lucille and Agnes and hurried into town.

Ten minutes later, when Agnes had cleared away the cups and saucers, she picked up her granddaughter and the pair of them went next door to see their neighbour.

For the next few hours the Elliot household was unusually still, with only Tramp and the pup left indoors, happily curled up in their basket by the side of the range, enjoying the warmth from the dwindling fire, and a rare bit of peace and quiet.

Bel, Joe, Agnes, Arthur and Polly may have been truthful about *where* they were all going, but none were being particularly honest about their reasons *why*.

Of course, they all knew that Bel's decision to go and thank Kate for the wonderful dress she had made for her wedding day was really an excuse for her to head into town and go walkabouts looking for her ma, but none of them admitted that they too were visiting places and people that might well help in the search for Pearl.

Joe had gone to see Major Black – not about matters pertaining to civil defence but because he wanted to put the word out to the Home Guard to keep an eye out for a skinny, middle-aged woman, who was probably half-cut and wearing a fancy blue velvet dress; if such a woman was spotted, they were to immediately report her whereabouts, or better still, haul her back to Tatham Street.

Arthur had headed over to the Town Moor to see Albert so that the pair of them could check out the area's public houses, and in particular any places they knew Pearl had connections with. They too were going to put the word out that Bel's ma had gone AWOL, and that there'd be a box of veg should anyone spot her and tell them where she had got to.

Agnes had nipped next door to see Beryl, who, despite rarely leaving her house, always seemed to be privy to just about every bit of gossip doing the rounds on the town's grapevine. If there was any news about Pearl, Beryl would be one of the first to hear.

Even Polly, on her way to work, had popped into a few of the taverns and inns along the south dock and asked the licensees to put the word out that the family were concerned about Pearl.

Polly would also have liked to have made a trip over to Ashbrooke to give Maisie a good tongue lashing. She knew her sister-in-law and her brother better than anyone, and they hadn't pulled the wool over her eyes. Yes, they might well have been eternally grateful to her for shelling out a week's wages to spend one night in the Grand, but there was no getting away from the fact that Maisie had cast a dark cloud not only over their wedding day – but also their first night as a married couple.

Polly was not best pleased – nor was she the only person to be furious with Maisie . . .

The front door of the bordello slammed shut.

'Where's Maisie?'

The call sounded out down the hallway and was loud enough to rise up to the third floor.

Lily immediately stopped what she was doing in the back reception room. A frown appeared on her forehead as she walked towards the doorway and into the main hallway.

'Kate, is that you?'

'Yes, Lily,' Kate's voice softened a fraction, but not much. 'I'm looking for Maisie, do yer know where she is?'

Lily was a little taken aback. She had given Kate a number of elocution lessons and was pleased with the result, but today, for some reason, she had fallen back into her old ways and sounded exactly as she had when she'd first arrived at the bordello, fresh from the doorway of one of the town's department stores.

'*Ma chère*,' Lily said, going over to Kate, 'are you all right? You seem . . . upset?'

Lily looked at Kate – her shoulders were hunched up to her neck and her fists were in balls. Her hair was a mess, and from her flushed cheeks and dishevelled clothing, she looked like she had just run the half a mile from town.

Before Kate had time to answer, Maisie appeared from the back parlour. Her voice sang out as if she were answering the telephone without a care in the world.

'Maisie here, Kate. Whatever is the matter?' Maisie wore a mustard and black print dress with three-quarter-length sleeves, and her hair had been pulled into a roll, kept in check by two hair combs. Her face was made up with the pale-coloured foundation she normally wore. As always, she looked stunning.

'*What's wrong?*' Kate's skinny arms swung as she marched over to where Maisie was standing.

'*What's wrong?*' she repeated, still breathless as she had, in fact, run from the shop in town to the bordello.

Before leaving the Maison Nouvelle Kate had spent half an hour with a very upset Bel, who had come into the shop to say thank you for the dress, but when Kate had asked her how she was – and how Pearl was – she had promptly burst into uncontrollable tears.

'*I'll tell yer what's wrong . . .*' Kate was almost snarling as she spat out her words.

Lily stood in the hallway in shock. She had never seen this side of her *petit enfant* before.

'*Thanks to you,*' Kate was now shouting, 'Pearl's gone missing . . . She's not come home and everyone's worried sick about her.'

Kate drew breath. 'And it's all your fault, Maisie. Yer selfish cow. Oh, but I forgot, *poor old Maisie . . .* ' she said with a heavy dose of sarcasm, ' . . . got adopted out and now she has to come back and punish everyone.

'Well, let's just hope Pearl turns up – otherwise you may well have blood on yer hands . . . And worse still – it'll be *yer ma's* blood.'

Kate's voice was reverberating round the house and had caused some of the girls to come out of their rooms and start peering down at the scene below.

Kate turned dramatically on her heels and stomped over to the coat stand by the front door; she yanked her coat off, then grabbed her woollen hat and her long knitted scarf and gloves.

'I'm going out to try and find her. And if you've got anything about ya, you'll get yourself over to the Elliots and beg forgiveness fer completely ruining yer sister's wedding day – then you'll get yer sorry backside back out there and look fer Pearl yerself. She won't survive another night out in this weather – not with just that soddin' velvet dress on her.'

Lily's mouth had dropped open. Her head was swinging from Kate to Maisie.

'Wait!' Finally Maisie found her tongue.

She ran the length of the hallway and grabbed her own coat – a beautiful brown muskrat fur – off the stand, along with a matching fur hat.

'I'm coming too.'

Kate looked at her before yanking the heavy front door open and hurrying down the steps and along the path.

As Lily tottered to the door she caught Kate and Maisie as they disappeared out the gate and on to the main road.

'*Mon dieu*,' she mumbled, shutting the door. She looked up at the girls and waved them away with both hands.

'Show's over, everyone,' she shouted out.

As she headed towards the kitchen in search of a stiff drink, she muttered under her breath, *'Let's hope to God the old girl turns up – otherwise there's going to be war on.'*

Chapter Forty-Eight

As Maisie ran through the town centre, trying to remember the directions that Kate had barked at her as to how to get to the Dun Cow as quickly as possible, she felt the first real stab of genuine remorse.

What had she done? This hadn't really turned out the way she had expected.

She had never imagined the consequences of her long-sought-after retribution would be this serious. She had wanted to humiliate her mother – to shame her – to scream and shout at her. But not for one minute had she ever wanted to cause her mother serious harm.

She certainly hadn't expected her to go missing. It was bloody freezing – and if Kate was right, and she only had a dress on . . . and had been out all night. Well, that did not bode well.

As she rounded the corner, she saw Bel

'Isabelle . . . Sorry – *Bel* . . . Stop . . . It's me . . . *Maisie!*'

Bel was just marching away from the Dun Cow on High Street West. It was one of Pearl's favourite pubs in town. Not because of its beautiful copper-domed tower, or its plush Edwardian interior, but because she knew Max the landlord from way back, and he would always give her a few on the house.

Maisie ran to catch up with Bel, who had stopped on hearing her name called.

'Kate told me . . . ' Maisie said breathlessly as she reached

Bel, 'that you were coming here . . . ' Maisie was clutching her chest as her lungs felt as if they were burning.

Bel looked at Maisie and for the first time she saw the resemblance to her ma. She looked different to yesterday. Her curly hair had been reined in by the fur hat she was wearing, and she had plastered the make-up on. Her skin now looked much paler, giving a mere hint of her true ethnicity.

'What do you want, Maisie? Don't you think you've caused enough trouble as it is?'

Maisie looked at her half-sister and could tell she had been crying. She had faint smudges of mascara around her eyes, but she still looked pretty. Maisie marvelled at her ivory-coloured skin untouched by even a speck of powder, and she felt a stab of envy.

'I know . . . and I'm sorry, Isabelle. Sorry – Bel,' Maisie quickly corrected herself. 'Honestly, I am. *Really sorry*. I didn't expect this to happen. I didn't know what to expect . . . ' She paused before adding, 'Actually, I didn't really think about what would happen after . . . ' Her voice tailed off.

And it was true. She'd put a lot of time and effort into finding her mother, and thinking about what she would do and say when she finally confronted her, but she hadn't really thought beyond that. Which, with hindsight, had always been her way: Act first – think later.

Bel turned and started to walk away. 'Well, the damage is done now, Maisie,' she shouted back over her shoulder.

Maisie ran and caught up with Bel, matching her fast march.

'I want to help.' Maisie coughed, she wasn't used to such ice cold air. It was quite literally breathtaking. 'I want to help you look for . . . ' Maisie hesitated, not knowing how to refer to the woman who had given birth to her, ' . . . *our ma.*'

Bel stopped in her tracks and swung around to glare at her half-sister.

'Help?' she spat the word out. 'Why would you want to help someone you clearly hate with a passion? The way you talked yesterday I would have thought you'd have been glad to see her six foot under!'

Bel's words struck Maisie hard.

'I do – I did . . . hate her . . . ' Maisie stumbled over the words. 'Honestly . . . I don't know what I feel at the moment . . . All I do know is that I don't want anyone getting hurt. Or worse still, dying – and it being my fault.'

Bel stared at Maisie dressed in her fur coat, looking like she was off to some kind of posh cocktail party.

'Well, Maisie, if you want to help look for "our ma", I can't stop you. Do as you want. But if you want to come with me, you might well find some of the places I'll be looking a tad – how would someone like you say it – unpalatable.'

Bel started walking again, as did Maisie.

Her half-sister's comments had annoyed her, though, and as they marched on, Maisie broke the angry silence between them.

'I've been in a few "unpalatable" places as well, you know, during my life.' Maisie shot a sidelong look at Bel. 'I wasn't born with a silver spoon in my mouth.'

Bel's head snapped round to look at Maisie as they approached the glazed tile frontage of the Three Crowns.

'Really? You could have fooled me.' Bel looked down at Maisie's perfectly smooth hands, which she was rubbing together to keep from going numb in the cold.

'Those hands look like they've never done a hard day's work in their life. And no one's born speaking with a plum in their mouth – it's learnt from an early age. As is that air of confidence and arrogance you carry off so well.'

Maisie opened her mouth to speak, but was beaten to it by Bel.

'You know, Maisie, you obviously think that you've had a hard time of it after Ma "gave you away" as you put it, but I've lost count of the number of times in my life I wished Ma'd had me adopted out. You have no idea what "our ma" was like when I was growing up. If it hadn't been for Agnes I probably wouldn't be here now, or at the very least I'd have ended up in the workhouse. You think you had it bad, well you don't know the kind of childhood I had to endure. But you don't see me moaning on about it – or ruining other people's wedding days to try and make myself feel better.'

Bel drew breath. Since Maisie's appearance and poor-little-me Orphan Annie performance in the snug, all her own anger and resentment about her childhood had been building up, as well as the anger she had forced down at having her wedding day ruined.

'If you had a hard time of it growing up,' Bel was leaning forward glaring into Maisie's startling hazel eyes, 'well then, you want to take a walk in my shoes.'

Suddenly Bel straightened up and let out an angry laugh. 'Ha! Actually, you'd be hard pushed to do that as our ma didn't think I needed shoes! God, I could tell you some stories that would make your hair curl. You weren't the only daughter our ma abandoned, you know!'

Bel stopped. The adrenaline and the cold had suddenly made her feel she was going to retch.

Maisie reached her arm out to help steady her sister, who had gone as white as a sheet and looked like she might faint.

'You know, Bel,' she said, trying to make her voice as soft and as caring as possible. 'I *am* sorry I ruined your wedding day. I really am. I shouldn't have involved you . . .

I can see now that I made a mistake. And that . . . let's just say . . . I misread the situation. I can see now that you've not had an easy time of it either.'

Maisie paused.

'The thing is, we could stand here all day, freezing our socks off, arguing about who got the worst deal, but that's not going to do any good. Maybe we could do that later, eh?' Maisie tried a smile. 'And then you can make my hair curl even more?'

Bel took a deep breath and felt the wave of nausea leave her.

'Why don't we just concentrate on finding our mother for now?' Maisie said. She could see she had talked Bel down. 'She mightn't have been much cop to you or me, but we need to find her. And at the end of the day she is our mother – whether we like it or not.'

Bel stood for a few moments looking at the woman who was her sister, and digested the words she had just said.

Then she nodded her head slightly, but didn't stay anything. Instead, she turned round and pulled open the door of the Three Crowns and walked into the busy, smoke-filled pub that was known to be particularly popular with sailors on shore leave.

Maisie took a deep, nervous intake of air and followed her younger sister inside.

Bloody hell, she hadn't planned for any of this.

By six in the evening Agnes, Ronald, Arthur and Joe had regrouped in the kitchen at Tatham Street and were exchanging information.

'Beryl's not heard anything, but will give us a shout straight away if she does,' Agnes said as she grabbed her oven gloves and swung open the door of the range to check on the stew and dumplings she was cooking that was made up with the assortment of vegetables Arthur had brought back from the allotment. He and Albert had gone on a long walk around the Town Moor and had been relieved not to find any sign of Pearl; if she'd staggered on to the moor last night and passed out, there would have been next to no chance of her surviving the night, especially as she had barely an ounce of fat on her, and was wearing a flimsy dress.

'I'm going back out to meet up with the Major and some of the lads from our squad,' Joe said, picking up Lucille. 'Once I've put this one to bed and we've done a few rounds with the Lambton Worm,' he joked as his stepdaughter's face lit up at the prospect of having her favourite story read to her.

'Good,' Agnes said, 'she's had her tea and she needs an early night after yesterday's excitement.'

Just then they heard the front door go and everyone fell silent.

'It's only me!' It was Polly back from work. 'And I've brought a visitor.'

Agnes's face lit up, thinking her daughter had found Pearl on her way home and that finally they could all get back to normal.

When Polly came into the kitchen, followed by Rosie, her face fell.

'Oh Rosie,' Agnes said, apologetically. 'Sorry, I thought you might be Pearl . . . come in and get warm.'

Rosie forced a smile, but the tense atmosphere in the house was evidence of the serious concerns they all had for Pearl's welfare.

'Nana?' Lucille asked, putting her thumb in her mouth and nestling into the crook of Joe's neck. She had been asking for her grandma sporadically throughout the day.

'Nana's not back home yet, sweetie,' Polly said, giving

her niece a quick kiss on the cheek. 'But I'm sure she'll be back by the time you wake up tomorrow.'

Rosie looked at the worried faces around the kitchen table and thought that none of them seemed convinced by Polly's hopeful forecast.

'Come on, I'll put you to bed and your uncle Joe can read you a story,' Polly said.

Lucille immediately objected.

'No, *Daddy*!'

Polly rolled her eyes to the ceiling. Joe carried an over-tired Lucille into her bedroom, thanking Rosie again for her kind wedding gift.

'I'm guessing that means you've still not heard anything?' Rosie said to everyone.

'Not a whisper,' Agnes said, looking at Rosie standing there in her dirty overalls, her hair tied up with a headscarf. She forced herself not to stare at the scars on her face. She'd had them well covered yesterday at the wedding and this was only the second time she had seen Rosie since that fateful night last year.

'Ronald's just nipped across to the Tatham to check Bill still hasn't heard anything, but that's doubtful, as I know Bill would have come over and told us himself if he'd got wind of anything. And Joe,' Agnes continued, 'said one of the local Home Guard lads heard Pearl'd been spotted coming out of the Norfolk House worse for wear late last night around last orders.'

There was a depressed silence. Everyone knew the pub that was in one of the poorest areas of the town. It was not a place a woman on her own should be frequenting, especially one in a 'mother of the bride' velvet dress.

'Honestly, Rosie,' Agnes suddenly blustered, 'I'm forgetting my manners. A nice hot cuppa tea? And what about staying for a bit of stew? I'm just about to serve up.'

'Ah, that's very kind of you, Mrs Elliot,' Rosie said, 'but I'm not hanging about. I just nipped in to see if Pearl had turned up.'

Seconds later they all heard the sound of the front door being opened and closed, and once again they fell silent in anticipation of Pearl's return home.

'Ma?' It was Bel's voice, sounding out down the hallway.

'Oh God,' Agnes mumbled under her breath.

'Bel . . . sweetheart . . . she's not here.' Agnes got up to see her daughter-in-law, who she knew would now be even more worried about her mother, but she stopped in her tracks when she saw Maisie following Bel into the room.

'Oh.' Agnes couldn't keep the shock out of her voice. It was the last person she had expected to see this evening.

Bel looked at everyone's bewildered faces.

'No introductions needed,' she said, turning to Maisie, who forced an unconvincing smile on to her face. 'Maisie's been helping me look for Ma, but so far we've not had any joy.'

Bel looked expectantly at everyone else.

'Sorry, pet.' It was Arthur; his voice was calm. 'Nothing at the moment, but everyone's out looking for her. Joe's rallied the Home Guard, Beryl's got her ear to the ground, Ronald's at the Tatham now – and me and Albert's been round the Town Moor.'

'And no one's even spotted her?' Bel asked.

There was an awkward silence.

'Just at Norfolk House.' Arthur knew it was important to be honest. Bel wasn't one to be soft-soaped and would be angry if they kept anything from her.

'Oh, God,' Bel said under her breath. Maisie looked at her for an explanation.

'Only the worst dive this side of town,' Bel said.

'There's someone else I know might be able to help,' Rosie chipped in, hopefully.

Everyone looked at her.

'He's one of the coppers down by the docks. He should be coming off his shift now . . . ' She looked at the clock on the mantelpiece. 'If I go now, I should catch him.' Rosie grabbed Bel's hand and squeezed it. 'The more people looking for her, the more likely she is to be found.'

Rosie completely ignored Maisie, who was standing by Bel's side. Rosie and Maisie had exchanged words late last night and it had not been pleasant. The whole house had heard them, although everyone knew well enough to stay in their rooms and keep out of the way.

After shutting the front door behind her, Rosie started jogging down Tatham Street towards the south dock. Her heart was hammering hard in her chest, although its pounding had nothing to do with the exertion of running in heavy hobnailed boots – and everything to do with her nervousness at seeing the man she still loved.

Chapter Forty-Nine

Rosie had just turned the corner on to Borough Road when she saw him.

Part of her wanted to turn back and run away – the other wanted to race to him.

She did neither. Instead she slowed her pace – and her breathing – and told herself to get a grip, and do what she had to do. For Bel's sake. For Bel's mother's sake.

'Peter.' She didn't have to shout as he had spotted her straight away, despite the darkness created by the enforced blackout.

'Rosie.' His voice was neither friendly nor hostile.

Rosie immediately picked up on a change in him.

'I didn't want to bother you . . . ' she said, trying to keep her voice even. She had to remind herself of the lies she had told him – that she no longer had any feelings for him. She had to play the part. And it was important she play it well – she didn't want him thinking this was her way of trying to resume their courtship.

'It's a bit of an emergency,' she explained, putting her hands together as she suddenly felt awkward and didn't know what to do with them.

'It's Bel's mother – Pearl. She got a bit of a shock the other night and she's been missing ever since. Everyone's been looking for her, but so far she's not turned up. I thought of you . . . ' Rosie voice trailed off.

DS Miller looked at Rosie. This was the first time he had seen her up close since they had drunk their final cup of tea together at Vera's. She looked tired and her face was still dirty from the yard. There was so much he wanted to say, but he knew this was not the time.

'Just rewind for a moment,' he said, putting his gloved hand out as if he were stopping her getting too close to him.

'You say Pearl got a shock the other night. What about?'

Rosie took a deep breath and tried to explain as simply as possible that the daughter Pearl had adopted out had made a sudden appearance at Bel's wedding and unveiled herself at the reception party.

'Afterwards Pearl just walked out – and hasn't been seen since,' Rosie finished.

'Did she have a coat or any other belongings with her?' DS Miller asked. His mind was now totally switched on to the present crisis. Last night the temperature had been below zero. He knew because he'd been out on patrol. And if the woman was, as Rosie had suggested, prone to drinking a lot, and had been wearing just a dress, the prognosis was not good.

'Right, I'm going to headquarters to organise a search party. Do you know where Pearl grew up?'

Rosie thought for a moment. 'As far as I know, the east end . . . Hendon,' she said. 'Why?' she asked.

'Just a thought,' DS Miller said, starting to move away. 'Go and tell the family we're organising a search. Tell them to keep looking themselves. Try and think of any places she might go to if she's upset – apart from the pub.'

As he turned to go, he stopped. His hand pushed his grey-streaked black hair away from his face and he looked at Rosie.

'I may be going out on a limb here, but tell Bel to think of anywhere her mother used to go to as a child – and to look there. It's worth a shot.'

He started to hurry away, but again stopped. 'What number Tatham Street do they live at?'

'Thirty-four,' Rosie shouted back, before adding, 'And . . . thank you Peter . . . Hopefully, I'll see you later.'

The words were out of her mouth before she had time to pull them back in.

She didn't see any reaction from Peter – only the back of his black coat swooping behind him as he hurried away.

As promised, DS Miller organised a search party for Pearl; he also sent a young police constable to the Elliots to be with the family and keep them informed of any developments.

Beryl kept bobbing in to see Agnes every now and again when she had any bits of tittle tattle to impart, although none of it amounted to much. A couple of fishwives had spotted Pearl last night in various pubs on the south dock, as well as at the Welcome Tavern on Barrack Street. They'd noticed her because they had thought she was 'a bit of posh' in her velvet dress, and had thought she was lost – that was until Pearl had opened her mouth and started gobbing off at them.

'Barrack Street? That's where Ma was brought up, I think,' Bel said when she and Maisie had gone back to Tatham Street to check that Pearl hadn't turned up.

Maisie had looked surprised. 'Don't you know where your mother was raised?' she asked, without thinking. She was tired and she hadn't been able to hide the criticism in her voice.

'No,' Bel snapped back. 'I'm not sure "where she was raised", but then again, my ma didn't bother telling me I had a sister either.'

Bel had glowered at Maisie, who was wise enough not to rise to the bait and bite back.

As they both headed back out into the dark, frosty night,

Bel had to admit to herself that she actually knew very little about her mother, or about the upbringing she'd had. Her ma had never talked about it – hadn't talked about much, really.

Rosie's detective friend was right, though – it did look like her ma had been going round her old haunts; probably because she knew she'd get a drink on the house 'for old times' sake'.

Joe had seen his new wife for just a few minutes when he'd caught her and Maisie leaving the house as he was coming back with a few of his mates from the Home Guard. On hearing that his mother-in-law had been drinking down by the south dock, they had done an about-turn and immediately gone back out to do a search along the quayside.

A chill had gone down their spines on hearing Pearl had been seen down by the river. It was not uncommon for drinkers there to have one too many and stumble on the cobbles in the darkness and end up in the ice cold river – and those that went in the Wear rarely came back out. At least, not alive.

Rosie and Polly, meanwhile, had been scouring the Villette Road area just up from the east end, and ended up calling in on Hannah, who lived near the Barley Mow Park, and then Martha in Cairo Street – and finally Dorothy, who lived further up in The Cedars.

Not one of them had hesitated – they'd grabbed their coats and gas masks, pulled on their hats and gloves, wrapped scarves around their necks, and joined the hunt.

Martha's mother had made a round of sandwiches for them all to share, and Hannah's aunty Rina had gone to see the local rabbi, who in turn had sent a group of young Jewish lads out to find Pearl with instructions to take her to the synagogue – and not to be deterred if she was drunk and abusive.

From the start of their joint search for their ma earlier on in the day, Bel and Maisie must have covered miles as they trooped from one pub to the next. They had gone to all the pubs their mother had been seen in, and cross-examined the regulars and the bar staff on what Pearl had said, done, and where she might have gone – but still, they'd had no joy. Most of the drinking dens they went to, the clientele could barely remember what day it was, never mind much about what Pearl had been up to, or where she had been going to next.

It was now nearly nine o'clock and, although neither of them would admit it, they were both exhausted, and becoming more worried by the minute.

DS Miller's advice to think about somewhere Pearl used to go to as a child kept stabbing away at Bel, but, try as she might, she couldn't think of anywhere.

'I just can't remember anything Ma's said about her own growing up . . . never mind any places she used to go to.' Bel spoke her thoughts out loud as they walked along Church Street East and passed the huge Trinity Church.

Maisie looked at Bel's worried face but didn't say anything. It was getting late. It had been pitch black for hours now. And the more places they went to, the more she learnt about her mother, and of the life she'd led – without any words being spoken. Maisie realised she was learning the hard way that the image she'd manufactured of her mother over the years was very, *very* wrong.

The words her mother had spoken to her in the snug kept coming back to her: 'The day I gave birth to you was the best day in my entire life – and also the worst . . . When they took you from me I thought I would die right there . . . I didn't think it was possible to love another human being the way I loved you . . . '

And, worst of all, she kept seeing her mother's distorted, pitiful face as she had told her that she had loved her.

Maisie realised now that her mother had meant it. Yesterday those words had gone over her head, been swatted away, spat at, and dismissed. Now she couldn't stop thinking about them. And the more she remembered them, the more wretched and guilty she felt. Now those feelings of guilt had overtaken those of anger towards her mother. And guilt was not something Maisie often felt.

And she didn't like it. Not one bit.

For the first time ever, she felt the need to talk to her mother – and not simply to scream and shout at her.

She just hoped to God that she'd get the chance.

Chapter Fifty

When Pearl had walked out of the wedding reception, she'd had no intention of going back. Either to the pub, or to the Elliots', or to either of her daughters. She was not wanted anywhere, or by anyone. She could have lived with that – had lived with that all of her life. But what she could not live with was the pure hatred she had seen in her elder daughter's eyes.

As she had wandered from pub to pub after leaving the party it didn't matter how much she drank, she still couldn't escape her thoughts and feelings. She kept rerunning the moment she had seen Maisie standing in the middle of the Tatham, how she hadn't been able to tear her eyes away from Maisie's face.

When she had come around in the snug and had again looked into her daughter's eyes, she had been filled with an overwhelming sense of euphoria.

The daughter she had given up had come back to her.

There hadn't been a day since she had handed her baby girl over to Evelina when she hadn't wondered what she was doing now, where she was. Had she met someone and got married? Had children of her own?

When she had staggered out of Norfolk House last night she had drunk enough to sink a ship, yet the devastation she felt – knowing that her daughter hated her – had not eased off. It didn't matter how much she drank, she just couldn't get rid of the image of Maisie as she had spoken to her. She could have stomached her daughter's anger, but not the deeply embedded hatred that emanated from every fibre of her daughter's being.

Pearl's recall of the words she had exchanged in the snug with Maisie kept swimming about in her head, and out of the chaos swirling around in her inebriated mind came clarity.

She had vague recollections of some of the bars and taverns she had drunk in over the past twenty-four hours. Last night she had passed out somewhere along Norfolk Street and had woken a few hours later in the shelter of a doorway, covered in an old blanket that someone must have put on her while she slept. Those few hours of oblivion had been blissful. And when she had woken up and been thrown back into the real world – back into the reality that was her life – she knew what she wanted.

She wanted peace – and she was going to get it.

She had no recollection of how she had got here – but here she was.

And it was exactly where she wanted to be.

As Pearl made her way down the grass embankment, the wind from the sea air pierced right through her velvet dress, which was now dirty, and torn. Ruined beyond repair. A sad reflection of the woman who was wearing it.

She understood so much now – how over the years she had tried to plug the emptiness with alcohol and men, but it had been futile. She knew it now.

As Pearl reached the bottom of the hill and her feet found the cold stone pebbles, she looked down at the dress, and thought about how it had brought her so much happiness – how it had made her feel special. Again the tears came. Never in her life had she cried so much. Her eyes felt itchy and swollen. Her lovely dress. Little Katie would be distraught. All that hard work, only to be ruined. But that was Pearl, wasn't it? Anything good that came along she spoilt.

Or gave away.

Well, now it was time for all that to stop.

As she walked across the pebbled beach, her eyes automatically looked for coal. The tide was going out, and her befuddled mind idly wondered if there had been good pickings today.

But when she looked further down the beach and saw it had been sectioned off with barbed wire she was reminded that she was not a young girl collecting sea coal, but a grown woman living through another world war.

The icy water washed over her dirty, bare feet and a shiver ran through her skinny body. She knew it wouldn't take long – the cold would get to her first, before the salt water had time to fill her lungs.

Soon it would all be over, and she could forget everything. The hurt and heartache she had carried around with her for her entire life would end.

She could escape – and, this time, for good.

Bel and Maisie had started walking down Commercial Road, heading for another pub that Pearl might, or might not, have frequented, and Maisie started to ramble on, as she tended to do when she was nervous or scared.

As Bel shone the little torch they had to help them find their way in the blackout, Maisie spoke her thoughts aloud.

'Makes you wonder, doesn't it? What life was like back then?'

'Back when?' Bel asked, irritated. Maisie had the really annoying habit of starting to speak about something, expecting you to know exactly what it was she was going on about.

'Well, you know, back when they didn't have electricity . . . it must have been so dark all the time . . . and bloody cold.' Maisie was thinking of the little electric heater she had in her room at the bordello, and how she would give anything to be in front of it now. She felt frozen to the bone.

'Gas, Maisie – God, you do talk a load of gibberish sometimes. People used gas – coal and gas,' Bel said as they reached Hendon Grange.

'Here we go again,' Maisie said with dread. The pub looked no better than any of the other dives they'd been in today, but at least she was getting used to the remarks the men would make on seeing her in her fur coat.

Opening the bar door, they walked into the warmth of the main bar. Bel saw the raging hot coal fire.

She stopped in her tracks.

'What's wrong? You all right?' Maisie asked. Bel looked even paler than normal. Almost ghostly white.

'Coal . . . it's the coal,' Bel said.

'Blimey, Bel, now who's talking a load of "gibberish"?'

Bel swung her head towards Maisie.

'I know – *I know where she is!*'

Maisie felt an instant flood of relief.

'Where?'

'Oh God!' Bel said. 'Come on. I hope we're not too late.'

Maisie took one last look at the orange glow of the blazing open fire in the pub and wished she could have stood in front of it for just a few moments – but the look on Bel's face said they didn't have a minute to lose.

Chapter Fifty-One

Hendon Beach, Sunderland

As the water lapped around Pearl's legs she felt the numbing cold shoot up her limbs and into the rest of her body. Her feet were just about frozen and she knew it would not be long before the rest of her body felt the same.

Her mind spun back like the swirling water around her fighting against the turning tide. For a brief moment she was just fourteen years old, picking coal from this very beach, and Maisie was growing in her swelling belly.

She had wanted to tell Maisie about the confusion she had felt on finding out she was pregnant – how she knew that she would be disowned by her family – and shunned by society – not only because she'd had a child out of wedlock, but because of the colour of that child's skin. Black and white didn't mix. It wasn't exactly accepted nowadays, *but back then* . . . Didn't Maisie realise this? She hoped one day she would forgive her and understand that she had done what she had done for love.

The freezing cold North Sea was now lapping around her scuffed knees where she had fallen when she tripped coming out of a pub by the docks.

The sea seemed relatively calm today, and she let her fingers lightly touch the tops of the small ripples of waves.

Then – just as a gust of wind caused her hair to swirl

around her tear-stained face – Pearl thought she heard a voice in the distance behind her.

'Ma!'

Was she hearing things?

She stood stock-still. There it was again.

'Ma!'

It was Isabelle.

Poor Isabelle. She had such a lovely voice. Had always tried to speak properly. She had been desperate to better herself. Desperate to run away from her upbringing. And who could blame her? How Pearl wished she had been able to love her more. To have been a good mother. But she hadn't. Not even half good.

Well, at least Isabelle would be better off without her now.

Pearl kept on pushing herself through the water, the waves still small but strong, knocking her a little off balance, causing her to stumble on the rocks and pebbles underfoot.

'Mother! Stop! For God's sake, stop!'

This time the voice was not Isabelle's.

Pearl stopped dead still.

It was Maisie.

She was here.

With Isabelle.

And she was calling to her.

Calling out for her mother.

When Maisie saw her mother against the outline of the blackness that was the North Sea, her whole body flooded with sheer panic.

What had she done?

She had been so stupid. So selfish. She had wanted to make her mother suffer for giving her up. But not like this.

Her mother was walking – or rather wading – towards death. And it was all her fault.

She may have hated her mother all of her life, but she had never wished her dead. Above all, she had never wanted to be the cause of her death.

A huge wash of guilt followed the wave of panic. This poor, pathetic woman wanted to end her life and it was all her fault.

'Mother! Stop! For God's sake, stop!'

Maisie shouted as forcefully and as loudly as she could. She tore off her heavy fur coat and tossed it to the ground. As she did so her hat flew off and into the surrounding darkness of the night.

As Maisie ran, pain shot through her as the sharp edges of rocks and pebbles stabbed into the soles of her feet. She slipped on some seaweed-covered stones, but her hands shot out in front of her as she went sprawling on to all fours. When she stood up Pearl had disappeared.

'No!' Maisie screamed out into the night's air, flinging her body forward. Her feet hit shingles and she knew then she was near the water's edge, but still she couldn't see anything – only a moving expanse of dark, murky sea.

Tears were running down her face. Her mind flooded with self-recrimination. Why had she been so bloody single-minded? So wrapped up in in her own pain and misery? Wanting everyone to pay for what life had done to her.

Her body shuddered with fear as she frantically stared about her. Willing her eyes to adjust to the darkness. To find her mother. The mother she had spent so long tracking down, and had then so heartlessly flung aside.

Behind her she heard Bel shouting out for her ma. She sounded desperate and Maisie knew that she too could no longer see their mother.

But then, all of sudden, her sister's tone changed. 'There!' Bel screamed out. 'There!'

Maisie's eyes scanned from left to right – and then she saw her.

The light from the half-crest of a moon glanced across the glass beading on Pearl's velvet dress and for a split second it glinted and shone out through the darkness.

Maisie sprinted into the water, swinging her arms to push herself forward as fast as she could. Pearl was not that far away. The darkness of the night had tricked them – its cruel sleight of hand had cloaked their mother from them, making her invisible for a moment. Pearl stood as still as a statue, her face white but dirty with grime and the remnants of old make-up.

'Maisie.' Pearl's voice sounded feeble.

'Maisie,' she repeated. Her daughter had no idea just how much her mother loved saying that name out loud.

'Ma, it's Maisie and Isabelle. Come here, *Ma*!'

Maisie knew she just needed to keep her mother engaged. Pearl looked like she wasn't all there – probably wasn't, with the amount Maisie could only guess that she'd consumed since she had seen her yesterday evening. Maisie felt the bitter cold water shock every nerve in her body as she stretched towards her mother, whose skinny body was being pushed about by the currents caused by the turning tide.

'Ma!' She had almost reached Pearl now, but Maisie could see her mother was about to go under. She looked finished. Pearl locked eyes with Maisie and smiled.

Maisie thought her mother looked content – at peace, almost.

And then, as if the sea itself was swallowing her up, Pearl was gone.

'*No!*' Maisie's voice bellowed out; her voice so loud even

Neptune himself must have heard. She propelled her body forward, forcing her legs through the grey water with the last ounce of energy she had left.

Maisie just reached her mother before she went under. Grabbing hold of Pearl's bare arms, she pulled her mother back up out of the water, and enveloped her in her own slender arms, hugging her hard.

'What are you doing? You madwoman,' Maisie was half laughing, half crying. The relief at having made it to her mother in time was overwhelming.

Since she had been a child she had dreamed of the time when her mother would come and find her, take her in her arms, and cuddle her. As she had grown up that dream had faded, and her hopes of her mother rescuing her from the wretchedness of her life had died. Her heart had hardened and become increasingly embittered.

Now, after all those years, here she was – finally reunited with her mother. And it didn't matter that she was frozen to the bone, soaking wet, and exhausted, she wanted to stay just as they were, for a moment at least.

As Maisie held her mother tight, she knew the hopes and dreams of her youth could never be resurrected. She had waited all of her life to feel her mother's arms around her, but she didn't care that it was she who was now cuddling her mother. Nor did she care that it was she who was rescuing her mother from wretchedness and despair.

None of that mattered.

All that mattered was that she had found her mother.

And that, thank God, she had not lost her again. And this time for good.

The water washed against both their legs, their feet sinking a little into the sand and shingles as they continued to hold each other, Maisie listening to her mother as she repeated her name over and over.

'Maisie . . . Maisie . . . ' Pearl's voice was unusually soft and fragile. 'Don't you think it's a lovely name, Maisie?' Pearl asked, and her voice sounded tired but happy.

'I chose your name, did you know that? I gave you your name. Did Evelina tell you?'

Maisie had no idea what Pearl was talking about, or who Evelina was, but she knew her mother loved her. These past few hours with Bel, out scouring the streets of the east end she'd had time to think and she'd had to admit to herself that she had been wrong. Her mother was not some hateful, heartless woman who had given her away like a child tossing aside a broken doll that was no longer desirable or of any use. She was not some two-dimensional uncaring bitch, but rather a woman who, it would seem, had led a chaotic, drink-addled, messed-up life.

'Ah, Maisie,' Pearl kept saying. 'You were the most perfect little baby ever. I loved you. Really loved you. You must believe me.' Her body sank into her daughter's arms.

Maisie held her mother. The water was now only up to their calves, having been drawn back by the receding tide and the pull of the moon.

'I know,' Maisie told her. 'I know.'

Mother and daughter stayed for a short while longer, standing in the half-light of the moon, in the shallow waters of the sea, simply holding each other.

Salty tears trickling down both their faces.

Standing on the beach, Bel shivered in the cold night air. She didn't think she had felt so exhausted in her entire life, but none of that mattered because they had found their ma. And she was alive.

As she saw Pearl and Maisie wade back on to the beach,

she grabbed Maisie's fur coat that had been flung on to the pebbles and hurried over to them. 'Bloody Nora. You two are gonna catch your death.' Bel held the thick fur coat out and Maisie reached out and took it.

Pearl was hunched up, her body shaking and her head down. Maisie put the coat around her mother's shoulders and then pulled it around her so she was cocooned. Pearl grabbed the lapels of the brown fur and pulled them to her neck.

Bel and Maisie guided their mother across the stones and rocks and on to the grassy embankment.

'Honestly, Ma,' Bel said, looking at Maisie and giving her the beginnings of a smile, 'you've pulled some stunts in the past, but this one takes the biscuit.' As she spoke she pulled her thick woollen scarf off and handed it to Maisie, whose designer dress was dripping wet from the waist down; like her sister, she was looking the worse for wear.

Maisie took the scarf and wrapped it around her neck and across her chest.

By the time they had reached the top of the promenade they were dropping on their feet. Pearl had lapsed into her own world and was saying the odd word which neither Bel nor Maisie could make head nor tail of.

'Do you think she's all right?' Maisie asked.

'That's the drink,' Bel said, 'but I think we need to get her somewhere warm – and quick.'

'How far is it back to yours?' Maisie had no idea where they were. They could have been in Timbuctoo for all she knew.

'Too far to walk with Ma in this state and you with just that dress on.' Bel looked around. 'There's a pub just up the road called the Blue House,' she said.

Maisie remembered the blazing fire in the last pub they had been to and felt a surge of energy. She felt for her mother's elbow through the fur coat and lifted her. Bel did likewise.

'Come on, then. What we waiting for?' She spoke across her mother's bowed head to Bel.

'Lead the way!'

Much to their relief, the pub was closer than they thought. The instant they got through the front door and the warmth of the bar enveloped them, Maisie felt she was in heaven. She didn't even mind the usual stares as people clocked the fact that they had a 'coloured person' in their midst.

'I don't think I've ever been so happy to walk into a pub in my entire life,' she said to Bel.

Within a few minutes, the landlord had got the three women into the adjourning snug and away from the stares of the locals, who were understandably fascinated by the sight of this odd trio of women who looked like they'd been put through the wringer a few times.

The older woman was clearly the worse for wear – more than a few sheets to the wind – and had not reacted kindly to being denied a brandy, especially as the two younger and very attractive women at that had been more than grateful when they were handed a good measure.

While the landlord's young son cycled to Tatham Street to let everyone know that Pearl had been found alive and well, but that they needed some warm clothes and a helping hand to get her home, Bel and Maisie started to talk to each other. The relief that they had found Pearl, along with the large brandies they were now drinking, allowed them to be amicable with each other for the first time.

'How did you know where she was?' Maisie asked Bel. She looked down at their mother, who was now gently snoring with her head crooked to the side and resting on the back of the leather armchair she had been put in.

Bel told Maisie that one of her mother's few skills in life was that of making 'the best fires ever', and that her mother had told her on countless occasions how she would be sent out as a child to collect bits of sea coal from Hendon beach.

'When Ma first came to stay with us,' Bel said, thinking about the day she had just tipped up on the doorstep, suitcase in hand, 'the only job she seemed able – or was willing – to do in the house, was to stack the fire up every night, ready for the next day. And every time she did it she would tell me how she'd go to Hendon beach as a child and spend hours picking up bits of smooth sea coal and carry them in a sack back home.'

Bel took a large gulp of her brandy. ' . . . I've heard the story of her coal-picking days so many times I sometimes feel like I was there with her myself!'

The two sisters chuckled. It was the first time they had laughed together.

'The thing is, she always made out it was a real chore, but I could tell by the way she talked about it that there was a part of her that had enjoyed the hours she'd spent looking for coal – the way she talked about the beach, what it was like in the summer when she would go for a swim, or in the winter when she and all the others down there picking coal would stand and watch the massive waves.

'Oh, and of course,' Bel added with a smile playing on her lips, 'Ma was the champion picker. Always got the best bits of coal. She had – how did she put it . . . That's it, "I had a real *eagle eye*," she'd tell me – and she would always spot the best and biggest bits before anyone else.'

Maisie listened, feeling more relieved than she had ever done in her entire life, and revelling in the heat from the snug fire and the hot burn of the brandy, even if it was a cheap one, and not one of Lily's finest.

'So,' Bel finished off her drink with a grimace, 'when

you started muttering on about "life back then" and electricity and the like, and we walked into that pub and saw the coal fire . . . well, it was like the penny dropped. I knew if Rosie's detective friend was right in thinking that Ma would be heading back to some childhood haunt – then it would be there. Hendon beach.'

'Well, thank goodness the penny did drop,' Maisie said, picking up their glasses and standing up to get a refill, 'otherwise this one here, quite honestly, wouldn't be here now.'

Maisie knew – as she squeezed around the chair in which her mother was sleeping – if that had been the case, then there would have only been one person to blame, and that was herself.

Chapter Fifty-Two

The next day when the women welders broke off for lunch, the chatter was nonstop.

Gloria was the only one who had no idea about the drama of the previous evening as she had been tucked up, warm in bed, with baby Hope, who, for once, slept soundly next to her in her crib the entire night. For the first time in a long while, she hadn't spent half the night awake, thinking about Vinnie or Jack – or Miriam.

When the women took their trays of food and sat round their self-designated table in the noisy canteen, Gloria was agog as she listened to everyone speaking over each other, telling their version of the night's events.

Everyone had had plenty to say about Maisie and what a total cow she had been, but how, at the end of the day, she had redeemed herself a little by joining Bel in her search for Pearl and for wading into the sea to save their mother.

'You should have seen the state of them all when we got to the pub!' Polly laughed out loud as she regaled everyone with a description of Bel, Maisie and Pearl in the Blue House pub, how the three of them had looked like a trio of waifs and strays, with Pearl snoring away in the corner, and Bel and Maisie supping on huge glasses of brandy and practically sitting on top of the open fire, they were that cold.

Gloria had been particularly curious to hear that Rosie had sought help from DS Miller, and that he had galvanised the whole of the town's police force into looking for Pearl.

'So, in a way,' Gloria said, 'it was your detective friend who saved the day. If he hadn't suggested that Bel look somewhere her mum used to go to as a child, she would never have gone to the beach at Hendon. No one would have. And, well . . . what could have happened doesn't bear thinking about.'

'Yes,' Rosie said, 'I guess so . . . '

'Eee,' Polly butted in, 'I feel awful, Rosie. I can't believe we've been so rude. There was so much happening last night. We managed to get word to everyone that we'd found Pearl and to say how thankful we were, but I don't think anyone got to thank Peter. I don't suppose you saw him afterwards?'

Rosie shook her head. 'No, it was so late by the time we got word that Pearl was all right that I just went straight home. I did tell the young constable at the house, though, to go and see Peter and tell him we'd found her, so he could call off the search party.'

'Goodness, how rude of us,' Polly said. She looked at Rosie. 'I don't suppose you could take him a home-made pie or something from Ma to thank him – and his men – on behalf of us all, could you?'

Rosie stuttered. 'Well . . . mmm . . . I'm not sure . . . ' She looked at everyone's faces – all looking at her, waiting for her to finish her sentence.

'Honestly, Rosie,' Dorothy blurted out, 'Polly's not asking you to wine and dine him for the night – just to give him a bit of pie and say "thank you".'

Her words were followed by a general murmur of assent.

Gloria looked at Rosie. She knew why her workmate was being so reticent, and she could understand.

'All right, everyone,' Rosie smiled. 'I give in.' She looked over at Polly. 'Whatever treat your mum bakes for Peter, I'll take it to him.'

As they started to leave their table, Gloria looked at everyone and said, a little mysteriously, 'Actually, I might be getting a treat of my own soon . . . ' She shifted her look to Dorothy, who was scanning the canteen. 'As *Dorothy here* is going to be buying me my long-promised "biggest cake ever" pretty soon.' She paused as her workmate's head swung back around on hearing her name.

'What's that, Gloria?' Dorothy said.

'I was just saying that I might be getting my "biggest ever" cake soon.'

Dorothy looked puzzled for a moment, then her eyes widened in comprehension.

'You haven't? Have you?'

Now everyone else looked puzzled.

Gloria solemnly nodded her head.

'Oh, but *I have*, Dor, and I think that means you now have to fulfil your end of the bargain.'

Yesterday, after work, Gloria had decided to go and see the vicar and book a time for Hope to get christened. She was on her own in this world now. She had to stand on her own two feet, without a man either propping her up, or knocking her down. And her first venture as a single independent woman was to organise this first important milestone in her baby's life.

'Yay! At long bloody last, Glor!' Dorothy threw her arms into the air as if she'd just won a race.

'Can someone explain?' Martha demanded.

Hannah stuck her arm up as if answering a question in class. 'I know!' she said. 'Baby Hope's going to get christened!'

'That's right, Hannah! And about bloody time!' Dorothy added

The klaxon sounded out and everyone groaned.

'This is turning out to be the best few weeks ever. *A*

wedding – and now my *goddaughter's baptism*,' Dorothy declared melodramatically as they all scraped their chairs back and stood up.

Gloria chuckled. 'But don't get too excited, Dorothy. It's only going to be a very small affair. Nothing like the wedding. And, hopefully, without all the drama –' she looked guiltily at Polly. 'No offence, Pol.'

Polly waved her hand and stifled a yawn. 'None taken. I'm just grateful that everything turned out all right – what's the expression?'

Dorothy butted in, '"All's well that ends well".' She nudged Angie. 'That's a play by Shakespeare.'

Looking at Angie's blank, uncomprehending face, Dorothy sighed, 'Never mind, Ange . . . More importantly,' she said as they all headed back out into the yard, '*where do you reckon we can get a really big cake?*'

As the afternoon wore on and the women tried to keep warm against the bitter cold winds now coming in from the north, Rosie kept thinking about Peter.

She was going to have to see him again.

Just when the aching of her heart was beginning to ease off a little, and the amount of time Peter came into her head during the day had lessened slightly – now, all of a sudden, after last night's drama, he was back in her life again. And she would have to see him, whether she wanted to or not. She had asked the favour of him. It was her responsibility. She couldn't push this on to Polly or Agnes, much as she would have liked to. She knew she had to go and thank him personally. It was the right and proper thing to do. Besides, he had gone beyond the call of duty and rallied practically the whole of Sunderland Borough Police Force in the search for Pearl.

It was just that, having seen him last night, and now that

she was going to meet with him again, all her hard work at trying to forget him had been undone in one fell swoop.

She felt as if she was heading back to square one.

'Bloody Maisie,' Rosie cursed into her welding mask, 'that woman has a lot to answer for. This is all her fault.'

But deep down, Rosie had to admit to herself that a part of her was secretly looking forward to seeing Peter again, even if it was just to hand over Agnes's home-made plate pie.

Chapter Fifty-Three

Shipyard hooters up and down the River Wear sounded out the end of that day's shift.

Each shipyard hooter had a different sound, but they all blared out at the same time.

Jack was just one of the thousands of shipyard workers that walked or cycled their way out of the nine yards, working flat out to keep up with the Allied need for new ships to be built and old ones repaired.

Jackie Crown's shipyard, Jack's new workplace, was on the north side of the river, which meant he only had a short journey home, past the Bungalow Café, along the top of the promenade, and then through Roker Park.

When he walked through the front door he was greeted by Miriam, who had already indulged in a large gin and tonic but had been sucking on an imperial mint to take away the smell.

'So, darling, how was work today?' she asked as she wandered over to the drinks cabinet and poured him a large Scotch.

Jack smiled and walked over and took his drink from her. He gave her a quick kiss, but only because he knew it was expected. Kissing – or any other kind of intimacy with his wife – still didn't seem right. Which was absurd.

Time, he kept telling himself. *It would just take time.*

'Yes, work's good,' Jack told Miriam, as he looked at the tumbler of single malt. He didn't really want a whisky, but took a sip from it all the same. At least, he rationalised, it helped with the growing feelings he'd had of late of being trapped. Which, frankly, he could not understand. Why would you feel trapped in your own home – with your own very loving and very attentive wife? Honest to God, he was alive, wasn't he? He had an enviable home life – and a job that he loved, and that, more than anything, was vital to the war effort.

'You getting used to Crown's now?' Miriam continued to prod. She knew she had been criticised behind her back for organising Jack's move.

'It's still feeling like I'm the new boy at school.' Jack tried to make light of the situation, even though he did feel the odd one out.

When he had been given the tour of Thompson's, some of the men's faces had rung distant bells in the far recesses of his mind. He had hoped that the tinkling of those bells would become more audible, and perhaps, in time, would even clang with clear remembrances of his past, but it looked unlikely he would return to Thompson's as Miriam had made it clear that it was important he should be at Crown's when the buyout happened.

'I'll get there,' Jack said with a tight smile.

'You *will* get there, darling,' Miriam purred, as she poured herself a large gin with just a splash of tonic. But her words were as false as the reality she was creating for herself and her husband – for Miriam had no wish for Jack to 'get there'. She wanted her husband exactly where he was now.

Under her control. And with absolutely no memory of the past.

As they drifted off to sleep later on that evening, Miriam lulled herself to sleep with thoughts of a grand dinner party she was planning to celebrate Jack's safe return. She was sick to death of all this warmongering and doom and gloom, of the constant BBC news reports about Hitler's seemingly successful invasion of Russia, and then there was the constant speculation as to whether or not the Americans would join the war. And that was besides all the home news about bombings up and down the country. A respite from all this death and destruction was needed, and she was the one to provide it.

Unlike Miriam, Jack, on the other hand, wanted to hear every news report, read every printed word on what was happening in every part of the world. He had been horrified to hear about what was happening on the Eastern Front, and prayed that the Yanks would step up to the mark – and sooner rather than later.

When Jack drifted off to sleep, his mind always seemed to find itself straying back to the expanse of the Atlantic Ocean. And when sleep finally won over, his dreams were filled with the panic of knowing he was drowning – that he was being pulled to his death. But lately his dreams had been swamped with another image – one which replaced the portent of death with a most wonderful feeling of serenity. And that was the vision of the baby.

The baby he had seen just before he thought his life was coming to an end – the baby, for some inexplicable reason, he had felt was his.

Chapter Fifty-Four

A week later

'Come on, *Mother*,' Maisie shouted up the staircase from the hallway at the Elliots'.

Since Pearl had been rescued from her drunken attempt to bed down in the North Sea, Maisie had become a regular visitor at the Elliots', although she would never stay long – just a few minutes while she waited for Pearl to fuss around. The pair of them would then have a walk into town, usually ending up in one of the tea shops, where Pearl would chain-smoke while they chatted about their lives.

If Maisie stayed more than a few minutes at the house in Tatham Street, she would have felt obliged to go and wait in the kitchen and even force down a cup of tea, which, if truth be told, wasn't really what anyone wanted. Agnes was always polite and would make a point of offering her daughter-in-law's newfound sister a brew when she came round, but Maisie was not fooled and knew her presence caused an unease in the house. She would, therefore, always tell Agnes, 'I'm not staying for long, but thank you all the same'. She knew her polite rebuttal of the proffered hospitality was secretly welcomed by Agnes, who, if she had genuinely wanted Maisie as a house guest, would have insisted she have at least a cuppa, if not a bite to eat.

This did not perturb Maisie – not in the least. Her reason

for calling round to Tatham Street was to see her mother, and, of course, her sister – and not because she wanted to ingratiate herself with Bel's in-laws. It was her opinion that the family her sister had married into – the family she had adopted, and who had adopted her – was Bel's world. It was *her* life, and not Maisie's.

If the Elliots wanted to be friendly with Maisie, all well and good. If they didn't, then they didn't. Maisie had grown a thick skin over the years and wasn't too fussed whether people liked her or not. Which was not unlike her mother. In fact, the more time Maisie spent with Pearl, the more she realised just how much alike they were.

This past week they'd managed to have a few honest talks. Her mother might not have remembered much about her twenty-four-hour drinking binge, but she could remember every word spoken in the snug and she had told Maisie that she had meant every one of them. She hadn't minced her words, nor had there been any tears. She'd just told her straight: 'What I said was true, pet!'. She hadn't elaborated and she hadn't got emotional. Maisie had known she was speaking the truth. And she had understood for the first time what her mother had meant when she'd said that she had given her up because she loved her so much.

Maisie still wished Pearl had kept her as a baby, but at least now she understood why she had not. The night of the search and the snippets she had picked up about the kind of life Pearl had led were enough to make her believe that her mother had – and did – love her. And had loved her as a baby.

'Dinnit hassle me,' Pearl shouted back down, 'I'll be down in a minute.'

Maisie let out an audible, theatrical huff.

'We're not going to the Ritz, you know, Ma.' Maisie

straightened the ivory rayon tea dress she was wearing under the fur coat that had taken an age to clean after it had been tossed about that godforsaken beach and then used as a blanket.

'Oh, sounds intriguing. Where are you two off to, then?' It was Bel emerging from her room with a sleepy Lucille in her arms. Maisie couldn't help but stare at the tatty toy rabbit her niece was clutching. She would have chucked it out a long time ago if it had been her daughter.

'Well,' Maisie said, quickly thinking up a little white lie. 'There's a place in town I've been told about that sounds quite nice. It's near the station.' Maisie paused as if trying to recall what the place was called.

'How annoying, I can't remember the name . . . '

There was nothing wrong with Maisie's memory, though, and she knew exactly where she was going.

'Ah, well,' Bel said, turning to go into the kitchen where she was to make Lucille a hot chocolate as her bedtime treat, 'I'm sure it'll be nice, whatever it's called. I'm sure Ma'll be telling us all about it in great detail tomorrow.'

As Bel walked into the kitchen, Maisie watched her sister as she started chattering to Lucille. She and Bel really were like chalk and cheese.

'At last,' Maisie said as she looked up to see her mother at the top of the stairs. She looked good – all things considered. Her appearance had been given a massive helping hand by Kate, who had knocked up a simple, yet stylish, little black dress for Pearl.

Maisie herself, however, was still very much in Kate's bad books and would probably stay there for the foreseeable future.

Rosie had also made it plain that she was far from happy with Maisie – and she had spelt it out to her in no

414

uncertain terms that not only had Maisie ruined Bel and Joe's wedding, but she had totally spoilt their honeymoon night at the Grand as well.

Guilt had never been something Maisie had been plagued with much in her life – a life, it had to be said, that had been far from blameless. Still, Maisie understood that it was right that she make amends to Bel – and Joe – for the irreparable damage she had done to their special day. And it was for this reason that she was taking Pearl out for a drink this evening to the Grand, where they were also going to find out how much a three-course dinner and an overnight stay would cost.

Maisie's motivations, though, weren't entirely selfless, as she was also intending to have a chat to the manager about the opening of the Gentlemen's Club. It was time to start spreading the word. George and Lily had, thankfully, decided to keep her on; and she was keen to prove that they had made the right decision.

'You look nice, Ma,' Maisie said, moving out of the way as Pearl came down the stairs.

'All thanks to little Katie,' Pearl said, turning to go into the kitchen. 'Just need to fetch my purse and fags and gas mask. Can't go out without the essentials.'

Maisie laughed out loud. 'I don't know about your purse, there's never anything in it.'

'Nana!' Lucille perked up on seeing her grandmother. Every time Pearl got ready to leave the house, Lucille would beg to go with them. Bel thought it was because her daughter was afraid she would go walkabout again and not come back, but Maisie thought that the little girl simply wanted to join in the fun and go into town and be treated to a glass of lemonade and a bag of crisps – like she'd done the other day when she and Pearl had taken her out for the afternoon.

While Pearl started hunting around for her fags, the front door went and Maisie turned to see Polly and Rosie walk into the house.

'Hello, Polly,' Maisie said in her sweetest of voices. She had learnt that if she put on a show of politeness with a hint of humility, Polly would be pretty amiable with her in return.

'Hi, Maisie, do you know if Ma's finished whatever she's baking for DS Miller?'

'I'm not sure, Polly, but judging by the lovely smells when I came in, I would guess so.'

Maisie smiled at Polly as she bustled past her and into the kitchen, but her face turned to stone when Rosie passed. The two women simply glared at each other – neither of them bothering to hide their true feelings.

Maisie knew Rosie was here to pick up what smelt like a savoury pie of some description and take it to her detective. She had been gobsmacked when she'd heard snippets about this Peter, and that there had been a possible romance but it had hit the buffers. For Rosie even to be just friends with the man, who, by all accounts, was straight as a die, was, in her opinion, complete lunacy. Women in their businesses simply did not hobnob with the boys in blue, unless those boys in blue were far from lily white.

'Hello, Maisie.' It was Arthur, coming through the front door. They smiled at each other and exchanged the usual pleasantries as the old man made his way into the kitchen, where he could be heard asking Rosie about one of the women welders called Gloria, and whether she was all set for the christening on Saturday.

'Come on, *Mother*!' Maisie trilled out.

'I'm coming, Maisie!' Pearl shouted back. 'And dinnit call me "mother" – makes me feel ancient!'

'Found them!' Pearl raised her packet of Winston's in the air like it was a trophy she had just won.

'Thank the Lord for that,' Maisie muttered. 'Come on, it's getting busier than Clapham Junction in here.'

Pearl laughed and then started to cough.

They could still her laughing and coughing as she and her daughter tottered down Tatham Street in the direction of the Grand Hotel.

Chapter Fifty-Five

The South Dock, Sunderland

Rosie was stepping from one foot to another to keep herself warm. Both of her hands were placed, palms up, underneath the cardboard box containing the leek and potato pie that Agnes had just made. It smelt delicious and she could feel the warm pastry through the bottom of the box.

The fret from the North Sea was just beginning to creep into the large gaping mouth of the River Wear and make its way inland. As Rosie tried to calm her growing nerves she could feel the beginnings of a fine drizzle on her face.

She had left the Elliots' ten minutes ago and had now been waiting for another ten for DS Miller to show himself. She was standing a little way along the quayside, not far from the ferry landing so that she could catch him leaving the police cabin up by the Sea Lock at the end of his day shift. She knew his routine and that he rarely went home before the start of his evening civil defence duties, preferring to go to the police headquarters in town to grab a cup of tea and a sandwich from the canteen and catch up with his former colleagues.

'Night all, see you in the morning.' Rosie heard the familiar sound of Peter's voice as he said his farewells to the other two police officers she knew worked the docks.

She squinted through the darkness and could just about make out the familiar outline of DS Miller's overcoat, which always flapped about as he never seemed to button it up, and his distinctive trilby hat. She watched as his darkened silhouette stepped out of the cabin and he closed the door shut behind him.

Rosie couldn't wait for him to reach her, so she started walking towards him.

'Hi Peter,' she spoke out into the darkness, the drizzle now starting to dampen the cardboard box she was carrying in front of her. She tried to force her voice to sound normal – nonchalant, even.

The surprise on the detective's face said he had not been expecting to see Rosie again, and his look was not one of joy.

'Ah, Rosie. How are you?' Peter still managed to sound professional, if not entirely friendly.

Rosie felt the smile she had forced to put on her face wane. This was not like Peter. The only time he had ever talked to her like this – so official and formal – was when she had first met him, almost exactly a year ago, the night he had knocked on her bedsit door and told her that her uncle's bloated body had been pulled out of the River Wear.

'I'm fine, thank you,' Rosie said, trying to match his formal tone.

She took a deep breath and straightened her back. 'The reason I've come to see you is to give you this present of thanks from the Elliots –' she put her arm out to hand him the pie '– one of Agnes's home-made specialities.'

On seeing the gift, DS Miller's face softened.

'Oh, she shouldn't have,' he said looking at the proffered box.

'To quote the family,' Rosie continued, now just wanting to end this awkward meeting, ' ... "it's the very least we can do to show how truly thankful we all are for your help in finding Pearl." There,' Rosie added, pushing the box into DS Miller's hands so that he had to take the pie from her, ' . . . the message has been delivered, word for word – as well as the present.'

Rosie turned to go. She knew when she was not wanted. Peter clearly was not exactly overjoyed at seeing her; that was for sure.

'So,' DS Miller's voice sounded panicky and he stretched his arm out to grab the woman he loved, but stopped himself. 'Is Pearl all right?'

Rosie looked at Peter. He was treating her like she was a complete stranger. Still, what should she have expected? She knew she had hurt him – deeply – when she had told him she did not want him. Of course, he was hardly going to be full of the joys of spring. But still, she felt there was something else going on underneath the surface.

'Pearl appears to have made a full recovery,' Rosie explained. 'She seems to be pretty much back to her normal self.' Rosie wanted to add that she was not sure whether that was necessarily a good thing.

'Actually, her brush with death seems to have given her a new lease of life,' Rosie added, thinking of seeing her this evening in her new black dress and how sprightly she was.

'Often the case,' he nodded, sagely.

DS Miller had picked up little bits of information about what had happened at the wedding, which had precipitated Pearl's disappearance.

'I suppose, being reunited with her daughter as well . . . ' he added, not needing to finish the sentence.

DS Miller actually knew more about the child Pearl had given up than Rosie realised. On the night Rosie had asked for his help and he had organised a search party, he had heard through the young uniformed officer he had sent to the Elliots all about the very beautiful and dark-skinned long-lost daughter called Maisie. DS Miller was not easily shocked, but he had been really quite flabbergasted by the coincidence that the stunning, mixed-race woman he had seen coming out of the house in Ashbrooke was the very same person who had revealed herself to Pearl at Bel's wedding.

'And everyone else well?' he asked. Rosie had caught him by surprise by turning up like this. 'Your girls?'

Rosie turned back, hearing the change in his voice. She looked him in the eye. Something was up and she didn't have a good feeling.

DS Miller returned Rosie's look and held it.

'I mean, your women welders . . . of course,' he added.

'Of course . . . ' Rosie repeated. The bad feeling in her gut was getting worse. 'They're all good.'

'And Gloria? Is she keeping well?' The concern in DS Miller's voice was genuine. He'd not heard of Vinnie kicking off again, but that was not to say he hadn't. If he had, it was unlikely that the police would have been informed.

Rosie felt herself relax a little.

'Oh, she's good. She's had the baby. Actually, she's having her christened at St Ignatius's on Saturday. Dorothy, who Gloria asked to be the godmother, has nagged her into submission.'

'That's great news.' He paused, then added, 'I'm guessing you're going – you and all your squad?'

Rosie nodded.

'And her ex, Vinnie, he's not been causing her any more trouble?'

Rosie shook her head. 'Not as such, but I don't think he's best pleased that Gloria's not letting him see the baby. She's just keeping her fingers crossed he doesn't get to hear about the christening until after the event. I think that's why Gloria's organised it at such short notice.'

DS Miller took in Rosie's words and sighed inwardly. Men like Vinnie never changed.

They both stood awkwardly for a moment, neither of them saying anything. Rosie so wanted them to start walking together, as they had done so many times before, and go to Vera's café and sit and chat.

But that was in the past. There was no going back.

Rosie looked at DS Miller's face. He looked like he was going to say something.

'Well, I better get going,' she said. As she turned and started to walk away, she heard DS Miller speak again.

'I know,' he said simply.

He hadn't been going to tell her, but the words just came out without thinking. It was as if he needed her to know.

After the night he'd seen her going into the house in Ashbrooke, it hadn't taken him long to find out what was really going on in there. He was a copper, after all. Had been a detective for longer than he cared to think. And it hadn't taken a genius to work it out, especially when he had gone round the back lane and found the 'other' entrance to the property that he now knew went by the name Lily's.

Rosie froze.

He knew? What? About her other life? Her other girls?
Had her worst nightmare just become reality?

'What do you mean, you "*know*"?' As she spoke Rosie turned around slowly.

Now it was her turn to sound a little hostile.

DS Miller walked towards Rosie – the woman who had stolen his heart, ripped it up and then thrown it away. He had been so pig-headed in his determination to find out her secret. To solve the puzzle. To find out the real reason she wouldn't be with him. Now his curiosity was satiated. But, how he wished he could turn back the clock and could have just let it be. Sometimes ignorance was bliss.

'I know about Lily's,' he said. His voice was flat and didn't give away any kind of emotion.

Rosie felt the bottom fall out of her world. It was what she had dreaded more than anything since the moment she realised she was falling in love with him.

For a second she felt sick. Nauseous. Afraid. Ashamed. Annoyed. Angry. All at once. All together.

She had worked so hard – had made so many sacrifices – to make sure this moment never happened.

But it had.

He knew the truth about her.

She had come to deliver a pie – had stupidly been excited about seeing him – and now her life, her livelihood, and that of those she loved, was under threat of being blown up right in front of her.

Immediately her thoughts went to Charlotte. Not only would she no longer be able to afford her sister's boarding school fees if she was behind bars, but she also knew the stuck-up head teacher would have her little sister marched out of those school gates quick as a flash if she found out that Charlotte's benefactor was in prison – and, more so, if she found out why.

Since her uncle Raymond had driven her to the depths of despair and exhaustion, and then nearly killed her, Rosie had worked hard at repairing her life. And over the past year she had not only salvaged it, but built on it, and was now doing extremely well for herself. She was managing the girls rather than working as one, and she also part-owned the business with Lily. She was easily affording to pay Charlotte's school fees, and was putting money aside for the future. Life was on the up.

Or rather, life *had been* on the up.

Until now.

Now, her lover had become her enemy. The man who had made her feel so happy and carefree had become a portent of misery – as well as her potential jailer.

Within the blink of an eye, her life – and that of Charlotte and those at the bordello – was in serious jeopardy.

Rosie had to think on her feet – and quickly. It was obvious Peter knew everything. There was certainty in his voice. This was no fishing expedition. He had somehow got to know about her work at Lily's.

They both stood there. Rosie felt unable to move, never mind explain.

'So, now . . . ' DS Miller broke the formidable silence, 'I find myself in an untenable position.'

Rosie had no idea what 'untenable' meant, except that it was not good.

How had he found out? She had a million questions, but she knew that whatever came out of her mouth next was going to be a game changer. If ever there was a time to play her cards right, then this was it.

'Well,' she said, trying to be calm and keep her dignity, although she could see the hurt and anger now showing in Peter's eyes, 'what does this "untenable" position mean you're going to do?'

Rosie was stalling for time to think. Panic was starting to surge through every pore. She could feel the drizzle start to become rain. A part of her wanted to sprint to the bordello and warn Lily that Peter knew and that the police could be bashing their door down at any time.

'To be honest, Rosie . . . ' Peter said. He looked jaded and a little defeated. The moment had come. He had been dreading it. Truly dreading it. The scene he'd known would have to be played out was now taking place, and it felt more than a little surreal. ' . . . I don't know what I'm going to do.'

And it was true. DS Miller had no idea what he was going to do. Or what would happen next. All he knew was that he felt a degree of relief. Finally, it was out in the open.

'I know what I should do as someone who enforces the law.' He didn't need to say that he should report the bordello to the authorities. That Rosie and Lily should be arrested for running an establishment of ill repute, and, more importantly, a place that was illegal.

'But,' he started to waffle, ' . . . sometimes it's hard.' As the words stuttered out of his mouth, all he could think of was that he didn't want to be saying this. He had only ever wanted to whisper sweet nothings into this woman's ear.

Had only ever just wanted to be with her.

God, he had wanted to marry her.

Have her as his. But that dream had been demolished. He had been living in cloud cuckoo land, and now he had been brutally chucked out of the nest and was having to sit up, dazed and confused, and face up to the reality of the situation.

Rosie looked at Peter. Neither of them moved an inch. The rain was getting heavier. Random thoughts went through Rosie's head: the pie would be getting wet if they stood there much longer. All of Agnes's hard work for nothing.

Rosie forced her mind back on track. She tried to interpret Peter's words. She wanted to shake him and ask what he meant. What was he going to do? Did he realise that it wasn't just her life he would be ruining, but Charlotte's as well? An innocent in all of this.

Rosie knew that she should tell him about Charlotte. Make him understand – beg him to understand. She should tell him about the events that had brought her to where she was now. Her parents' deaths. That Charlotte would be sent to an orphanage, or the care home run by the nuns. That she had done what she had done not for her own survival – but to save her sister.

Surely he would understand?

Surely this would stop him reporting her and Lily to the police?

She should throw herself on his mercy. Explain why she had done what she had done. Why she now did what she did.

Rosie opened her mouth to speak, but nothing came out. She tried to say the words, but she couldn't. Something steely and obstructive inside her was stopping the begging words from coming out. She couldn't do it. Couldn't bow down and beg for mercy. Especially to a man.

Flashes of her uncle Raymond on top of her as she gasped for air, aged just fifteen . . . Him threatening to do the same to Charlotte if she didn't let him do what he wanted . . . The years of working as a girl at Lily's . . . Being forced to hand over money in exchange for her uncle's silence last year . . . the repeated threat of exposure and, worse still, the unspoken risk he posed to her sister.

And then the moment she'd had her face held over a live weld and nearly died.

No.

She was never going to beg for any man's mercy.

Never.

Rosie opened her mouth again. 'Peter,' she said, without anger or shame, and with not a hint of contrition.

'You have to do what you think is right. It is your choice. It is your decision what you do. I cannot – will not – do anything to try and stop you or influence you.'

She took a deep breath and spoke the next words with a tremor in her voice.

'All I want to say to you is that I am sorry I lied to you. I'm sorry I was not honest about my *other life* – but everything else I shared with you was true.'

Peter was standing, rain now dripping down the edges of his trilby. Rosie looked into his eyes and thought she saw tears forming.

'Most of all, though, I am sorry for lying to you about how I felt. That was the hardest and most painful lie I have ever had to tell, because – and I think deep down you knew this – I *did* want to be with you . . . I loved being with you . . . When you tried to kiss me that evening, I didn't want to stop you . . . '

Rosie took a deep breath and told herself to be strong. 'When I told you that I didn't want to be with you – that was a lie. I wanted to be with you more than anything – but I knew I couldn't because of what you have now found out . . . and so I lied.

'Peter, do what you have to do. But know that I lied for a reason. I was falling in love with you. And try as I might I have not been able to force myself to fall out of love with you.'

With that, Rosie turned and walked away into the darkness of the night.

And Peter stood, still holding the pie, watching the woman he had also not been able to force himself to fall out of love with, walk away.

Chapter Fifty-Six

When Rosie got home that night, she quickly changed and went straight to the bordello. As soon as she was through the front door she found Lily and asked her to come for a chat in the front office. Lily could see by the look on Rosie's face that whatever she wanted to tell her was serious.

'George – George!' Lily called out, poking her head around the door of the reception room and finding her fiancé. Since they had announced their engagement, there had been great excitement in the house; it was something the girls couldn't easily forget as Lily was enjoying wearing her enormous diamond ring every minute of the day; there had even been speculation that she wore it in bed.

George took one look at Lily's face and knew something was up.

'Coming, my dear.' He pushed himself off the piano stool. He had been tinkling away, teaching himself a new tune. As he joined Lily out in the hallway, he looked at her and asked, 'What's up?'

'I don't know,' Lily said, opening the door to Rosie's office. 'But I think we're about to find out.'

'Bloody hell.' Lily had reverted to her East End twang. 'I knew that man was trouble from the start. Bloody, bloody, bloody . . . '

George took another drink of the cognac Rosie had poured out for them all before she broke the news that Peter knew about the bordello.

'Did he say anything else?' Lily demanded. 'How much does he know? Does he know how many girls we have here? How long we've been going for?'

Rosie looked flushed. She had barely had time to digest this new turn of events herself. All she knew was that she'd had to get here as quickly as she could and tell Lily. This affected Lily's life as much as it did her own. She had a right to know straight away. Rosie just hoped to God that Peter wouldn't do anything tonight if he was going to turn them in.

'No, he didn't go into any detail,' she said, racking her brains and going over every word they had exchanged, 'just said that he "*knew*".'

There was silence as Lily walked round the large desk and pulled open one of the top drawers, where she kept a spare packet of Gauloises. After she took a cigarette out of the packet and lit it with the large silver lighter that was kept on the top of the desk, she exhaled smoke, put a hand on Rosie's shoulder and squeezed it gently. This was not the time for blame, although she could bloody well strangle Rosie for ever becoming friendly with probably the straightest copper in the whole of the Borough Police. No, they had to pull together, and work out the best solution to the dire situation they now found themselves in.

Rosie put her hand on top of Lily's and squeezed it in return. She could feel Lily's ring against the palm of her hand.

'Well,' George said, 'I think the first thing we have to do is to put your ledgers somewhere they can't be found.'

Lily paced the room, cigarette in one hand and in the other her large glass of cognac.

'Yes, good thinking, George. Can you deal with that?' she asked, taking a slug of her drink, followed by a puff on her Gauloise. 'And I think we'll tell the girls that we're going to close shop for a week or so until we can work out what we're going to do. At least then we don't have to worry about having the girls here, or that they'll be nicked. They'd probably get off with a slap on the wrist and a fine, but it would be the humiliation that would be the worst for them . . . '

'And the fact they would never get another job anywhere else once it came out about their work here,' Rosie added.

Lily continued to smoke; as she did so she kept looking at her engagement ring. 'Mmm,' she pondered for a moment, ' . . . you wanting to make an honest woman of me, George, might just give us a bit of an advantage here.'

Within the hour the girls had been assembled. All the clients had paid up and gone home. Any other men seeking the services of the bordello were politely turned away with the explanation that there were problems with the plumbing and the bordello was going to have to close for the next few days – possibly the next week, if it was as big a problem as they thought.

Lily and Rosie were honest with the girls about the reason the business was suddenly closing its doors as they had agreed between them that everyone connected to the bordello needed to know the truth.

'But what about those of us who live here?' Vivian asked. She looked gutted. Life had been getting really interesting since Maisie had come on board, especially now the wedding fiasco was slowly receding into the background and it looked as though Maisie was going to stay.

Lily looked at Vivian. She knew she had nowhere else to go to. She originally hailed from Liverpool, but had shown no desire in the past year she had been here to return to her home town.

'Why don't we have a chat about that when Maisie and

Kate get back? We can put our heads together and work something out,' she said.

At the mention of Kate, Rosie felt awash with guilt. This was the last thing she wanted for her old schoolfriend. She had brought her here to help her, not get her arrested and put behind bars. And, besides, where would she go? Back on the streets? Back to her old ways?

Chapter Fifty-Seven

Friday 21 November 1941

The next morning when Rosie went into work she had dark rings around her eyes, evidence that she had barely slept a wink.

'Rosie looks a bit rough today,' Dorothy said under her breath to Angie. 'Haven't seen her like this since all that trouble she was having with her uncle.'

Gloria, next to them, had been thinking the same. 'I agree,' she said quietly. 'I'll have a chat and see what's up and if there's anything we can do.'

As they all worked through the morning shift, Rosie's mind kept looping around and around.

When Kate and Maisie had got back last night – Maisie from her trip to the Grand, and Kate from working late at the shop – they had all sat around the kitchen table with Vivian. The rest of the girls had already gone home and the small red light at the back of the house had been switched off.

It had surprised Rosie that Kate didn't seem too perturbed by everything. She wasn't sure if it was because Kate didn't feel that she had any other option other than to stay, or because the thought of being hauled off by the police was nothing new for her. George seemed to think that, if the place was raided, they would not be able to find anything to charge Kate with. But, you never knew, especially with her previous misdemeanours.

Maisie, however, could not hide her anxiety. Rosie had a feeling that Bel's half-sister might already have felt the pull of her collar in London, and that was why she appeared more than keen to remove herself from the situation. Maisie said she would sleep on it and work out what she was going to do in the morning.

Vivian, on the other hand, seemed pretty resolute about staying. It was clear she did not want to go back to the Wirral, and in her words, spoken like a true Mae West, was 'willing to take her chances'.

Lily and George had gone off for a walk for an hour. Rosie suspected they had gone across to the Ashbrooke sports and social club for a chat. They weren't regulars there but George was a member and they occasionally popped in for a quick drink.

When they returned they had told them that – as a newly engaged couple – they were going to live together in the house in an effort to give it some semblance of a 'normal' family home. And that, instead of children, they had lodgers in the form of Vivian and Kate – and Maisie, of course, should she choose to stay.

They all knew that Peter might already have enough evidence of their illegitimate business to have them hauled immediately in front of the magistrates, and whatever they did now to try and erect a veneer of respectability would make no difference. 'But,' Lily had declared, 'best to do something rather than nothing. That's what I say.'

And so it was agreed. George would move out of his bachelor pad, where he rarely spent any time as it was, and Vivian, Maisie and Kate would assume the role of lodgers.

When Rosie had gone back home she had felt physically sick that it was all her fault. She had caused this horrendous situation.

Throughout the night and into the early hours of the morning she had repeatedly berated herself for ever agreeing to go for a cup of tea with Peter. She knew from the start the risk she was taking – and yet she took it. And now here she was – and it wasn't just herself who was paying for that mistake, but a whole bunch of other people who had done nothing wrong, other than want to get by and earn a living.

Her self-admonishment had continued all morning at work, and now the horn was sounding out for lunch, she was glad to be with the women. Her mind needed a rest.

'So, Gloria,' she asked as they traipsed over to the canteen. They all had several layers of clothes on as it was turning out to be another bitterly cold winter. 'Are you all set for Hope's christening tomorrow?'

Gloria grabbed the door of the canteen and swung it open as they piled in.

'I certainly am. Not much to organise, really, just turn up with the baby at the arranged time,' she said. 'It's Dorothy,' she added, casting a look over to Hope's godmother, 'you should really be asking. She's the one who's got her work cut out.'

Rosie's mind was feeling sluggish and tired and she glanced at Dorothy with a quizzical look on her drawn face.

'The *cake*,' Dorothy said. 'She means I have to keep my end of the bargain and get "the biggest cake ever". You know, like I promised when she had Hope?'

'Ah, yes, of course,' Rosie forced a smile.

'Anyway, I keep meaning to ask,' Polly said, 'did you manage to catch Peter last night?'

Rosie felt her face turn crimson.

'Oh, yes, yes, I did,' she hesitated, not sure what to say. 'He was really pleased . . . grateful . . . said all the usual things – "you shouldn't have" and "only doing my job" and all that – but I could tell he was really, really chuffed.'

Rosie hoped Polly hadn't picked up that she was lying, and that in reality the potato and leek pie had been like a shield between the pair of them. Rosie didn't want the Elliots – and Agnes in particular – to know that her thank-you gift was the last thing on Peter's mind and that it was probably ruined by the time Peter got home, thanks to the heavens opening as soon as they had parted company.

As they made their way along the queue, telling the dinner ladies what they wanted, the women looked at each other discreetly. They were no one's fools. They knew something was up. It was too much of a coincidence that Rosie had come into work looking like death warmed up the night after seeing the man they all knew she had more than a soft spot for.

When they had settled round the table, Martha looked at Rosie and then at her friends and asked matter-of-factly, 'The Admiral?'

Her question was followed by unanimous agreement.

Rosie was especially glad. She might as well enjoy her freedom while she still had it.

Chapter Fifty-Eight

On hearing the lunchtime klaxon sound out, Jack pulled open his desk drawer and took out his sandwiches that had been wrapped up in greaseproof paper and tied with string. Mrs Westley had told him they were a surprise when she had handed him them this morning after breakfast. She told him they had always been his favourites. He was curious to know what he used to like, and was just untying her neat bow when there was a tap on his office door, which he always kept open.

When he looked up he saw an old man standing in the doorway. He was tall – very tall, in fact – for a bloke of his age. And he still had a full head of silver hair. For a moment Jack stared at the old man's face. There was something familiar about him. Was this someone he had met recently? Or a face from his past?

'Hello, there.' Jack stood up, abandoning his sandwiches. 'Can I help you?' He moved round his desk and walked across to the man and stretched out his arm to shake hands. 'Or, what I should really say,' Jack smiled a little awkwardly, 'is do I actually know you? Because if I do I apologise in advance as the old memory's not working properly at the moment.' Jack had learnt that it was best to just come out with it up front. It saved a lot of misunderstanding and time.

'Aye, Jack,' Arthur shook the proffered hand energetically, 'you do know me. It's Arthur Watts. I used to work with you down the docks when I was under the employ of the Wear Commissioner,' Arthur let out a gruff laugh, 'many years ago now, mind you. But we always stayed in touch. My grandson Tommy was dock diver at Thompson's until recently.'

'Ah,' Jack said, 'now I do know of Tommy.' Jack saw Arthur's face light up. 'But I'm afraid that's not because I remember him as such, only that I was told he's engaged to one of the women welders. Polly, I believe her name is. Polly Elliot.'

Jack looked pleased with himself. 'See. Nothing wrong with my present-day memory. Just the blasted past I'm struggling with.'

Arthur looked at Jack. He seemed so vulnerable. Like a man floundering around in the dark, not able to find the light switch to see where he was going.

'Aye, well,' Arthur said, getting straight to the point, 'that's why I'm here. See if I can help. Do yer fancy a walk along the river?' He looked across at Jack's sandwiches partially unwrapped on his desk. 'Bring yer bait along and we'll eat it by the quayside.'

Jack looked at the man called Arthur. He wished he could remember him; he seemed like a man who knew what was what.

'Sounds good to me,' Jack said, turning and grabbing his lunch, and then his jacket from the back of the door.

Within five minutes they were walking along the edge of the Wear, heading towards the north dock that was just on the cusp of the mouth of the river.

'So,' Jack said, 'when did we first got to know each other?'

He looked at the old man and felt the same familiarity with him as he was beginning to feel about the place he had lived and worked in all of his life. As if there was a whole batch of memories just lying out of his reach, but if he could just drag them forward a little, they'd be within snatching distance.

Arthur suggested they sit by the quayside. 'One of my favourite views,' he said. 'Actually, this was where me and you used to come to eat our lunch when you were working as a plater.'

Arthur eased his old body down so that he was sitting on the side of the quayside, his long lanky legs dangling over the side. He laughed. 'Sitting down is easier than getting up, so you might have to give us a hand when it's time to go.'

Jack looked at Arthur and for a moment an image flashed across his mind of a middle-aged man with a thick mop of brown hair wearing a cumbersome, dark green canvas body suit, and huge lead boots.

'Aye,' Arthur said, looking out at the south pier and then up at the large grey barrage balloon that was looming above them like a heavy storm cloud. 'It feels like it's been a long life.'

Arthur looked at Jack, who was staring intently at him, much like he used to as a young lad, and he began to talk. He started by telling Jack how he had actually seen him on his first day at the yard, standing in front of the head foreman, asking to be taken on as an apprentice.

As Arthur spoke another image darted across Jack's consciousness. This time the middle-aged man was standing on the diver's pontoon being helped out of his huge 12-bolt copper helmet by two smaller men wearing dungarees, rolled-up cigarettes dangling from their mouths.

As Arthur chatted on, Jack listened, unaware of everything around him – the slight wind coming in from the North Sea, the bitter cold, the usual incessant squawks of the seagulls above.

'Aye, you were a determined little bugger,' Arthur smiled at the remembrance. 'I remember asking you if you had taken up residence at the yard, as yer were always there. Working every hour God sent.'

438

'What about my mam and dad?' Jack asked, captivated by Arthur's story. His story.

Arthur chose his words carefully, but reading in between the lines it would seem that Jack's parents had been glad to see the back of him; his da a big drinker who spent most of his time in the taverns lining the south dock; his mother trying her best to bring up her brood of children that was added to each year. Jack asked Arthur what had happened to his many brothers and sisters, but he didn't know.

'It was like the yard became yer home,' Arthur said, thoughtfully. 'Yer never liked to leave it.'

Arthur related how Jack used to come and watch the divers whenever he had a break and that was how they had become friendly. He described his wife Flo, and told him briefly how their daughter had killed herself after her husband had died in the First World War, and that Jack used to come round for his tea and kick an old leather football around with Tommy.

'Sounds like I spent a lot of time with you all?' Jack asked. He was curious as Miriam had not mentioned anything about Arthur or his closeness to him and his family.

Arthur nodded. 'Aye, yer did that.' Arthur chuckled. 'I used to joke that yer were like part of the furniture. Flo loved having yer there, though, loved having someone else to fuss over.'

Arthur was quiet for a moment as he held on to the image of Flo bustling about the kitchen, cooking and chatting, or singing along to some new tune she'd heard on the wireless.

'And Miriam?' Jack asked tentatively. 'Did you know Miriam?' It seemed strange to be asking about his wife, felt almost a little disloyal, but the question was out before he could stop it.

'Aye, Miriam,' Arthur said. He paused for a moment. Jack waited. 'Miriam,' Arthur repeated. 'Well, I'm sure you know this already, but yer met Miriam through Thompson's. She'd come with her da, ya know, old Mr Havelock.' There was another pause. 'Well,' Arthur continued, 'you and Miriam courted, and got married. Just like yer do at that age.'

Jack looked at Arthur and felt he was holding something back.

'I dinnit want ta overload yer with information,' Arthur said, a little uncomfortably.

Jack felt a stab of panic, as though the old man was thinking about giving him something precious but wasn't sure whether he should or not.

'I *want* to be overloaded,' Jack said. 'Go on.' It was more a plea than a request.

'Well,' Arthur said, starting to haul himself back up on to his feet. Jack jumped up and gave the old man a hand. 'There was someone else before Miriam came along,' Arthur puffed as he straightened his tall frame.

'Who?' Jack sensed his heart beating faster. The pair of them were now walking back to Crown's as it was only a few minutes before the end of the lunch break.

'A young woman called Gloria, although . . . of course . . . she's not so young now,' Arthur said. He looked at Jack, who had stopped in his tracks.

'Gloria?' Jack sounded shocked. 'One of the women working at Thompson's – one of the women welders?'

'Aye, that's the one,' Arthur said, trying to sound nonchalant. 'She's been working at Thompson's for well over a year now. Was one of the first women to be drafted into the yards.'

Just then the klaxon bellowed out. Jack panicked. They were out of time.

'Bloody hell,' Jack said, 'I can't believe how fast that hour's just gone.'

Arthur sensed Jack was troubled. That he wanted – needed – to hear more.

'I tell you what,' Arthur said. 'I know you'll probably be working tomorrow, but if you can get an hour off in the morning, we could have a cup of tea and some breakfast together.'

Jack couldn't agree fast enough. 'Definitely,' he said.

'Grand,' Arthur said, 'I know you won't remember, but me and you would often pop into a little café just up from the south dock on High Street East. It's called Vera's. It's a canny place – even if the old woman that owns it isn't exactly the most hospitable. See you there around nine?'

'See you then,' Jack said, feeling happy for the first time in a long while. 'But the bacon baps are on me!' he shouted as he hurried back to the yard.

Arthur felt a jolt. That was what they used to always get – bacon baps and two mugs of hot steaming tea.

He knew it!

Jack's memory was there. It just needed coaxing out.

Chapter Fifty-Nine

'I don't bloody believe it!' Vinnie announced as he took his key out of the front door and stepped over the threshold to the flat that was Sarah's, but which he now treated like his own.

'*I don't bloody believe it!*' Vinnie repeated, with more volume. Not that Sarah could have failed to hear his lament in the first place. The neighbours two doors down would have easily caught every word if they were in.

Sarah stood by the counter in her little kitchen, rustling up something to eat for their tea. She wasn't the best, or most enthusiastic cook in the world. Too much like hard work. Her attitude was: she did her day at the factory, why should she then have to slave away when she got home? Not that she would ever dare express her beliefs to Vinnie – or anyone else, for that matter. Women were meant to be superhuman these days – working like a man all day, and doing all the cooking, laundry and cleaning, as well as looking after any children they might have.

And talking about kids, she would bet her weekly wage that Vinnie's obviously foul mood had something to do with the baby or Gloria – or both.

She took a deep breath and left the refuge of her kitchen to face Vinnie.

'What's up, pet? Who's got yer goat?' she asked, with a concerned frown, as she went to give him a kiss.

Their lips had barely touched before Vinnie was off ranting again.

'That bloody cow has gone and organised my daughter's christening and hasn't had the decency to soddin' well tell me. How dare she! I mean, for God's sake, that's not right, is it? I'm the bloody father after all!' Vinnie spotted Sarah's cigarettes on the coffee table and snatched them up, pulling one out and jabbing it into his mouth.

'That is *not* the behaviour of a normal woman, is it? Makes me look a right moron! Like she's just stomping all over me, like I'm nothing. Nobody. Doing whatever the hell she wants! Like I have no control whatsoever of my wife and child! People'll be saying I'm a right wimp.'

Vinnie was winding himself up a treat and Sarah knew if she let him freewheel, he would be out of control in no time at all. God, it was at times like this she wondered if being with a fella was really worth it. Tonight all she wanted was to warm up the mince and onion pie she'd bought on the way home, eat it, and then get down the pub for a bit of a laugh and a few bevvies.

'Vinnie, calm down,' Sarah said, lighting his cigarette – at the same time taking the packet off him and shaking one out for herself.

'Tell me . . . how do you know about this christening? Who told you?' Sarah sneaked the much-needed cigarette into her mouth, lit it quickly, and blew out smoke.

'One of the women from work knows that nosey parker, what's-her-name . . . Muriel, I think she's called – she works in the canteen over at Thompson's. It's a right little gossip shop over there. They know the far end of a fart—'

'And *when* it is?' Sarah interrupted.

'Tomorrow! That's the point! Tomorrow!' Vinnie said, stomping into the kitchen and flinging open the cupboard doors hoping to find a bottle of beer.

'Bloody hell, Sarah, hasn't a bloke even got a beer to come home to after a hard day's graft?'

Sarah bit her lip, something she seemed to have to do a lot lately. She hated herself for thinking this way, but sometimes she believed she'd been happier when she had just been Vinnie's bit on the side. Taking another long drag on her cigarette she said calmly, 'Why don't we just go down the pub and have a chat about all this over a beer or two?'

Vinnie's ill temper dissipated a little.

'Sounds like a good plan. You got any dosh on you?' He patted down his jacket as if he expected to feel a wad of notes bulging through his inside pocket.

Sarah grabbed her handbag, along with her gas mask, and flicked her cigarette in the ashtray.

'Yeah, Vinnie, I've got enough for a couple,' she said, trying to keep the weariness out of her voice. *Another reason*, she thought, *why I'd be better off on my own – I'd have some more bleedin' money!*

As Sarah got her old winter coat that was hanging on a hook in the hallway, she saw the letter that had arrived for Vinnie in the post which she had put on the little shelf where she kept her keys. It looked official.

'This arrived for you today,' she said, picking up the white envelope and wafting it in front of Vinnie's face like a fan. He immediately snatched it off her and tore it open.

They stood in silence as Vinnie unfolded the thick paper on which the letter had been typed. Sarah feigned a lack of interest and stood smoking her cigarette down to the butt.

Vinnie looked up and she glanced away and started checking her nails, which were chipped and in a right state.

'You couldn't make it up!' He glared at Sarah, his anger now back in full swing.

'So now *I'm* being divorced? Bloody hell, I was the one who was supposed to be divorcing her! She was the one who bloody chucked me out!' Vinnie puffed out his chest.

'Divorce papers in the same week as my daughter gets christened! Well, how's that for bloody good timing, eh?'

Sarah noticed that his hands were trembling, and gingerly took the letter. Quickly she scanned the contents. Gloria was indeed starting divorce proceedings. From what she could see from this letter it was just a formality, saying that this was her intention and that Vinnie would be hearing from her lawyers soon – but it was the start.

Sarah thought she would have felt happy, or at least a little excited about the fact Vinnie would soon be a free man, and would therefore be able to make an honest woman out of her – but she didn't. All this baby talk had worn her out, and was ruining what she thought was a good relationship.

'Come on,' she cajoled, opening the front door and tossing her cigarette outside, 'let's get down to the pub and chat about it there.'

Vinnie huffed and when he followed her out she shut the door behind them. 'Makes you wonder where she's getting all this money from – to pay for all of these fancy lawyers and christenings?'

As they hurried down the road, Sarah wrapped her woollen coat tightly around herself as the wind whipped up.

Perhaps, she thought, *that's because she's keeping what she's earning for herself. And no one else is getting their greedy hands on it.*

When they reached the pub and Vinnie opened the door and she followed him in, she watched him strut to the bar and order their drinks. At the bar, Vinnie turned to her impatiently.

'Well, pay the nice young gentleman behind the bar, Sar. He's not got all day.'

Sarah had to force a smile on her face as she delved into her bag to get her purse.

Chapter Sixty

When Polly got back home after the girls' get-together at the Admiral she was surprised to find Arthur up and sitting at the table chatting to Agnes.

'You two look very conspiratorial?' Polly said, dumping her gas mask and bag down on the floor, then going into the scullery to find her mum had made her a sandwich.

'Ah, thanks, Ma. I'm starving.' Polly grabbed the plate, came back into the kitchen, and plonked herself down at the table.

'Nothing new there, then?' Agnes smiled as she watched her daughter hungrily tuck into the sausage and tomato sandwich she had made with the leftover bangers and mash from tea.

'Are you sure you're all right with having everyone back here tomorrow?' Polly asked, wiping her mouth and pulling over the teapot so she could pour herself a cup.

'Of course I am,' Agnes said, 'I don't have to do anything. I don't even have to bake – thanks to Dorothy and Angie.'

'I'm guessing they're bringing the cake over first thing?' Polly asked as she took a big slurp of tepid tea.

Agnes nodded. 'It'll be nice to just enjoy the ceremony, and then for everyone to come back here. All very civilised.'

'Let's hope so. As long as Vinnie doesn't show his ugly mug, everything'll be fine,' Polly said, thinking about the women's chat in the Admiral and how the conversation had turned to Vinnie. Gloria was doing a convincing job of being a strong, self-sufficient woman – as well as hiding the heartache she must be feeling about Jack – but she had admitted that she was worried Vinnie would get wind of the christening. It was why she had organised it at such short notice.

'Come to think of it, Hope getting baptised at St Ignatius will actually be like a rerun of the day of her birth – with her first stop being the church, and her second here.' Polly took another bite of her sandwich.

'God willing, this time without the added trauma of an air raid,' Agnes added, thinking of how fraught she had felt that day in August while they had waited for the air raid to be over, knowing that the Luftwaffe had bombed the north side of the river where Polly was working.

Her thoughts were broken by Arthur's croaky voice asking, 'Do you think Gloria would mind if I brought a friend along to the christening? I don't know if yer have to have formal invites to these occasions?'

Agnes was just about to ask Arthur who it was that he was going to bring to the church, when Polly piped up, 'Of course she wouldn't mind,' then suddenly jumped up.

'Oh goodness, how could I forget? I got a letter from Tommy today. He's started to send them to the yard to see if they get here any quicker.' Polly leant down to get her haversack and scrabbled around, before pulling out the letter. She pushed her plate of sandwiches away – all her thoughts and attention now on the words of her betrothed.

Arthur looked at his grandson's fiancée and felt happy. When he had left Jack today he'd felt a great sense of relief. He had completed a task that he had been quite anxious about doing, but having done it, felt it had given him a lift. And even more so, as it had gone so well. Better than he'd expected.

What better way to end the day than by hearing about his beloved grandson.

On the other side of town the bell for last orders had just gone and Vinnie was at the bar with Sarah, trying to catch the attention of the barmaid.

Sarah had enjoyed the evening chatting away to their friends, but now she and Vinnie were on their own again and the conversation had steered back to the same old, same old: Gloria. Baby Hope. The christening. And now the divorce.

Vinnie had started to go on and on about how *he* should be the one divorcing her . . . how *he* didn't even get a say about the bab's name . . . how *he* hadn't even been told about the soddin' christening . . .

'Bloody hell, she's my flesh and blood!' Vinnie was working himself up into another rant.

'Flesh and blood!' Change the sodding record! Sarah wanted to scream her thoughts but knew better. For God's sake, this baby was doing her nut in. Why couldn't Vinnie just let Gloria get on with it? Sarah knew what she would do if she was Vinnie – and that would be to keep her trap shut.

Was Vinnie thick, or what? Gloria would be round soon enough when she needed some dosh for the baby, or wanted shot of it for a few hours.

But Vinnie just didn't seem to be letting this go. The baby was now – what? Four or five months old and he was still harping on about not seeing it.

All evening Sarah kept thinking about how she and Vinnie had been rubbing along just nicely since they had started living together – that was until this damned baby had come along. Now, Vinnie seemed to be drinking more, which in turn meant he never had any of his own money and, worse still, he was on an increasingly short fuse most of the time.

The more she thought about it, the more she believed that if she could just somehow get shot of the baby, they could get back to normal. They might even finally get married if this divorce went through.

But, if the baby kept getting in the way, and spoiling their lives, her whole house of cards would come tumbling down and she could well be left with nothing and no one. This baby could well be the ruination of her hopes for her future.

Her thoughts were broken by Vinnie's loud exclamation.

'I should just snatch her!' he declared.

'Who – Gloria?' For a moment Sarah was confused.

'No, yer stupid mare, the baby,' Vinnie laughed nastily. 'No one can stop me – *the bairn's mine after all.*'

It was at that moment she was struck by an idea.

An idea that might well stop Vinnie going on and on about this damned child.

'I know you might not want to hear this, Vinnie?' Sarah was treading on very thin ice and knew it.

Vinnie looked at her. He was in a better mood but still had that dark, angry look about him.

'But have you ever considered . . . ' Sarah paused while Vinnie ordered their drinks and asked for them to be put on his tab.

'Yeah, considered what?' Vinnie asked, a little impatiently.

'Well, I was just thinking—' The conversation was interrupted by the arrival of their drinks.

Vinnie took a big glug of his pint of Vaux.

'I was wondering if . . . perhaps . . . Gloria's baby might *not* be yours.'

There. She had said it.

449

Sarah took a drink of her port and lemon and mentally crossed her fingers that Vinnie didn't flare up.

Vinnie looked at Sarah as if it was taking him a while to understand the meaning of her words.

Sarah looked at her lover and wondered if she had just made a catastrophic mistake.

She didn't really think that Gloria would have really taken a lover while Vinnie was still at home. She just wasn't the sort. She'd seen her a few times in town and on the buses, and she looked a bit of a frump. Very ordinary looking, boring brown hair, and having a baby later on in life had certainly done a job on her figure.

'What you saying?' Vinnie asked, looking a little confused. 'That Gloria's had someone else?'

Sarah looked at Vinnie and took another sip of her drink. She would have to play this one very carefully and very cleverly if it was to have the desired effect.

'All I'm thinking . . . is that I *know* you, Vinnie,' Sarah lowered her voice. 'You're always very *careful*.' She stressed the word 'careful'.

Vinnie nodded his head slowly.

'Aye,' he said. His hand was around his pint glass but he didn't make any effort to take a drink.

'Aye, you're right, I am. Always get off at Gateshead.'

Sarah didn't say anything, knowing when to keep quiet.

Sitting quietly, surrounded by the growing chatter and clashing of pint glasses as the pub landlord tried to get people to sup up and leave, Sarah felt a wave of anger rise up in her that she fought to suppress. If Vinnie had done what he had said he had done (or rather *not* done) and hadn't had anything to do with his wife in the bedroom department, then they wouldn't be in the situation they were now in.

When Sarah had got to hear that Gloria was pregnant,

and the paternity of the child was not in question, she had been hurt that Vinnie had clearly still been sleeping with his wife – something he had denied throughout the whole of their affair. Sarah had foolishly believed him. When he had told her, a little shamefaced, that Gloria had a bun in the oven, his excuse was that it must have been a one-off, after he'd had one too many. And who was Sarah to argue?

'You know what, Sar,' Vinnie said, pausing to neck his pint. 'I had actually wondered that myself . . . a while back . . . ' He took another glug of beer and put his empty pint glass down.

It had gone through his mind that the bab might not be his not long after he had found out Gloria was in the family way. But he had dismissed the possibility almost at once. There was just no way in a million years that Gloria, out of anyone, would have had a bit on the side . . . But now that Sarah had pushed the idea back into his head, it had made him think again. And this time he wasn't so quick to dismiss it. It would certainly explain a few things – the way she had been with him this past year, the fact she wouldn't let him see the bairn, and now she seemed in a hurry to get a divorce . . .

Sarah finished her drink quickly and they both climbed off their bar stools and threaded their way through the smoky lounge and out of the pub.

Outside, the wind had really got up; rubbish that had escaped from some of the bins was swirling around in the growing tempest.

Sarah staggered a little to the side of the road, but stopped herself from stumbling into the gutter. 'Bloody blackouts!' she mumbled, trying to blame her near fall on the lack of light as opposed to several bottles of beer followed by a chaser.

As they battled their way down the street, both of then

451

holding on to the fronts of their coats lest the wind try and tear them off their backs, Sarah stole a glance at Vinnie. He looked deep in thought, which was unlike Vinnie. She wasn't sure whether that was to do with the drink, or the doubt she had placed in his head.

If he had any sense at all about him he would be jumping at the idea that he could be freed from the responsibility of this new baby – from having to be a dad. Again. Twenty years on from being a father to his two boys. To be footloose and fancy-free. Not shackled to something that only screams its head off, sicks up and sleeps.

When they reached the flat and Sarah started fumbling around for her front door key, her thoughts swung to Gloria. She knew she wouldn't be bothered if she or her baby never saw hair nor hide of Vinnie again. The divorce papers had proved that.

Finally Sarah found her front door key and pushed it into the lock.

Gloria quite obviously wanted to wipe her hands clean of her ex, which would leave the way clear for her and Vinnie to start their life – hopefully *married life* – afresh: no mitherings from his ex and, most of all, no screaming baby in the background.

Chapter Sixty-One

As the rain started to lash down on the windows and the winds howled outside, Jack looked across at his wife as she lay in bed. She was out for the count. He could smell the gin on her now and knew she kept some tablets in her bedroom drawer to help her sleep. He also knew he could get up out of bed without any questions or cajoling to come back and join her.

Still, just to be on the safe side, he manoeuvred himself gently and quietly out of bed, making sure he put the bed-clothes back around Miriam so that she would not feel the cold and wake.

Grabbing his thick night robe Jack pulled it on, then slipped out of the room. Quiet as a mouse, he padded down the carpeted stairs and into the main living room where the drinks cabinet could be found.

Jack put one of the side lights on – just enough to see what he was doing. Then he went over to the walnut cabinet, fully stocked with just about every kind of alcoholic beverage, more than they should have had, considering wartime shortages.

He took the bottle of Glenfiddich and poured himself a good measure, immediately taking a mouthful and swallowing hard. He needed this. As the burn travelled from his mouth, then throat and down into his stomach, he started to feel a little calmer.

Now that he was on his own, in the semi-darkness, with no one distracting him, asking him questions, or telling him things, he could try and think clearly. Go over what he had learnt today.

He'd had to sit through another mind-numbingly boring dinner party at some high society house a few streets down, and all he wanted to do was simply be on his own, with his own thoughts, mulling over what Arthur had told him today.

Jack sat on the leather chesterfield and said a silent prayer of thanks that his daughter had gone up to Scotland for a few weeks to see relatives and to have a break. The poor girl had been working her socks off at the yard while he had been away in America, by all accounts, and when he'd been in hospital she had barely left his side. He loved his daughter dearly, but he was glad that this evening he knew he would be undisturbed.

'Arthur.' Jack said the name quietly to himself, as if saying it would bring back the memory of this old man he had apparently known so well for most of his life.

Chatting to him today he had felt a few green sprouts start to peek their way through the barren wasteland of his memory. For the first time since he had come out of his coma he had a sense of his past. It was still pretty murky, but he had felt that there might be the slightest possibility that his memory, or at least a part of it, could come back. For once he had felt some kind of connection with the past.

When Miriam chatted to him, it was like listening to the story of another person's life, but with Arthur he had a feeling of reality.

But what had really made him think – and was the reason he was now sitting here, late at night, on his own, in the semi-darkness, unable to sleep and in need of a large whisky – was Arthur's mention of Gloria.

He understood now why she had visited him in the hospital, but what he didn't know was why she hadn't said as

454

much when he had seen her in the yard that day. Wouldn't it have been normal to mention it? Or did she not say anything because of Miriam? And, come to think of it, Miriam had acted like she didn't even know Gloria.

Nothing made sense.

Jack finished off his whisky and as he made his way back up to bed, he hoped he'd be able to get some sleep. He needed to get into work early tomorrow to arrange cover while he went to meet Arthur. He didn't want their meeting to be rushed.

He wanted – no, *needed* – time to hear more about this woman called Gloria. He had a lot of questions he wanted to ask his old friend, Arthur.

Chapter Sixty-Two

Brookside Gardens, Sunderland

In the early hours of the morning, DS Miller got up and used his work boots as a doorstop to prevent his bedroom door from opening and shutting. The wind was so bad it was penetrating the house. He'd even had to peg his black-out curtains together as they kept flapping open with the wind forcing itself through any available nook or cranny.

As he climbed back into the bed he had once shared with his wife, he thought back to the day she had died and the following weeks and months when he had tried to deal with the heartbreaking grief that had overtaken every part of his being. He had felt desolate and so angry at the injustice of it all – his beautiful, kind wife had been taken from him when she was still so young and they had so much of their lives ahead of them.

As he lay with his eyes open, having given up on sleep, DS Miller looked at the ceiling and the wall with the rose-patterned wallpaper. He had not felt this bereft since Sal had died. He knew, of course, that the feelings of melancholy that now afflicted him could not be compared to those he felt over the death of his wife, but still it was as if, in a way, he was mourning a loss – the loss of a person he thought he knew. A person he had loved.

As if it was not enough that the world around him was at war, his mind too was in constant conflict. For the past week or so since he had discovered the truth about the house in West Lawn, and about Rosie's part in the goings-on there, there had been a civil war going on in his head as to what to do.

One army of thoughts argued that he should do what he had sworn an oath to do at the beginning of his career with the police force: that he should do things by the book and arrest and charge Rosie – and Lily – with running a brothel.

He had been more than aware of how ironic it was that he'd felt relieved when he had found out that Rosie was managing the place rather than being a working girl – even though it would probably be better for her if she was simply providing services to those who visited, as the sentence she would receive would be far less.

Then there was a second army of thought that fought valiantly against the first, which proposed that he turn a blind eye to what went on at Lily's; after all, what harm were they really doing?

The part of him that still loved Rosie said that he should simply walk away and erase from his mind what he had found out. That was the preferable option.

But – and it was a big 'but' – he had devoted his whole life to the pursuit of justice and the enforcement of law and order.

And there was no getting away from the basic fact that both Rosie and Lily had broken the law of the land – and, as such, justice needed to be served.

DS Miller forced himself to close his eyes in an attempt to get some sleep. He had a busy day tomorrow.

He had a christening to attend.

Chapter Sixty-Three

Saturday 22 November 1941

When Vinnie woke he looked at the bedside clock. It was half past eight. Normally on a Saturday if he wasn't working overtime he would have a long lie-in with Sarah, then have a fry-up if there was any bacon or black pudding on the go and then he'd head off to the pub with his week's wages.

Today was going to be different. He'd thought about it on the walk home last night and the same thoughts had stayed in his head until he had fallen asleep. Now, he was awake and he was still adamant. It was time for him to take control. He was going to see the bab if it was the last thing he did on this earth. No one was going to stop him. He was sick to death of Gloria calling all the shots and telling him what he could and couldn't do. He'd had enough.

Vinnie subconsciously clenched his fists as he lay in bed, his mind going over all the scenarios. He would know if the child was his by looking at her. Of this he was sure. His two sons had looked the spit of him when they were babies. Same deep brown eyes. Both chunky. Like little barrels, they were.

Feeling energised by his anger, Vinnie flung the bed-clothes off him, causing Sarah to grumble about the cold.

After picking up his clothes from the floor and quickly pulling them on, he leant over the bed and kissed Sarah on the side of her head.

'I'm just nipping out, pet,' he said, 'you stay here. I'll see yer later on.'

There was no way he wanted her to know what he was up to. She'd get to know soon enough.

As he let himself out of the flat, he grabbed the solicitor's letter, screwed it up into a ball and shoved it in his coat pocket.

'So, Detective Sergeant Miller, how many men do you need?'

DS Miller thought Detective Inspector Young looked dead on his feet. They were stretched thin these days with so many of the police officers volunteering to go to war.

'Just the one, sir . . . Just need to make an arrest. Shouldn't take long.'

'Take special constables Hargreaves and Jenkins. They're both free this morning, and they've got a bit of muscle on them – should you need it.'

DS Miller shook his head. 'I'm sure I won't, but thank you, sir. We'll be back by midday at the latest. Is the custody suite free?'

Detective Inspector Young nodded. 'We've got vacancies – there's one of our regulars in there at the moment, stinking the place out to high Jesus, but he should be gone soon enough – just waiting for him to sober up before we send him on his way.'

Ten minutes later DS Miller, and the two special constables were heading down the Hendon Road at a brisk pace. It had just gone nine thirty. The weather had not eased off at all: it had actually got worse. Although it was almost mid-morning, the high winds were pushing dark clouds across the sky making it feel like they were heading towards early evening.

'Sarge,' Special Constable Jenkins had to shout to be

heard through gusts of winds. DS Miller looked a million miles away.

'Sarge,' Jenkins repeated, tapping his superior on the shoulder to get his attention.

DS Miller turned sharply.

'Where exactly are we going?'

'St Ignatius Church on the corner of Bramwell Road.'

Jenkins and Hargreaves looked at each other, both their faces showing surprise.

'Come on, Lily,' Rosie chided, 'otherwise we'll be late. The vicar's only just managed to squeeze Hope's baptism in between a couple of others.'

Rosie had come over to the house early to get herself ready for the christening. Over the past few days since Peter's revelation to her that 'he knew', she had been spending a lot of time at the bordello. She had felt the need to be there, should there be a raid on the property. This was, after all, her doing, although no one had so far had a go at her for bringing it upon them all. The only comment Lily had made was one of surprise that it had been *Rosie's* love life that had brought such trouble to their doorstep – and not Vivian's or one of the other girls'.

'I'm coming!' Lily's voice sounded croaky as she came down the stairs slowly, taking care with each step because the shoes she was wearing had a higher than normal heel. She was also a little unsteady on her pins, as she'd had a big swig or two of brandy. She was feeling particularly reckless due to the prospect that she might soon be residing in a six by eight cell with no chance of access to any kind of liquor, never mind the best French brandy that money could buy. Her philosophy was: if she was going to go down, then she was going to go down tanked up.

'Come on,' Rosie said. Taking Lily's arm as she reached

the bottom step, Rosie was immediately overcome by a mixture of Coco Chanel perfume and Rémy Martin. 'George has got the engine running. He'll be using up his meagre petrol ration.'

Lily barked a laugh. 'He'll have the engine running to keep himself warm. It's bleedin' freezing out there. And if that wind gets up any more, George's beloved motor car won't need any petrol because it'll be *flying* us to the church.'

At the front door, both Rosie and Lily looked behind them as if it was the last time they would see the place. As if to mark the occasion, Lily stopped and rummaged around in her handbag.

'I'll just have a quick puff before we go,' she said.

Rosie noticed Lily's hands were shaking as she lit her Gauloise.

'Kate meeting us there?' she asked, while Lily stood and smoked, and looked around the grand hallway with its twelve-branch chandelier and polished parquet flooring.

Lily nodded as she exhaled smoke. 'Yes, she went to the Maison Nouvelle early doors, then she's walking down to the church from there.'

She took another deep drag. 'Vivian's gone shopping in town – not that I think she really wanted to – not in this bloody awful weather anyway. She won't admit it, but I know she doesn't want to be here on her own in case the Old Bill come knocking.'

'And Maisie?' Rosie asked. 'Has she gone?'

Lily took another drag.

'Yes, she left just before you arrived ... ' Lily looked unusually thoughtful. 'You know what? I think this is probably the first time ever that the house has been left empty.'

Lily was now sounding maudlin.

'For heaven's sake, Lily,' Rosie chastised her, 'cheer up, we're going to a christening – not a funeral, you know. Now finish that cigarette and let's go.'

But as they shut the door, Rosie couldn't stop herself having one last look. It surprised her just how much she had grown to love this house, and her life here, and – more so – the people in it.

Making his way into town and towards the east end, Vinnie could feel his anger building up inside of him. He knew it had to come out and, by God, it would – either way. Whether the baby was his or not. There was no two ways about it, Gloria was going to get it big time. She'd had no right at all to keep his baby from him. If indeed it was his baby. She'd been bang out of order. He should have simply knocked down the front door from the off and seen the baby for himself, regardless of any repeat visits from the man in the balaclava who'd given him a right hiding. Nothing nor no one was going to stop him. If anyone tried to get in his way, they would rue the day.

It was about time everyone knew who was in control. And it was *him*. Not Gloria.

Vinnie looked at his watch. It was just after nine thirty. He should easily make it in time. In the next half an hour he was not only going *to see* this bloody baby – but he was also going to find out if it really was *his*.

And if it wasn't – *then there would be murders*.

'Bloody bitch!' Vinnie clenched his fists at the thought that his wife – his wife of twenty years – might have slept with another man. How dare she? He would skin her alive. Give her the biggest thrashing she had ever had in her entire life. And she would deserve every single blow.

His anger was now bubbling, ready to explode.

Gloria having it off with another man ... Having another man's baby ... All while still married to him!

Making a mockery of him!

As he stomped down the road he deliberately knocked into a couple walking in the opposite direction.

'Hey, mate, watch where you're going!' the man shouted out.

But when Vinnie turned on the couple and snarled, 'What yer ganna dee about it then, mate?' the man immediately backed off, grabbed his girlfriend's hand and hurried off.

Chapter Sixty-Four

Vera's Café, High Street East, Sunderland

'Good morning, Vera. How yer doing?' Arthur smiled at the old woman, who responded with her usual scowl.

'Two bacon baps and a cup of tea?' she barked the question.

Arthur let out a hoot of laughter. 'Aye, Vera, yer still sharp as a button.'

Vera managed to maintain her scowl while pointing her bony finger over to a table by the window.

'As is the tongue, *Arthur Watts,*' she batted back quick as a flash. 'Now you and Jack go and sit down over there, and keep out my way.'

Arthur and Jack did as they were told.

'How did she know we wanted bacon baps?' Jack asked.

Arthur chuckled. 'It was what we always ordered. Without fail. Every time we came in, Vera wouldn't even ask what we wanted. She'd just take our money and then point over to where she wanted us to sit.'

Jack felt frustrated that he couldn't remember any of this, but it was a frustration he was getting used to.

'Can you tell me more about Gloria?' Jack decided the best way forward was just to come out and say it.

Arthur clasped his hands together as if in prayer and put them on the table. Just then Vera arrived with two small round plates, each one containing a big white buttered bun with two large rashers of bacon stuffed in the middle. She returned seconds later with two big mugs of steaming tea.

Both men said their thanks and Arthur took a big bite of his bap, followed by a slurp of tea. Jack hadn't had any breakfast but just didn't have an appetite. His mind was on other things.

'Gloria,' Arthur mumbled through a mouth full of bread and bacon. 'Well –' He swallowed hard, then went on. 'My Flo always said you two made a good couple. We always thought the two of you would get married.'

Jack was staring at Arthur, shocked. So, they really had been a couple. A serious couple.

'Really? What went wrong?' Jack asked, desperate to know more.

'Actually,' Arthur said, 'we thought you were going to get engaged, but then you had some kind of a fall-out – "lovers' tiff" is what Flo called it – and ...' Arthur paused. 'That's when yer started to step out with Miriam. If my memory serves me right, I do remember Flo saying that ya had got back with Gloria, but then all of a sudden yer were with Miriam again. And then,' Arthur continued, his mind now back at that time, remembering how puzzled Flo had been about the turn of events. 'Before you knew it, you and Miriam were married.'

Jack took a swig of his tea. His mouth felt dry. This was nothing like the story Miriam had told him.

'Sounds to me that Miriam and I got married quickly. *Had* to get married?' Jack asked.

Arthur nodded. 'Aye, yer right in what yer thinking. There was talk ... Yer know, that yer had to do the right thing and all of that.'

'My daughter, Helen?' Jack asked, but as soon as he said the words he knew that couldn't have been the case as

Helen hadn't come along until they had been married a couple of years.

'I dinnit know about that,' Arthur said, 'you'd have to ask Miriam.'

Jack knew Arthur was not letting on as much as he knew.

Arthur took another big bite out of his sandwich as if to fortify himself for what he had to say next. What he had really come here to tell Jack. He just hoped he was doing the right thing. It felt wrong to meddle. But this didn't really feel like meddling. Jack had been like family to him and Flo. He had a right to know the truth. The truth about his present life, rather than his distant past.

Jack looked at Arthur and noticed the old man's face had clouded over.

'There's something I have to tell you,' Arthur said gravely, 'something that I think you have to know.'

Jack was sitting, barely moving, his eyes clapped on Arthur. He nearly jumped out of his skin when Vera suddenly appeared at the table. 'Either of you two in need of a top-up?'

'No thanks, we're just fine, Vera,' Arthur smiled up at the café proprietor who was staring down at Jack's untouched bacon butty. Jack saw the look and took a bite out of his bun, which seemed to do the trick as Vera waddled back off to the counter where she now had a line of customers.

'What?' Jack swallowed hard and put the bap back down on the plate. 'What do I have to know?'

Arthur looked around him to make sure there were no nebby noses earwigging in on their conversation. He dropped his voice and began.

'Before you went off to America,' he said in a near whisper, 'you and Gloria started to meet up again.'

There was a pause.

'Meet up?' Jack asked.

'Aye,' Arthur said. He was totally out of his depth, but he knew he just had to keep wading on. 'By the time yer left the country, Gloria had become very important in yer life once again.'

Jack sat back.

Arthur didn't need to say any more.

There was a pause as Arthur's words hung in the air. Then all of a sudden he looked around him. 'What time is it?'

Jack glanced at the clock on the wall just above the big shiny copper urn on the counter. 'Ten to ten,' he told him.

As soon as the words were out of his mouth, Arthur stood up.

'There's a christening I've got to go to at St Ignatius's.'

'What? The parish church in Hendon?' Jack asked.

'Aye, that's the one,' Arthur said, taking another quick glug of his tea.

'Come with me,' Arthur said, turning to wave his goodbyes to Vera. They were out the café door before Arthur added, 'Gloria's going to be there. She can tell you everything. Much more than I can.'

'Come on then,' Jack said. There was no hesitation. He needed to see Gloria. Talk to her. Find out more. 'We've not got much time.' As a huge gust of wind almost knocked Arthur off his feet, Jack grabbed him. 'And in this weather, it'll take us even longer.'

Both men buttoned their coats up and started walking as fast as they could against the strength of the brewing storm.

Nothing, though, was going to stop Jack from getting to the church.

Not even a force ten gale.

Chapter Sixty-Five

St Ignatius Church, Bramwell Road, Sunderland

'Oh, isn't she gorgeous?' Angie leant into the pram and cooed at Hope as she wiggled about, her little thumb stuck in her tiny mouth.

'I don't think she likes her christening gown, she keeps shuffling around and won't settle,' Gloria said, concerned that Hope might get grouchy and end up screaming the church down.

'Well, she'll have to stay in it until after she's been baptised. My goddaughter is going to have to learn that sometimes looking good does not go hand in hand with feeling comfortable,' Dorothy said in all seriousness, as she gently brushed Hope's dark brown hair to one side.

Angie chuckled and Gloria rolled her eyes. They were already at the church. Due to the windstorm outside and the beginnings of a downpour, they had come to the church early and were waiting inside. They kept their voices low as there was another christening taking place, not that they really needed to keep quiet as the building itself was huge and the baby presently having holy water sprinkled on to its head was demonstrating just how good the acoustics were.

'So, I'm guessing you got the cake sorted, then?' Gloria asked with a mischievous smile. She didn't dare tell Dorothy that her sugar cravings were finally abating and that all she seemed to want to eat now was meat and veg.

'Oh, yes, Ange and I took it round to Agnes's just before

we came here. I think you're going to love it,' Dorothy said, clearly proud as punch at keeping her side of the bargain.

'Yeah, and it's massive!' Angie added, excitedly.

'Where did you end up getting it from?' Gloria asked, genuinely curious.

Dorothy put her finger to her nose and tapped it, wanting to keep the unveiling of their prize cake as much a mystery as possible until after the christening when she could present the cake to Gloria personally. Only then would she tell her that she and Angie had gone together to see the sour-faced woman who ran the bakery on Dundas Street – the one Angie got her penny bag of broken-up pastries and bread from every Sunday. They had actually seen the semblance of a smile appear on the woman's face when they said how much they could afford to pay her if she could bake them a super-large cake. The woman had stood for a few moments with both her hands on the counter, her shoulders hunched up, deep in thought. Then she had suddenly clapped her hands together and said, 'I have an idea!'

And what a great idea it was. She was to make three cakes in the largest cake tin she possessed, then put them on top of each other so that the cake would be almost as thick as it was wide.

This morning, the woman's husband had even been persuaded to transport the freshly baked triple-layered cake to Tatham Street. When Agnes had answered her front door, she'd let out a loud whoop, which had pleased Dorothy and Angie no end. They had achieved their aim and procured probably the biggest Victoria sponge the town had known since the outbreak of war.

'All will be revealed after the christening,' Dorothy said to Gloria, with an air of mystery.

'What is to be "revealed"?' It was Hannah, who had arrived along with Martha and Olly.

'Blimey, Hannah, you gave me a shock,' Dorothy looked up at Martha and then down at Olly. 'All right, you two?' They both nodded.

Angie did a double take. Martha was wearing a thick tweed skirt and polo neck jumper. 'Sorry, Martha,' she said, realising she had been staring, 'I don't think I'll ever get used to seeing you in anything but an overall.'

Martha chortled. 'Me neither.'

Just then the heavy oak door opened and let in a swirl of cold air and a few leaves. It was Agnes and Polly.

'Where's Bel and Joe and little Lucille?' Gloria asked. Bel had played such a big part in her daughter's life, Gloria would be gutted if for some reason she was not able to make the ceremony.

'Don't worry. They'll be here before ten. They've gone to see Pearl and Maisie off at the station.'

Everyone turned to look at Polly for an explanation.

'They're going to London for a week or so . . . a sort of mother–daughter bonding trip, I think.'

Gloria looked at Agnes. 'Bet you'll be pleased to have a little peace and quiet?'

Agnes sighed. 'Well, there has been rather a lot going on lately, that's for sure.' She looked towards the front of the church and at the tall grey-haired vicar who was now making the sign of the cross over the baby that had expended all its vocal energy and now looked half asleep in its mother's arms.

'Oh!' Agnes suddenly remembered. 'Arthur's on his way. With this friend of his. Someone from his past, I think. I hope you're all right about him bringing a guest? He asked Polly to check you didn't mind . . . '

Gloria waved her hand. 'Of course not, the more the merrier. Besides, by the sounds of this cake, there's going to be more than enough to go around.'

Chapter Sixty-Six

The Railway Station, Athenaeum Street, Sunderland

'Have a good time!' Bel shouted out to Pearl and Maisie as the train let out a huge puff of steam and the piercing sound of the conductor's whistle screeched through the smoggy air.

'And if you can't be good – be careful!' Joe added, letting out a loud laugh.

Lucille was balanced on his shoulders, loving the view from such giddy heights, giggling along, happily waving both her little hands at her nana and aunty Maisie, who were squashed together, leaning out of their carriage window.

'The same goes to you too!' Maisie hollered back, adding cheekily, '*Enjoy the Grand!*'

Bel looked at Joe and blushed a little.

'We will,' she shouted back. ' . . . And thank you!'

Everyone, Bel thought, looked like they had been dragged through a hedge backwards due to the stormy weather that had hit the north-east coast overnight. Still, it certainly hadn't bothered any of them, and especially not Maisie, who had seemed particularly happy, and also more than a little relieved as she'd boarded the London-bound train to King's Cross.

As Bel waved back at Pearl and Maisie, she thought how happy her ma looked. The pair of them looked so at ease with each other – as if they had known each other all of their lives, and it was she, Bel, who was the newcomer – the one who had just popped up out of nowhere.

Looking at Maisie now, with her mass of chestnut brown curls and her coffee-coloured skin, Bel knew that they were poles apart, like night and day, not only in looks – but in personality as well. They'd probably never become bosom buddies – but, all the same, they were now a part of each other's lives whether they liked it or not.

'Bye, Isabelle!' Bel was jolted out of her thoughts by her ma's loud, gravelly voice.

'Bye, Ma!' she shouted back.

'Bye bye, LuLu . . . ' Pearl waved her skinny arm up at her excited granddaughter.

' . . . And Joe,' she said shifting her gaze down, 'make sure you look after that little granddaughter of mine . . . '

Pearl's final words were lost as the train started to chuff slowly out of the station.

As Bel stood waving and watching the train pull away, she wondered what the future would hold for them all – for her ma, her sister, and her little girl. Three generations of women, all bound by blood, yet all so very, very different.

As Pearl and Maisie settled down in the carriage that they had to themselves until at least the next stop, they sighed in unison.

'Back to the Big Smoke then, eh?' Pearl said. There was a slight hint of nervous excitement in her voice. The last time she had made this trip, from this very station, in a carriage not unlike the one they were in now, her daughter was in her belly. Now, twenty-eight years later, her daughter was, unbelievably, here with her, sitting opposite her, making that exact same journey with her.

'Aye,' Maisie said, cheekily mimicking the north-east

accent. 'To the city where the streets are paved in gold,' she added, tongue-in-cheek.

Pearl felt herself freeze. They were the same words her brother had used when she had told her family that she was travelling down to London for a temporary job in a posh hotel. For the briefest of moments Pearl was transported back to her fourteen-year-old self on her way to a place called Ivy House.

As if reading her thoughts, Maisie mused, 'So, do you think this Evelina woman's still alive?'

As the train gained speed, Pearl thought for a moment.

'God knows,' she said, her mind still loitering in her distant past. 'She must have only been about your age when I knew her, although she seemed older to me then.'

'Let's see,' Maisie said, doing the maths in her head, 'that would make her now in her mid-fifties, so there's a good chance she's still about.'

Pearl stared out the window that was being lashed with wind and rain as they left behind the town's red-brick houses and smoking chimneys. She would never have thought in a million years that she would do this trip with the daughter she had given up. Her Maisie. The child she had never expected to see again in her life. The baby girl she had never stopped loving. The daughter who had broken her heart as a baby and then again as an adult, but had ended up bringing her a joy she had not known existed.

'Well, if this Evelina's popped her clogs, it'll still be good to have a look at where I was born,' Maisie said.

Maisie had listened to her ma as she had told her a little about Ivy House, and the women there who had been so kind and caring towards her. She had come to realise that her mother had done the best she could for her, given the dire circumstances she was in. And that those running the unmarried mothers' refuge had believed they were doing the right thing in having her adopted out. They weren't to know what would happen in the future. No one could have.

As she had grown up, Maisie had so wanted someone to blame for the life she'd had foisted upon her, but now she knew that sometimes there was no one to blame. Sometimes it was just bloody bad luck. That was just life. Her life. And she was going to continue to do what she had always done – as she had done all of her twenty-eight years – she was going to turn her luck around. Make what was bad into something good. And if she couldn't make it good, then at least something that would work in her favour.

'Aye, it will,' Pearl agreed, looking out the window. The thought of going back to London and to Ivy House, and perhaps even seeing Evelina again, was more than a little unnerving, but she would deal with that when she was there.

Pearl had to laugh at the irony that she had spent the whole of her life running away from her past but now here she was actually running – or rather travelling – full pelt back to it. Still, she would rather be here now, facing up to it, than lying in some morgue, or worse still, on the bottom of the North Sea. She couldn't believe she had been so stupid as to go off on a bender. She could barely remember a thing after she had left the Tatham that night, and she had no idea what had possessed her to go for a midnight stroll down Hendon beach. Well, that was the booze for you. Beer in, wits out.

As Pearl looked at Maisie staring out of the window as the train steamed through the lush, green landscape towards Durham, she knew that there was more to this trip than met the eye. Maisie might have been able to fool everyone else with her sweetness and light declarations that she wanted to spend time with her old ma so that they could really get to know each other, but not Pearl.

No, this trip down to the Big Smoke for Maisie was not just about revisiting the place of her birth, and spending time with her long-lost ma – there was something else going on. Pearl was no one's fool. She had sensed her daughter's anxiety when she had come round the house the very morning after they'd been to the Grand to have a drink and sort out Bel and Joe's honeymoon suite. Maisie had tried to paste over her nervousness, but Pearl had been lied to and conned too many times in her life not to know when someone was not being honest with her.

When Maisie had suggested this trip to London – and that she would pay for it – Pearl knew, for sure, that, for some reason, Maisie needed to disappear for a short while.

At some point during their journey she would ask Maisie the real reason why they were heading down south. And why they'd had to leave so quickly. Whatever it was, it was unlikely Pearl would be shocked. Perhaps now would be a good time for Maisie to be open about the kind of work she had done in her life – and was possibly still doing – work that had enabled her to afford such swanky clothes, a honeymoon suite in a top hotel, and an expensive trip to the capital.

Whatever she had done in her life, Pearl would not judge, just as she hoped she too would not be judged for her many wrongdoings.

And whatever the problem was that had caused Maisie to leave town in such haste, they would deal with it. Together.

'Oh, my goodness!' Bel's words were snatched away by the violent winds now whipping up.

'Mammy!' Lucille screamed out as her tatty toy rabbit went somersaulting down the street as soon as they stepped out of the train station's main entrance.

'You hold on to Lucille, I'll get the rabbit,' Bel shouted across to Joe while chasing her daughter's beloved toy as it tried to make its escape and careered down Station Street.

As Bel ran, the bottom of her coat flailing in the air as the wind swirled around her, the thought ran through her mind to let the rabbit win; it was dropping to pieces, and looked more like a rag than a rabbit. She knew that Maisie would. The look on her face every time Lucille had it in her grip said all there was to be said: the toy had seen far better days and was not far off disgusting.

Still, Bel thought, lunging down to grab it before it went into the gutter – that was the difference between the two of them. As she grabbed the toy, now dripping wet, having rolled in at least half a dozen puddles during its desperate fight for freedom, she sometimes wished she had a little bit more of her sister's ruthlessness about her.

As she hurried back, Joe, having given up on speech as they seemed to be walking in some kind of natural wind tunnel, pointed in the direction of Fawcett Street as the best route to the church. From the state of her husband and her daughter, Bel thought that by the time the three of them tipped up at the church they'd all look like they had come to beg alms and not see little Hope baptised.

'You all right?' Joe shouted across as they reached the end of the town's main shopping street and turned into Borough Road.

'Yes,' Bel hollered back. Lucille was between them, holding both of their hands, her little rabbit stuffed securely in her coat pocket.

As they battled their way towards the east end, Bel thought once again about her sister and her ma, and, like this wretched weather, what a truly turbulent week it had been.

Maisie had told her yesterday the little she had gleaned

from Pearl about the young sailor boy who had put her in the family way – and Maisie had said to Bel that she was determined to find out if he was still alive and, if so, track him down. Knowing Maisie, Bel thought, she would succeed.

All the talk of long-lost mothers – and fathers – had made Bel wonder afresh about who her own da was. Pearl had said he was dead, but Bel knew she was lying.

Perhaps when Maisie and Pearl came back from their impromptu trip down to the capital, Bel could start trying to find out the truth about her own parentage.

As Bel, Joe and Lucille leant forward against the force of the wind and struggled along the Hendon Road, Joe spotted two uniformed police officers and a plain-clothes copper on the opposite side of the street to them, hurrying in the same direction. The three men did not have a little girl to slow them down, though, and it wasn't long before they disappeared from view.

Five minutes later, Bel, Joe and Lucille were within sight of the church. The rain was starting to come down heavily now and they caught sight of George's red MG pulling up outside St Ignatius's. Rosie and Lily hurried from the car straight into the church. They were followed by George, holding on to his hat with one hand and his ivory walking stick with the other.

'I'm not jealous . . . ' Bel shouted across to Joe, her hands now red raw and clutching the lapels of her coat around her neck, ' . . . *really, I'm not!*'

'Just think of tonight and that lovely three course meal –' Joe shouted back with a smile on his face as they finally reached their destination, '– and that gorgeous suite!'

Bel felt a shot of nervous excitement at the thought of her evening at the Grand with her new husband.

It would be the honeymoon they'd never got to have.

Chapter Sixty-Seven

Mowbray Road, Sunderland

DS Miller was striding forward, head down so as to fight his way through the wind and rain. His two special constables were struggling to keep up and had fallen a few yards behind him. Pulling his pocket watch out of his waist-coat, he squinted through a blur of harsh drizzle to see the time. It was nearly a quarter to ten. He was cutting it fine. A short sharp shock of adrenaline coursed through him.

Should I be doing this? Is it the right thing to be doing?

He had lain awake last night undecided, his mind chopping and changing, like this damned weather.

Well, he was committed now. He had made his decision. And he had to stick to it.

Now he just had to get to the church in time. Or rather, before time. He had found out from the vicar that the christening was being slotted in at ten o'clock. It was imperative he got there before it started. There was no way he wanted the ceremony spoilt for Gloria. The woman had had enough to contend with, by all accounts. He had heard through one of the other officers with the Dock Police the news that Jack had survived his ship being bombed – but at a cost. The poor man had lost his memory – and with it his chance of love.

Not unlike himself. Only he hadn't the peace of not knowing.

As he turned the corner from Mowbray Road on to

Suffolk Street his heart started to thump loudly in his chest. He could just make out a figure; recognised the distinctive gait. He broke into a jog, desperate to get to his collar before his two fellow officers. He needed to say a few words before slapping on the handcuffs.

DS Miller pounded the pavement. His breathing was heavy. He saw the outline of the church and panicked. He needed to do this now. Anyone waiting outside the church or arriving would see – and that was the last thing he wanted.

The person ahead of him was walking fast.

Determined.

DS Miller stepped up his pace. For the briefest of seconds he looked up to the skies and saw the dark clouds above him, and heard the first deep rumble of thunder, followed by a distant flash of lightning.

He lurched forward and grabbed the shoulder of his potential captive.

'What the bloody hell are you doing?'

Vinnie's words were spat out. Spittle mixed with droplets of rain flew out of his mouth, his face pure vitriol. Malevolence oozing from every pore in his body.

Seeing the undisguised desire for violence, DS Miller knew he had made the right decision. When Rosie had mentioned the christening during their last meeting, he'd been in no doubt that Vinnie would hear about it – any kind of gossip concerning a married woman, who'd had a baby late in life, *and* had chucked her husband out, was guaranteed to do the rounds at the speed of light. And Vinnie, being the kind of man he was, would be seething mad that he'd not been invited. That he had been left out. Made to look a fool.

'Sir –' he had to shout so as to be heard through the wind and rain, 'Detective Sergeant Miller.' He pulled out his badge as proof of identity and held it up close in front of Vinnie's face.

'I have to ask you where you are going and exactly what your intentions are?' He purposely made his voice sound official and unfriendly; his tone was also more than a little antagonistic.

Vinnie glared at him, his eyes bloodshot and wild.

DS Miller hadn't expected him to be so irate – so puffed up and stuffed full of violence. Thank God he had got to him before he reached the church. The man was clearly beyond any rational behaviour.

The decision, as a copper, to get involved in a domestic had been right.

'It's none of your business, mate! Now sod off!' Vinnie shouted, squaring up to DS Miller, his hands clenched tight.

Sensing that the two special constables had caught up, DS Miller shouted over his shoulder, 'Leave this to me,' before turning back to Vinnie.

'I think it is very much my business, *mate*,' he bellowed back, 'especially if you are about to become the cause of an affray or – worse still – an assault.'

Vinnie was seething. His anger reaching boiling point. 'Affray? . . . Assault? . . . ' he practically screamed. 'More like bloody murder when I get my hands on that bitch!'

It was exactly what DS Miller needed to hear. He stepped forward.

'Vinnie Armstrong, I am arresting you—'

The words were barely out of his mouth when Vinnie snarled, 'Like hell you are!' He then pulled his right arm back and threw all his weight behind a punch aimed at DS Miller's face.

His knuckles glanced the side of the detective's head but it didn't prevent DS Miller from doing a quick sidestep and grabbing the arm Vinnie had tried to clobber him with. He wrenched it up his back.

'Argh!' Vinnie screamed out.

'Not so easy trying to deck a bloke, is it, Vinnie?' DS Miller was leaning heavily on him from behind, forcing Vinnie to bend forward to ease the pain shooting through his shoulder and down his arm. His muscles felt like they were slowly being torn apart.

'But then again you wouldn't know, would you?' DS Miller spat the words into Vinnie's ear. 'Much easier bashing a woman, isn't it?'

As DS Miller's words filtered through the excruciating pain coursing down his right arm, for a brief moment Vinnie thought he recognised the voice. It sounded familiar.

'Get the cuffs on him!' DS Miller ordered the two specials, who had been waiting, braced for action while being buffeted by strong whirlwinds and lashing rain.

The two uniforms jumped to it, positioning themselves on either side of Vinnie, who was now hurling obscenities.

'Right, let's get this one back to the station,' DS Miller said, allowing the two officers and a caterwauling Vinnie to march on ahead.

Another clap of thunder sounded, this one louder and nearer, followed more or less immediately by a slash of lightning that pierced the sky. DS Miller could see Vinnie kicking off, but his efforts to escape were fruitless. He had to admit to himself that he was glad the DI had given him Jenkins and Hargreaves; the energy seemed to have drained out of him, and tiredness from not sleeping the night before was starting to make itself felt. He hurried along the street that was, unsurprisingly, empty due to the foul weather.

People have got more sense, he thought, but as he turned

up Mowbray Road he spotted two exceptions: two lone men. A tall old man with dripping wet hair hurrying along the street with a middle-aged man with slicked-back dark hair and wearing a grey suit and waistcoat. DS Miller wondered if perhaps they were heading for the christening. If they were, they were pushing it to make it there on time.

After a few more minutes, DS Miller found himself striding along Grange Terrace and, as he always did whenever he came along this particular road, he sought out the tenement where he had first met Rosie almost exactly a year ago. He had thought her intriguing that day. Now he knew why.

Last night he had thought long and hard. He had mentally walked through all the possibilities of what he *could*, and what he *should* do, and he had realised that it didn't matter what the law stipulated, it made no difference – he could not become Rosie's jailer.

He could not ruin her life. He could not do that to her.

Nor could he do that to himself – for he would have to live with his conscience.

Last night, as he'd lain awake staring at the walls, listening to the turbulence outside his home, as well as that inside his very soul, he had replayed Rosie's words in his head – her words of love. For that is what they amounted to. She had declared her love for him.

Even though those words were harshly delivered, and were even uttered with a degree of bitterness, she had still said them. And moreover, he knew she meant them.

She had loved him.

He had been right. The deep, intuitive feelings that had caused him such confusion when she had rejected him he now knew were true.

Of course, now he knew she'd had no choice but to

rebuff him – if she had given free rein to the love she'd felt for him, she would have been risking her life, her livelihood, and at least a few years behind bars. His choice, however, the decision he had to make since he'd found out the truth about the woman he had fallen for – well, that was less clear-cut.

The choice he had to make was between the law of the land – and love.

Love or the law?

He had argued with himself that Rosie was not hurting anyone; the women who worked at Lily's did so of their own volition.

And he had to admit that he himself had bent the rules many times over the years in his dealings with the likes of Vinnie.

Was it really justice for Rosie to be arrested?

He knew she was a good person. Did she really deserve it?

The law might dictate that she did – but his heart said she did not.

As DS Miller looked ahead of him he saw that the battle had been won between Vinnie and the two constables; Vinnie's body was now limp and compliant.

Sometimes, he mused, life seemed to be one battle after another. And he knew from experience that there was wisdom in knowing when to fight – and when to give up.

He had tried everything to keep his wife alive, but he had been forced to surrender. He could not beat the disease that was ravaging her.

But with Rosie it was different.

He felt there was still hope. That their love might somehow survive.

Chapter Sixty-Eight

Suffolk Street, Sunderland

Arthur was bent double, heaving for breath, both hands placed on his knees as the thunder rumbled above them and the lightning clashed across the distant skies. Gunmetal grey clouds stretched across the sky like distorted bullets.

'Are you all right?' Jack shouted at Arthur, the concern in his voice deep and genuine; the old man was looking like he might breathe his last. Jack might only have spent a short amount of time with him, but Arthur had given him – knowingly or not – the hope that his memories of the past might break through to the surface of his mind. They were there now, just starting to peek through.

Arthur had had to stop and catch his breath halfway down Suffolk Street. They were now just a few hundred yards away from the church.

Arthur knew his breathing was getting worse of late; all those years spent underwater. He knew time was catching up with him. Still, it didn't perturb him. He was just glad he had managed to get Jack this far. If he keeled over now he would have no regrets.

'Go ahead!' he insisted, waving one hand at Jack as if trying to shoo him away. 'You might miss it!'

'I'm not leaving you here,' Jack said, matter-of-factly. 'Just get your breath back. We're nearly there – and then you can have a rest and get out of this blasted weather.'

Arthur knew Jack was not going to leave him, which didn't surprise him. Jack had always watched the backs of the men he worked with.

'All right,' Arthur said, standing up straight. 'I'm ready.'

Jack took the old man's arm and helped him walk the last stretch to the sanctuary of the church. It was unlikely to be warm in there, but at least it would be dry.

As Jack squinted against the onslaught of rain, and felt fat droplets of water dribbling down his face and neck, for a moment he was transported back to the ice cold waters of the Atlantic Ocean. To what had nearly become his watery grave.

He breathed deeply and forced his mind back to the present reality. He needed to focus on what was happening now. Arthur had told him as much as he could in the little time they'd had, but it was Gloria that Jack really wanted – needed – to talk to now. He had a great sense of trepidation. A premonition that something momentous was about to happen.

'Made it!' Arthur said. His words self-congratulatory. They were now just yards away from the Church of St Ignatius.

Jack glanced at the old man, who looked ready to drop, and, with his own heart racing with nerves, he grabbed the wrought iron handles of the heavy wooden doors of the magnificent house of worship – and, with one huge tug, pulled them open.

Chapter Sixty-Nine

At five minutes to ten, just as the previous christening party was leaving the church, the slightly harried vicar signalled for Gloria and her guests to come and sit themselves down at the front of the nave, ready for a prompt ten o'clock start. He had agreed to slot Hope's christening in before the next one at half ten, which meant, if he got a move on, he might have time for a quick cuppa and some of that lovely home-made apple pie one of his elderly parishioners had made for him.

As everyone started to amble towards the front of the church, Gloria looked over to Polly and Agnes, and asked anxiously, 'What about Arthur?'

Gloria knew Arthur would want to be here, that he loved Hope to pieces and always kept a watchful eye on her when she was at the Elliots' during the day. She also knew the old man was not in the best of health, nor was he getting any younger.

'Don't worry about Arthur,' Polly reassured her. 'He'll be here soon.'

'The weather's probably slowed him down,' Agnes chipped in, ' . . . or this friend of his he's bringing might be running late . . . Don't you worry, just get up there and enjoy your daughter's special day.'

Gloria smiled a little nervously. She would actually be glad to get this all over and done with. She'd had an awful feeling Vinnie might turn up, and was having to stop herself from looking over at the entrance every few minutes. She had worked hard to keep the christening under wraps, but she knew these things had a way of getting out and becoming fodder for the local gossipmongers. It was looking hopeful, though. If Vinnie hadn't turned up now, fingers crossed, he wouldn't turn up at all.

'Come on, Glor.' It was Dorothy, looking stunning in a classy, but rather figure-hugging black dress. She had been gassing to Angie and the rest of the women welders but on the vicar's signal to get ready for the beginning of the ceremony, she had immediately donned a serious, holier-than-thou façade she obviously thought appropriate for her role of godmother.

'We've got to go and stand at the font,' she said and pointed a gloved hand at the large marble basin in front of the altar. Dorothy had, of course, read up on everything to do with the formalities of a baby's baptism – something Gloria was thankful for as her mind seemed to be all over the place, and she could barely remember either of her sons' christenings, they had been that long ago.

The vicar cleared his throat as everyone settled into their places on the hard wooden pews.

'Oh, doesn't Hope look lovely?' Kate whispered to Lily. She was sandwiched between Rosie and Lily.

'Kate O'Donnell,' Lily spoke out of the side of her mouth, keeping her eyes focused on the ceremony taking place in front of them. 'I know you have next to no interest in babies and what you really think lovely is that wonderful hand-sewn broderie anglaise christening gown the baby's wearing.'

Kate looked at Lily and frowned, before admitting, 'Well, it *is* a work of art, isn't it? Gloria told me it was made by her Scottish grandmother. She lived in some village in Ayrshire known for its embroidery . . . '

Any further chatter between Lily and Kate – and anyone

else, for that matter – was drowned out by the booming voice of the vicar.

'Good morning, all!'

There was a pause as his eyes scanned the modest – and, he thought, rather diverse – gathering of people for this hastily arranged christening. There was a very eccentric-looking lady with what could only be described as a mass of orange hair, who was sitting with an older, dapper-looking man dressed in an expensive three-piece suit. In the next row there was a young woman who was taller and more muscle-bound than any man he knew, and a young girl who looked east European and was most certainly Jewish. Squashed on at the end of their row was a skinny young boy, with a thick mop of black hair and wearing a pair of incredibly large, thick, round glasses.

'I would like to welcome you all here today … ' The vicar smiled at Joe, who was in his Home Guard uniform and was clearly the husband of the pretty blonde woman and father to the child, who, for some reason, was holding some sort of rag.

Suddenly the vicar's facial expression changed, and he looked about him as if he had forgotten something. He turned quickly to Gloria and Dorothy who were standing in front of the large ornate font that had already been half filled with holy water.

'We're not expecting anyone else, are we?' he asked, in a much quieter voice.

Both Gloria and Dorothy knew that he was really asking if the baby's father was going to make an appearance.

Before Gloria had time to say anything, Dorothy leant forward, pulling on the long black elbow-length gloves she had bought for the occasion, and said in the snootiest voice she could muster, 'No, vicar, the baby's father would have, *of course*, loved to have been here, but sadly – through unavoidable reasons – has not been able to make it. So, please, do carry on.' She ended her reply with the most endearing of smiles.

'So then . . . ' the vicar's voice returned to its normal volume and he looked ahead at his attentive audience. 'We are gathered here today for the christening of baby Hope . . . '

As the vicar spoke, Dorothy cast a look over to Angie and gave her a wink. Dorothy was revelling in every minute of this day, and more than anything she was where she loved to be – centre stage – even if that stage was actually the middle of a church.

Angie, who was seated next to Martha, Hannah and Olly, threw back a look of disapproval. It was only about the second or third time Angie had been in a church in her life, which not only made her feel very self-conscious, but also that she – and her friend – should be on their very best behaviour. This was, as Gloria had called it that day when Hope was born, 'God's house', after all.

The vicar cleared his throat. 'We will now begin with a blessing,' he announced.

'The grace of our Lord Jesus Christ . . . '

Rosie had caught Dorothy's cheeky wink, and had to suppress a smile. The girl really was incorrigible. Still, she deserved her moment of glory as she had been the one to bring this baby into the world – and had done so in the most challenging – and most dangerous – of circumstances imaginable.

As the vicar continued with the blessing, Rosie looked at Gloria with baby Hope swaddled in her arms. Gloria was the only one she had told that Peter knew about her 'other life'. She'd managed to get Gloria on her own a few nights ago when they had all been at the Admiral and had asked if she would be her unofficial banker, and take on the responsibility of paying the fees for her little sister's education should Rosie find herself behind bars.

Gloria had hardly batted an eyelid, which was what Rosie loved about Gloria. And when Rosie told her she had the money in her haversack, wrapped up in newspaper like a fish and chip supper, Gloria had put her own work holdall next to Rosie's and told her to pop it in there when no one was looking.

Rosie had felt a massive relief knowing that if she suddenly found herself in one of His Majesty's Prisons, Gloria would see to it that the bills from the boarding school were paid on time.

As her mind wandered back to the bordello, Rosie turned her head and looked along the pew at Lily and George and saw that they were holding hands. She felt so happy for them, and yet so sad. Their love affair was now out in the open and they had even started to plan their wedding, but it was all on hold. They didn't even know if they were going to be together, never mind become husband and wife. Their future, which until a week ago had seemed so bright and exciting, now looked ominously uncertain.

And, worst of all, it was all Rosie's fault.

As the vicar came to the end of his reading, he took a deep breath.

'And now a few words on—'

But before the vicar had the chance to start his sermon, there was an almighty bang as the church's huge oak doors clashed open and slammed against the sides of the entrance porch. A gust of wind immediately raced in and swirled around the church in a flurry of mischief, ruffling the thin pages of the hymn books and bibles.

The sudden loud noise caused everyone to jump in their seats, and heads to turn to see who it was that had come to the ceremony late. As they took in the vision of the two men struggling to push the heavy church doors closed, there was the sound of shocked gasps.

'Jack,' Gloria said in a whisper.

Dorothy grabbed her friend's hand and squeezed it hard.

'Oh my God, it's Jack,' she said, unconsciously mimicking Gloria's hushed tones.

Gloria stood stock-still. Even Hope had stopped wriggling about in her arms and had fallen unusually quiet as if sensing that something important was happening.

Everyone had now focused on the drama at the far end of the church. Jack had managed to force the doors closed, but it had been a struggle against the strength of the wind that seemed to be trying to batter down everything in its path.

'Please, come in!' The vicar's voice boomed out to the back of the church. 'Get out of this terrible storm that's been brewing up all morning!'

Arthur staggered to the nearest pew and plonked himself down, leaning forward on the backs of the seats in front of him, struggling to get his breath back. Bel and Agnes jumped up and hurried up the aisle to tend to him.

Seeing that the elderly gentleman was being looked after, the vicar's attention turned to the man he had come with and who was now walking slowly down the aisle. He looked a little disorientated. As if he didn't quite know where he was.

'Please,' the vicar said to the confused-looking man coming towards him, 'come and have a seat. We've only just got started.'

But the man didn't look as if he had heard his words. He certainly didn't look as if he was going to take a seat with the rest of the congregation. He was heading straight for the altar – his eyes fixed on mother and baby.

Chapter Seventy

Jack sensed everyone's eyes on him as he walked down the centre aisle of this magnificent church, but he could not drag his gaze away from the woman he knew to be Gloria – and, more importantly, the baby she was holding in her arms.

So, this was what Arthur had really wanted to tell him.

Of course, it all made sense now – why Arthur had come to see him yesterday at work, and why they had met this morning at the café.

This was where he'd really wanted to bring him.

Jack could just about make out the baby's profile. He could see two small clenched fists, and the long, very beautiful ivory christening gown the baby was wearing – but that was all.

He had to see this baby.

As he approached the altar, he glanced at the vicar and the young woman welder in the black dress, but still he could not pull his attention away from the baby.

As he neared mother and child he had the sense of being surrounded by water, and for a split second he was propelled back into the ocean – but then he was once again in the present and only a few yards away from the baby.

The air in the church was still – serene, almost – and there was not a sound to be heard.

As he slowly walked up the three stone steps to the font, the woman he knew he had loved – both as a young lad, and again as a middle-aged, married man – stepped forward and carefully lifted the baby up.

She was handing him the baby.

He was aware of his own arms stretching out to take hold of the treasure being offered to him.

He heard the slight gurgling as the child sensed movement.

As he took the baby in his arms, and looked down at the face of the cherub, he knew for certain who the baby was.

It was the baby he had seen when he had nearly drowned at sea.

The baby with the grey-blue eyes that had looked at him when he had thought he was facing almost certain death.

And he knew – just like he had known when he had been gifted the vision of the baby as he fought for his life in the dark, icy cold ocean. He knew that the child that he had seen then – and the child now lying in his arms looking up at him – were the same.

But, most of all, he knew, with absolute certainty, that this baby was his.

As he stood and gazed at his child, Jack was aware of the vicar's arm on his shoulder. The man's old but kindly face smiled at him and he said a few words, before stepping back and speaking once more to the small congregation.

Jack allowed his eyes to break away momentarily from the child to see that Arthur and the two women, who had gone to help him, were taking seats next to a man in a soldier's uniform.

His eyes, though, were soon pulled back to the child in his arms. He continued to hold her and gaze down at her in awe and adoration.

And the child stared back at him, the beginnings of a smile on her rosebud lips.

And they both stayed there, simply looking at each other, while the vicar gave his short sermon.

When there was silence again, Jack looked up to see

Gloria. Tears were forming in her eyes. And as they looked at each other he knew he loved this woman. He still could not recall his past with her, but he knew in his heart that he *had* loved her – and moreover that he *still* loved her.

As Jack felt Gloria take his hand into her own, he continued to look down at his daughter – the baby with whom he had finally been reunited.

' . . . *Shine as a light in the world to the glory of God,*' the vicar read from his script.

Jack remembered the light he had seen when he was drowning. He had learnt when he was in hospital that the light had come from a fisherman's trawler and that it had been the men in it who had saved him.

As the vicar started talking to the pretty woman welder about her responsibilities as the baby's godmother, Jack looked again at Gloria and moved to her side so that they stood next to each other, shoulder to shoulder, together with their baby.

' . . . *and you promise to continue to support this child from this moment.*'

Jack heard the words and knew that no matter what happened, he would love, cherish and care for this child for the rest of his days.

The vicar allowed a few moments' silence, then turned to Jack and Gloria. He didn't have to ask if this was the child's father. He also knew not to question the absence of a wedding ring on the woman's hand, or why the baby's father was wearing an expensive gold band on his.

The vicar moved towards Jack and Gloria and dipped his thumb lightly in the font's holy water. He gently made the sign of the cross on Hope's forehead, and told the baby lying happily in her father's arms, 'Christ claims you for his own. Receive the sign of the cross.'

There was another short pause.

Angie, Martha, Hannah and Olly all sat in a row, their eyes glued to the scene in front of them, all with silent tears running unchecked down their faces.

The vicar looked at his attentive congregation and saw that there did not appear to be a dry eye in the house. He realised that there was much more to this ceremony than a simple christening, but he was not one to probe, or to judge. The baby was here to be baptised. That was all that was required of him today. Besides, they were running out of time. The next christening party would be in soon.

'And, now,' he said, 'it is time for Hope to be baptised in water . . . ' he turned to Jack, who took his cue and stepped towards the white and grey marbled font, ' . . . in water which is blessed.'

As baby Hope was held over the font her eyes still focused entirely on her father, as if she was in a trance. Only the holy water, trickling across her forehead, caused her to break her stare, her little face crunching up in discomfort at the feel of its cold on her warm, dry skin as the vicar spoke the age-old words: *'I baptise you in the name of the Father, and of the Son, and of the Holy Spirit. Amen.'*

The vicar looked at Jack and then at Gloria and told them, *'This is your child's baptism. It is a sign of a new beginning . . .'*

Gloria looked at Jack and her baby and thought how true the words of the vicar were.

This *was* a new beginning. It was a terrifying, exciting beginning. A beginning she had only dreamed of. It was the beginning of a new life. Not just the new life of her baby daughter, but a new life for them all – for her, Jack, and Hope.

Gloria knew the road ahead of them would not be an easy one. There would be huge hurdles to overcome and many battles to be fought. She could see in Jack's eyes that he still did not know her – but she had also seen love, and that was enough for her. If they had love, then they had a foundation on which they could build a future. They could face their new life together.

After the vicar said a short prayer for Hope and for all those who would support her, everyone recited the words printed on the Order of Service leaflet that had been put out on their seats at the start of the ceremony. As they did so, Gloria caught Arthur's eye and mouthed 'thank you' to him. He smiled back at her, before closing his eyes and saying a few words to his beloved Flo, who he knew would be pleased with what he had done.

Lily pulled out a hankie from her bag and handed it to Kate, whose face was now wet with tears. Rosie put her arm round Kate and gave her a little cuddle, thinking that for someone who had endured such a hard life, she really was a big softie. Rosie kept a protective arm around her old schoolfriend as she watched the vicar light a candle and hand it to Dorothy, who took it with a look of great seriousness and listened intently as the vicar told her that, as godmother, she was holding the light for her goddaughter.

As the vicar brought the ceremony to an end, Gloria looked across to Dorothy, who looked as though she didn't know whether to laugh with joy, or cry with sheer emotion.

Gloria then looked at all the people she knew and loved, who were sharing with her the most wondrous moment in her life. Hope had been the one to be blessed by the vicar with his holy water, but it was Gloria herself who felt truly blessed.

Blessed to have her baby daughter.

Blessed with the return of the man she had loved her whole life long.

And blessed with her family of friends.

Epilogue

Peter was standing on the corner of the street, awaiting Rosie's return home.

He was frozen to the bone, and his hands and face felt numb, but the wind had finally exhausted itself and dropped to a mere bluster and the dark clouds were starting to drift away, allowing splashes of aqua blue sky to show through.

He had guessed Rosie would be heading home around now. Enough time to have enjoyed the christening and then to have gone somewhere afterwards for a little celebration. Probably the Elliots' would be his guess.

It had given him the chance to bang Vinnie up, for a while at least. His work for now was done, although he knew Vinnie would be an ongoing problem. But, at least today Gloria and baby Hope had been able to enjoy their special occasion.

As Peter stared down the cobbled main road, presently glistening in the sheen of fresh rainwater and a wealth of patchwork puddles, his body leapt to life as he spotted Rosie walking up the street.

He knew it was her, even though she was some distance away. He knew the way she walked – her confidence, the way she marched rather than walked, in spite of the fact she was wearing heels and not her usual rubber-soled boots.

He watched transfixed as Rosie transformed from a grey and red blur at the bottom of the road to the beautiful woman she was. Her crimson trousers peeking through her long grey gaberdine mackintosh and her corn-coloured curly hair shining in the sunlight that was starting to break through the gloom.

He watched, barely able to breathe as she hurried across the road.

Only then did he move out from the shadows.

'Rosie,' he called out.

Rosie turned quickly, her eyes searching.

And then she saw him.

She stood still, watching him as he strode towards her, his trilby hat in one hand, his black woollen coat, as always, flapping open. When he reached her they both stood still, facing each other, looking each other in the eye.

Then Peter gently took her hand in his, and as he did so, kissed the woman whom he had tried to stop loving.

And, this time, Rosie lifted her face up to his and kissed him back.

Dear Reader,

I hope you have enjoyed this third instalment of the Shipyard Girls series. If you've been with the women welders and their nearest and dearest (and not so nearest and dearest!) from the start, you'll know that for each book there is a subtle underlying theme – for *The Shipyard Girls* it was love, for *Shipyard Girls at War* it was hope, and for *Secrets of the Shipyard Girls* it is charity.

I love the Winston Churchill quote I have used at the start of the book. In my opinion, it encapsulates the true meaning of charity. And how wonderful that someone in such a powerful position could say this during a time that was dominated by so much hatred and warmongering.

Love, hope and charity have been around from the beginning of time, but I believe that in this day and age – more than at any other time in our history – they really are needed.

I wish you all three – love, hope and charity – and lots of it!

With love,

Nancy x

History Notes

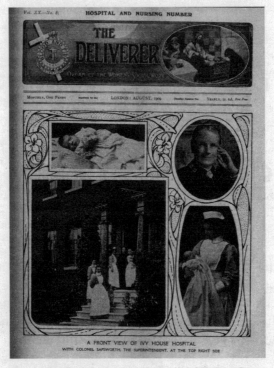

Here is the front cover of the *Deliverer*, the magazine published by The Salvation Army back in the early 1900s. It is the same one that was handed to Pearl in the novel and which led her to Ivy House – the country's first ever maternity hospital for unmarried mothers, financed and run by the charitable organisation, The Salvation Army.

During my research for *Secrets of the Shipyard Girls*, I was amazed to learn about the truly inspirational and ground-breaking work carried out at Ivy House, which was not just a maternity hospital for unmarried mothers, but also a refuge for vulnerable women from all walks of life who had fallen on hard times and had nowhere else to turn.

Nancy Revell
June 2017

Dying to know what the future holds for

Gloria, Jack and Hope?

Look out for Nancy's new novel

Shipyard Girls
in Love

Nancy Revell

Available to PRE-ORDER now

in paperback and e-book

Out 22 March 2018